PIRATES

OF THE

NARROW SEAS 3

Iron Men

SECOND EDITION

M. KEI

KEIBOOKS
PERRYVILLE, MARYLAND, USA
2011

ISBN 978-0615520841

Printed in the United States of America, 2011.

KEIBOOKS
P O Box 516
Perryville, MD, USA
Email: Keibooks@gmail.com

PIRATES OF THE NARROW SEAS

BOOK ONE : THE SALLEE ROVERS
BOOK TWO : MEN OF HONOR
BOOK THREE : IRON MEN
BOOK FOUR : HEART OF OAK

The ebook versions of the series are published by Bristlecone Pine Press, Portland, Maine

.

POETRY BY M. KEI

Slow Motion : The Log of a Chesapeake Bay Skipjack (2nd edition)

Heron Sea : Short Poems of the Chesapeake Bay

Take Five : Best Contemporary Tanka, Volume Three (editor)

Take Five : Best Contemporary Tanka, Volume Two (editor)

Take Five : Best Contemporary Tanka (editor)

Fire Pearls : Short Masterpieces of the Human Heart (editor)

Atlas Poetica : A Journal of Poetry of Place in Modern English Tanka

TABLE OF CONTENTS

CHAPTER 1 : LAUNDRY DAY

Lieutenant Peter Thorton, acting-captain of His Britannic Majesty's frigate *Ajax*, was stripped to the waist on his quarterdeck. He had a blue and white checked cloth tied over his blond hair and was barefoot. His officers were in a similar state of undress. All around them hung their dripping laundry. Shirts, jerseys, waistcoats, stocks, cravats, breeches, drawers, stockings, nightshirts, bed sheets, blankets, tablecloths, and napkins were flapping in the breeze. On the weather deck the laundry was a good deal more colorful; a rating could wear a striped jersey or a red shirt if he felt like it. Indeed, along with the usual petticoat breeches, trousers and short jackets, a number of bright colored ribbons and kerchiefs were hung. The men loved to deck themselves with such things; a great deal of red ribbon could be bought for a few pence when a shirt cost a shilling or more.

The Mediterranean sun shown down relentlessly and there was a great deal of horseplay with the water as a consequence. It was a sign of the boredom of their station that laundry day was celebrated as a source of entertainment. For two weeks they had been patrolling Algeciras Bay. After the destruction of the Mediterranean fleet under Walters, they had assumed that the Spanish would want to follow up their victory by striking at the hated British barnacle clinging to the butt of the Iberian Peninsula, otherwise known as the naval station of Gibraltar. Yet they did not molest the British in spite of outnumbering them.

"Do you think they're afraid if they attack Gibraltar the Turks will come after them?" Perry asked. He was the acting first lieutenant.

The actual first lieutenant, Albert Forsythe, and the *Ajax's* temporary captain, Ebenezer Horner, were currently assigned to the *Resolute* "until the pleasure of the Admiralty be known" and were working like fiends to repair her. The *Resolute*, doomed to be forever known as the 'Irresolute' because she had run from the Battle of Majorca, had been badly damaged, and most of her senior officers, including captain and lieutenants, were among the dead. Horner, who had been filling in for Bishop, the *Ajax's* rightful captain who was on furlough to recover from a heart attack, had been temporarily transferred to the *Resolute*. The destruction of the British fleet in the

7

Mediterranean had left the squadron at Gibraltar with no resources to call upon. Officers were spread thin.

"I don't know," Thorton replied. "I was four years in the Spanish navy, but that was on the West Indies station. 'Tis different here. Especially with the revolt in Portugal."

Lieutenant Alan Abby was lounging in a hammock chair. He had survived the sinking of the *Adamant* but lost his sight. His shirt was open on account of the heat and the bandages around his ribs showed. "Victory at Majorca or not, these Spaniards have got to go out. The French have taken Barcelona," he opined.

"They'll have to pass the Turks, though. And the Turks outnumber them. Speaking of which . . ."

The *Ajax* had reached the mouth of Algeciras Bay. They could see the dim brown coast of Africa seven miles away and the thunder of gunnery sometimes came to them when the wind was right. The Turks were very methodically blockading Sebta, the Spanish enclave on the coast of Africa. Sebta was the southern Pillar of Hercules, just as Gibraltar was the northern. To lose Sebta would mean losing control of the Strait of Gibraltar. Spain would not yield.

"Deck! Boat coming!" the masthead lookout called.

Immediately all the officers on the quarterdeck reached for their spyglasses, but with their coats hanging with the laundry, their glasses were not to hand. Only the officers actually on duty were properly dressed and equipped. Midshipman Jackson, acting third lieutenant, used his good hand to raise his spyglass to his eye. His left arm was still in a sling. A senior midshipman, he was also a survivor from the *Adamant* and now assigned to the *Ajax*.

The vessel proved to be a Turkish brigantine, in other words, a small galley. With only fifteen pairs of oars, she was something like a large gig or wherry. She sped across the water. The red Turkish ensign with its crescents and stars flew at her stern. She raised a green flag and dipped it once.

"Raise the green signal and dip it twice," Thorton ordered.

The signal midshipman quickly made the sign.

"Heave to. Pass the word for my steward. I want my coat." Thorton unpegged a damp linen shirt from the line pulled it on. The cool cloth felt good against his skin — his broad shoulders were coppered by the sun. All around him the officers hastily righted their clothes and got themselves into proper uniform. By the time the Turks drew alongside they were damp but presentable.

The lieutenant in charge of the brigantine hailed them in very bad English. "Dispatch Gibraltar having!"

Thorton swore at him in Arabic and commanded, "Speak plainly man!" His Arabic was scant, but it was better than the Turk's English.

The Turkish lieutenant was a wiry, bow-legged man in a dark blue coat and clean white turban. He was clearly surprised to be accosted in the Prophet's tongue and let loose a spate of Arabic Thorton couldn't understand at all.

"Speak slowly!"

Through halting Arabic and English they made out that the man had dispatches for Commodore Whittingdon.

"Carry on," Thorton said.

"What ship?" the Turkish lieutenant wanted to know.

"*Pegasus*," Thorton replied.

"What ship?"

"Do you want me to go with him?" Abby asked.

"Why? You can't see," Thorton replied.

Abby hauled himself out of the hammock chair. "So what? I'm bored. I'm sure I can help. Where is the flagship?"

"Past the little mole where the boats tie up." He shook his head, but Abby was a passenger, not a member of his crew, and could go if he pleased. "Go if you will. How are you getting back?"

"I'll find a way."

With unerring accuracy he went down the windward stair and made his way over the side into the Turkish vessel. He knew his way around the *Ajax* by heart, but once he arrived on the brigantine he knew nothing, not even what sort of vessel she was. The Turks were dismayed to see the gauze he wore wrapped around his eyes and were not reassured by Thorton's explanation that a blind man would show them the way to Whittingdon.

Perry stood at Thorton's elbow. "Do you think it wise?"

"What can happen? If worse comes to worst we'll send a boat to fetch him. A little exercise will be good for the men."

The Turkish vessel kept well to the inside and skimmed along the eastern shore at the foot of the legendary Rock. The water shoaled there, but that was no concern to a shallow vessel like the brigantine.

"Stand by to wear ship," Thorton said.

"Aye aye, sir. Stand by to wear ship!" Perry repeated.

The *Ajax* swung ponderously around with her stern to the prevailing west wind. It was a light breeze and she ambled slowly through her turn. Heading north up the bay the sun now shown on the opposite side of the deck and shifted the laundry shadows to new locations. The men dragged their laundry tubs into the changed patches of shade and continued their work. The brigantine swept away from them and ran swiftly up the bay towards Gibraltar.

"Deck! Spanish xebec three points off the larboard bow! She's on course to intercept the Turk!" The excitement in the man's voice broke through the stupor of heat and boredom. Properly dressed, Thorton now had his own spyglass. He pulled it out of his pocket, placed it to his good eye, and studied the enemy.

The *San Idelfonso* had changed her patrol to cross the inviolable center line with the goal of intercepting the Turkish messenger. She made three and half knots with the wind on her starboard quarter. Her studding sails broke out as they watched and she gained speed. Thorton swiftly lowered the glass.

"Make all sail! Clear for action!"

The topmen lay aloft while marines pulled down the clotheslines complete with laundry and passed them below. The wet clothes were tumbled willy nilly together into the hold. They would be sorted out later.

"Toss the log."

"Aye aye, sir! Toss the log."

Thirteen year old midshipman Jones came scrambling up to the quarterdeck to take his position at the quarterdeck guns, but Thorton had not yet given the order to beat to quarters. There was too much laundry to move. All around him the officers' stewards were frantically pulling down their masters' clothes and trundling them below.

"Ra'uf! Stow my papers, my rug, and my chandelier!" Thorton told his steward in Arabic. The man had come with him after his brief service as a captain of a Sallee rover. The rug and chandelier were also courtesy of his brief but lucrative Sallee service. They were the nicest things he owned.

"Aye aye, Captain," the man replied. He hurried below with a bushel basket of Thorton's damp laundry.

In about fifteen minutes the ship transformed into something that looked like a warship instead of a laundry.

"Beat to quarters," Thorton ordered. He clasped his hands behind his back and braced his legs to the rolling of the deck as she caught more wind.

The snare rattled and the pipes called. He had a very small marine band composed of a drummer boy, a fifer, and a blind fiddler. "Let's have 'Heart of Oak,' lads," he called to them.

The crew sang along, "Come cheer up, lads, 'tis to glory we steer . . ."

Thorton calculated the speed and angle of the approaching vessels. He had the advantage of being nearer to the brigantine, but the Spanish had the advantage of the weather gauge. Still, he would be able to intercept and cover the brigantine. He smiled grimly. A show of resolution on his part and the Spanish would break off. He was sure of it. He had whipped them before.

CHAPTER 2 : TO GLORY WE STEER

A second Spanish xebec was well up the bay, but when she saw her consort tearing toward Gibraltar, she made haste to support her. She was far enough away that both *Ajax* and the *San Idelfonso* would reach the brigantine before she came up.

"Two xebecs, Captain. Both frigate-rigged," Perry said in a worried voice.

Thorton had whipped a pair of Spanish frigates on this very bay two months ago. He had had the advantage of surprise, darkness, and the Spanish being damaged and undermanned, none of which was the case now. But then he had had a galiot and now he had a frigate; conversely, the Spanish had had frigates, now they had somewhat lighter xebecs. The *Ajax* carried twenty-four guns in broadside compared to the galiot's archaic bow battery. He felt better about the current contest than the former, and he had been victorious then.

Midshipman Bettencourt at the signal box was white. He could see as plain as anyone that if the Spaniards persisted, the *Ajax* was going to be doubled. The slim little brigantine would be of no practical help. Would the British come off station to support them? Or would they fear a feint to expose Gibraltar while the Spanish attacked? Thorton swung his spyglass to study Algeciras and the Spanish line.

"Signals from Algeciras," he commented.

"What do they say?" Perry asked.

"I can't make them out. 'Tis too far."

Handsome Perry was starting to sweat in his wool coat and lace cravat. "Damn me. They're finally going to fight."

"Fire a warning shot, if you please, Mister Perry."

"Gunner, warning shot!" Perry repeated, passing the message to the gun deck. "Damn it, Thorton, we've got boys on the gundeck, not even lieutenants!"

"Mister Jackson is an experienced officer. He's qualified to be a lieutenant."

"Chambers isn't!"

One of the small bow guns barked out, punctuating their conversation.

"What would you have me do, Lieutenant? Abandon our ally? He has dispatches for Gibraltar."

"Forgive me, sir. You are correct." Turning to watch the progress of the enemy, he muttered, "Whittingdon had better support us."

The British fleet was outnumbered, outgunned and outmanned by the Spanish fleet. They beat to quarters but remained at anchor. On the other side of the bay, the Spanish beat to quarters and several battleships came out and formed a screen across the front of Algeciras. The brigantine, frigate, and xebecs continued on courses that would meet somewhere in the vicinity of the little mole at the south end of the town. They would be right under the guns of the anchored British if they persisted.

The *San Idelfonso* fired a shot of her own. It splashed down not more than two cables from the brigantine. A lucky shot would shatter the little vessel. The Turk knew the danger and his oars held water. He lost headway, then began to row in reverse to retreat from the Spaniard and run back towards the *Ajax*. Minutes ticked by as the *Ajax* overtook the smaller vessel.

"Sea anchor. Give me three knots."

The Turkish rowers were getting tired, but they paced the British frigate. They hid behind the *Ajax* like a bashful boy hiding behind his mother's skirts.

The buckets were sent over and dragged behind the *Ajax* to slow her. To the Spanish further up the bay it would appear that she was losing her wind; she had all sail set and was coming on, but slower. Thorton kept one eye on the little mole — if the brigantine could get behind it, she would be safe. The other eye he kept on the Spanish. The third eye he kept on the wind and sails. Thorton only had one good eye, so it darted from scene to scene as he calculated everything.

"Mister Perry. I would count it a favor if you would lay the bow guns yourself. I want to bloody that Spaniard's nose. Let's show her we can shoot better than she can."

"Aye aye, sir."

Perry went forward. The *Ajax* had had three captains in six months, but they had all had a passion for discipline, and two of the three were avid fans of gunnery. The crew was competent. But were they excellent? Thorton intended to find out.

People on shore were gawking at the sight of the ships racing towards each other. Some of them brought out beer and cold beef to make a picnic of watching. The brigantine dashed for the shelter of the mole. Half a mile — ten minutes — and they would have it.

"Close-hauled. Run right at her. Cut the sea anchor."

An axe thudded down and the line parted. The *Ajax* suddenly leaped forward as the pent up energy of her sails rushed her towards her destiny. Thorton kept his eye on the Spaniards; the consort was going to arrive at least twenty minutes after the *Izzy* and *Ajax* met.

"Pass the word to Mister Perry. Fire the bow chasers on my command."

The Spaniard luffed up so that she could bring her larboard battery to bear. She fired, and eighteen guns belched flame and smoke at them. The balls splashed into the sea a cable away.

Thorton smiled grimly. "She wasted her best shot."

Still he did not give the order to fire. The *Izzy* snaked around to present her starboard broadside. The two had closed sufficiently for her balls to tear through the *Ajax*'s rigging.

The *Ajax* didn't answer. She continued charging right at the Spaniard. "Signalman. Hoist the following." He translated it into Spanish so that the enemy could read it plain as day, "To glory we steer."

The *Izzy* had lost much of her headway by yawing around. She tacked and attempted to bring her larboard guns into play again, missed stays, and hung dead in irons. A cheer went up from the British seamen. The brigantine had almost reached the mole.

Blakesley, the sailing master, smiled at him. "Capital bluff, sir. The brigantine is safe."

"I'm not bluffing," Thorton replied. He turned back to face the Spaniard. She was falling off and exposing her spent starboard broadside as she tried to gain headway. "Bow guns, fire!"

Perry crouched on one leg with his left leg straight out to the side to take one last look along the barrel of the gun, then hopped out of the way. "Fire."

The four bow chasers barked and their six pound shots flew across the half mile to the *San Idelfonso*. Perry shaded his eyes with his hands.

"A hit!" somebody next to him crowed.

Two of the balls tore through the fore corner where the Spanish hands were desperately hauling the lines to try to bring her head around before the *Ajax* came up. The Spanish captain gave up trying to tack and gave the order to wear ship. Thorton saw her yawing further to her larboard and divined her intention.

"Prepare to tack! Helm hard over! Fire as she bears!"

The *Ajax*'s head came into the wind. For a heart stopping moment she wavered, then her head swung through the eye of the wind, and she presented her starboard to the Spaniard. The *Izzy* was still cumbrously trying to get around when the British guns roared and raked her stern.

Thorton calculated his headway, the wind, his ship, and his seamanship. He did not have enough way on to tack back and bring his larboard to bear as the Spaniard had done to him. There was no use dwelling on it; indeed, the calculations were hardly conscious in his mind. His grasp of the situation was instinctual, as if the ship were a part of his body whose capacity and use was of the utmost familiarity to him. Just as an ordinary man did not need to think to lift a mug or use a spoon, so Thorton did not need to think to maneuver the *Ajax*.

"Wear ship," was his instant answer.

The larboard guns roared and hit, pounding the *Izzy*'s stern for a second time. Thorton felt the way the *Ajax* moved over the waves, felt the wind, and checked the nearness of the shore (uncomfortably near). The wind was over her larboard quarter; it was one of her best points of sail. A creamy mustache foamed at her bow as she made four and a half knots and the land rushed toward them.

"Helm hard over. Fire as she bears."

The frigate swung around close-hauled. She heeled, and the starboard battery spoke again. A cloud of gunsmoke trailed away as thin and white as a wedding veil.

Perry was back at his side. "We hit again, but I can't see much damage from the last broadside."

"Maintain pursuit. We shall hound her and if Allah wills, we will take her," Thorton replied.

Perry stared at him. "With all due respect, sir. You've driven her off and the Turk is safe. Her consort is coming up!"

Thorton glanced at him, then glanced at the British line at anchor with their guns run out.

"Give chase."

"You can't take two Spanish xebecs! Peter, you have none of the advantages you had before! 'Tis folly!"

Thorton's jaw set. "I gave you an order, Mister Perry."

Perry straightened. "Aye aye, sir." Turning away, he passed the order. "Make chase!"

CHAPTER 3 : RUNNING BATTLE

The Spaniards both turned tail and ran. The British sailors jeered and made rude gestures at them.

Thorton peered through his glass. "We hurt her," he said. "I can't make it all out, but the *Idelfonso* is sending a damage report to the *Casilda*."

Nobody else could read the Spanish flags, but Thorton had the Spanish signal book memorized. If he could see the flags clearly he would know the Spanish moves as soon as the Spaniards did. He kept his glass fixed on the signals. A new message broke out on the *Santa Casilda*. He peered at it, lowered the glass and rubbed his good eye, then raised the glass again.

"I can't make it out . . . there!" The wind blew the signal flags straight out. "The *San Idelfonso* is returning to port, and the *Santa Casilda* will attack us to cover her retreat."

He snapped the glass shut and gave the shore a good look. They were passing Gibraltar with her line of battleships. If he got in over his head, it would not be easy for the ships to rescue him; they would have to beat against the zephyr. He was on his own with all the squadron watching him. He was happy.

"Stand by to tack." That would bring his starboard broadside to bear. "Fire on my signal."

The orders were given and the men waited tensely. The Spaniards continued running north up the bay with the *Ajax* in pursuit. They ran on and on and Thorton smiled grimly.

"They're trying to lure us out of range of the British guns," he remarked. He kept track of the shore passing under his lee. He opened and shut the spyglass a couple of times. "Are both broadsides loaded, Mister Perry?"

"Aye, sir," his lieutenant replied promptly. The breeze stirred Perry's curls under the brim of his hat. A scar crossed from his left eyebrow across his nose and onto the other cheek.

"Helm three points to larboard."

"Three points to larboard, aye." The head swung around and the *Ajax* ran close hauled to the northwest. Her course put her between the Spanish frigates and their escape route to Algeciras.

The *Santa Casilda* turned around promptly and ran on the other tack. The *San Idelfonso* swept in a slow curving arc as she labored to come around on the new course.

"Her steering's damaged!" Perry chortled as her laborious turn revealed damage not visible to the eye.

"Good work, Mister Perry," Thorton replied.

The *Izzy* could not run close-hauled. She elected to run south on an oblique course that would take her to the Spanish line. She had to get past the *Ajax* first, and the *Ajax* had the weather gauge, but she had no choice. She could run north and be trapped at the head of Algeciras Bay, or try to claw her way back to port with her consort for cover. That was the option Thorton would have tried, too. She was not without defenses; her broadside was fully operational. She was wounded but not helpless.

The *Ajax* had her own problems. The *Cassy* was south of *Izzy* and screening her. The *Ajax* had to cross her to get at the wounded xebec.

"Fire!" Thorton barked.

The starboard broadside roared out. The officers watched through their glasses as the long shots peppered the water around the *Cassy*. A line parted and the foresail's larboard brace began to flap. Her yard yawed around and her course veered. Spanish hands leaped to retrieve the loose end and bend a new line to it.

"At least one hit," Perry reported.

Thorton grunted in dissatisfaction. At that range it wasn't reasonable to hope for more, but still he had. "Make a note: more gunnery practice, Lieutenant."

"Aye aye, sir." Perry was a keen fan of gunnery; he was pleased to accept the order.

"Keep the starboard guns working, but see that her larboard battery is loaded and ready."

"Aye aye, sir." He passed the word below.

The guns leaped and roared again. Gunsmoke blew in an acrid cloud past the quarterdeck. The scent of brimstone made Thorton's eyes water and he smiled. The smell appealed to him. The *Cassy* altered course a little to bring her own broadside to bear. Fountains of water bloomed all around them but none struck. The minutes ticked by. The *Ajax* belched forth another broadside before the Spanish replied.

The smile grew on the acting-captain's face. "We are faster than them."

Thorton watched the movements of the two vessels closely. He planned to thump them as much as he could get away with, then run back to the protection of the British line. He glanced at the west side of the bay, but he was still well clear of the Spanish line. He glanced at the east side, but the British would not leave Gibraltar unguarded for the sake of a mere frigate.

"Helm two points to starboard," Thorton said.

The *Cassy* crossed their bows at an angle. "Here it comes," Perry muttered.

The Spanish xebec raked them at an angle from bow to midships. Men screamed and timbers shattered. Wooden splinters the size of knives flew through the air. Blood spilled on the sanded deck.

Thorton was privately relieved; his move had not let the *Cassy* get a full rake on them. "Fire as she bears." A moment later and the *Cassy* had to pass through their arc of fire, and received a thumping in return.

"Here comes the *Izzy*," Perry warned him.

"I know. Prepare to tack. Fire as she bears."

The *Ajax* answered her helm promptly and ran close-hauled with a proud white mustache at her bow and foam creaming her sides. The *Izzy* fired on her as they came abreast. Debris rained down from overhead and somebody shouted. The *Ajax's* starboard guns ran out raggedly and boomed out an irregular broadside. With less than five cables between them, her shots told on the *San Idelfonso*.

The *Cassy* came around and threatened to cross their bow again, but Thorton said, "One point to starboard. Take the weather gauge."

If the *Cassy* persisted, they would trade broadsides as they passed, and the *Ajax* would come between the *Casilda* and the wounded *Idelfonso*. They could double the British. She didn't, instead the *Cassy* wore ship and ran after her consort. The maneuver took time and the *Ajax* nearly caught up to her.

The three vessels ran down the bay. The *Ajax* was the fastest of the three and she was gaining on them. The *Izzy* could not keep close to the wind and fell off, running due south. The *Ajax* gained on her inch by inch, but the *Santa Casilda* kept between them. The gun crews on each vessel worked frantically. Thorton debated possible courses of action. If it had been him on the *Cassy*, he would have luffed up so as to let the pursuing vessel catch up and be broadsided before she was ready, but that would only worked if the Spanish could load and run out their guns faster. He knew and the Spanish captain knew that the British were swifter with the guns.

The *Ajax* drew abreast, and the *Cassy* fired the half broadside she had ready. Shot came whistling across the quarterdeck and smashed one of the gun carriages on the starboard side. The gun toppled and he heard the shrieks of wounded wood and men. His heart leaped in his chest.

"Damage report!"

"One gun dismounted. Three wounded. Lost a studding sail, two or three wounded on the weather deck."

Thorton grunted. "Fire as she bears."

The English broadside roared out and their smoke blew across the gap to wreath the Spaniard. When the smoke cleared they could see the *Cassy* bore multiple wounds. Her starboard rail was shattered in three places and her mizzenmast was leaning. The boy Jones was leaping to reload, swearing at his gun crews like an officer. Thorton did not like Jones, but he was afflicted with a moment of nostalgia. Once he had been such a midshipman.

Balls from musket fire whined around him and he finally noticed that the Spanish marines were in action and had been for a while. He had been busy with more important things. He glanced up into his own rigging and saw the red coats of his marines and the small puffs of smoke as they did their duty. He swept his glass along the deck of the Spanish ship. She appeared to have a full complement and no obvious invalids aboard her. The Spanish fleet had recovered from their wounds. He could not take her by boarding.

He looked through the *Casilda's* rigging towards the *Idelfonso*. He narrowed his eyes. If he took the Cassy, he would have two frigates under his command. The wounded *Izzy* could not hope to escape. The wind was favorable to his course. His gunnery was superior to the enemy. His ship was faster. If he kept pressure on them so that they could not escape back to their own lines, both of the ships could be his.

"Praise Allah from whom all good things come. Helm, match her speed for speed. Mister Blakesley, press her to lee. See that we do not overshoot her. We are going to pound her into submission and take her."

By covering the wounded *San Idelfonso*, the Spaniards had given up the advantage of their numbers. The *Santa Casilda* endured being smashed by the British guns over and over again. She worked her guns as fast as she could, but the British outshot her three for every two.

"Nine pounders," Perry observed as one of the Spaniard's spent balls rolled around the quarterdeck. He put his foot on it. "Eighty-one pounds to our gross weight. She's small." The *Ajax's* broadside was almost double the Spaniard's.

For twenty minutes they ran side by side down the middle of Algeciras Bay. The *Cassy* was unable to draw ahead of the *Ajax* who clung to her like a bloody barnacle. The *Izzy* fell behind as the two embattled ships slugged it out pistol shot range.

Thorton never lost sight of his prey. As the *Izzy* dropped behind he worried that she might come up into the wind and rake his stern. She would have to get her steering repaired to do it, but it could happen. Then he would be doubled. Algeciras was three miles away on his starboard. Puffs of smoke and the rumble of gunnery announced action by the fortress. Shore mounted batteries had extensive range, but still fell short of the *Ajax*. The British did not fire; they were too far away to do any practical good. The *Ajax* was on her own.

Smoke blew heavily from the *Ajax* to the *Santa Casilda* and fogged her decks. Thorton had good visibility on his own deck, but sometimes he saw the flash of a scarlet cuff as the Spanish captain waved his arm to clear the smoke from around his head. The rumble of the guns was continuous as the broadsides broke up. Each gun was firing as fast as it could and the Devil take the hindmost.

"Pass the word to Lieutenant Barnes, 'Prepare boarding party.'"

A musket ball went through the brim of his hat and knocked it askew. He merely straightened his hat. He had too much to think about to worry about a missed shot. Meanwhile the redcoats massed at the rail.

"Take us alongside."

The *Ajax* came along side the *Santa Casilda*. The *Ajax's* guns roared and blew through the Spanish defenders at the gunwale. Barnes had kept his own marines low to try to avoid a similar fate. Thorton heard the screams of wounded men and could not tell if they were Spanish or English. "Take her!"

The boarding party swarmed over the rail. Spanish grenades exploded among them.

"Keep those guns working, Mister Jones. Keep pressure on their quarterdeck."

The *Izzy* opened fire. When the *Ajax* grappled the *Casilda*, the wounded xebec cut across their wake and laid her broadside into the *Ajax's* stern. Jones leaped to aim the sternchasers. "Kill them, you sons of bitches! Shoot them!" he screamed.

The *Idelfonso* clawed past, but she could not keep her course and made dangerous leeway. She was drifting onto the *Ajax's* starboard.

"Starboard broadside!" Thorton bellowed. He bent over the starboard quarterdeck guns and aimed them himself.

The captain on the *San Idelfonso* shouted in Spanish, "One hundred pieces of eight to the man who kills the English captain!"

Thorton ducked down behind the binnacle as Spanish musket fire rained on the quarterdeck. The starboard battery boomed out and the *Ajax* rocked, but being grappled with the *Casilda*, her movements were constrained. The *San Idelfonso* had spent her larboard battery on their stern and was helpless to reply as the *Ajax* savaged her at point blank range. The Spanish captain disappeared, but Thorton didn't know that; he was pinned behind the binnacle.

Perry was shouting orders when three balls struck him and he went down in a bloody heap. On the *Izzy,* the Spaniards cheered to see him topple — they had mistaken him for the captain. Thorton leaped up and roared in perfect Castilian Spanish, "I'm not dead, you Spanish dogs! For England and for Allah!"

The *Izzy* bumped gently against the *Ajax*. The frigate was sandwiched between the two vessels. Thorton wanted to leap onto the quarterdeck of the *San Idelfonso* — she was that close, he could have done it. But he was the acting-captain. He could not leave his post. Perry writhed on the deck, bleeding from the body and arm. He had Jones and Blakesley for able-bodied officers. Abby was safe with the Turkish brigantine and a good thing, too. A blind man would never have survived such slaughter.

"Jones! Board her! Secure their quarterdeck!"

Thirteen year old Midshipman Niall Jones looked up at him in disbelief and blanched, then looked across to the Spaniard. He shouted in his high-pitched boy voice, "*Ajax!* Follow me!" and with a pack of red-coated marines behind him, swarmed over the rail and onto the *Idelfonso*.

More musket fire whined around Thorton and he felt the pain of a ball passing through his upper arm. He pulled out his checked kerchief and tied it around the wound.

"She's struck! Praise Jesus, she has struck!" somebody shouted in his ear. He snapped his head around. The *Izzy's* ensign was coming down.

Thorton shouted across, "Mister Jones, take her into Gibraltar! Fend off! Get her off us!"

Jones had hardly enough crew to secure the Spaniards in the hold, let alone get her under sail. She did not want to answer her helm and the wind kept pushing her against the *Ajax*. Thorton was at his wit's end.

"I need another fifty men and officers to lead them! God damn the Admiralty for sending us to sea with a peacetime complement!"

Perry was sitting on the deck, "'Twas peacetime when we were commissioned," he pointed out, holding his wounded arm against his chest. "I told you 'twas folly!"

Just then the *Santa Casilda* struck her colors.

CHAPTER 4 : SPOILS OF WAR

The victorious officers of the *Ajax* were dining aboard the *Pegasus* in the commodore's large and commodious cabin. China and crystal glittered. The commodore himself was a portly gentleman of no great height with a fine dark blue dress coat laden with gold lace. His waistcoat and cravat were of the purest white. Thorton had the post of honor at the foot of the table opposite the commodore. He wore his right arm in a sling. Captain Horner was seated at his right hand and Perry, looking peaked, was propped up to Thorton's left. Midshipman Jones, who had suffered a slash to the leg, had limped along with them, while Midshipman Jackson, who had a broken arm to begin with, had survived in much the same condition. Midshipman Chambers had a black eye and broken finger. Lieutenant Barnes of the marines was miraculously unscratched.

They had just finished giving the commodore a lively account of the action.

"Mister Perry, you are the luckiest man to ever be shot three times!" Whittingdon exclaimed.

"I know, sir. I thank God for my deliverance!" One ball had grazed his upper arm, another had struck him in the ribs and been channeled around to the back where it exited, but the third had buried itself in the copy of *The Adventures of Roderick Random* he had put into his breast pocket when getting dressed that morning.

"I'll tell you this," Perry continued. "I am very much looking forward to winter. I'd like a nice peaceful blizzard." Perry had been wounded several times this year, none serious until now, although the slash across his face that marred his good looks caused him considerable unhappiness.

There were chuckles around the table at that.

"No rest for the wicked, I'm afraid. The Turks inform me they plan to besiege Sebta through the winter. They want our support," Whittingdon replied. He shook his head. "Although what Whitehall is going to do about Minorca and the destruction of the Mediterranean fleet, I don't know. Still, the Turkish letters have to go to England. As soon as you've mended the *Ajax*, you'll have to run the dispatches for me."

"Aye aye, sir," Thorton replied.

Horner was properly the captain of the *Ajax*, he being the substitute sent to replace Bishop, the actual captain. Bishop was furloughed at home due to complications after his heart attack. In the meantime, the battered *Resolute* needed a captain, and the British in Gibraltar were short on qualified officers, thanks to the mass casualties of the English debacle. Horner merely sipped his wine and did not contradict Thorton's assumption that he would be acting-captain for the trip to England.

"'Twas a smashing victory, Peter, but now I have three disabled vessels on my hands and none of them fit to run a message to England!"

"The *Santa Casilda* is not badly damaged, sir."

"She's a prize and will be confiscated by the Admiralty. The *Naiad* will have sailed by the time you get there, so you would be stranded. I can't afford to have you sitting in a public room in Portsmouth. I need you here! By God, you've done it again, Peter. Two for one! You are the very deuce!"

"The Spanish are not very good gunners, sir," Thorton replied modestly.

"The first time could have been luck — you've heard it said, I'm sure — I trust I'm not offending you to mention it. Dark, and the Spanish undermanned and wounded. Yes, you ought to have prevailed in such conditions. But two xebecs in the broad light of day! Damn me, but that's something! A bit of prize money for all of us, too. Don't worry, you'll get a captain's share. Ebenezer will get the *Resolute's* share."

The British system shared the prize money among all vessels in sight regardless of who actually secured the prize. Even though the British line of battle had done nothing they were to profit by Thorton's actions.

Horner merely inclined his head in acknowledgment. He hadn't the slightest objection to continuing as the temporary captain of the *Resolute* until the pleasure of the Admiralty be known. The longer he held the temporary post, the more likely the Admiralty would make it permanent.

"You're such a hotspur, Peter. I should like to send you out cruising and make us all rich, but the Turkish dispatches must go to England. We need supplies, men and officers. I hope the *Naiad* brings me a boatload. Get the *Ajax* fixed up as much as you can, then you can escort the *Elf* and the prizes home. Three days. No more." He held up three fingers for emphasis.

"Aye aye, sir," replied Thorton.

"I'll send the orders over in the morning."

Horner finally spoke. "I believe the *Resolute* will be fit to sail in a few days. With your permission, I'd like to accompany the *Ajax* and the prizes to England."

"She's leaky," Whittingdon replied.

"Better now than wait for autumn gales."

"True enough. Very well. You can take her home. Spithead will make her right again."

The rest of the evening was given over to conversation on various topics. Thorton was by nature a laconic man and said little. Horner, his superior officer, was even more taciturn. A natural disinclination for conversation had been reinforced by years of privation and service to the point where he was a dour man in the estimation of his fellow officers. Perry could generally be counted on to enliven the conversation, but his ribs were aching. Although Roderick Random had stopped the bullet, it had still kicked like a mule. He drank to numb the pain. Chambers was of too little rank to contribute much to the conversation and the boy Jones was drinking away his battle-shock. As a result the officers of the *Pegasus* did most of the talking. At last Horner rose and begged leave to depart, at which point the junior officers were happy to take their leave.

A tired Thorton entered his cabin. A single lantern was burning. It was a very modestly furnished room. He had no curtains for his sleeping area and his bed was an ordinary hammock that differed in no way from those used by the sailors. The carpenter and his mates had been at work and mended the damage. His steward had fetched the glass windows from below and reinstalled them, along with the blue gingham curtains, and the rude table, desk, and chairs the carpenter had made for him when he received the warrant making him acting-captain. The 'sofa' beneath his windows was a wooden locker topped with plain canvas cushions made from old sailcloth stuffed with oakum. His two luxuries were a crystal chandelier and a blue and red carpet that were part of the prizes he had acquired during his brief tenure as the captain of a Sallee rover. It had happened only a few months before, but already it seemed a lifetime ago. He was glad they were all in one piece, even if they looked like a duke and duchess among the rabble compared to his other furnishings.

Sitting on the locker was Alan Abby. When he heard the door he rose quietly from the bench. He was casually dressed in a blue satin dressing gown over his shirt and breeches. "Captain," he said.

Thorton startled. "Alan! I didn't see you! What are you doing here?"

"I wanted to congratulate you on your victory. By the time I got back to the *Ajax* you'd already gone to the the flagship."

Thorton hung up his hat and sword and coat on the pegs in the bulkhead near the hammock. "Thank you, Alan," he said warmly.

"The *Ajax* is really shot up. I went below decks and there was so much daylight down there I could almost see."

Abby's blindness was such that he could see shadow shapes against a bright background but little more.

Thorton sighed at that. "We have some futtocks to repair. After that we can put some planks on her." He crossed to meet the other man.

"Are you all right? They told me you were wounded." Abby's hand gently brushed against the sling.

"Creased my right arm. 'Tis minor, but it aches."

"Poor Peter. That's where you got the splinters last time, isn't it?" He stepped a little closer.

Thorton caught his breath. He was taller than the blond lieutenant by several inches and naturally inclined his head when speaking to him. "'Tis nothing, really. It will be better in a week."

Abby's hands slid gently up his arms around his neck. His blind eyes searched Thorton's face almost as if he could see. "Do you have any idea how much I worried about you, how sorry I was I'd gone with the Turk? I wanted to be here with you, Peter. I heard the guns and tried to imagine the scene, but the Turks could hardly tell me what was happening."

Thorton smelled of gunsmoke, cigars, and brandy. His shoulders beneath the searching hands were broad and strong in the wool coat. Abby worked his fingers into the hair where it was tied at his nape in a long queue bound with black ribbon. Thorton's arms went around the slender waist and gently pulled the man against his chest. His neck bent and he kissed the other lieutenant full on the mouth. He did not mean to, yet somehow the moment seemed to require it. Abby returned the kiss with ardor. Thorton felt his blood pulsing hot in his veins and longed for more, but at the same time, he worried.

"Alan. We shouldn't do this."

The other lieutenant brushed his lips against Thorton's. "I want to. I have wanted to ever since you found me in the cockpit of the *Resolute* half out of my senses."

"I have a lover."

"I know. But he's not here, is he?"

"But — "

Another kiss blocked Thorton's reply. His arms tightened on the smaller man. His body ached for the kind of soothing that Abby could provide. He was tired and sore after his victory, how good it felt to have those arms around him! The evening air was growing chill; to have someone to warm his bed would be delicious.

"Article Twenty-Eight," he whispered. The *Articles of War* prescribed the death for any man convicted of sodomy or buggery.

"Feh. Do you think I care about that? Nobody will dare raise his hand against me. My father is the Earl of Falmouth."

Thorton envied him the privileges that came with status. Even though Abby was an illegitimate son, he had an allowance that was double a lieutenant's yearly pay, not to mention his father's patronage and support in the navy.

"Maybe they won't touch you, but they've already shown they're more than willing to touch me." He broke away.

"I won't let them hurt you, Peter. You know that. I've written to my father and I'll write him again. You captured two Spanish xebecs right under the guns of Algeciras! After the disaster of Minorca, the public will be hungry for heroes. You'll be in all the papers! Tell me what you want to say, and I'll write it and send it to friends of mine. They'll publish it. Nobody will dare speak against you if you're a public hero."

"I don't want to be a public hero!" Thorton exclaimed.

Abby pulled his pigtail and gave him a lopsided smile. "You are innocent, Peter. I like that about you. You aren't motivated by political considerations. You're a good and decent man and an able officer. But somebody has to watch over you because you haven't the sense God gave a goose!"

"Perry has said the same. But why can't I be an able officer and have that be the end of it?"

"Because you like kissing men and that is going to get you into trouble. Unless powerful men take an interest in you," Abby replied sensibly. "I want you, Peter! Don't you want me? I can help your career and I will."

Thorton wavered. He was flustered to discover his hands had slipped below the waist to cup the other lieutenant's rump of their own volition. His thoughts were galloping over fertile fields of imagination. How nice it would be to —

"No," he said roughly but untruthfully. He didn't let go. His hands seemed stuck where they were.

"Not even a little bit?" Abby whispered, stroking his face.

"I have a lover," Thorton whispered. "I have to be true to him. Allah knows if I didn't — " He stopped.

"You'd choose me?"

Thorton nodded. He realized Abby couldn't see his nod and breathed, "Yes. I wish I'd met you before. Maybe — "

"You've met me now." Abby's lips brushed his again.

His wayward hands were massaging the delicious roundness of Abby's rump. "I can't. Please, Alan. You know I can't."

Abby took hold of his ruffles and tugged them petulantly. "You'll make me jealous!"

Thorton was flattered. "I don't see why. I'm nothing special. I'm not any different than I ever was."

Abby gave the ruffles a little jerk. "You *are* special. Everybody knows it. I know it. Perry knows it. Horner knows it. Whittingdon knows it. And yes, even that damn Moor, Shakil, knows it."

Thorton blushed a little. "Not like that. Not Perry, anyhow."

"Are you still sweet on Perry?"

Thorton blushed even redder. "He's a ladies' man. You know that."

"You may not have noticed, but there's a shortage of ladies at present. Roger Perry likes a warm bed."

Thorton snorted. "You know what happened when I tried to kiss him. I'm lucky it didn't ruin my career."

Abby sighed and fluffed his ruffles. "You are an idiot. Even Jackson adores you."

"Huh?"

"Men are attracted to success. And you, Peter Thorton, are very successful. You're our dashing corsair. Who wouldn't want you?"

The next kiss was an extremely long one. Thorton's blood raged within his veins and he was sorely tempted: to the victor go the spoils. Hadn't Captain Tangle said something of the sort once upon a time?

How could he face Abby, or Perry, or Horner, or any of them on the morrow if he did?

Thorton pushed him away. "No," he said raggedly. "I like you, Alan, but no. Shakil is counting on me."

The blind lieutenant stroked the rough texture of taller man's five o'clock shadow. "Are you certain?" he wheedled.

"Yes," Thorton said with quiet conviction.

Abby heaved a dramatic sigh. "Then I may have to seduce Perry. I'm tired of sleeping alone!"

"You're wicked!"

Abby gave him a sunny smile. "So my father says. He enlisted me in the navy to remove me from bad influences. It almost worked. I was starting to think I was the only sodomite in the service."

Thorton was thoroughly scandalized. "You shouldn't say such things!"

"Why not? They're true." Abby laughed, then he turned and pressed his backside against Thorton's front. He threw a coy look over his shoulder. "Mm. A good fit, don't you think?"

Thorton's hands automatically gripped the other man's hips. His animal half thought it a very good fit indeed. It took a great effort to push the smaller man away. He swatted the impertinent rump for emphasis. Abby wiggled it at him.

"Stop that! Now go to bed and leave me in peace!"

Abby threw a last look over his shoulder. He blew a kiss. "Tell Shakil I'm jealous. If he decides he doesn't want you anymore, I'll be waiting."

Then he opened the door and stepped out. Thorton groaned. It required the comfort of his own hand before he could sleep.

CHAPTER 5 : THE NEW LIEUTENANT

After breakfast a boat arrived from the flagship bearing a lieutenant, his sea chest, and dispatches. He was obliged to wait for acting-Captain Thorton to emerge from the hold where he was meeting with the carpenter about repairing the ship. The wounded had been taken off and some fresh hands sent by the *Pegasus*. Now the men were moving all the guns to the starboard side so that the strakes could be stripped from the larboard, the futtocks mended, and the new strakes put in. It was the sort of job that ought to have been done in a dry dock, but there was no dry dock in Gibraltar.

As brief as Thorton's career as a Sallee rover had been, it had instilled in him the notion that what must be done, could be done, if only a man would apply himself to the task.

"Lieutenant Andrew Posonby reporting for duty, sir."

The new arrival was a tall, good-looking man with sandy brown hair, a bluff face, broad shoulders, a soft middle, an excellent frock coat, perfect blue breeches, and solid silver buckles on his shoes. His hat had a tasteful bit of gold braid around the brim and a crisp new naval cockade. He was at least thirty-five and maybe even forty. His hairline had retreated to give him a high brow and fine crow's feet marked the corners of his eyes.

"Peter Thorton, acting-captain of His Britannic Majesty's frigate *Ajax*," Thorton replied, returning the salute. "Your papers?"

The papers were handed over and Thorton inspected them. Posonby spoke, "Commodore Whittingdon said you needed another lieutenant, sir."

"I do," Thorton replied. Reading the man's commission he said, "I see you're nearly as junior as we are." He looked at the man who was ten years older than himself.

Posonby interpreted that look as a question and smiled affably. "I was six years a midshipman, but I didn't like it. Then I was six years a subaltern in the cavalry, but I didn't like that either. Then I was then married six years, which I didn't like any better, but my wife was a heiress so I was obliged to reconcile myself to the life of a gentleman of leisure. It was a hardship, but I managed to get through it. Unfortunately, my wife died without issue. The inheritance went to her cousin, a large gentleman with a larger estate. He didn't need mine, but alas, he was kin and I'm not. Therefore, I am left only with the widower's portion."

Thorton listened to this tale in puzzlement. "But the widower's portion must be far more generous than a lieutenant's pay."

Posonby gave an almost Gallic shrug. "So it would be, but it is encumbered by debts. His Majesty's bailiffs cannot touch a man safely aboard His Majesty's ship of war. From which you may deduce that I will not be asking for shore leave when we reach England. I'm sure your other officers will want it, but I am content to remain aboard."

Thorton folded up the commission and returned it to the man. "Very well, you're our second. This is Roger Perry, acting-first. This is Alan Abby, who was our second but who is now on furlough. This is Midshipman Lemuel Jackson, our acting-third. Sorry, Jacky, but you'll have to share with Posonby. Abby's got the first lieutenant's cabin because he's blind," he explained to the new arrival.

Posonby nodded, "I had wondered."

"Get him stowed. Gentlemen, will you all join me for dinner so we may get acquainted with our new lieutenant?"

Naturally they assented. Not that Thorton's table was any more commodious than the wardroom's, but he did have couscous and oranges and served an excellent cabbage salad a la Mahonnaise. It was a frugal mess full of impoverished officers, officers who had become even more impoverished by losing nearly all of their possessions in the Spanish attack on Minorca. They were happy to eke out their board by mooching off his.

The windows were swung up on their hinges to admit cerulean light and air and bugs. Posonby was the best-dressed of the shabby officer corps. Each of the *Ajax's* officers was looking forward to the prospect of prize money; the lieutenants would be able to re-equip themselves with uniforms, navigational instruments, food, wine, and other necessities of shipboard life. With luck they would end the year no worse off than they began it.

"So you are not fond of the matrimonial state?" Barnes was asking the newcomer. Barnes was brilliant in his scarlet uniform. Although it is the duty of a marine to shoot and be shot, he had come through unscathed.

"I am exceedingly fond of it. I think it suits women very well," Posonby replied. "As for myself, I give support to the state of matrimony by admiring other men's wives. They can have the expense of keeping them and I the pleasure of their company."

Thorton did not know what to make of such a frank discussion. "I fear you'll be called to the dueling grounds, Lieutenant," he observed primly.

Posonby shrugged his shoulders. "In every case, when a husband has told me to desist or be shot, I have been happy to desist as I would rather not be shot."

"What? You decline the challenge?"

"Not at all. Proper challenges are always accompanied by a demand for an apology. Since I freely admit it is wrong of me to seduce other men's wives, I have always made the requested apology and quitted the married lady's company." He waggled his fork at Thorton. "Which is why you should never seduce an unmarried woman. You can't get off with an apology but must marry the creature. 'Tis an unhappy ending."

Thorton could only stare at the man in astonishment.

Perry's wounds were aching, but Posonby was balm to his mood. He smiled and said, "He has a point, Peter, and I shall keep it in mind for my next affair. You must admit, the butcher's wife was more generous than the pastry girl."

Thorton peered at them both. He suspected they were making sport of him. He was about to make a hot remark when a scurry of footsteps was followed by a knocking on the door.

"Bother. What is it now?" Thorton asked no one in particular. "Enter!"

The midshipman burst in and blurted out, "Mister Blakesley says to come quick, sir! The Spanish are coming out!"

The table erupted as all the men leaped up and boiled out of the cabin. They rushed to the quarterdeck and took out their spyglasses. The Spanish ships were hauling their anchors. A northwest wind filled their sails and they sailed majestically down Algeciras Bay towards the Strait of Gibraltar. Fifteen ships, half of which were ships of the line, accompanied by xebecs and frigates and their tenders, left the protection of the Spanish fortress. Thorton couldn't do a thing to stop them. The *Ajax* was tied up at the mole with so many planks missing she looked more like a rail fence than a ship. Her guns were all lashed together on the starboard side and useless; worse, if her guns were returned to their proper places, one good heel would send them and their crews tumbling out the gaps in her larboard.

"Make a signal, 'Enemy fleet on course due south,'" Thorton snapped. "When you have it up, fire a gun, Mister Perry."

A moment later the signal flags broke out. One of the bow guns barked to draw the attention of the British to her, just in case they hadn't noticed for themselves.

"Prepare to cast off." Thorton said.

"Prepare to cast off!" Perry called. The cry was passed from one end of the vessel to the other.

"Set topsails."

The *Ajax* eased away from the mole

"Sinclair! Tell the carpenter to get some planks in place so that the guns won't go over when we run them out. Do it quick." The boy ran off. "Mister Perry, clear for action."

The British fleet was already raising anchor and unfurling their sails to go in pursuit of the Spanish. Five line-of-battle ships, a ship-sloop, and the *Ajax* were the fighting force. They had no hope of victory if they engaged the Spanish, but the Turkish navy was investing Sebta. If the Spanish engaged the Turks, the British could harry their rear.

"Signal, sir. Our number, 'make course due south.'" It was the duty of the frigate to scout the enemy, even if she was shot to hell.

"Acknowledge."

The *Ajax* scudded lightly before the wind. With all her guns to the starboard, she listed to that side, which proved helpful since the wind was from the northwest and the listing counteracted the heeling.

"Make all sail. I'll have the stuns'ls, if you please, Mister Perry."

Perry loved a fast ship as much as Thorton. He shouted the orders and the hands swarmed aloft. The men borrowed from the *Pegasus* were confused and had to be pushed to the correct places. They were stout from guard duty and panted for breath as they ran up the ratlines and into the rigging. Down below the sound of hammering told Thorton that the carpenter was at work rigging some sort of guardrail to keep the guns from going over board when they were run out.

"Mister Perry, have a look below. As soon as safe, return the guns to the larboard. Double shot, please."

Perry disappeared for a couple of minutes. "They've got the after portion ready and the guns are moving." The rumble of the carriages told the news as clearly as Perry did.

"How's Posonby?"

"He's getting the starboard guns in order. We've got two guns ready on the starboard now."

"Does he seem to know what he's doing?"

"He does."

"I wish you were working the guns, Perry. I know I can count on you."

"Do you want me to trade places with him?"

Thorton shook his head. "I hope we don't have to engage them. Let's try to run past and see what there is to see in the Strait."

"Aye aye, sir."

CHAPTER 6 : THE SPANISH COME OUT

The Spanish fleet was beautiful and terrifying. The great battleships were clouds of sail scudding before the wind while their xebecs and frigates ran with them like greyhounds coursing alongside huntsmen. Thorton paced them two miles off, but a frigate-rigged xebec broke off to angle her course across his. He bent his course more to the east, towards the great Rock, and she left off menacing him. With the Rock only a mile away on his beam, he ran down the bay well ahead of the much smaller British fleet.

"The Spanish are signaling, sir," Midshipman Chambers reported.

Thorton trained his glass on the flagship. The wind caused the flags to stream out clear as could be, and he had a good glass. His command of Spanish was excellent. He lowered the glass and slammed it shut.

"The xebecs are ordered to intercept and sink us."

He had a sick feeling in the pit of his stomach that today would be the day he got his comeuppance. For a moment he thought about running back to the safety of the fleet, then banished it from his thoughts. He had a duty to do.

"Make a signal, 'Relay, Spanish flag to xebecs, sink, our number.'"

"Aye aye, sir," Chambers replied. He went through the signal box to pick out the necessary signals. He had to spell out 'xebec'. X was not a commonly used letter and he found it in the very bottom of the drawer.

"Mister Perry, kindly put the boarding netting over both sides. We don't want the Spanish to have an easy entrance to the gun deck."

"Boarding netting, aye!" he replied.

The boarding netting probably wouldn't hold a rolling gun, but it would keep the men from being pitched over board or the Spanish from crawling through the gaping holes in the *Ajax's* side.

Chambers reported, "British flagship acknowledges, sir."

"Mister Perry. How many guns do I have ready?"

"I'll find out." He ran below.

Thorton watched three frigate-rigged xebecs altering course to intercept him. They were big, muscular vessels unlike the corvette-sized *Casilda* and *Idelfonso*. That they sent three xebecs after him even when they knew he was shot up was a very great compliment. His blood was up and he longed to rush straight at them, but he had orders to scout. He must try to run past them.

"Signal from British flag, sir. 'Disengage.'"

"Damn." He was disappointed.

Disengaging was not so simple. If he wore ship that would bring him closer to the Rock and the shoals at the foot of it while the closest xebec would gain on him. He would then have to beat back to the British fleet while the xebec could run with the wind on her larboard quarter to intercept him. Had it been a regular Spanish frigate he would have trusted his shallower draft among the shoals, but the xebecs were shoal-draft vessels themselves. He appraised the situation. Every moment he hesitated would bring the xebecs closer to him. Very well. If he was going to be intercepted by the Spanish, let it be on his terms.

"Very good. Make the following message, Our number to Spanish flagship, 'Fortuna favet fortibus.'"

Chambers hurried to obey.

"Helm due west."

The *Ajax* charged straight at the Spanish line, close-hauled and heeling. Profanity erupted from the gundeck below and the thunderous crash of a loose cannon explained why.

"Spanish flag acknowledges, sir. She replies, 'Deus nobiscum.' 'God is on our side,'" he translated. He had a schoolboy's command of Latin.

"It is often thought God favors the powerful, but my experience has shown me He loves good gunnery more," Thorton replied.

Perry came scrambling back up to the quarterdeck. "Seven guns ready starboard. I told Posonby to haul the larboard guns out of the way so that he can at least work his side. The carpenter's still rigging rails on the larboard. We're shipping some water below, sir."

"I expect we'll ship quite a lot before we're through. String life lines on the gun deck and see it well sanded," Thorton replied.

It would be the devil's own work to serve the guns while slipping and sliding across the wet deck.

Chambers spoke, "Signal from British flag, sir. 'Disengage.'"

"Respond, 'Disengaging in force.'" Thorton's mind was working at a high rate of speed. "Mister Perry, fire the bow guns as follows, One, pause, two, three. Attend to it yourself, there must be no mistake."

"Aye aye, sir." He ran forward.

The xebec had the weather gauge but Thorton didn't care. He did not plan to be on her lee for long. A moment later one of the bow chasers spoke, followed by a short pause, then two more guns one after another. Perry came running back.

"Perfect, Mister Perry."

"What does it mean?" Perry asked.

The xebec answered their shots with guns of her own. Her shots fell into the sea well short of the British frigate.

"It may mean nothing at all, Mister Perry. Notify me the instant we have the larboard battery ready."

"Aye aye, sir." Mystified, Perry had to do his duty.

Thorton clasped his hands behind his back and stood braced on the slanted quarterdeck. The xebecs continued to close with him and the Spanish line continued its majestic course down the bay towards the Strait of Gibraltar. The British fleet was coming after them with all sails out. The *Pegasus* showed her name was true as she rushed over the waters of Algeciras Bay. She was a handsome third rate of eighty guns with all sail clapped on. Her bevy of fourth rates followed her like pearls on a string, each exactly in her wake. It was a brave sight, and braver still for being outnumbered by the Spanish three to one.

Why today? Why had the laggard Spaniards finally decided to come out? They had repaired their vessels and their wounded had recuperated, yet they had delayed and delayed until now. If the goal was to keep the last British force in the Mediterranean pinned at Gibraltar, they could have done it with half the fleet. With five or six battleships at Algeciras the British would not dare to leave Gibraltar undefended.

Today was a good day to come out; the wind favored the Spaniards. It would send them scudding across the Strait to fall on the Turkish fleet investing Sebta with a hammer blow. If he had been on patrol, he might have been able to run out and warn the Turks. Now he was caught in the bay with a damaged ship and no way to warn their Muslim allies. The sea ghazis would be taken by surprise.

His only hope was the warning he had already given. The chance that any Sallee vessel was close enough to have heard it was small, but real.

"Mister Perry. Repeat the signal, please. You might as well aim at the xebec so they think the shots are for them."

"Aye aye, sir."

A gun spoke, paused, and two more spoke. Gunsmoke drifted from the foredeck.

"Larboard guns ready, sir," the messenger informed him.

"Stand by to tack. All idlers to the windward rail."

The *Ajax* came around smartly and the idlers ran to the opposite rail.

"Do you think it mattered?" Perry asked him.

Thorton shrugged. "Maybe. I think I felt a difference. These shallow vessels are sensitive to where the weight is placed. Stand by to fire the larboard battery."

"Stand by larboard guns!" Perry shouted the order down the deck. It was passed man to man below decks.

Thorton watched the xebec coming into the angle his guns could traverse. "Fire."

"Fire!" Perry roared.

The larboard battery thundered. A cloud of gunsmoke blew across the deck. The crew cheered as their shots told on the xebec at a distance of half a mile. The xebec replied in kind and a few shots landed near them and one smashed through the gunwale and went clattering across the deck. A shriek announced the first casualty. Thorton's gut tightened.

The second xebec was a mile out. She fired a single gun. He did not see the fall of the shot, but the warning was clear.

"Fire at will."

The *Ajax* was now running close-hauled on the other tack. They reloaded and ran out and fired again before the Spaniard had reloaded. Her reply came half a minute after the British broadside. They traded broadsides and received some Spanish damage, then they were too far ahead of her and she could not traverse her guns far enough. The *Ajax* continued to shoot at her; with so many strakes out of her sides the guns could traverse further than usual.

"Damage report."

"Minor. Three wounded," Perry replied.

They were running for the British line. The xebec did not care to meet the British fleet and crossed their wake. They received her raking shot in their stern and Thorton groaned as if it had been his own body that had been hit.

"Signal from British flag, sir. 'Take position two cables to windward.'"

"Acknowledge."

Now that they were covered by their own fleet, the xebecs broke off and ran back to the protection of their own line. The *Pegasus* was not inclined to let them go unpunished though. Her bow guns spoke and the mizzenmast fell on the closer of the two xebecs.

"Lucky shot," Perry said.

Chambers spoke. "Signal from flag, sir. 'Our number, pursue xebec.'"

Thorton grinned. "Acknowledge!"

With the wind on his quarter he raced after the wounded vessel. Without her mizzen the Spaniard had lost way but was still clipping along. Her companions were beating back towards her. Thorton calculated relative speeds.

"I don't think we're going to catch her before her friends arrive," he remarked. "Let's cross her wake and see if we can rake her."

The larboard guns were slewed around and fired twice as they crossed her wake, then the starboard battery fired and they came around on their new course. The second xebec replied from a distance and a few balls whistled through their rigging. The third xebec was gaining on them. He looked back to the British fleet a mile distant, then to the mouth of the bay where the head of the Spanish line was already reaching the strait.

"Do you know how a wounded grouse will drag her wing to lure the hunter away from her nest, Mister Perry?"

"I do, sir."

"The next time they fire, bring our fore topsail down fast — I want them to think they have hurt us. Leave the crow's foot rigged. Make damn sure she doesn't foul."

"Aye aye, sir." He passed the word and went among the men to make certain they understood.

Next time the Spanish shot flew through their rigging, the fore topsail came down fast and hard.

"Keep it fair! It must be ready to go up in an instant!" Thorton shouted at them.

They understood what was wanted but exactly how to accomplish it was a puzzle. Thorton left it for them to solve. He was the captain; his duty was to give orders. Theirs was to figure out how to obey.

"Helm, two points to larboard."

The *Ajax* ran but she'd lost a couple knots of speed with her fore topsail billowing loosely over the fighting top. The three xebecs ran after her. They wanted revenge for the humiliations the *Ajax* had heaped upon them. They were determined she would not make it to the safety of the British fleet.

"Stand by fore topsail!"

They ran for ten minutes and the xebecs continued to gain on them. They were within range of the *Pegasus'* guns but the battleship did not fire. Thorton steeled his nerves. Shot from the xebecs' bow chasers peppered the *Ajax*. The larboard gallery was shattered and splinters flew everywhere.

"Raise the fore tops'l!"

The sail went up and billowed out full of wind. The *Ajax* increased her speed. She went scudding across a quarter mile in front of the *Pegasus'* bows.

The *Pegasus* made signals. The *Resolute* broke away from the line and charged the xebecs.

The Spaniards had not expected the *Resolute* to leave the line of battle; that was simply not how battleships behaved. The etiquette of war meant that battleships matched themselves against battleships and ignored smaller vessels, unless the smaller vessels were foolish enough to fire on them first.

The *Resolute's* broadside was thirty-two guns. She pounded the lead xebec. The smaller vessel replied in kind, but her nine pound balls bounced off the thick oak of the battleship's hull. The men of the *Resolute*, so shamed and disheartened by their defeat and flight off Majorca, thirsted for revenge. They mauled the xebec. The others fled, but the wounded xebec was overtaken and boarded by the *Resolute*.

CHAPTER 7 : THE ARROW OF LOVE

The deep throated roar of guns sounded somewhere beyond the mouth of Algeciras Bay. The Spanish were meeting resistance. Thorton cocked his head as he listened.

"Sounds like thirty-two pounders, don't you think?"

"'Tis heavy metal to be sure, but I wouldn't wager on the caliber," Perry replied.

"The Turks must be on patrol. The Spanish have lost the advantage of surprise."

The British fleet was halfway down the bay and approaching the mouth as the last of the Spaniards ran out. As they watched, a lateen-rigged vessel ran into the mouth of the bay and hugged the eastern shore. The Spanish took potshots at her, then one of the xebecs ran to intercept her.

"That's the *Arrow*!" Thorton cried. "We can't let them take her! Make a signal, 'Submit, aid Turk.'"

"'Permission granted,'" Chambers reported.

Thorton let out all sail. The *Ajax* left the *Pegasus* behind as she ran a path intended to come between the xebec and the galiot. Unfortunately, the xebec had a good head start. The *Arrow* ran close-hauled among the reefs of the eastern shore and the xebec turned to pace her outside the reefs. She let loose a broadside which the galiot could not answer. The two raced on parallel courses and the xebec began to headreach her.

Thorton swore heartily. The galiot was a lively vessel, but she was shallower than even the *Ajax* and carried correspondingly less sail. The xebec could run her under.

"Helm a point to starboard. We will take the weather gauge and rake her as we cross her bow."

The xebec saw them coming and clawed to windward. She was nimbler than the *Ajax* and succeeded in getting up wind. That separated her from the *Arrow*. The galiot kept running until she gained the shelter of the British line. The *Ajax* traded broadsides with the Spaniard, but she broke off and ran back to the Spanish line when the *Resolute* fired on her. The *Ajax* returned to her position two cables off the *Pegasus'* starboard.

"Signal from the flagship, sir. 'Scout. Do not engage.'"

"Acknowledge."

Even though he'd been ordered to sit it out, Thorton was not one to assume that battle would not come to him. His palms itched; on a day on which fleets clashed to be left entirely out seemed impossible to endure. Even if it was the prudent course.

"Pass the word for the carpenter."

Meanwhile the *Arrow* was coming alongside. Her purple clad officers stood on her poop deck and the purple ensign with the white crescent and star fluttered astern. The tallest officer was a figure well known to Thorton: Commodore Isam bin Hamet al-Tangueli, known to the English as 'Captain Tangle.' A white turban capped his lean figure. The long purple skirts of the Turkish coat stopped just short of the top of his knees to reveal buff-colored pantaloons tucked into tall black boots. His scimitar hung on his right hip — the corsair was a left-handed man. His face and hands were burned the color of mahogany by long exposure to the sun while his eyes were lively and brown.

"Ahoy the *Ajax*! What the hell happened to you?" Tangle spoke reasonably good English as he pointed at the gaping holes in the frigate's side.

"Took two Spanish xebecs yesterday," Thorton called back. "How is it with you?"

"Patrolling," Tangle replied. "We heard your signal." The gun-pause-gun-gun signal was the Sallee rovers' warning for an enemy vessel.

The two small vessels were being left behind in the wake of the battleships. "Are you going to fight?" Thorton asked.

Tangle tugged the white streak that ran down the middle of his short black beard. "If I come across anything my own size, I will. What about you?" He eyed the stripped strakes dubiously.

"Dispatches. We've been ordered to observe and carry the news to England."

"I'll stay with you then. You look like you could use some cover."

Thorton smiled at the man. "We'd like your company. Care to join us for dinner? Bring a few of your officers over."

"I will!" He knew which officer in particular Thorton wanted to see and grinned at the blond lieutenant.

They reached the mouth of the bay and saw a line of small fore-and-aft rigged vessels. The Sallee commodore made signals. A pair of galiots and some galleys fanned out to wait and watch for the opportunity to pick off wounded vessels and stragglers. The small lateen craft were no match for battleships. Then the *Dart* was lowered from the *Arrow's* deck and Tangle and several men went into it.

Thorton went down to meet his guests. The first aboard was Shakil bin Nakih, purser's mate from the *Arrow*. He wore a plain purple coat and simple white turban. He was lightly tanned and his hazel eyes were warm. He smiled and put his hand to his forehead as he bowed deeply.

"Salaam, Peter Rais," he said in Arabic.

"Salaam, habibi," Thorton replied, daring to use the Arab endearment no Englishman would understand. "Thank you for joining us for dinner," he said in English. His heart was full of feelings he could not express in words — not in Arabic, Spanish, nor English. Thorton suddenly seized the Moor by the shoulders and kissed him on both cheeks in the French fashion. Shakil blushed and grinned at the familiarity. It would not do to show too much favoritism to his lover; Thorton's relationship with the Moor was not public knowledge. With a gulp he realized he was going to have to kiss all the guests like a Frenchman so they did not think he had singled out Shakil.

Lieutenant Archibald Maynard Aruj scrambled on board and stood on his peg leg looking around. The men of the *Ajax* recognized him — he had been one of their midshipmen until he'd deserted and taken the turban.

Thorton said, "Archie, you've grown!" It was true. The boy-lieutenant's wrists were sticking out of the bottom of his purple sleeves. Thorton grabbed him by the shoulders and gave him a peck on each cheek. Aruj smiled back at him and returned the kiss.

Lieutenant Joshua Foster, another English renegade, came on deck next. He was a stout and hairy man with red hair grizzled grey. He had bushy grey muttonchops as if to make up for the hair disappearing from the top of his head. He, too, wore the turban.

"I hope you don't mind if I don't kiss you," Thorton said.

"I'll be jealous, but I'll forgive you," Foster said jovially.

Thorton blushed. "I don't want you to feel left out." So he lightly pecked Foster on each hairy cheek. "'Tis good to see you again, Joshua."

"And you, sir. We've been worried about you."

Last came Tangle. He was the tallest man on either of the two vessels. With his boots and turban he loomed even larger.

Thorton found himself unable to speak as he stared into the man's eyes and felt the lightning in his soul. Tangle felt it, too, and his brown eyes glowed as hot as coffee about to boil over. How closely Thorton's fate had entwined with this man's for half a year! A lifetime of adventure crammed into a few short months.

The Sallee rover spoke in a deep baritone, "Peter Rais, peace be upon you and all within this vessel."

Thorton saluted smartly. "And also upon you, sir. I trust you have been well since I saw you last?"

"Very well. But bored with blockade duty. I thank you for the dinner invitation. We are on the dull end of our stores."

"My table isn't big enough and I think we all want to watch the action. Let's have a picnic on the quarterdeck," Thorton suggested.

"Capital idea!" Tangle agreed.

As he turned away from the corsair commodore, he saw Shakil watching them with narrowed eyes.

"Shakil, will you help me?" he asked in Spanish. Turning to the others he said in English, "Please go up to the quarterdeck. I'll speak to the mess servants."

The British and Sallee officers climbed up. Thorton and Shakil went quietly into the cabin and helped the servants pack the baskets and trays to take them up.

When the servants were gone, Shakil said, "You still carry a torch for him."

"I don't!" Thorton protested.

"I saw the way you two looked at each other."

"I don't want him."

"He wants you."

"He can't have me! I love you, Shakil. I jilted him for good reason and I don't regret it. I have been faithful to you. Ask Abby. He set his cap for me but I turned him down. You are the only one I want."

"Look at me, Peter. I'm not tall and dashing. I'm not the heroic *Kapitan Pasha*. I'm nothing like him!"

"That's why I love you!" Thorton said fiercely. He seized him in his arms. "You are good and kind and noble and brave and honest and loyal and helpful and cheerful and sweet and clever and everything I like."

Shakil was two inches shorter than Thorton with a slim frame. His porcelain skin was fine; he had not been weathered by years at sea and hardened by rough living. He felt good in Thorton's arms, and the blond lieutenant was filled with the urge to protect and cherish him.

Shakil slipped his arms around Thorton's neck. "Do you really mean it?"

"You know I do. I miss you all the time. I wish we didn't have to go up to dinner."

Shakil melted and let Thorton kiss him long and passionately. Thorton closed his eyes and let all that he felt in his body and his soul burn itself in his memory. If ever he was tempted by another man, he would pull up this moment as armor against temptation. "I will be true to you and only you," he whispered.

Shakil stroked his face. "I know how hard it is to resist Isam, but he needs a friend, not a lover. He's only human. He has bad dreams and catches cold. Remember that, Peter. Sometimes he forgets."

Thorton smiled crookedly. "I'm still a little afraid of him."

Shakil laughed an honest laugh at that. "I was petrified of him for years. I got over it. You will, too." He hooked his arm in Thorton's elbow. "They will wonder what we are doing. We have to go up."

It was crowded around the tablecloth, but the midshipmen were dislodged to make room for the guests. The middies perched on the guns with their plates balanced in their laps. Tangle got the foot of the tablecloth as the guest of honor and Shakil was shoehorned in next to Thorton. Abby managed to insert himself next to the famous corsair. The other officers jammed in so close together that nobody paid any attention to the fact that Thorton's and Shakil's knees touched throughout the entirety of the meal. Likewise nobody objected when Tangle served cold beef and couscous onto blind Abby's plate. It was a jolly gathering as they shared stories with one another about their activities of late.

"I'll run with you through the Pinch, but then I must go back to Tettiwan for supplies," Tangle was telling Thorton.

"May I go with you, sir?" Abby asked.

Tangle smiled. "I'd like that. How about it, Peter Rais? May Abby come with us?"

"I'm afraid not. He has to go to England for the inquiry about the loss of the *Adamant* and the rest of that business," Thorton replied.

A shadow fell over Abby's face. Although he was only the fourth lieutenant, he was the *Adamant*'s senior surviving officer. A court of inquiry would not be a pleasant.

"Jacky has to go with me," he countered. Lemuel Jackson was the only surviving midshipman from the *Adamant*.

"Yes, he does," Thorton agreed.

A pall fell over the picnic. The British officers sat in glum silence, except for Posonby, who had been safe at Gibraltar and hence untouched by the stain of the British defeats at Minorca and Majorca.

Tangle spoke. "If you help me get supplies, I will go with you to England. I was a witness to the battle and since I am not an Englishman, I am as close to an impartial observer as you can find."

"Do your orders permit it?" Thorton glanced at Shakil out of the corner of his eye and gave his lover a hopeful look.

"I am on station in the Strait to seize the cabotage, but with such heavy fleets in the Pinch, nothing dares move without an escort unless it is far larger than we can take. This has not been a profitable cruise for us. So although it stretches orders to cruise all the way to England, as long as we take prizes, I can make my excuses. Supplies are the issue."

"We'd like your company, rais, but we can't go into Tettiwan. That is the wrong direction for us. We must pick up the *Elf* and the prizes in Gibraltar. Maybe we can get supplies for you there."

Tangle gave him a lopsided smile. "You will be selling my own casks back to me, I think. Ah well. I'll leave Shakil with you to make the arrangements." He switched to Arabic to explain to Shakil what was wanted because the purser's mate knew only a few words of English.

The rumble of gunnery halted their chatter. They all froze with their forks or spoons in hand and cocked their heads to listen.

"What is it, Chambers?" Thorton asked.

From his vantage point on the starboard gun the youth reported, "The Spanish have reached the Turkish line."

Everybody stood up and watched. Tangle picked up his plate and ate the remains of his food hastily. So did Thorton and the rest of the officers. They gulped their food and washed it all down with wine as they watched the spectacle of the Spanish fleet paralleling the Turkish line. The British fleet nipped their heels and kept harassing them. A pall of gunsmoke developed that obscured most of the action in the fog of war. The thunder of the guns became continuous.

Tangle handed off his empty plate. "I thank you for your hospitality, but I must return to my ship. I'll send Shakil's dunnage over."

"Thank you, Commodore."

CHAPTER 8 : SURVIVORS

The battle lasted most of the day. When it was over, the drifting and battered hulks of Turkish and Sallee vessels littered a stretch of sea three miles to the east of Sebta. There was nothing for small vessels like the *Ajax* and *Arrow* to do but follow in their wake and pick up survivors. They fished up Turks, Moors, Sallee rovers, and a few Spaniards. The Muslims they treated with kindness, but the Spaniards they locked in the hold. Shakil was helpful as a translator. He recorded the names of the rescued men, their nationality, and whether they were wounded.

"At least we'll get some head money," Perry commented.

Thorton shrugged. "'Twill not be much, but I suppose 'tis better to arrive in England with prisoners than without."

The sun was sinking in the west when a British battleship came up on them.

"The *Resolute* is making signals, sir," Chambers informed Thorton. "'Relay from flagship, 'Captains report in half an hour.'"

Thorton checked his pocket watch, made a note of the time, then went below to write a brief report and append the names of the prisoners and rescued seamen. By the time it was done the cutter was ready. The wind picked up and the boat skimmed over the whitecaps to the *Pegasus*. They were fishing a new yard and reeving new lines on her. The carpenter and his mates were at work plugging holes. Her ensign was torn but still flying. She had a Spanish battleship under her lee, *Nuestra Señora de Buen Consejo,* 74 guns. Several small boats converged on the battleship, including one flying the purple pennant of the Sallee rovers. The British captains stood aside and let Commodore Tangueli hook on first. He climbed up the side and went in through the entry port. He was greeted with six sideboys, the trill of the pipe and ruffle of drums. Thorton, being only a lieutenant acting as a captain, was the most junior and last to board. He saluted anything that moved.

They were admitted to Commodore Whittingdon's cabin. It was large and had a ceiling high enough for even Tangle to stand upright. The wainscoting was painted white with blue trim and the chairs had blue cushions on them. A brass chandelier with crystal pendants hung over the table. The oak table had enough room to seat them all.

The captains who had fought the Spanish gave their reports first. Action, damage, casualties, prisoners. Thorton listened carefully. The taking of the *Buen Consejo* was the only notable action for the British. Then the non-combatants reported their survivors and prisoners. All told the British had picked up over a thousand men, more than two hundred of which were Spanish prisoners. The question was, what to do with so many Turks, Moors, and Sallee rovers? Gibraltar could not easily receive them.

"So we would be grateful if you would land them at Tettiwan or Zokhara," Tangle explained. "The able men can go into Tettiwan but the casualties must go by ship to the hospital at Zokhara."

Whittingdon shook his head. "We can't leave Gibraltar defenseless — out of the question. We can land the casualties at Tettiwan for humanitarian reasons. You'll have to ferry the rest yourselves."

Tangle shook his head firmly. "No hospital in Tettiwan. Wounded men cannot travel by land to Zokhara. They need to go by ship."

Whittingdon checked his figures. He had nearly two hundred Muslim casualties in his care. He hmmed and hummed. "Quite. But we agree that you must take the able-bodied men yourself?"

"We do not agree. I am low on supplies. I need them tonight. I want to turn the corner of the Modiq Peninsula before the Spanish come out again. Mark my word, they will be cruising for us tomorrow. We are bound to meet disabled Turkish or Moorish ships and must help them. That will slow us down. I'd like the *Resolute* and the *Ajax* to escort us."

Whittingdon made a steeple of his fingers. "That is a large request."

Tangle shrugged. "'Tis a large number of men. We are loaded with survivors and prisoners ourselves. The *Resolute* and *Ajax* are shot up. They are no good for battle, but they can transport men. It is time our British ally did us a service. I insist."

Whittingdon humphed again. "Very well. I will send the *Resolute* and the *Ajax* to carry as many men as possible in exchange for supplies for Gibraltar. With the Turkish fleet in disarray the Spanish are sure to blockade the Strait again. We need powder, shot, and food. We cannot afford to assist you unless you supply us."

Tangle tugged the white streak in his beard as he thought about it. "Very well. That can be arranged. My purser's mate speaks a little English. He'll take care of it."

They returned to Gibraltar. Thorton moored alongside the Old Mole and spent the rest of the afternoon and evening making repairs. He wanted a proper dry dock with the ability to steam planks, but no such facility existed at Gibraltar. The new planks were bent into place by the brute force of fifty men throwing their shoulders against them. Meanwhile Shakil shuttled between the shore and ships; he had the British letters of credit Horner had used to buy supplies off the Sallee rovers a month ago. He redeemed them for supplies for the *Arrow*. The rovers were not happy with British salt beef and hard tack, but they took what they could get.

At midnight the Sallee-British convoy got under way. It consisted of the *Arrow*, two other galiots, a pair of galleys, the *Resolute*, and the *Ajax*. The *Arrow* flew the purple pennant of a Sallee commodore. It was a cold night with the wind out of the northwest. The wind was favorable for Zokhara and they made excellent time. Sadly the *Ajax* did not have any covers for the new gunports. Canvas port covers made of old sailcloth cut the breeze but it was unusually chilly and drafty belowdecks. The hammering and sawing went on all night as one by one the new wooden covers were made and fitted.

Dawn found Thorton and Shakil curled up together in a makeshift bed on the floor of great cabin. They had been much too tired to do anything but sleep. They huddled together to keep warm through the crisp September night. At eight bells Ra'uf knocked on Thorton's door, then entered with the wash water. If he was surprised to find the two of them together when he lit the lamps, he didn't show it. He laid out Thorton's shaving kit and brushed his uniform coat.

Shakil woke blearily, then stretched and yawned. He washed in the basin. Thorton dragged himself out of bed into the pre-dawn chill and washed himself as well. They shaved side by side at the mirror.

When they were clean and dressed, Shakil asked, "Will you join me for prayers?"

"I will, but we must pray quietly."

The Moor nodded. "For your sake, all right."

"Ra'uf, do you want to pray with us?" Thorton asked.

"I will."

The three turned to face forward. It was their best estimate as to the position of Mecca. Shakil chanted the Arabic softly and they answered him in equally soft voices. They bowed and turned, then knelt and prostrated themselves in the prescribed manner. They were only halfway through the prayer when a knock came at the door.

Thorton froze in alarm. "That will be Perry for the morning inspection. Ra'uf, tell him that I have overslept and to return in fifteen minutes."

Ra'uf went to the door and in his bad English said, "Captain sleep late. He not ready. Come back fifteen minutes."

Perry had overslept himself and dressed in haste. He was pleased to be given fifteen minutes grace to shave and drink some tea. When he returned he found Thorton coming out of the cabin with a cup of coffee in his hand. They fell into their morning routine and walked the ship attended by various mates and officers.

All the ports on the larboard side finally had covers, but the starboard side did not. Not as many planks had been damaged on the starboard side, but three covers were needed.

"Get the covers on the starboard gun ports this morning. We can omit holystoning the decks to make it so. I want the guns situated properly."

"Aye aye, sir." The ship's carpenter was bleary-eyed and swaying with fatigue as he walked.

Thorton said, "I know you're tired, Ferrell, but the wind is kicking up. We must get the ports sealed. You can have whatever men you need."

"Aye aye, sir."

They went below, checked the hold, took the measure of water in the bilge, and visited the wounded. Eventually they came up on deck. The sound of hammering reverberated through the ship. "Up hammocks," was piped. Thorton was very tired and his stomach rumbled. Perry had the first watch and was just as tired. Dawn broke in a crimson sky while clouds piled up in the north. The day remained chilly even as the sky lightened. They counted three Turkish additions to their convoy. The mixed lot of square-riggers and fore-and-afters were making about seven knots. With the wind astern the square-riggers could have made more speed, but the lateeners did not run as well on that course. They had set their sails in "hare's ears" with the foresail on one tack and the mainsail on the other to make the best of the situation.

"Looks like rain," Perry observed. He turned his collar up against the clammy air.

"As long as it doesn't veer around to the east," Thorton said. "Not until we've turned the corner and are sailing up Modiq Bay, anyhow."

The wind they were running before would turn into a headwind once they rounded the tip of the peninsula and had to beat up to Zokhara.

By breakfast time all the gun ports were covered. It didn't rain, but it did drizzle and a cold northwest wind flew fitfully. The hands were just as tired as the officers and trudged to their messes to eat. Perry and Thorton retired to the great cabin where they found Shakil sitting at Thorton's desk. He was working his figures with a reed pen.

"I hope you don't mind me using your desk," Shakil said in Arabic.

"Not at all. You'll join us for breakfast?" Thorton replied in the same language.

Perry dropped his hat on the table and stood watching Shakil with hooded eyes.

"Yes?" Shakil asked politely in English in response to Perry's look.

Perry shook his head. "Nothing."

Ra'uf was setting bowls of oatmeal on the table. A few slices of orange accompanied each bowl as well as toast, bacon and coffee. "Not many oranges left," he told Thorton.

Thorton nodded. "We'll have to make them last."

"We have plenty on the *Arrow*, do you want some?" Shakil asked in Arabic.

"Yes, and more couscous if I can get them," Thorton replied.

Shakil cleaned his pen and came over to the table. "You need some bed curtains and a bed, too."

"Can I get some more of that checked cloth to make bed curtains?" Thorton asked as he settled into his place at the head of the table. He switched to Spanish to supplement his meager Arabic.

"Yes, I think there's a bolt left." Shakil made the change easily.

Perry spoke French well enough that he could make out some of the Spanish. He ate his oatmeal quietly. When Thorton and Shakil stopped talking and started eating he asked Shakil in French, "Will you be staying with us until England?"

Thorton had to translate into Spanish for him. "I don't know," Shakil replied. He glanced at Thorton.

Thorton chewed his lip. He wanted very much to have Shakil with him as long as he could, but he knew Perry knew why. He racked his brain to come up with an excuse to justify keeping his lover with him, but his effort was in vain. "Until we get to Zokhara, I think. I don't see any reason why you would be needed after that."

"I need to go over to the *Resolute* and the *Arrow* about the accounts. May I borrow a boat?" Shakil asked.

"Yes, of course. Abby wants to go over the *Arrow* for a visit, too. You can take him with you."

"Thank you, Peter Rais." Shakil smiled warmly. Thorton smiled back. Perry pointedly ignored them.

The purple-clad Moor finished his breakfast and went up to make ready for his trip, but Perry lingered at the table.

Thorton scraped the last of the oatmeal from his bowl. "What?"

"People will talk. It won't be long before they realize you're sleeping with him."

Thorton stiffened. "There is nothing wrong with sleeping. He must be housed somewhere."

"But not with the captain. 'Tis too much favor for a mere purser's mate."

"He's the Sallee commodore's brother-in-law," Thorton pointed out.

"This is how rumors start."

"Not if you keep your mouth shut, Lieutenant."

Perry glared at him. The scar across his face made him look even angrier. "As you wish, Captain," he snapped.

Thorton put his hands on the edge of the table and pushed his chair back. "I don't like your tone, Lieutenant."

Perry sighed. "Peter, come to your senses. He's not even British, for God's sake!"

"I love him."

Perry scowled at him. "Once you said you loved me, then you were making eyes at Tangle, and now you 'love' Shakil. You're fickle."

"You're jealous!"

"I am not! I'm angry. You toy with people's affections with no concern for the trouble you cause. You nearly ruined me."

"You tried to entrap me in Mahon!"

"That was your fault!"

Thorton jumped to his feet. "I'll hear no more of it. I had my court martial. The matter is settled."

"Feh. You've been made acting-captain of the *Ajax*. That's not much of punishment, is it?"

"They busted me back to midshipman and fined me twenty-five pounds!"

"Tangle paid the fine and Whittingdon made you a lieutenant again. You didn't suffer."

"I paid the fine out of my Sallee prize money. Besides, you know we're short on officers."

"They should have made Forsythe acting-captain, not you. He was senior here. Whittingdon is playing favorites. 'Tis not fair to Albert."

"He's better off where he is. He's a good clerk. He is exactly the kind of help Horner needs on the *Resolute*. You know he lacks the nerve for command."

"I don't lack the nerve! I've got more seniority than you, too."

Thorton stared at the man who had once been his friend. "What do you want? To trade places with me? Would that end your grudge?"

Perry was silent for a while. "No."

"Can't we put this behind us and be friends again?"

Another long silence. "No. You abused my friendship. I can't forgive you for that."

Thorton sat in his chair again. "I'm sorry, Roger."

Perry rose from his place. "By your leave, I have work to do, Captain," he said coldly.

"Dismissed."

CHAPTER 9 : ZOKHARA

Two days after they left Gibraltar they beat up Modiq Bay. It proved an onerous chore for the square-rigged ships. They were obliged to set their staysails and put out their sweeps if they had them. The galiot danced ahead of them. The more flexible lateen rig was adapted to the undulations of the twisty bay. It was full of shoals, dotted with islands, and laced with coves, points, and necks. The *Arrow* could have left them behind, but didn't. Instead she waited patiently for the *Resolute* and *Ajax* to struggle through the winding roads. The Turks had an equally difficult time of it; a generation before they had adopted square-rigged battleships in an effort to modernize and compete with the rising empires of the West, but it had not done them any good.

"I see now why the square rig never became popular with the corsairs," Perry observed. Once again the *Ajax* had to put out her sweeps to work around a corner.

"Oh, they have square sails too," Thorton replied. "It depends on the voyage. If they're going to make a long trip running before the wind they'll adopt a polacre rig. Say from Zokhara to Alexandria. On the way back they'll rig lateen because they have to beat against the prevailing wind."

Perry looked dubious. "That sounds like an awful lot of changing sails."

"I like having the option myself," Thorton replied.

"What's that fortress?" Posonby asked as a new sight came into view.

"Star Fort. It was built on an artificial island in the middle of the shoals. Deep-drought vessels have to go around it to get into the harbor," Thorton replied.

The fort was a substantial construction in the modern 'star' style. It enfiladed a two mile long approach during which a ship would exposed to heavy artillery with no chance to respond in kind. If they succeeded in reaching the island, they must still work around it, exposed to gunfire all the while. It was a formidable defense.

The galiot fired the Sallee rovers private signal. The four smallest guns cracked out, boom, boom, boom, pause, boom. There were some houses and fishboats scattered on the western shore and the people came out to wave.

"That's Pearl Point," Thorton said, indicating the point they were passing. "And that's Mosque Point."

As the *Arrow* passed the cove between them, Thorton pointed out a single story house with Greek columns at the bottom of the cove.

"Bessilama House. Shakil and Jamila own the farm. That is to say, Mistress Tangueli. It is the Muslim custom to address people by their given names."

Children trooped out of the house and ran down to the water to wave and shout. A woman in sky blue veils accompanied them, along with female servants and a big black barking dog.

"The wife and children of Commodore Tangueli."

As they watched, the woman and a black servant got into the boat tied up at the dock and cast off. The little boat with its single lateen sail skimmed before the wind. The woman stood straight and tall with her silks blowing about her.

Perry trained his spyglass on her. "God, she's beautiful!"

"I suppose she is," Thorton replied indifferently.

As they watched, she took off her veil and waved it at the *Arrow*. Streamers of auburn curls blew back from her face. She was smiling and her eyes were intent on the purple figure at the rail of the *Arrow*. The tall, turban-topped figure waved back enthusiastically.

"She's taking off her veil and waving it!" Perry exclaimed. His glass was glued to the spectacle.

All the officers of the *Ajax* were crowded along the rail to watch: Perry, Posonby, Abby, Jackson, Chambers, Pettigrew, Bettancourt, Jones, Sinclair, Ferncastle, Pennybrigg, Blakesley and more.

Shakil stood next to Thorton and asked, "What did he say?" After Thorton translated for him, Shakil tapped Perry on the shoulder.

Perry looked around, "Yes?"

Shakil said in English, "She is my sister."

Perry lowered the spyglass. "I was just saying," he replied.

Shakil had recourse to Thorton for help with what he wanted to say in English. "Don't ogle her. She is a wife and mother. She is a Muslim woman. Show respect."

Perry closed the spyglass and put it in his pocket. "I meant no disrespect. My remarks were born of admiration."

Shakil waited for Thorton to translate, then said, "Apology accepted."

The *Arrow* held water and waited.

"Back sails," Thorton said.

They kept their position and watched the little boat overtake the commodore's vessel. The woman pinned her silk back over her hair. By the time she reached the vessel she was properly veiled.

Perry watched her as she climbed up the battens to the deck. "Damn the Turk for a lucky man," he muttered under his breath.

Blind Abby changed the subject, "What does the country look like?"

Thorton was happy to answer him. "The fields have been harvested. There's a forest to the north and an orange grove to the south. 'Tis a large farm. In Maryland we would have called it a 'plantation.' They sell produce directly to the ships, so they receive a better price, but the corsairs, buying it from the farm, get it cheaper than they would in the city. All the farms around here cooperate in supplying Commodore Tangueli and his squadron. There is a thriving town on the other side of Mosque Point. It has chandlers, coopers, caulkers, shipsmiths, couscous makers, sailmakers, butchers, ropers, anything needed to equip the corsairs. This side has cottages for fishermen and oyster divers and so forth."

"Arabic signal from the *Arrow*, sir," Chambers reported.

Thorton raised his glass to his good eye. He translated for them, "*Arrow* to fort, 'Escorts are British and Turkish allies.'"

British naval vessels were rare visitors to Zokhara. They came to deliver and pick up consuls and little else. Usually they landed their dispatches at Tettiwan, a small town on the other side of the Modiq Peninsula from whence they traveled overland twenty or so miles to Zokhara. It was faster than trying to round the peninsula in a ship, a route that added seventy-five miles and a day to the trip — if the winds were fair.

The *Arrow* saluted the fort. Her guns boomed one by one and smoke drifted lazily on the breeze. The fort returned her salute. The puffs of smoke were seen first, then a second later the sound of the report. The salute for a commodore was substantial, eleven guns, fired several seconds apart. The *Arrow* came up to the fort before it was finished. She put out her sweeps and swept gracefully around the bend.

The *Resolute* came up next. She delivered her salute, then made the turn around the shoal. She stalled and sent out her boats to tow her. Slowly she crept around the horseshoe bend.

Next the *Ajax* came up.

"Prepare to salute the Sallee colors," Thorton directed.

One by one the *Ajax* boomed her honors to the host nation and its purple flag.

The *Ajax* put out her sweeps to help her make the turn. Thorton knew that her shallow draft did not garner much respect from the British navy, but she suited him very well at the moment. Her dozen oars were enough for her to sweep gracefully around the horseshoe bend with the Turkish and Salletine ships following in her wake

The sailing master, quartermaster, and their mates were all clustered together. They had a chart, but it was an old chart and not very accurate. Blakesley had been making soundings and corrections all the way up the bay. The resulting document would be a vast improvement.

They glided around the north side of the shoals and the road of Zokhara opened up before them. It ran northwest and another long point delineated its northern shore. "North Point," Thorton said.

Ahead of them the galiot made signals in Arabic, then the Latin alphabet. "'Maintain course northwest,'" Chambers reported.

"Acknowledge."

The *Arrow* pulled in her sweeps and swept close-hauled in a sudden turn to the north. She ran up opposite of North Point, then turned and skimmed southwest on a beam reach with her sails full of wind. She was as beautiful and light as a bird as she made her board — but her sails were on bad tack. They pressed against the masts because Tangle had not bothered to lower the antennas then raise them again on the proper side. The reason was soon apparent. Reaching the southern side of the road, she tacked again and shot up close-hauled on a good tack into the Arsenal of Zokhara on the northwest shore. She spilled her wind and put out her oars with perfect timing as she approached the entrance. She glided between the towers with the dignity of a royal barge and disappeared from sight.

The *Resolute* and *Ajax* continued the laborious feat of towing and sweeping into Zokhara against the wind. It took them two hours to creep over the distance the *Arrow* had covered in a mere thirty minutes. The *Ajax* could not sail as close to the wind; it would have been futile to try and make the northern board necessary to set up the broad reach. As for the *Resolute*, there was simply not enough water to the north to even think about it.

They dropped their anchors and found a good sandy bottom mixed with some mud and weeds. The anchors set well. Officials from the

Lazaretto came out to make arrangements to take off the wounded and prisoners. Meanwhile Tangle finished his own arrangements in the Arsenal and the *Dart* skimmed across the bay and hooked onto the chains of the *Resolute*. Shortly thereafter the signal was made for Thorton to come aboard.

Acting-Captain Thorton was admitted to the great cabin of the *Resolute*. Patchwork was much in evidence, but it had all been painted over. The cabin was sparsely furnished; Horner had never been a rich man. His mahogany and brass barometer-thermometer was the most precious thing in the cabin. His small chandelier was brass and his desk well worn. The cabin was as thin and threadbare as the man himself.

Horner himself was getting thin on top while his face had a perpetually dour expression. He could have been a handsome man had he ever smiled. His build was tall and gangly. His uniform was perfectly decent although it had it had never been fine, and his shirts were plain, without ruffles or lace. He might have been thought a Quaker, if there were such a thing as a Quaker naval officer.

Looking between them Thorton was struck by the vitality of the rover. Although Tangle was in fact several years older than Horner, he looked younger. The grey in his black beard made him appear distinguished, not worn. His purple coat was made of good quality hemp, fit well, and adorned with a fair amount of gold braid in stripes across his chest in the Turkish fashion. His black knee-high boots were well polished and his turban was crisp white. He had an energetic air about him even when he stood still.

Horner said, "Lieutenant Thorton, you will be my liaison in Zokhara since you know the city and the language. Commodore Tangueli tells me that we may be able to use the Arsenal to make repairs, but we must get permission from the Minister of Marine. I understand you know him."

Thorton was confused. "I do?"

Tangle smiled at him. "Zahid Amir."

"Ah," said Thorton. "Yes, I know him. Lord Zahid was educated in England and speaks English," he told Horner. "He admires the British navy. He will be a friend to us."

Horner gave the briefest of nods in acknowledgement. "Thank you, Commodore. May I impose on you to escort us to the palace?"

Tangle's eyes darkened and he shook his head. "You may expect me to do as much for you as the British did for me at Mahon," he replied coolly.

The British hadn't done anything for him. On the contrary, he had fought a duel with Admiral Walters.

Horner replied delicately, "'Twas not I who quarreled with you. Walters is dead."

Tangle's jaw worked and he folded his arms over his chest. "That does not change what happened. England has not treated the Sallee Republic like an ally. They wanted to hang Thorton."

"The matter was resolved satisfactorily. I trust you have no complaint about Commodore Whittingdon."

"I have no quarrel with Whittingdon. But it irks me that he formerly paid no attention to the Sallee Republic but now wants us to supply him. It seems we matter to the British only when convenient."

Thorton touched his purple sleeve gently. "Isam Rais. It will do Sallee no good to short Gibraltar on supplies. If Gibraltar falls, the Strait will be even more firmly in Spanish hands. Will you cut off your nose to spite your face?"

Tangle did not understand all that he said and Thorton had to repeat it in Spanish.

The Sallee rover sighed and unfolded his arms. "I will not accompany you, but I will give you letters of introduction. I suggest you call on Lord Naseed in the Arsenal yourself and send Peter Rais to the Minister of Marine. I will not do more for you. Thorton is your partisan. You will have to depend on him."

That made Thorton nervous. He was not accustomed to associating with anyone of higher rank than a captain. Ministers were out of his ken. He knew Zahid, it was true, but he could hardly be called a bosom friend. He was one of the sons of the Bey of Tanguel, and that made Zahid a sort of prince or at least a lord.

"Thank you, rais. You are very gracious." Horner bowed politely.

"If I may use your desk and paper, I will write out the letter."

"Certainly, Commodore."

Thorton wasted no time in calling on the Minister. Zahid wore a naval uniform in purple and a large white turban. His carriage was as erect as any man schooled by the British system, as indeed he had been. He was a graduate of Cambridge University. He spoke excellent English with the accent of the upper classes.

"Peter Rais! I am delighted to see you alive and well. You must tell me everything that has happened."

They settled on the divans and crossed their legs. The carpets were three thick on the floor and richly colored brown, tan, and red. The walls were decorated with brown and white tiles and fretwork filled the windows. Crimson and gold brocade cushions added to the comfort of plush divans. A great bronze lamp of intricate filagree cast a warm light. Outside it was grey and threatened rain, but inside it was warm, thanks to a brazier loaded with charcoal. Pomegranate trees were setting their first ruddy fruits just outside the window and they gleamed redly in the damp. Thorton and Zahid drank frothy sweet Turkish coffee and ate baklava and grapes while Thorton told him all about his court martial and adventures. Some how it was easier to talk to Zahid than an Englishman of the same rank.

"Of course you may use the Arsenal to refit. I will send a letter immediately."

"Tonight?" Thorton asked.

Zahid smiled. "British efficiency, eh? That will not go over well with Lord Naseed, I'm afraid. He is a Turk. I wish we had a more energetic man in his place."

"Some one like Isam Rais."

Zahid shook his head. "He would languish like a leopard in a cage if we tried to give him a desk job. That one will die on his quarterdeck like his father before him."

Thorton shivered. He had not thought much about the manner of another man's death; he had been preoccupied with his own affairs. With his court martial safely past, he was very much alive and likely to remain so for a while. He began to wonder how he might reach his final end. A desk job didn't sound half bad. He thought about the mortality of the people he knew: Tangle, Shakil, Perry, Horner, Abby, Forsythe, Jamila — even little Miss Tahirah, Tangle's daughter. Another little girl, Miss Gertrude FitzGerald, was paralyzed for life after a moment's accident. Thorton himself was blind in one eye. He put his hand up to the milk-glass eye and sighed.

Zahid watched him, then said, "You're going to the hospital, aren't you?"

Thorton looked at him in surprise. "For what?"

"To have the cataract removed."

Thorton gaped at him. "How? 'Tis my eye."

Zahid chuckled a little. "I am an ophthalmologist." He had to use Arabic because no such word existed in English. "An 'occulist,' so to speak, except much more highly skilled. After completing my degrees in philosophy and biology at Cambridge, I entered the University of Al-Karaouine in Fez where I completed my medical degree. I did my internship at the Charity Hospital here. It is one of the greatest hospitals in Africa and I dare say our ophthalmology department is superior to that of the Qalawun Hospital in Cairo, even if the hospital itself is not nearly so large. I will arrange for you to be admitted on Sunday before you break your fast. You'll be bandaged for a week, and your eye should be completely healed in two weeks."

Thorton was amazed. "How much does it cost? Will it hurt?"

"It will not cost anything, Peter Rais. All the services of the hospital are free to the residents of Zokhara. You are one of us. You took the turban and swore your oath of citizenship. It will hurt a little bit, but we will give you anesthesia. You will sleep through the operation."

"I have to have my captain's permission."

"By all means. Invite him to witness the operation. I think he will be impressed. As a gesture of good will I perform cataract surgery on any British seaman or officer who needs it as long as the fleet is in Zokhara."

Thorton gaped. "That is a generous offer, sir!" He knelt on the carpet before the man and grabbed his hand and kissed it. "If you can restore my sight, I will be forever in your debt."

Zahid patted his hand. "I am a great admirer of British industry and efficiency, but you must admit, your medical science and hygiene are deficient. An alliance between our countries will be good for both of us. We will improve our industry with British help, and British medicine will improve with our help. The result will be two countries that are healthier, happier, and more prosperous."

"If you say so, sir."

CHAPTER 10 : CHARITY HOSPITAL

Thorton presented himself at Charity Hospital. He was comfortably dressed in a loose-fitting white tunic and pantaloons as directed by the doctor. A blue-checked cloth was tied over his hair. He hadn't eaten. The operating table was padded and covered with leather and a clean white linen sheet over it. Natural light streamed in from the clerestory windows supplemented by lanterns on stands with reflectors to direct and intensify the light. The room had a clean soapy smell. A small gallery ranged along one side and various medical students, doctors, and well-wishers filled the benches. Tangle and Shakil were right in front. Captain Horner did not attend.

Dr. Ferncastle was beside the nurse to observe everything. He had already had an extensive conference with Zahid and a tour of the ophthalmology clinic. He was fascinated by everything. Very few doctors in England attempted such things. He was well aware that when his tour of duty ended he might go home and become a celebrated eye surgeon. If he could heal the blind, people would come from miles around and pay any price for his work. He was zealous to learn everything the Muslims could teach him.

The nurse was a round-faced man with a cheerful countenance. He spoke kindly to Thorton, then put the sponge full of ether over his mouth and nose. Thorton inhaled the strange scent and grew drowsy. The room wavered but the voices continued. The audience hushed and he could hear Dr. Zahid speaking distantly in Arabic, but he could not understand it. Then he heard nothing at all.

Only after he was asleep were his limbs and head bound to the table to keep him secure. They had not told him about that part; it was deemed better to not alarm the patient. The nurse held Thorton's eyelids open and the doctor used a magnifying lens to minutely examine the surface of the eye. He passed the glass to Ferncastle.

Zahid straightened and addressed his audience in both English and Arabic. "There are numerous minute particles embedded in the surface of the eye. I will not be able to remove them. They may work themselves out over time, or they may remain as spots in his vision. However, the cataract itself is fluid and contiguous, so its removal will be simple."

Zahid was wearing a leather apron over his plain white clothes. His sleeves were bound up above his elbows to keep them out of the way. He wore a white cloth over his hair to bind it back. Since his hair was short it seemed a needless measure, but he did it all the same. By contrast, Ferncastle was wearing his green wool coat, powdered wig, and high-heeled shoes. Being a gentleman he would not deign to adopt the simple linen garments of the Muslim medical men at work.

An array of more than twenty delicate steel implements lay on the tray next to the operating table. Zahid selected one. He carefully inserted the tip of a suction needle under the surface of Thorton's eye. Slowly, gently, he drew the fluid out. He laid the needle aside and used the magnifying glass to examine Thorton's eye again. With the obscuring cloud of fluid gone he could see more clearly. The nurse held a lantern with a focussed beam so that he could look inside the dilated pupil. Then he straightened up and the lantern was set aside.

"An excellent prognosis. The damage appears to be all superficial. He will see much better immediately after surgery. The surgery itself will heal within two weeks. Thereafter the surface of the eye should continue to improve. I cannot promise that his vision will be perfect, but I think he will recover at least eighty percent of it."

Applause broke out. Zahid took a small bow. "Thank you."

The nurse placed a soft white pad directly against Thorton's closed eyelid and wrapped a bandage around his head to hold it in place. The restraining straps were removed and hidden. With the ether gone Thorton began to wake up. He heard the chatter of several languages and blinked groggily.

"How much longer?" he asked.

"All finished," Zahid told him cheerfully.

"Already?"

"A simple operation," Zahid assured him. "You have an excellent prognosis. You should recover at least eighty percent of the sight in your left eye."

"Really?"

The nurse helped Thorton sit up Zahid asked, "How do you feel?"

"Sick."

"That is the ether. How is your eye?"

Thorton blinked beneath the bandage. "A little tender."

"Any pain?"

He shook his head, regretted it, and said, "Only if I move quickly."

"Very good. You will convalesce today. If you continue to improve I will let you go back to your ship tomorrow. However, you must remain on light duty until the bandage comes off. Dr. Ferncastle will attend you."

"How long?"

"Five to seven days."

Jackson and Ra'uf helped Thorton down the hall to the ward. His bed was one of ten in the room. The room was dimly lit by tall narrow windows piercing the thick stone walls. The room was a pleasant temperature and very neat and clean. The plastered walls were painted pale blue and the floor was covered with a simple octagonal pattern of dark blue and white tiles. Well-wishers came crowding around to see him.

Shakil dared to sit on the side of his bed and squeeze his hand. He smiled at Thorton. He whispered in Spanish, "I told you it would be all right."

Thorton couldn't help but smile back at him. "I hope it worked! 'Tis a little sore, but I can't really feel anything."

Ferncastle was saying to the British visitors, "It is quite a simple operation, in truth. I could do it myself if I had the proper tools. I wonder if I can buy them here . . ." Then he went back to the operating theater to witness more of the miraculous operations.

There were two other British sailors with cataracts. One was the *Ajax's* blind fiddler and the other was an old man from the *Resolute* who caulked by feel. Zahid operated on each of them and they were brought to the ward to recover. After a while Ra'uf brought Thorton his dinner. The patient was ravenous but the meal was light: soup, fruit, and couscous. No meat. Zahid assured him if he continued to do well he could have more substantial food on the morrow. One of the ship's boys had been left to care for the two other men. They had portable soup, hardtack, cheese, and fruit. The hospital orderlies took care of the men's medical needs, but food, bathing and dressing were the duty of the patients' friends and family. The ratings ate ship's fare and ignored the Muslim doctor's dietary advice.

Abby settled on the other side of the bed. Thorton grabbed his hand. "Alan! Have you seen Dr. Zahid? Perhaps he can help you, too!"

Abby smiled and shook his head. "I did, but he can't. There is nothing wrong with my eyes, he says. I was struck on the head when a portion of the *Resolute's* deck collapsed. My head still hurts and I can't see more than shadows. The injury is inside my skull. He says that my vision should continue to slowly improve. He is uncertain if I will make a full recovery or not. He says it is in God's hands." He spoke quietly, but a needle of grief stitched through his words. "I'm glad for you, though, Peter. 'Tis marvelous what he has done. Three men will see again because of him."

Thorton squeezed his hand. "Time, Alan. You are getting better."

Shakil did not understand the English. He waited politely, then asked in Arabic, "What did he say?"

Tangle stepped up and translated in a soft baritone for him.

Shakil smiled softly at Abby and spoke Arabic. "I am sorry that Zahid Amir could not help you. Allah provides a cure for every disease, but we have not discovered all of them yet."

After Tangle had translated, Abby said, "Thank you. I wish I could speak Arabic."

Shakil smiled. "We can teach you, if you'd like lessons."

Abby's gaze strayed past Shakil up to the tall form of the Sallee commodore. "Yes, I'd like that very much."

Tangle took up the invitation and expanded it. "In fact, we'd like it if all the British officers would join us to shoot peacocks when Peter gets out of the hospital. We have so many they are a nuisance, and I think the gentlemen might like a little sport. They taste like . . . Peter, what is the English word?"

"Pheasant," Thorton supplied.

The invitation caught the attention of the officers hanging around Thorton's bed. "Pheasant is very tasty," Perry agreed.

"Will Horner let us?" Forsythe asked. "He already gave us leave today!"

Tangle smiled. "I'll send him a written invitation. I plan to invite Lord Zahid and other dignitaries. I'll be offended if he refuses. Surely he can spare a day to improve relations between the Sallee Republic and England?" His eyes strayed back to Abby.

Sourly Perry said, "When you put it that way, I don't see how he could refuse."

"Lieutenant Abby. If I may impose on you, I'll write the letter now and you can take it to the captain," Tangle said in his persuasive baritone.

Abby rose swiftly. "I'd be delighted to attend you, Commodore."

The other visitors took that as their cue to say good bye. Slowly they filed out. Shakil and Thorton were left alone, aside from the other sailors lying in their cots. Because they were only ratings, they were on the opposite side of the room so that the officer had as much privacy as the ward could offer.

"Get well, *habibi,*" Shakil said in soft Arabic.

Thorton grinned happily. "I'll try," he promised.

"I'll visit you tomorrow," the Moor said as he rose.

Thorton held his hand tightly. "Stay a little longer. Help me with my prayers. I am forgetting them because I can't pray on board ship."

Shakil could not refuse such an appeal, so he resettled on the bed. "Don't you have the notes I made for you?"

"I do. But I want to hear it from your lips."

Shakil smiled down at him. "All right. The call to prayer goes like this: *Allahu Akbar. Allahu Akbar. Allahu Akbar. Allahu Akbar.*"

"God is great," Thorton replied.

Shakil continued to chant in a plaintive tenor. "*Ash-hadu alla ilaha illallah. Ash-hadu alla ilaha illallah.*"

"I bear witness that there is none worthy of worship except God."

"*Ash-hadu anna Muhammadar Rasulullah. Ash-hadu anna Muhammadar Rasulullah.*"

"I bear witness that Muhammad is the Messenger of God."

"*Hayya alassalah. Hayya alassalah.*"

"Come to prayer."

"*Hayya alal-Falah. Hayya alal-Falah.*"

"Come to success."

"*Allahu Akbar. Allahu Akbar. La ilaha illallah. La ilaha illallah.*"

"God is great. There is none worthy of worship but God."

Shakil held both of Thorton's hands in his as he gazed into his one good eye and smiled.

The blond lieutenant whispered, "Peace and blessings upon you, O Messenger of God."

"And also upon you, *habibi,*" Shakil replied. He gave the ratings a quick look, but with their eyes bandaged they could see nothing. He swiftly bent and kissed Thorton full on the mouth.

Thorton's arms went around his neck and held him tight. He kissed him ardently in return, but Shakil broke the kiss and rose. "I'll see you tomorrow, beloved." Then he was gone.

CHAPTER 11 : PEACOCK SHOOTING

Thorton, with an eyepatch over his left eye, Abby, Horner, and the whole British party, landed on the dock in Pearl Cove and marched up to Bessilama House at the appointed hour. The mist was still on the stubbled fields, the air was pleasantly cool, and the neighborhood dogs barked themselves silly. The Sallee members of the party were arriving as well. Several of them, being Shakil's kin, had spent the night in the house and were already on the lawn to discuss the day's prospects, fowling pieces loosely crooked in their elbows.

Tangle came up and greeted him with a firm buss on each cheek. *"Salaam, rais,"* Tangle replied. "I'm glad you came. It will be a fine party. The weather is excellent."

"Salaam, kapitan," Thorton greeted him. "Peace be upon you and all within this house. Unfortunately, Dr. Ferncastle has forbidden me to shoot. I am to do nothing more strenuous than stroll. I am on light duty."

"That's too bad. Still, we will try to entertain you."

Lord Zahid came over to inspect his patient. "How is your eye?"

Thorton touched the leather patch holding the linen padding in place. "A little sore still. A couple more days and the dressing may be off."

"I will look at it before you leave today."

"Thank you, *hakim,*" Thorton replied.

"Let me introduce you to the other guests," Tangle said. "You already know Achmed, of course. You remember my father-in-law, Nakih bin Nasir. And my brother-in-law, Kasim Rais, son of Nakih."

Nakih was not particularly tall and had curly black hair well grizzled with grey. He had a comfortable paunch and a ready smile above his curly beard. His nose was hooked and his eyes were brown and deep set. He wore a brown coat over matching pantaloons and a neatly wrapped and stitched turban. His son Kasim looked very like him, but younger with even curlier hair and eyes that were shifty and tense compared to his father's more open countenance. He wore a dark red jacket and dark-blue pantaloons striped with crimson and grey.

"I am delighted to see you again," Nakih said in Arabic. Kasim merely grunted. Tangle passed over that without remark and introduced Thorton to still more Salletines.

There was a short, powerfully built captain as black as Africa with a head shaved down to a smooth nap. Next to him was a skinny redhead that spoke Arabic with an Irish lilt. There were a pair of swarthy Moors, or perhaps they were Turks, and a man with frizzy blond hair, green eyes, and full lips that bespoke ancestry from three continents. The Muslims were men of every hue, height, build, eye color, hair style, and background. They shook hands or kissed him on the cheek when Tangle introduced him as a brother in Islam.

A carriage rolled up and discharged Lord and Lady Fairchild, the British envoy to the Sallee Republic and his wife. Tangle greeted them and made introductions, then the servants showed the lady into the house where the women were gathered in the courtyard. Fairchild was a man of average height, well fed, and dressed in brown tweed, spatterdashes, woolen stockings, and equipped with a handsome fowling piece chased with silver. His servants stood discreetly in the distance.

The men naturally divided into two groups with Muslims on one side, British on the other. Thorton looked back at the knot of British gathered around Captain Horner and Lord Fairchild. Although the English ranged from the blondness of Ebenezer Horner to the darkness of Roger Perry, there was something alike about them, something pale and elegant, that made him feel he did not belong. Even the impoverished Captain Horner had something genteel and British about him in stark contrast to the rich colors and hearty demeanors of the Muslim men. Reluctantly he left the Muslims to rejoin the Christians.

"Is that you, Peter?" Abby asked him. "I see a light blue blur."

Thorton was in civilian dress in a short French blue jacket and wide legged breeches. He was very far from fashionable. "'Tis I," he replied.

"We invalids are not allowed to shoot. Will you stay with me and tell me all about it?"

"I will," he replied.

Abby tucked his hand into Thorton's elbow and they stepped away a few feet so that Thorton could describe the scene in a low voice.

Everyone was dressed casually. The officers were in frock coats of various colors — mostly blue, since half the officers had lost their sea chests during the debacle in the Mediterranean and had to wear their undress coats. Posonby had an actual hunting outfit consisting of a brown and green tweed coat and dark brown breeches. He had a small caliber fowling piece. Horner was wearing an old naval frock coat and looking shabbier than usual because of it. Thorton felt badly for him and hoped that when they got their prize money the man would invest in some new uniforms. Perry and Abby were wearing naval frock coats as well.

Most of the Muslim men were dressed in short jackets like Zouave tribesmen with their pantaloons wrapped with canvas spatterdashes from knee to ankle and buttoned down the back. Tangle was dressed in tan and grey striped pantaloons and a tan jacket and white turban. He had a pair of gazehounds with him. The dogs were so tall their withers came up to his thighs. They were like greyhounds in build, but not as lean, with longer coats and flop ears. One had a fawn saddle and head cap, the other was charcoal grey on top and white below. They were erect and alert, but unlike the mongrels kept by the fisherfolk, did not bark or prance. Posonby and Horner came to inspect the dogs.

"What kind are they? I have never seen the breed before," Horner asked.

"Turkish Tazi dogs. They hunt by sight and are swift enough to run down their prey," Tangle replied. "I hunt ground prey with them, but they will start the peafowl if we need them to. Although I think we will find plenty of them perching in clear view. Still, the dogs need exercise."

"We all need exercise," replied Horner. "I have never hunted peafowl before. It will be a novel experience. What is our plan of attack?"

The fowlers gathered around Tangle. He spoke Arabic and English, but he did not know all the terms he needed in English. He resorted to Spanish and Horner translated for him. Everything settled, they trooped across the stepping stones in the stream, then spread out in a line across the field. The servants followed behind with panniers of supplies and empty bags to gather up the game. Abby and Thorton brought up the rear. Thorton had to practically carry Abby across the stream since he couldn't see the stepping stones.

Once across the stream the men paused to lock and load. The British with their pistols had the benefit of paper cartridges they tore open with their teeth, but Posonby and Tangle and others with long guns had to pour powder from their horns into thimbles to measure, and from there into the muzzles of their guns. They patched and put the balls in, then tamped them down. A little powder went into the flash pan and they locked.

The handler released the dogs. The grey one darted ahead. He ran like lightning and suddenly a great bird started up in a flash of iridescent blue. It glided a few yards but could not truly fly. Half a dozen guns came up and a volley cracked the peace of an autumn day. The smell of brimstone drifted beneath the warm sun. The peacock dropped and the dogs ran to it.

Tangle called out in Turkish, then Arabic and English, "Guns up! Hold your fire!" When all the weapons were secured, he trotted out to meet the dog and retrieve the dead bird. He held it by the neck and showed them what a large creature it was. The train was nearly six foot long and trailed on the ground as he held it up. He showered praise on the dog in Turkish, and the animal wagged its tail and jumped up on him. The men surged forward to examine the kill and debate who had brought it down.

"No matter. The first bird goes to the table anyhow!" Tangle pronounced. The servants field-dressed the magnificent bird, then carried it back to the kitchen. It would be ready to eat by the time the men got back from hunting.

The commotion had startled away any game birds or small mammals that might be lurking in the field, so they reached the woods without starting any more prey. They came together to file in a single line into the trail leading under the eaves of the woods. It was cool and dry amid the evergreen oaks. They had not gone far before they spotted peacocks roosting in the trees.

Tangle said, "Wait. There's a clearing up ahead we will use for our camp."

They reached a grassy meadow and the servants spread the rugs and set down the panniers. Tangle gave directions for the line. "There are houses on the other side of the woods, so we will shoot to the west, in case any one from the houses is about. They shouldn't be, but they trespass all the time."

The hunters disappeared into the woods and Thorton and Abby settled on the blue and gold rug spread by the servants. The air was cool and still in the woods. The scent of loam and decaying leaves was strong, but the evergreen oaks around them remained green in all seasons. It was dry and dusty. Abby laid down and Ra'uf brought him a mustard-colored pillow for his head. Thorton settled next to him.

"I want a lover," Abby announced.

Thorton gave him an amused look. "Who's the lucky man?"

Abby made a face. "Nobody! You turned me down."

Although it pained him to think of his friend and his former lover together, Thorton said, "I thought you and Isam Rais were getting along rather well."

Abby made a face. "He flirts with me, but he goes home to his wife every night. I think he could slip me in between his prayers and paperwork, but I'm holding out for something better." He sighed. "I don't think I'm going to get it. Nobody wants a blind man for a lover."

Thorton's heart went out to his friend. "I'm sure you'll find someone. You're very handsome and gallant."

Abby sat up and peered at himself. "Maybe the uniform is the problem. I should try a dress. I look very fetching in a skirt and bonnet. Do you think Isam would like me that way?"

Thorton's eyes grew wide. "A dress? Wherefore a dress?"

Abby explained, "Because married men like pretty boys and they'd rather their wives thought they were cheating with a hussy than a man. I don't know why, but somehow they think 'tis worse to cheat with a man than a woman. You should see me primped and corseted. I would make any wife jealous!"

Thorton peered at him. "You're teasing me, aren't you? You like to scandalize me and make me blush!"

"Are you blushing?"

"A little," he admitted.

"Would you like to see me in a bonnet and corset? With stockings and garters and no dress at all?"

Thorton gawked, then gave a short answer, "No."

Abby sighed heavily. He began to pull at the threads of the carpet. "I'm lonely, Peter. I was flirting with a marine officer back in Mahon, but nothing happened. Before I went to sea I had a lot of men, but not many lovers. I know how to wiggle my bum so that men pounce on it, but I am tired of being a plaything. You treat me well. You never act like my butt is the only thing you want."

"Well, 'tisn't."

"Don't you want it even a little?"

The memory of Abby's previous seduction attempt leaped immediately into Thorton's mind and he felt his blood stir. "No," he lied. Then he told the truth. "I love Shakil."

Abby pouted at him. "I wish I could see him. Then I'd know if he was as pretty as me."

"You are vain and terrible! You say these things to torment me for no good reason!"

Abby gave him a wry smile. "You are half right. But that doesn't mean I'm not telling the truth."

"I wish you wouldn't tease me so much."

"It keeps me from thinking about things I don't want to think about."

"What sort of things?"

Abby turned away from him. "The court martial."

"You have nothing to fear. You were very brave and stood your post on the *Adamant* until it sank, then you stood a post on the *Resolute* until the deck collapsed and knocked you down. You did nothing wrong. Unlike me. I deserved to get in trouble, even though I didn't mean to."

"I am the senior surviving officer from the *Adamant*, Peter. They will hold that against me. More than that, I am the senior surviving officer from the Battle of Majorca. Walters is dead and Wolfe is in a Spanish prison. All those ships and officers, lost. Gone to the bottom of the sea or languishing in a Spanish gaol. They will need someone to blame. That will be me." The blind lieutenant continued in the same melancholy vein. "My father won't save me. Not from this. He pays me two hundred pounds a year to stay out of sight and not embarrass him. He can't ignore this. It will be in all the papers. People will point at me on the street. They will either pity me because I'm blind or blame me because I lived."

Such an interpretation had never crossed Thorton's mind. He wrapped his arms around his friend and pulled him into his lap. "They won't!" he said fiercely. "We will tell them how brave and honorable you were and how hard you fought!"

"Peter, I love you. I have loved you ever since you found me in that hellhole at the bottom of the *Resolute*. You have been good and kind and never made me feel like a cripple or degenerate. I want you more than anything, but you won't have me!"

Mere words were not sufficient to express how Abby felt. He grabbed Thorton's face in his hands and kissed him long and hard. Thorton closed his eyes and let Abby kiss him. He knew he shouldn't allow it, but he was flattered as well as troubled by his friend's confession.

A sudden thump on the carpet next to them made them both jump and open their eyes. Shakil stood at the edge of the rug, fowling piece in the crook of his arm and a furious expression on his face. The brown coat did nothing to lesson the severity of his appearance.

"Shakil!" Thorton exclaimed.

The dead peahen lay on the rug. "I made my shot. 'Tis a good thing my gun isn't loaded," he snarled in Arabic.

"It isn't what you think!" Thorton cried in English.

Abby should have removed himself from Thorton's lap, but he understood Shakil's mistake and was delighted to take advantage of it. He smirked at him, which made the Moor even angrier. Thorton swiftly removed his arms from around his neck and shoved him out of his lap.

"I was comforting Abby. He's worried about the court martial," he explained in Spanish. It did not sound convincing, not even to him. "I swear it, Shakil. There is nothing between us."

In Arabic Shakil said, "I want to slap his smirking face."

"Alan, tell him nothing happened!" Thorton begged in English.

Abby crossed his arms over his chest and tilted his chin up defiantly as he met Shakil's glare. "If you don't want Peter, I'll take him."

"That's not helping!" Thorton got to his feet and tried to mollify his lover. "Please believe me when I tell you there is nothing between Alan and me. He flirts with me, but I say no to him."

"That didn't look like you were saying 'no' to me!" Shakil snapped back.

"He's persistent!"

Abby couldn't understand Spanish, but he knew they were quarreling. He kept quiet and hoped for the best — that Shakil would jilt Thorton and he'd get to comfort the wounded Englishman.

Shakil scowled at Abby. "You're a fool, Peter Rais. You can't trust him. He's taking advantage of you."

Thorton glowered at him. "You say that about all my friends. You said it about Roger Perry, you said it about Isam Rais, and now you're saying it about Alan Abbemarle! You're jealous, that's what you are! I won't abandon my friends for you, and you are wrong to ask it!"

"I'm not jealous! You know Roger betrayed you and tried to entrap you for the court martial. Isam will sleep with you in a heartbeat if he catches you with your pants down. And that pasty-faced Englishman has got his hooks in you and you don't even know it! You can't trust any of them."

Thorton said, "They are my friends, and I trust my life with them. I won't stand by and listen to you insult them."

Shakil set the butt of the musket on the rug. He leaned it against his shoulder and took a deep breath. He closed his eyes and let the breath out slowly. "Peter. See reason. You have not made wise choices."

"You're right. I'm not a wise man. But I know who my friends are. I don't care what you say about them."

Shakil's face crumpled in exasperation. "I was wrong to love an Englishman!"

Those words cut Thorton deep. He blanched and staggered back as if shot. Abby was listening intently. He could not understand the words, but he understood the feelings. They were hurting each other by the things they said. He felt bad then.

"I'm sorry," he said. "Peter loves you, Shakil. I wish he didn't, but he does. I've done my best to seduce him, but he keeps turning me down."

Shakil understood only part of the English. He turned to Thorton to explain the rest. "What did he say?"

"He's says you're a fool who's mad for no reason," Thorton told him in Spanish.

Shakil rolled his eyes. "He didn't."

"He did. He said I keep choosing you over him and you're blind to not see it."

Shakil digested this information. "You shouldn't have let him kiss you."

"He didn't ask permission. He just did it. Besides, it was only a kiss. Surely that's no crime?"

"It leads to other things," Shakil muttered.

Thorton grabbed Shakil's hand and brought it to his lips. He pressed an ardent kiss to the back of the Moor's hand. "Only when you're involved."

Shakil's lips quirked. He was not ready to be mollified, but he couldn't help himself. "You vex me."

"But you love me anyhow."

"Allah help me, I do."

They embraced. Abby couldn't see them clearly, but he could tell what they were doing. He turned away and started walking. He tripped over a basket. Ra'uf came and helped to pick him up.

"Take me back to the house. I can't find my way," Abby said wearily.

CHAPTER 12 : AUTUMN GALE

Dr. Ferncastle removed the bandage from Thorton's eye. Thorton blinked and looked around him, then shut his good eye. A broad smile crossed his face. "I can see!" His left eye darted to take in his surroundings. "I can see your face, the table, the rug, everything!"

Ferncastle smiled at him and held up fingers. "How many fingers am I holding up?"

"Three!" Thorton announced happily. "I can see them as plain as the nose on your face!"

"The operation is a success. However, you must guard against the weather. Continue to wear the eyepatch when you are on deck. A few more days should do it."

Rain drummed against the quarterdeck overhead. The *Resolute* and *Ajax* were beating against a west wind and the Gibraltar current. It was nearly a gale and the square-riggers were making no discernible headway. The sea heaped up white horses everywhere. Spindles of spray broke from the foamy crests. The *Ajax*, being a low vessel, shipped waves over the bow on a recurring basis. It was cold and wet with the ship bucking along under courses and double-reefed topsails. Anyone prone to seasickness was thoroughly sick.

Thorton was so pleased by recovering his sight that he put on foul weather gear and went on deck. He found sailors huddled in the coach and the deck beneath their feet wet with rain. He smiled warmly at them. "Cheer up, lads. 'Tis not the North Atlantic!"

"Aye aye, sir," they replied. Then one puked on the deck.

"Clean that up."

"Aye aye, sir."

Thorton stepped around the mess and went out.

Lifelines were strung the length of the vessel. He took hold of one and clawed his way forward. The wind filled his oilskin and he was cold in spite of having a knitted smock under his shirt and coat. His feet were soaked as a wave broke over the bow and sent a surge of water coursing the length of the deck. It sloshed into the waterways and poured out the scuppers. The men knuckled their foreheads to him and answered his questions. They had to shout to be heard over the roaring of the sea and the thrumming of the rigging. The *Ajax* was holding her own. He would have been content were it not for her mended bottom.

"Pass the word for MacDonald!" he called. The boatswain appeared. Rain dripped from his nose in spite of the protective gear. "How much water?" Thorton asked.

MacDonald reported, "Three feet in the well, sir."

"Man the pumps."

"Aye aye, sir. Begging your pardon, but our speed is forcing the leaks."

"I think so too." The faster a vessel moved through the water, the more the planks deformed and the more they leaked — especially if there was a pre-existing weak spot. The *Ajax* had been bilged and mended on the fly that summer. "Very well. We'll reduce sail."

He made his way up to the quarterdeck and found a rather green-looking Posonby on watch. "Reduce sail. Close-reef the topsails and take a reef in the courses."

"Aye aye, sir. Close-reef topsails and another reef in the courses." The word was passed.

The *Ajax* had been lucky with fair weather this year, so there was some grumbling by landsmen who thought it was a terrible storm, but knotted ropes swung by their the soggy midshipmen started them moving. The topmen lay aloft. The wet sails were even heavier than usual, but they got them in.

"Make a signal to the *Resolute*. 'Leak, am reducing sail.'"

Chambers picked out the flags and ran them up. With the *Ajax* following two cables behind the *Resolute* the flags could not be seen on account of the *Ajax's* own sails intervening, but he made the signal anyhow. It would be duly noted in the log. The *Ajax* slowed a little and the *Resolute* began to pull away.

A messenger ran along the deck from the bow. "The *Resolute* is making the query signal, sir."

Thorton said, "Helm two points north."

That brought the wind more directly over their beam and let their flags stream out so that they could be read. After a minute the *Resolute* acknowledged, then sent, "Resume position."

The *Ajax* acknowledged. She resumed her old position in the *Resolute's* wake. The larger vessel reefed to match her speed, and they continued cruising at a slower speed.

Half an hour later MacDonald came up to report, "She's pumped out, sir. Just as I thought, she's taking water where she was mended. We've got several other seams working, too."

"Is she holding?"

"Aye, sir."

"Sound the well every half hour. If it rises a foot, start the pumps and let me know."

"Aye aye, sir."

MacDonald went away. The rain came down more fiercely but there was no thunder nor lightning. Thorton was pleased about that. He stood his quarterdeck calmly and even experienced a certain amount of pleasure. Another wave broke over the bow and weighed her down. Water poured along her deck. Men slid with it, fetched up against the bulwarks, and clung to the side as the water roared out the scuppers in white waterfalls.

Posonby swore. "She's a damned strumpet, she is, going down for every wave that comes along."

Thorton glared at him. "She's a fine vessel and I like her well!"

"Pardon me for saying it, sir, but she's as wet as that hussy I had before I left London." Defending himself from Thorton's glare had caused him to forget about his stomach. That unruly part, finding itself unsupervised, seized the opportunity to rebel. Posonby whirled and hung his head over the leeward rail.

"Serves you right, insulting her like that," Thorton told the lieutenant's posterior.

Posonby finished vomiting and pulled himself up right. "As you say, sir."

Thorton wasn't sure if the weather was turning colder or if he was chilled from standing on the quarterdeck. He began to pace to warm himself up. Posonby stayed clear of him and hung by the leeward rail in case he needed it again.

"Signal from *Resolute*, sir. 'Strange sail one mile to windward, course due east.'"

"Acknowledge." Thorton took out his glass, but the *Resolute* was between him and whatever was out there.

"Lookout! What sail?" There was no answer. "Damn it, is that man dead at the masthead? Get his name. He'll be flogged on punishment day."

The message came down at last, "Lateen."

That was a minimum of information. Thorton longed to run up the to the masthead himself, but he was the acting-captain. Jackson's arm was still in a sling. He sent the master's mate instead. "Wallace, take my glass and go up."

Wallace was a short and stout young man who normally kept quiet and did as he was told. He was startled to be assigned such a duty and the look of dread he gave the masthead told Thorton why. The man was afraid of heights.

"Get up there," he snapped.

"Aye aye, sir," the man replied tremulously. He took the glass with a shaking hand and tucked it into the pocket of his oilskin. Slowly he made his way down the ladder to the deck. At the windward rail he paused and clung to the shrouds.

Thorton bellowed, "Move!"

Wallace turned, saluted, and began to climb. He had not made it halfway up when he froze. He went neither up nor down. There he clung as the ship gyred through her rolls.

"I can go up, sir," Posonby said.

"Get that man down first. Pass the word for Wiggins. We may need him." Wiggins was the other master's mate.

Blakesley, the master, replied, "Aye aye, sir. Pass the word for Wiggins."

Posonby went up the larboard ratlines until he reached the petrified man. No one could hear him, but they could tell by the motion of the two heads that they were talking. Blakesley watched in tense silence. He was certain the poor performance of the mate would reflect on him.

Thorton was thoroughly exasperated by the foibles of his crew. He was understaffed and his officers were all too junior. Even he was too junior to properly hold the post he was holding. On top of that, Abby, who was a skilled and experienced officer, was blind. Jackson, who was a good midshipman, had a broken arm. Perry, a good lieutenant, had been shot three times. Posonby was seasick.

All the same, Posonby had gone up. He knew his duty. Step by step he helped the frightened mate down to the deck. The man was very pale when he arrived on the quarterdeck. He wouldn't meet Thorton's eye. He stood shivering and miserable before the acting-captain. Thorton gave him a hard look. "Attend your master."

"Aye aye, sir." The man saluted and went hastily over to Blakesley, who boxed his ears for good measure.

Thorton ignored them. "Thank you, Mister Posonby. I'd appreciate it if you would go to the masthead, please."

"Aye aye, sir." Posonby went up to the masthead with easy motions. He paused when necessary to ride out a violent swoop, but the man's demeanor was brisk and matter of fact. He pleased Thorton. Posonby's soft middle had caused him some concern, but Whittingdon had not sent him a fool. Posonby was a useful addition to his diminutive body of officers.

Thorton glanced over at the mate. He felt sorry for the man, but Wallace had failed at the task to which he was assigned. What if he failed at some critical juncture? Thorton could not stand that.

"Mister Wallace. When I give an order I expect it to be obeyed promptly and cheerfully."

"Aye aye, sir," Wallace replied faintly.

"Therefore as soon as the weather clears you shall climb to the masthead every day until you can do it with alacrity."

"'Tis not my job to go to the masthead!" the man protested.

"You will do whatever I tell you, mister!"

"I'm afraid of heights!"

"I'm afraid of officers who don't do as they're told in the middle of a crisis!" Thorton barked at him.

"'Tis not a crisis, sir."

"'Twill be if you do not mend your tone!"

"I beg your pardon, sir."

Wiggins arrived. He'd been huddled in the gunroom and had to get properly dressed to come up. He hung back and waited to be noticed.

"You are relieved for the rest of the watch, Wallace. Go below. Wiggins, you're on duty. I'm sorry to inconvenience you, but there's no help for it."

Wiggins saluted and said, "Aye aye, sir."

Wallace fled.

Thorton took the speaking trumpet and called up, "What do you see?" but Posonby was already climbing down the ratlines.

"Two sail, sir. There's a three-masted lateener being chased by a frigate. The frigate's about two miles out. I wasn't entirely sure I saw her at first, given the rain, but she's out there."

There was several possible explanations for such a scenario, but the most likely was a Spanish coastguard in pursuit of a Sallee rover. Just then the *Resolute* hoisted the British colors.

"Hoist the colors, Lieutenant."

"Hoist the colors, aye."

The white ensign flapped with a racket like thunder as the wind tormented it.

"Signal from *Resolute*. 'Clear for action.'"

"Make it so." The pipes shrilled and the hands came running on deck.

When the lateener saw the British ensign she altered her course to run towards them. By turning more directly east to meet the British she was allowing the frigate to gain; a lateener could not run as well before the wind as a square-rigged vessel. As Thorton peered through his glass a strange sense of familiarity began to penetrate his vitals. He lowered the glass and looked at the vessel with his good eye, then lifted the eyepatch so that he could peer at her with both eyes. He got spray in his eyes and it stung, so he covered the repaired eye with the patch again.

"Damn me, but I think she's the *Sea Leopard*."

CHAPTER 13 : THE GREAT WAVE

"Rogue wave coming!" the masthead shouted. From his vantage point he could see it swelling five fathoms high. It dwarfed the other waves as it rolled from west to east.

"Secure all hands!" Thorton bellowed. "Head to wind! Secure the wheel!"

The *Ajax* turned into the wind. Rope swiftly went around the spokes of the wheel and secured it to either side. More rope was passed around the waists of the two helmsmen and another around the mizzenmast to secure the officers. Thorton saw the *Resolute* turning her bow to the wave as well. Thank Allah it was day time and they could see it coming. Unfortunately like Ulysses, Thorton wanted to hear the sirens sing. "I'm going up."

"Sir!" Blakesley and Posonby protested. Thorton ran for the shrouds and swung himself up. He climbed rapidly and made it to the masthead in time.

The lookout shared his rope with him. They were binding it around their middles when Thorton said, "My God."

The great wave pooped the Spanish frigate. Her bow went down and her stern went up. She was carrying all sail in pursuit of the Sallee rover and it proved her undoing. With the force of the wind pressing her forward as the wave lifted her stern up, she pitched forward onto her bowsprit. She stood on her nose for a moment, then completed her summersault as she toppled over and landed upside down. She was keel up with her masts under water. Great bubbles appeared in the sea around her as the air escaped from her hull. Debris floated around her. The waves washed over her, and then she was gone.

"Poor devils," said the lookout. "They never 'ad a chance."

Thorton transferred his attention to the xebec. She was turning to bring her bow to wind, but she wasn't going to make it in time. The vessel was carrying large lateen sails that were only supposed to be used in fair weather, but with the frigate in pursuit she had not dared to reduce sail. Given a choice between the storm and the Spanish, the captain had chosen the storm. The great lateen yards went to the deck, but before they could be secured, the great wave caught their starboard bow and rolled them. The xebec laid down on her beam ends and the sails and spars went overboard. The mountain of water broke over her. The ship disappeared. Thorton had no time to worry because now it was the Britons' turn.

The *Resolute* took the wave bow on. She lifted high on the mountain of water and sent up immense sprays that obscured her bow. The *Resolute* was made in the traditional English way with a high, bluff bow and forecastle. She rode up the wave and only a portion of it foamed across her deck in white cascades. She bucked and tipped as the wave passed under her middle and then she slid down the backside. Her bowsprit went under and Thorton held his breath.

She dug deep into the trough, shuddered, and her fore course flapped. Then she heaved herself up and shed water like a retriever coming out of a lake.

The *Ajax* caught it next. Her low sharp bow sliced into the wave and water engulfed the vessel in a mighty roar. The entire deck and quarterdeck below him disappeared as a cataract of water surged halfway up the mast. Everything loose was carried away, men, tools, lines. Anything that was not strong enough to withstand the crash of tons of water broke and scattered. Lines came loose and the courses shredded. Long tatters of sail streamed in the wind and snarled around the masts and lines. The masthead swung crazily as the *Ajax* wallowed beneath the weight of water. Thorton was sick then. The foul stuff disappeared instantly into the rain and spume and water. He coughed and raised his good eye to look.

The *Ajax* struggled up and shed water in cataracts of white, but there were men in the sea around her and behind her. Her deck was awash. Spars and shreds of sailcloth trailed over the side and into the sea.

The lookout said, "Glory be. The rover's up again."

The xebec on the surface. Her spars and sails were gone; her masts were bare poles. Men were in the water around her with a great deal of debris.

"She might make it," Thorton replied.

He had his own ship to tend. He untied himself and went down the ratlines on shaky legs. The rain was coming down in sheets as if the passing of the great wave had been the signal for the heavens to open up. He found his helmsmen nearly drowned but still at their posts. His quarterdeck staff were all accounted for.

"Damage report!" Thorton bellowed over the rising wind and roaring of the rain.

Posonby replied, "I don't know, sir! Shall I launch the boats?"

Thorton hesitated. To launch the boats in such a sea was dangerous. He could easily lose the boats and their hands. He needed everyone to tend the ship. He looked over the rail and saw the debris dragging alongside, lines and sails and men all tangled together. The frigate began to fall off the wind.

The helmsmen fought the wheel and called, "Sir! We need more help!"

"Put two more men on that wheel," Thorton snapped. "If we broach we're done for!"

Perry came on deck and Abby, too. They were drenched. "The wardroom is flooded, sir. The companionway hatch is broken."

"Posonby, you're the most able-bodied of the lieutenants. You will supervise rescue operations for the men overboard. Get those fellows that are clinging to the debris a line first. Then we must cut the debris loose. Use your judgment about the other men. We must save the ship before we can save them. Perry, you will take over as executive officer while Posonby supervises rescue operations. Get those sails and spars replaced. Chambers, see that the companionway is sealed. Abby, get me a damage and casualty report."

A chorus of "Aye aye, sir," answered him.

There was nothing more for Thorton to do but wait for his subordinates to do what they had been assigned to do. Slowly the sky darkened as night came on.

Posonby did not want to lose any more men overboard. His gang cast lines to the men clinging to the debris and fished them aboard. Three were recovered that way. Then he gave orders to cut away the debris. Thorton felt the lines part and the ship immediately behaved better. He watched the retrieval of the castaways with mixed feelings; Captain Bishop had cut the lines and Thorton had been stranded aboard a sinking galley on that fateful day six months ago. Now he was in Bishop's shoes. Did he dare to risk his ship to save the men? His stomach knotted.

"Full and by, sir!" Perry reported.

"Keep her that way," Thorton replied, banishing the past.

"Aye aye, sir."

They were now on a course south of west with the close-reefed topsails full of wind and several splits. So far the canvas was holding. Thorton was glad he'd reduced sail. He could have gone over just like the Spaniard and the rover.

Perry reported, "We've lost all the headsails and snapped the forestay. Good thing the courses were already shredded; the mast would have toppled if it had to bear the full strain." He had to shout to be heard.

"Reeve a new forestay," Thorton shouted back.

"All ready working, sir!"

"Carry on, Lieutenant."

Abby came up with his report. "Four men unaccounted for and believed washed overboard, sir. Another three were rescued by Lieutenant Posonby." He had to lean in close to Thorton to make himself heard.

"Did he launch the boat?"

"No, sir. By the time he got the three hauled on board there was no sign of the others."

Thorton grunted. "How much water in the bilge?"

Perry said, "I don't know, sir."

"Find out. I don't like how she's wallowing." Another wave swept over the bow and flooded the deck into the coach.

Perry shouted for MacDonald, then came back. "Four feet, sir. The pumps are running."

Thorton rubbed a hand across his face and tried to brush the rain out of his eyes. "Is the bottom holding?"

"So far, sir."

"Praise Allah for that."

"Signal from the *Resolute*, sir," Jackson's voice broke in. "'Damage report.'"

"Reply with, 'Headsails gone. Four men missing. Four feet in bilge.'"

The flags went up and were immediately drenched by the rain. The *Resolute* replied "Keep station two cables to windward." She lit her stern lanthorn as a beacon in the gathering gloom.

"Acknowledge. Light our lanthorn."

The golden glow made their faces appear even more haggard.

"Deck! The rover is fine on the starboard bow! Half mile!"

Thorton clapped his glass to his good eye and stared at her. She had her head to the wind and was making sternway as the wind and water pushed her to the east. With no sails she was at the mercy of the weather. That posed a new danger. What if she collided with them?

"Curse Kasim Rais for feeble-minded lout who should have never gone to sea!" Thorton exclaimed.

"Sir?" Perry asked.

"Give me a point more south."

"Aye aye, sir," the helmsman replied.

That would cause them to converge with the *Resolute*.

"Make signal, 'Gang way!'"

Before the hoist even went up the *Resolute* was altering her course two points south.

"Belay that signal. Horner's awake. Helm another point south."

"Signal from the *Resolute*, 'Stand by to wear ship.'"

"Acknowledge."

The *Resolute* slowly curved through her turn and set herself on a course to parallel the drifting xebec. The *Ajax* matched her. They were now running with the wind over their larboard quarter.

"Steer small, damn you!" Thorton snapped.

The helm corrected. The three vessels wound up on parallel courses with the *Ajax* nearest the drifting xebec.

The lookout sang out, "Deck! Men clinging to debris fine on the larboard quarter!"

Thorton swung his glass around but saw nothing but the white horses of the waves. "I'm going up."

He scrambled up to the masthead again. Men were still afloat, but wallowing in a trough. With the sea running so high they couldn't be seen from the deck unless by coincidence they rose to the top of their wave at the same time the *Ajax* did. Once it turned full dark they would be invisible. So would the great spar they clung to — it could strike the *Ajax* like a giant spear. It was the main antenna from the xebec.

Thorton shot down the backstay to the deck and called, "Posonby! Prepare to make a rescue. There are two Sallee rovers clinging to a large spar about one and a half cables off the larboard quarter."

"Aye aye, sir." Posonby was drenched and cold, but he made no complaint. He hurried down to launch the cutter.

"Make a signal to the *Resolute*. 'Am launching rescue.'"

The xebec drifted three cables off their larboard. Thorton swept his glass over her and said, "'Tis the *Sea Leopard*, all right." She was still making sternway with her bow to the wind and waves. No sails of any sort had been set on her. She was a naked hulk.

"Reduce sail. I don't want to outrun our boat. Is that forestay up yet?"

"Checking, sir," Perry replied. He ran down to the weather deck.

The *Resolute* wore around again. Jackson announced, "*Resolute* to cutter, 'Follow me.'"

"Their lookout can see the men in the sea," Thorton guessed immediately. "She will lead the cutter to them." The cutter was such a small boat she could not see over the waves.

"Stand by to wear ship," He waited until Perry came running back to him. "Well?"

"Finishing now, sir. Give them a few minutes."

"Run back. The minute it is done we are wearing ship." He'd been lucky that he'd not lost his foremast the first time. He did not intend to turn head to wind until he was sure his forestay was set. Perry ran back. A few minutes later the word was passed.

"Wear ship," Thorton commanded. The *Ajax* came around and followed the *Resolute* at a distance.

CHAPTER 14 : KASIM RAIS

In the morning the seas had moderated to three or four foot swells. The sun rose in a blue sky as clear as crystal. Thorton washed carefully, then wound his turban around his head. Ra'uf gave him a surprised look, but Thorton said, "Not a word to the crew."

A knock sounded and Ra'uf went to the door and cracked it open. He spoke Arabic, then told Thorton, "'Tis Lieutenant Suhail, of the *Sea Leopard,* sir." Suhail was one of the men they had fished out of the sea the night before.

"Let him in."

The man who entered the room was a powerfully built blackamoor. He had a medium brown complexion, almond shaped eyes, flared nostrils, full lips, and short kinky hair cut close to his head. He had covered his head with a white kerchief; his turban had been torn away by the sea. The clothes he wore consisted of a borrowed blue checked shirt, tan breeches, and woolen stockings. A set of rope sandals were the only footgear found in the ship that would fit his big feet. The man was about a fathom tall and weighed at least sixteen stone. His chest was big, his waist stout, and his thighs thick. He stopped in surprise as he saw the English officer wearing a turban.

"Peace be upon you," Thorton greeted him in Arabic.

"And also upon you, rais," he replied in the same language.

"Will you pray with me before we dine?"

The man was even more surprised. "You are a believer?"

"There is no God but Allah and Mohammed is his prophet," Thorton replied. Then he sighed, "But you must not discuss it with the other British officers."

"I will pray with you, sir, but I am astonished."

The three Muslims, the two officers and steward, prayed together as brothers in Islam. Afterwards, Thorton removed his turban and sat down to breakfast with Lieutenant Suhail. They had oatmeal and oranges and coffee served by Ra'uf.

Suhail was happy to have the Moorish food. He had been dreading salt pork and peas which he had heard were all the British ever ate. He asked, "How did you come to be a believer?"

"A long story. I rescued Isam Rais from a Spanish galley." His Arabic wasn't good enough to relate the entire adventure. He pointed his spoon to the starboard. "I own one share of that xebec, too."

Suhail was astonished all over again. Thorton turned to Ra'uf and said, "Explain to him."

So Ra'uf told him the tale of how Isam Rais Tangueli had been rescued from a Spanish galley by the *ferenghi*[1] lieutenant, how Thorton had been captain of a Sallee rover for a short period of time and taken many prizes, and used his prize money to buy a share of the *Sea Leopard* at the request of Jamila bint Nakih and her brother Shakil. The *Sea Leopard* was owned by a party of investors who had selected Kasim Rais as their captain. Eventually Tangle's friends hoped to buy enough shares to force a vote to replace Kasim and return control of the *Sea Leopard* to Captain Tangle.

Suhail ate his oatmeal and listened carefully to this tale. "Kasim Rais has not been a profitable captain," he said. "There is no letter of marque or there wouldn't be any profit at all."

Thorton's Arabic was imperfect, but 'letter of marque' was one Arabic term he knew by heart. "No letter of marque? He's a pirate?"

"A letter of marque requires a bond of a thousand sequins and a share of the profit goes to the government."

Thorton understood that perfectly well, too. It was the difference between a corsair and a pirate; a corsair put up the bond as proof that he would obey the law and raid only his nation's enemies. He shared a portion of the proceeds with the government. A pirate was a robber on the high seas and nothing more. He shared with no one, was accountable to no one, and could commit any crime and get away with it. As long as the pirate raided only his country's enemies nobody was likely to inquire into his business — but should he be captured by the enemy, he would be hanged from the yardarm. Kasim Rais had had good reason to pile on all canvas in spite of the gale.

Thorton said slowly, "The investors think he has a letter of marque. They think they invest in an honest corsair."

Suhail gave him a bitter look. "I thought so, too. I have learned many things on this cruise I am not pleased to know."

Thorton ground his teeth in mute fury. "He can risk his own life if he wishes, but he has no right to risk the money of his family and friends!"

---

[1] *ferenghi* Turkish, lit.' French,' by extension, European

"The crew is unhappy. They would welcome a new captain."

Thorton had recourse to Ra'uf to make certain he understood. When did he sat back in his chair. At first he thought there was nothing he could do, but then his brain began to cogitate. He had been a Sallee rover only a little while, but he had served under the most redoubtable of corsairs, the man the English called 'Captain Tangle.' He was certain Isam Rais could do something. He racked his brain to think what it might be.

"I am positive that I represent the majority of the shareholders when I protest the lack of a letter of marque. The question is, will the crew agree?"

Again Ra'uf translated to make certain both sides understood what was being asked.

"I think most will. But Kasim has his hand-picked men."

"I have British marines I will happily throw against his hand-picked men. But I require your assistance to get them on board."

"The men will not help you if they think they will be taken as pirates," Suhail warned him.

"They have been deceived by Kasim. No blame attaches to them."

Suhail squared his shoulders. "I will do it. What do you want from me?"

Thorton went across to the *Sea Leopard*. Suhail and Ra'uf accompanied him, not to mention, half a dozen British marines. There was a load of British seamen in the boat, ostensibly to pull the oars through the rough sea. Thorton wanted back up. He clambered over the gunwale and looked around. He noticed the guns were missing. Well, a prudent captain would have sent them below when the weather got rough. The guns of a xebec were worked from the weather deck. He also noticed the many gratings set into the deck. He puzzled at them, then remembered that Tangle had told him that a xebec laid a false deck over the real deck and the gratings lead the water below decks into the scuppers, thereby clearing water from the deck quickly. He watched his step that he did not catch his heel in one.

The Sallee rovers on board seemed tired and dispirited. The officer of the watch came to meet Suhail and Thorton. They exchanged Arabic comments too rapidly for the Englishman to understand, then he was conducted to the captain's cabin. The marines covered the coach and Suhail told the men loitering there to leave. There was no sentry at the captain's door. Suhail opened it and Thorton entered.

The first thing Thorton noticed was the high deckhead that let him stand up straight even with his hat on. He removed it as he crossed the threshold and stepped into a world of Oriental splendor. Brilliantly colored gold and crimson carpets covered the floor, crimson and gold cushions were stacked up in piles, intricate bronze lamps hung from the ceiling, the walls were yellow and painted with red Arabesques, and small pieces of elaborately decorated brass and ebony furniture were scattered around the space. The windows had colored panes of red and yellow to form geometric patterns. Where an Englishman like Thorton kept a locker under the stern windows, the cabin had a divan. Seated upon the divan was Kasim Rais.

He was a fleshy man about thirty years of age. He had a curly brown beard and short brown hair under his large turban. He wore a yellow and brown striped shirt and a red vest over it. Loose brown pantaloons covered his legs. A gold medallion hung around his neck from a heavy chain. He sat cross-legged with one hand resting on the head of his dog. The dog was a great ugly beast, extremely large and bulky in the body with short dun colored hair, flop ears, heavy jowls, and a short tail that curled over his back. He raised his head and watched the strangers alertly. He looked most like a mastiff, but that was like saying a bull looked like a bison. True as far as it went but otherwise inadequate. On his other side the Moor had a girl that was only half the size of the dog. She was as dainty and delicate as the dog was robust and muscled. She wore green veils that covered everything but her eyes, but the veils were sheer enough for the Irish to show through. Her hair was red and long and her face was freckled. The wrists and hands that protruded from the green silk sleeves were as small and slender as a child's. She wore pantaloons beneath her dress and knelt beside the corsair.

Thorton stopped short and blinked at this apparition. Nothing he had encountered in Zokhara had prepared him for the barbarous splendor of Kasim Rais. *"Salaam,"* he finally said. "I am Peter Rais Thorton of His Britannic Majesty's frigate *Ajax*. I am here to inspect your papers."

Kasim Rais gave him a contemptuous look. In Arabic he said, "I know who you are. You're Isam's pet." His bass voice was unfriendly.

Thorton stiffened. His Arabic was not equal to all that he wanted to say, so he told Ra'uf, "Tell him I am the one that sent the cutter to rescue his castaways and that I have his antenna. Now I need to inspect his papers."

Ra'uf spoke lively Arabic and gestured with his hands for emphasis.

Kasim shrugged. "I don't need them. I have plenty more. You need not have bothered."

Thorton was struck dumb by the callousness of his statement. He could only goggle at someone who affected so little concern for his men and ship.

Suhail broke in, "We need every man we can get! We are short-handed, and we need those spars to re-rig! Why on earth would you say such a thing?"

Kasim glared at him. "I don't need the help of an English catamite who kisses my brother-in-law's ass!"

The pulse beat visibly in Thorton's temple. He had rarely encountered Kasim Rais, but every time he did, the man raised a choler in him. He wondered how Captain Tangle had managed to refrain from throttling the man during the ten years in which he had been married to his sister.

"Your papers, or Allah help me, I'll tell the marines to beat you!" he burst out.

"My papers are none of your business. You do not have permission to come on board my vessel."

"Hah! I am one of the owners this vessel, I can set foot on it whenever I please!" He jerked his thumb at Barnes. "Lieutenant, search the cabin. I want his papers and I want them now."

Kasim gave him a startled look, so Thorton knew Shakil had managed to buy the share on the sly. If Kasim had known what they were up to, they never would have been able to make the purchase.

"You lie!"

Barnes and the marines pulled out drawers and dumped them on the floor. Then they turned back the rugs and pawed through the cushions. The Irish girl quailed and drew away from them.

Suhail said, "He keeps the papers in a wooden box about this big." He held up his hands to indicate something about eighteen inches long. Barnes couldn't understand Arabic and Suhail couldn't understand English, but they understood one another well enough.

"I will protest to the Minister of Marine!" Kasim complained.

"I doubt we'll need to go that high," Thorton replied. "I am happy to refer the matter to Captain Horner. He is a stickler for the law. If your papers are in order, you have nothing to fear."

He saw the look that flickered across Kasim's face and knew Suhail had told the truth. Kasim began to sweat, but there was nothing he could do. Two of Barnes' marines had found the box. Barnes stood guard with pistol and sword in hand.

Thorton laid it on the carpet and knelt beside it.

"The key." He held out his hand to Kasim.

Kasim crossed his arms and glared. "I refuse. This is an illegal search."

Thorton rose and stepped back. "Open it."

Barnes took aim at the lock,and fired. The shot sounded loud in the cabin and it brought men to knock on the cabin door. The marines stood guard on either side of it.

Suhail shouted Arabic through the door, "Stand down! Captain's business!"

Barnes reloaded.

Arabic voices called queries, but Thorton ignored them. He knelt and went hastily through the papers. He found Kasim's passport on top; it was legal. He had a Sallee passport of his own and knew what they looked like. He hunted through all the Arabic papers. He couldn't read them but he didn't have to. The Sallee Republic, like all other governments, used pre-printed letters of marque. The corsair's personal information was written into the blanks. Thorton had one of those, too.

He riffled the papers with a sound like a deck of cards being shuffled. "No letter of marque." He stared at Kasim Rais. "You have one minute to produce it or I hand you over to Captain Horner as a pirate."

Kasim was sweating. "You fool! You went right past it!"

Thorton stared at him with a hard level grey stare. "No, I didn't. You have thirty seconds left before I order your arrest."

Kasim blustered. "You can't!"

Thorton took out his watch and watched time sweep past. Kasim stared at him. When the minute circled back to its starting point, he said, "Arrest him."

The marines leveled their muskets at the pirate. Kasim glared back at them. "You'll never leave my ship alive!"

"Seize him and carry him over to the *Resolute*."

Kasim spat at him. The spittle landed on Thorton's shoe and slowly dribbled down the side. Barnes raised his hand to slap the pirate, but the dog raised his hackles and stood up with a low growl. The girl covered her face with her hands and gasped. The marines grabbed

Kasim and hauled him to feet. The dog sprang. A musket cracked. The dog gave a single high pitched yelped, then sprawled on the deck and lay whining and twitching. Kasim swore in Arabic and a marine clubbed him in the face. Barnes cocked his pistol, took careful aim, and dispatched the dog. The great beast lay still with his blood soaking into the rug. The marines bound Kasim's hands behind his back and dragged him from the room.

"Traitor," Kasim spat at Suhail.

"Acting on behalf of the other investors, I appoint you captain until you can return to Zokhara and submit the matter to their scrutiny. I will write you a warrant," Thorton told the lieutenant.

Suhail nodded grimly.

CHAPTER 15 : THE FATE OF PIRATES

Horner listened as Thorton completed his report. The captain's cabin aboard the *Resolute* was the opposite of the great cabin on the *Sea Leopard*. The only adornment was a painted canvas rug on the floor. The furniture was rustic stuff made by the ship's carpenter. It was as serviceable, plain, and sturdy as the man who occupied the cabin.

Horner himself was tall and thin and going bald. His uniform was neat but old; it was out of style with its big boot cuffs. He looked through the papers, but he knew no Arabic at all. He had no idea whether he was looking at amorous verses or a grocery list.

"You're positive he has no letter of marque?"

"We will have to consult the authorities in Zokhara to be sure, but I sincerely doubt it."

"Still, I can't hang the man without substantial evidence. He is Commodore Tangueli's brother-in-law."

"I don't think Isam Rais will miss him."

Horner put the papers back in the box. "I think we had better turn him over to the Admiralty. The seizure of a Sallee rover is bound to strain relations between the two countries. Is there any evidence he has raided British shipping?"

"There's the Irish girl, Emily McKinley. She was on a Spanish ship when she was taken."

"We'll restore her to her family, of course."

Thorton coughed. "She was going to her family in Spain. They're Catholics."

Horner sighed. "So was my grandmother. Very well. We'll turn them both over to the Admiralty. It is a matter for the politicians."

"If you wish, sir."

"Given the reasonable suspicion of piracy you have brought before me, I cannot release the *Sea Leopard*. We will put a prize crew on her and take her into Spithead with us."

Thorton spoke quickly. "I am certain the owners are innocent. It would be unfair to deprive them of their investment due to the folly of one man."

"I sincerely doubt that they are unaware of a little fact like a missing letter of marque," Horner replied drily.

"Sir, I know some of them. Shakil Effendi, Mistress Tangueli, Commodore Tangueli, they all own shares. Even I own a share and I certainly thought he was a properly commissioned corsair. I never dreamed he might not be!"

Horner pinched the bridge of his nose and sighed. "Mister Thorton. You have gotten yourself hopelessly mixed up with these corsairs."

Thorton was puzzled. "'Tis nothing new. I bought my share with my Sallee prize money before I was arrested. Nobody said I couldn't invest in a privateer."

"A pirate. You have invested in a pirate, Peter. You have brought the evidence yourself."

Thorton's face fell.

"You are the most naive officer over the age of sixteen I have ever met."

"I trusted Jamila bint Nakih when she asked for the money to invest. She is trying to buy back the *Sea Leopard* from the other investors so she can return it to her husband, Commodore Tangueli. It was his ship until the Spanish captured him."

Horner waved his hand. "That is neither here nor there. Who among your crew understands how to sail a lateen vessel?"

"I do. My man Ra'uf, and MacDonald was on the galleys with me."

Horner's steely gaze pinned him to the spot. "Do you think you can perform the duty of prizemaster to bring the xebec into Spithead? It isn't easy for a man to act contrary to his affection and the interest of his friends."

Thorton's face drained of color. "There are men aboard who are honorable men. I cannot hand them over to be hanged as pirates!"

"It is our duty to deliver them to the law. A trial will settle the matter."

Thorton swallowed hard. "But how will the investors even know? 'Tisn't fair!"

"You will have to write them a letter. The *Ajax* can land it at Tettiwan. I think I can trust Perry to act as captain for that much. He needs seasoning. He can't get into much trouble on a mail run. Select your crew, and I'll give you a party of marines. We'll move the officers from the *Sea Leopard* to the *Resolute* and lock the native crew in the hold." He rose from his desk.

Thorton said, "Aye aye, sir."

They went on deck. Horner said casually, "Beat to quarters. We are arresting the *Sea Leopard*, Mister Forsythe."

Forsythe leaped to obey. He had steadied under Horner's leadership; he was no longer terrorized by the arbitrary and tyrannical Captain Bishop. When Horner gave an order, it made sense, and he stood by it. A man knew what was expected of him, and as long as he did it to the best of his ability, Horner would not find fault with him.

A wild tattoo rattled through the ship and the men ran to their stations.

"Lock and load. Case shot."

On the two gundecks men labored with big eighteen pounders. They rammed the wads and shot home and waited behind the closed ports.

"Make a signal. '*Resolute* to *Sea Leopard*, 'We require your surrender.'"

The flags went up.

"I don't know if anyone on board understands English, sir," Thorton said worriedly.

The *Sea Leopard* raised a signal in reply.

"'Don't understand,'" Thorton translated.

"Translate it into Arabic, Mister Thorton."

Thorton sorted through the flags and sent up the Arabic message using Latin letters.

On the quarterdeck of the *Sea Leopard* Suhail and the others studied the message nervously. They had heard the rattle of the snares and seen men running to their posts; the *Resolute* was a beehive of purposeful action.

"'Don't understand,'" Thorton translated again.

"Run out the guns. I think that will make our meaning clear."

The gun ports flew open and thirty-two black-mouthed long guns ran out with a sound like thunder. Thorton could feel the vibrations in the wood beneath his feet. The *Sea Leopard* was under bare poles with no sails. She could put out oars to run, but she would be pummeled at close range by heavy metal.

The *Sea Leopard* had not been flying her flag, but the purple ensign ran up, paused, and immediately ran down again.

"They're surrendering, sir."

"Excellent. Take your prize crew and secure her."

Thorton could not look Suhail in the eye as he accepted the man's scimitar. Suhail glared at him and spat in low Arabic, "Traitor."

Thorton made no answer.

The crew of the *Sea Leopard* was a mixed lot of Moors, Turks, Africans, and European renegades. They were sullen and restive as they were bundled into the narrow confines of the hold. The smell of the bilge was rank and the air fetid. The officers were taken across under marine guard and delivered into confinement aboard the *Resolute*.

Dispatches were exchanged, then the *Ajax* wheeled away and headed south toward the coast of the Sallee Republic. With a heavy heart Thorton ordered the British ensign to be placed over the purple flag of the Sallee Republic and hoisted up. The *Sea Leopard* was a captive. Tears gathered in his eyes and he blinked them away before turning back to look at his crew.

He had Abby again, pressed into service once more due to the need for a prize crew. He had Jackson and some midshipmen. He had MacDonald for a boatswain and some other hands from the *Resolute* and *Ajax*. Both ships were undermanned as it was; Horner did not want to strip either one too badly. Those sent were men Horner trusted; they were insurance for Thorton's uncertain loyalty.

Thorton inspected the *Sea Leopard*. He found her deeper than the *Arrow*, and beamier, too, but she was still narrow compared to English vessels. Her bow was exceptionally fine and her keel was raked so that the heel bit deeper than her toe. The foremast looked down on her bowsprit, the mizzenmast canted over the transom and only the mainmast was vertical. Her lazyboard continued the long graceful sweep of her sheer so that it narrowed like the tail of a pintail duck, as opposed to Spanish and French xebecs where the lazyboard flared a little. The lines of her hull were extremely beautiful. She was built of African teak in shiplap construction: no caulking needed. Her decks were made of a tan African hardwood and the seams sealed with pitch. The gratings in her deck were grids but interlaced with wooden work in the form of a floret. Each grating was about three feet by five. They were spaced along each side of the deck in between the gun ports.

She had no guns. The Sallee rovers had thrown them overboard to lighten the load when they were being chased by the Spanish. She had very little in the way of spare spars; they were carried in outriggers along side her quarters and the rogue wave had ripped them away. Most of her sweeps were gone. She had a suite of small lateen storm sails in her locker, but precious little in the way of supplies. Everything had been thrown over to try and escape the Spanish.

Thorton signaled to request water, food, and spars. They were sent to him and he set about re-rigging the vessel. It took all day to get the stores aboard and the new rig set up. The spare antenna he had saved came in very handy; it was separated into its constitute pieces, each of which he used as antennas to set the storm sails. They weren't very large, but at last, late in the afternoon, she was moving under her own power. The *Resolute* sent her orders, and they settled into her wake two cables' length behind. The battleship's high stern with its double-deck galleries and sculpture dwarfed the *Sea Leopard* in size and power, and Thorton felt sad and helpless as he guided the captive rover toward England.

CHAPTER 16 : THE WOULD-BE KING OF PORTUGAL

The *Resolute* and the *Sea Leopard* ran the Spanish blockade of the Strait of Gibraltar in the dark. With only storm sails the *Sea Leopard* could not make more than four knots; she had to fight against the Gibraltar current. Without guns she was defenseless and kept close under the *Resolute's* stern. The *Resolute* hung a lantern in the cove of the captain's cabin but lit no other lights. The wind shifted around to the north and they were able to cruise through the Pinch on a beam reach. They saw lights in the night but were apparently unseen themselves. They made it through unmolested.

Thorton spent an uneasy night. He could not bring himself to sleep in Kasim's bed and hung a hammock instead. The ivory, gold, and crimson decor grated on his nerves. He was positive Tangle had not had the cabin painted in such colors. The following morning he had all of Kasim Rais' furnishings packed up and stowed below. He tasked the carpenter's mate to make him some simple furniture: a table with benches, a desk and chair, a tin lantern. He put his sea chest under the windows for a locker. He had no cushions for it. He did have a tablecloth but no china. He had a wooden trencher and a pewter mug. Breakfast was couscous from his personal store.

Horner kept close to the Spanish coast as he wore around Cape Surprise. True to its name, they surprised several small coastal vessels. The *Resolute* succeeded in running one down. It was a small coastal schooner loaded with hardtack. It wasn't worth much, but it would put a little extra money into their pockets when they reached England. A day later they spotted a ship, but she showed a clean pair of heels. They gave chase but never caught her. Had she been alone the *Resolute* probably could have overtaken her, but she would not abandon the *Sea Leopard* and the prize.

Day by day they followed the Iberian coast northward. On the third day they were crossing Setúbal Bay and fighting close-hauled against a northeast wind. That was when they met the squadron of xebecs.

The *Resolute* altered course to run northwest and the *Sea Leopard* followed her. They had made a jib out of an old foresail and rigged a square topsail on the mizzen to give them a bit more speed, but they could not run like a fully canvased xebec. The *Resolute* changed tactics; she fell back and let the *Sea Leopard* lead. The prize followed the *Sea Leopard*. The strange xebecs would have to get past the *Resolute* to reach the prize. Four xebecs would be a challenge for the *Resolute*. If they succeeded in closing they could overwhelm her by boarding. The *Resolute* must make them keep their distance where her superior gunnery could score on them while their lighter guns could do little damage against her thick hide.

Hour after hour they ran. The xebecs had been spotted just after noon; they were miles away but closing. By late afternoon the xebecs had gained on them until they were little more than a mile away. Suddenly the *Resolute* wore ship and charged them. Horner fired a single gun and the British colors ran up. The xebecs turned aside and spread out into a V-formation and hoisted their colors; the black and white gyronny of Portugal flew from their sterns. They saluted the *Resolute* and their flagship made signals.

The British vessels slowed and the xebecs continued to close. Thorton watched tensely over the tafferel; the Portuguese colors could be a ruse to allow the xebecs to get close enough to rush the battleship. As they closed to half a mile, the *Resolute* ran out all guns on both sides. Again she fired a warning shot. The flagship of the approaching squadron made signals again. Thorton studied them through his glass.

"What's happening?" Abby asked.

Thorton quickly explained. "They are asking our identity." He raised his spyglass again. "The *Resolute* is replying, 'R-e-s-o-l-u-t-e and prizes.' Now he's asking, 'Who are you?'"

"What do they answer?" Abby asked anxiously.

Thorton suddenly shouted, *"Royal Guardian!"* He capered across the quarterdeck in the delight. "'Tis the *Royal Guardian!*"

"Who?"

Thorton clapped his glass to his good eye. "There's the *Loyalty!* I don't know the other two."

The *Resolute* knew them, too. She pulled her guns back inside. More signals were made and Thorton exulted again. "Admiral Henrique do Coimbra is the commander!"

The vessels came together in a friendly cluster. Horner and Thorton were both called aboard the admiral's flagship and Thorton was happy to go. He donned his best uniform and went swiftly over in the cutter. Horner beat him to the flagship by virtue of being closer, but when Thorton scrambled over the gunwale, Henrique was there to greet him.

The admiral was the ugliest man that Thorton had ever seen, but he was delighted to see him all the same. Henrique received Thorton's salute, then grabbed him by the shoulders, kissed him on each cheek, and greeted him in a spate of Portuguese. When the admiral finally let him go, Thorton got a proper look at him.

Henrique, Duke of Coimbra, was a fathom tall but stooped a little. He had broad fleshy shoulders, a large head that hung forward, crossed eyes, and a gangly physique. He leaned on a gold-headed cane and waved his hand as he spoke. His sky blue uniform was loaded with gold lace. The reverses were primrose yellow and trimmed in gold. His three-corner hat was ornamented with too many ostrich feathers and a broad band of gold lace. Diamond earrings studded his ears, and he wore more diamonds on his hands. The lace cuffs of his linen sleeves flopped over big-knuckled hands while the cuffs of his coat were turned up in deep boot cuffs nearly to the elbow. His breeches were yellow and his waistcoat was white. A pair of gold epaulettes so heavy with bullion they could have ransomed a lieutenant weighed down his shoulders. It was a ridiculous uniform suited to a penny opera, but it pleased the duke.

"I am delighted to find that you have not been hanged," he told Thorton warmly in Spanish.

"I'm glad I wasn't hanged, too," Thorton replied.

Henrique touched the gold braid on his collar. "You're still a lieutenant? They didn't do anything terrible to you?"

"They disrated me back to midshipman and fined me twenty-five pounds," Thorton replied. "But Commodore Whittingdon restored my rank. I was the acting-captain of the *Ajax* because we're short on officers, except we have taken prizes and I'm the only one who knows how to command a lateen-rigged vessel, so I had to be the prizemaster. Perry's got the *Ajax*. He might catch up."

Henrique marveled. "You must join me for supper and tell me all about it."

So they dined with the flamboyant duke and heard his story as well as telling him theirs.

"And so, the Count of Oeiras has supported that dastard, João, and he's going to being crowned in Lisbon this spring. I protested, of course, but he's got seven daughters and he's marrying them off to all the major houses of Portugal. I am to marry his oldest daughter, Antónia. I'll be his heir if none of his daughters produces a male heir." He grunted in dissatisfaction at that. "In the meantime, he made me

Admiral of the Portuguese navy. I designed the uniform, do you like it?"

"Blue is nice," Thorton replied. Gaudy as the duke's uniform was, it was considerably tamer than the calico dress the duke had been wearing when they met.

The china that littered the table was expensive and bright-colored Chinese porcelain — the real stuff, imported across thousands of miles of ocean. The linen on his table was intricate lacework of purest white. The crystal chandelier hanging over it refracted the light and sent diamonds of light dancing over the walls. Mirrors in ornate frames and oil paintings were hung around the cabin. A genuine box bed with snowy white curtains, linens, and a yellow coverlet was only partially obscured by the tapestry curtains that divided the sleeping chamber from the day cabin. The cabin of a xebec was small, but the duke had stuffed it with every comfort without concern for expense.

"Congratulations on your impending nuptials," Horner replied.

"I have to do my duty and beget an heir, but Antónia is not an attractive woman."

"I'm sure you make the perfect couple," Horner replied in fluent Spanish.

Thorton eyed Horner, but the captain sat with his hands neatly folded in his lap and a demure expression on his face. Thorton couldn't decide if Horner was twitting Henrique or not.

Henrique was apparently oblivious to the irony of a homely man complaining about the looks of his prospective bride. He was talking again. "I am delighted to find you alive and well, Peter. I am very fond of you and I hope your captain will give you leave to visit me. In fact, I have a blank commission here. I need men like you in the Portuguese navy. You too, Ebenezer. I may call you 'Ebenezer,' mayn't I? I can offer you preferment. You'll have to become Catholic because João is currying favor with the clergy, but that's a minor matter."

"I am overwhelmed by your generous offer, but I must decline. I am already a commissioned officer of His Britannic Majesty's navy, and so is Lieutenant Thorton. Lest we have a repeat of this summer's misadventures, let me make it clear that Lieutenant Thorton does not have permission to resign his current commission, or to accept a new one." Horner's voice was firm.

Henrique flipped his wrist and made a face. "Dash it all, don't you want to wear something more stylish than that drab coat you've got on?" He turned to Thorton. "I appeal to your sense of fashion and the friendship that is between us. Join us in liberating Portugal from the heel of the Spanish despot!"

Thorton shook his head. "I am a Muslim, Your Grace. I sincerely believe it to be the most correct religion. I cannot convert. Even if I could, I am honor bound to fulfill my existing commission."

Henrique twined a curl of his blond wig around his finger. "You disappoint me. I admit there are certain charms in the harems of Africa, but I will make you a commodore. You can have as many lovers as you want."

Thorton replied stiffly, "I don't want a harem, Your Grace. I will be faithful to my love."

"Are you still with Shakil?"

Thorton wanted to slide under the table and hide. His relationship with Shakil was not a secret he kept from the captain, but he did not feel comfortable drawing his superior officer's attention to it, either. Better if it were forgotten.

"Aye, sir," he replied shortly. He avoided looking at Horner.

Henrique lowered his hand and removed a diamond ring from his finger. He pressed it into Thorton's hand.

"I owe my life and liberty to you and Shakil Effendi. I have already given him a token of my esteem. This is for you." He closed Thorton's hand around the ring. "If you ever need a favor, send the ring to me, whatever it is, if it is within my power, I will grant it."

"All I really need are some new antennas and sails, Your Grace," Thorton replied.

"Done. I'll send them over immediately.

The admiral-duke rose, signaling that the meal was over. Horner and Thorton returned to their respective vessels.

Henrique was as good as his word. Sails and spars were promptly sent. Each of the Portuguese xebecs sacrificed a portion of their supplies, so Thorton was able to re-rig the *Sea Leopard*. Applying the Pythagorean theorem he deduced that his mainsail was five thousand square feet; Tangle had assured him that as originally rigged the *Sea Leopard*'s mainsail was seven thousand square feet. The *Ajax*'s entire suit of plain sail was about twelve thousand square feet. The *Sea Leopard*'s undersized mainsail was the biggest sail with which he had ever grappled — it required forty men to raise it up. There was no capstan on the *Sea Leopard*; they hauled like demons.

He smiled as the large lateens bloomed over head. He felt her take the wind and a thrill rushed through him; she was built for speed.

Captain Tangle had designed her and supervised her construction; he had spared no expense in creating the perfect rover. She was a living creature and Thorton loved her. He understood why Tangle had been wroth to lose her, and why he was willing to go to any lengths to get her back. If he could claw to windward he could easily outrun the *Resolute*. He could fly home to the Sallee Republic where his lover, glory, and freedom waited for him.

Chapter 17 : Cape Finisterra

The *Ajax* caught up with them. Horner was running north up the coast of Portugal with the north star as his guide. Three days later they were off Cape Finisterra. The Portuguese frontier was left behind. This time it was a Spanish squadron that gave chase to them. The British had been sailing with the *Resolute* in the lead, but the battleship made signals and dropped back to protect her smaller consorts. The unarmed *Sea Leopard* led the way, followed by the prize and then the *Ajax*.

"Pile on all sail," Thorton ordered.

"Shall we clear for action?" Abby asked.

"Clear what? We haven't any guns."

"All the same, we should stow the valuables below. It will occupy the men and make them feel useful. Chases are wearing on the nerves."

"Very well. Make it so," he said.

The snare rattled and the pipes blew. Managing the big lateens took all the hands they had. Ra'uf was captain of the main and much too busy shepherding his *ferenghi* sailors to worry about stowing the glass from the captain's windows or anything else. Thorton assigned the marines to do the clearing. Marines always did a great deal of the clearing since there was nothing else for them to do until battle was actually joined.

Thorton said to Abby, "You have the conn. Keep us on course to round Cape Finisterra. I'm going below to secure my papers. Midshipman Sinclair!"

The midshipman bounded after him. Thorton went below and looked in vain for something he could use to weight the dispatch pouch. Finally he settled on a bottle of olive oil. It was a far cry from a four pound shot, but it was all he had.

"Mister Sinclair. If the enemy attempts to board us, you will drop this bag overboard. I'm leaving it right here on the locker where it will be easy to find. In the meantime, take the glass out of my windows and stow them. I have no idea where the glass covers and deadlights are, you'll have to find them or make do."

"Aye aye, sir." The young man began by taking the windows off their hinges and setting them on the floor. Thorton left him to it and went back up top.

The *Sea Leopard* flew across the sea. A bow wave threw spume on either side as she sliced through the water and the great lateens bellied over his head. He grinned happily. "We're making good time. Toss the log."

The line was run out and Chambers reported, "Ten knots, sir."

"By Allah. Tangle might be right. If she had a proper suit of sails, she might be capable of fourteen knots!"

Chambers gave him a skeptical look.

Thorton watched over the tafferel. The *Ajax* and the *Resolute* were making every stitch of sail, but the Spanish xebecs were gaining. The *Sea Leopard* was slowly leaving her escorts behind. The wind was very fresh out of the grey northeast and the English square-riggers were running close-hauled. Horner made signals and altered course to run northwest.

"Helm, four points west."

"Four points west, aye."

"Steady up."

"Steady up, aye. Course northwest."

The wind was now blowing over their starboard beam. The *Sea Leopard* heeled moderately and rushed over the waters.

"Toss the log."

"Eleven knots a quarter, sir."

Thorton adjusted the trim of the sails. "Toss the log again."

"Eleven and a half, sir."

Behind him the *Ajax* was going all out; Perry was setting her studding sails. "Lace on bonnets,"

The hands rushed below to examine the sail locker. Thankfully, she had bonnets. They carried them up and hastily lashed them to the bottoms of the lateen sails.

"Log."

"Just shy of twelve, sir."

Thorton looked back. The prize, the *Ajax*, and the *Resolute*, were falling behind while the Spanish xebecs continued to catch up to them. The *Sea Leopard* was leaving them all behind. It disheartened him to fly away from danger and leave his consorts behind, but what else could he do? He had no guns. He checked the sky; the northeast was turning dark as clouds piled up. It might blow a gale before it was all over, too. That would benefit the square-riggers; they were hardier than xebecs when it came to surviving a storm. A storm did not bode well for him. Yet the *Sea Leopard* had survived being knocked down by a rogue wave. Thorton decided he would rather trust God and His storms than the Spanish.

"Mister Abby. See that all hands are on deck and that the watertight bulkheads are sealed. String life lines."

"Aye aye, sir." The blind lieutenant did not know his way around the *Sea Leopard* and had to feel his way below. He collected a marine as his guide and gave him instructions. A little later he returned. "Bulkheads sealed and lifelines run, sir."

Thorton did not want to run too far away from his consorts. "Reef the bonnets."

"Reef the bonnets, aye." That was done and their speed slowed a trifle.

The minutes dragged by. After an hour Thorton raised his glass again. The *Ajax* had gained a little. The xebecs were closer. The Spanish battleship was further behind. The clouds continued to mount in the sky. The wind gusted and their coattails fluttered around them. The sails slatted and boomed. The sun was hot but the wind was cold.

"Keep her full and by."

"Full and by, aye."

The sails quieted. Thorton checked his watch. He swept his glass around the sea. There was nothing to see but the distant coast of Spain, the sea, the sky, the clouds, and the ships.

"Send the hands to dinner. After they've eaten, douse the galley fires."

Soon the smell of food was wafting over the vessel. Thorton went below and had his own dinner. It was couscous and boiled mutton with some chopped vegetables mixed in. It was tasty in spite of the British meat being tough enough to make his teeth ache. Half an hour later he came on deck. He studied the sea and sky and ships again. Nothing had changed.

The master's mate said, "They've gained on us, sir."

"Loose the bonnets."

Another hour dragged by. Thorton was bored and tense and so were the men. On the *Ajax* under Horner they had danced to while away the long hours before battle was joined.

"Have we got a fiddler?" he asked. No one on board could play an instrument, but one of the sailors owned up to singing. "Let's have it."

The sailor had a strong tenor and knew plenty of Irish folk songs they could dance a reel to. Thorton had the honor of being head man dancer while Abby took the spot of head woman dancer. The other couples were made up of midshipmen and mates. Abby knew the dance well enough, but Thorton had to watch out not to collide with him since Abby had no way to watch out for himself. The sailors laughed when Abby got turned part way around and bowed to nobody in particular, and they laughed even more when Thorton grabbed him by the arm and whirled him around and around. Thorton grinned.

Abby began to simper and prance and swoon like a delicate lady, "I should have brought my ballgown!" he said in a high falsetto. "'Tis all ribbons and lace and I have a wig three stories high topped with bird nests!"

Thorton laughed again as he danced attendance and exaggerated the gentlemanly bows and the difficulties of keeping his blind partner straight. The master's mate Wiggins bumped his butt with Abby's on purpose and pretended surprise as he went staggering across the deck. The sailors threw him back and after that the whole thing degenerated into a rowdy burlesque.

By the time the glass was turned and the bells rung, the dancers were sweating and panting. The men were in high spirits. Beer was served to quench their thirst and they mopped their faces with their handkerchiefs. Thorton drank deep, then went back up to the quarterdeck. Abby followed him.

The xebecs had gained on the battleship and frigate. Thorton checked his watch again, checked the sky, the sails, the log, and everything else.

The wind was growing fitful. Sometimes it dropped so that only a faint breeze was felt for minutes at a time, then it would blow hard and roar through the rigging. Sometimes it veered and took the sails aback with a wild flapping thunder. He had learned to handle the sails on the galiot, but those were small compared to the *Sea Leopard*. He worried and wondered if he should reduce sail. He could not forget the sight of the Spanish frigate pitchpoling with all canvas set. The same wave had laid the *Sea Leopard* on her beams ends.

The rover had been saved by water tight bulkheads below decks that kept her buoyant and shiplap strakes that needed no caulking to keep her dry. Her African teak hull was nearly as hard as iron and her galley construction reinforced the weather deck with a second deck close beneath it. Isam Rais Tangueli had built her to embody all that was best in North African naval architecture. Thorton had an almost superstitious faith in the nautical knowledge of the man the English called 'Captain Tangle,' so he gritted his teeth, held his course, and kept his sails up.

A spit of rain stung his cheek. He prayed for a good hard rain that would obscure them from the Spanish, but there was no such luck. The wind whipped his pigtail around his face and he jammed his cocked hat more firmly onto his head. He went below and got his boat cloak. It blew around him and he donned his gloves and wrapped a scarf around his neck to keep warm.

The Spanish had nearly caught up to the *Resolute*. The British were about to pass Finisterra and enter the Bay of Biscay. The northeast wind would be blowing unimpeded all the way across the bay, building up chop and making conditions worse. The xebecs might not have the stomach for the harsher environment of the Bay of Biscay. He prayed they had the weak constitutions of other Spaniards he had met in northern waters. Yet that meant exposing himself to risks the Spanish were right to fear.

"Mister Abby, I am going to give some very strange orders. See that they are obeyed with alacrity. I do not have time to explain myself."

"Aye aye, sir," the startled Abby replied.

The Bay of Biscay began to open on their right.

"Douse all sail. NOW. Get it in as quick as you can. Every scrap!"

Behind them the xebecs had not paid much attention to the *Sea Leopard* so far ahead of them, but when she doused all sail in a hurried panic, they were thrown into confusion. Why in the world would she suddenly reduce all sail with the enemy in hot pursuit? She had a battleship to defend her, but all the same, why? She was well ahead. She could have rounded the point and escaped while the xebecs engaged the battleship. Dousing sail caused her to hang on the point. The pursing Spaniards would overtake her shortly.

She must see something they could not . . . something that frightened her more than the possibility of being outnumbered by the Spanish. The Bay of Biscay was on the other side of that point, and the Bay, with a northeast wind blowing, was not a friendly place. The clouds were covering half the sky and a rain curtain was stretching below them. The other side of the point must be engulfed in a full blown storm, a storm she feared to face. That was the only explanation that made any sense.

The xebecs doused their sails and sent their antennas down. They lashed them in the davits and worked busily to set the small storm sails on the shortened antennas so that they could ride out whatever was going to blow around that point any minute now.

Thorton watched them through his glass. "Yes!" he crowed. "We have tricked them! Make all sail! Smartly, lads, smartly!"

The great lateens sails billowed over head and were sheeted home. The *Sea Leopard* kicked up her heels and flew around the point close-hauled. The *Ajax* and *Resolute* followed her.

Furious, the Spaniards ordered their antennas up again. They had fallen far behind the English while they reduced sail, and now they were under storm sails. They had to bring them down again, wrestle the full-sized antennas into place, and haul them up again. It took a long time. The *Sea Leopard* and her consorts bowled forward and disappeared into the curtain of rain.

CHAPTER 18 : SEVEN STARS

The Bay of Biscay was windy, rainy and chilly. The sun that came out the next day was bright and clear, but it was an autumn day in the north, not at all like a balmy Mediterranean autumn. Thorton kept his cloak on and wrapped a wool muffler around his throat. The other officers were gloved and cloaked as they walked the quarterdeck. Walk it they did; exercise kept them warm.

They had company that morning. Far to the west, a barely discernible triangle of white, was a strange vessel. Over the course of the morning its course slowly converged with theirs until it became apparent that it would pass to the west of Eel Buff as they passed to the east. At a distance of only two miles it could be seen to be a xebec with the lofty lateen rig of a Sallee rover. The vessel disappeared behind the bulk of Eel Buff. As they rounded the island and turned in toward the harbor, they met her again.

She beat them to the harbor entrance but did not go in. Instead she hove to and waited for them. At such a close distance they could see the purple ensign flying at her stern and the broad purple pennant of a commodore at her masthead.

"Tangle," Thorton breathed.

Abby couldn't see and desperately wished he could. "Why do you think so?"

"What other Sallee commodore would come north in pursuit of the *Sea Leopard*?"

"You don't know they are pursuing the *Sea Leopard*."

"They're waiting for us," Thorton said with conviction.

Abby was skeptical. "Anyhow, it can't be Tangle. He couldn't have beaten us to Eel Buff. The message had to go to Zokhara, and if he was in Zokhara, he would have to beat around the Modiq Peninsula to come after us. Even if he'd left on the instant he'd be two days behind us."

"We spent two days rigging the *Sea Leopard*. First, the storm sails in the Strait of Gibraltar, and second, the new antennas and big lateens off Lisbon."

"I suppose it is possible," Abby conceded. "But still, he made good time."

Thorton swept his glass over the other xebec. "*Seven Stars*," he made out her name in Arabic upon her bow. A star before and behind the name helped him. "That's Achmed's xebec."

The *Seven Stars* challenged them. It was customary for the larger ship to challenge the smaller, and so the prerogative should have belonged to the *Resolute*, but the commodore's pennant outranked the sixty-four guns of a British battleship. The *Resolute* replied with her name and captain. She queried the stranger in return.

"*Seven Stars*, Commodore Tangueli," was the answer.

"Told you so," said Thorton as he read the exchange of signals.

"Yes, you were right," Abby said a little crossly.

Next Horner was summoned aboard the *Seven Stars*. It was an order, not an invitation. Most British captains would take umbrage at being ordered to do anything by a Sallee rover, so it was several minutes before the *Resolute* acknowledged. Thorton bit the edge of his muffler and wished he were the one to go, but there was nothing he could do but wait.

The minutes ticked by. Thorton consulted his watch nine times in twenty minutes. After an eternity, the *Seven Stars* signaled for Thorton. Thorton hastily called for the *Leopard's Whelp* and the ship's boat was brought along side. A few minutes later and Thorton was clambering over the *Seven Stars* gunwale and onto the deck.

The deckhead of the great cabin of the *Seven Stars* was of normal height; Thorton had to duck under the beams. Achmed was sitting upon a divan with his legs crossed while Tangle stood next to him. Horner was seated upon a small divan of the sort that was known to the English as an 'ottoman' after its country of origin. A four-legged tray was next to him with papers upon it. The wainscot was varnished to a mellow shade of Mediterranean oak. Bronze lamps hung from the beams and swayed gently as the vessel bobbed on the waters. A kilim rug of green, brown, tan and cream covered the floor. Achmed himself was wearing a green Turkish coat and fawn colored pantaloons. The skirts spread gracefully around him as he sat on the divan.

Thorton stopped just short of the carpet. He knew it was customary in Muslim countries for people to remove their shoes before entering a residence; it seemed rude to track dirty shoes over such magnificent rugs. He did notice that Tangle was wearing his tall black boots; he was there on business. Only a little of his buff-colored pantaloons were revealed beneath the sweep of the full skirts of the purple coat. The man was tall and the turban on his head made him even taller. He had to stoop under the deckhead.

Achmed bin Mamoud smiled warmly. *"Salaam.* Peace be upon you, Peter Rais. I am delighted to see you again." He seemed like a gracious host greeting an old friend.

Thorton was uncertain whether to bow, salute, or press his hand to his forehead in the Muslim fashion. He settled for holding his cocked hat under his arm and standing at attention. "Your Excellency," he replied.

"Please, have a seat, Captain Thorton."

Achmed's black eunuch brought another ottoman over. Thorton hesitated and looked at Tangle and at Horner, but the men's expressions were inscrutable. "Thank you, sir." He sat cross-legged on the small divan and arranged his tails and cloak so they hung over the sides. He put his hat in his lap.

"Coffee?"

"Thank you, sir."

The eunuch served him a cup of fine celadon porcelain. Horner and Achmed had coffee also, but Tangle stood by in silence. The coffee had been boiled to a froth and allowed to cool just enough to be drinkable. It was sweetened with honey. It warmed him up and made him decide to spend some of his prize money laying in a stock of Turkish coffee.

Horner let him drink, then picked up the paper from the top of the stack. "His Excellency has brought a copy of Kasim Rais' letter of marque. Since I cannot read Arabic, I would appreciate it if you would examine the document for me." He cleared his throat politely and explained to Achmed, "I'm sure you understand that although I have the utmost faith in the Sallee bureaucracy, I must satisfy my superiors that I have taken every proper step."

Achmed smiled indulgently. "Of course. I expect nothing less." He had a genial, round face with curly beard sprinkled with white. He looked like somebody's kind-hearted uncle.

Thorton took the paper in surprise. He glanced back and forth between Tangle and Horner. He set the coffee cup down on the four legged tray that magically appeared at his elbow and studied the form. He said cautiously, "It looks like the other Sallee letters of marque that I have seen, sir."

Although Thorton was not fluent in Arabic, he was familiar with those aspects of the language that impinged directly on himself; he too had a letter of marque. Once, for a little while, he had been Sallee rover and captain of the *Arrow*.

"Can you read it to me?" Horner asked.

"Not all of it, sir. But I can read the names and dates. It is issued to Kasim bin Nakih, captain of the *Sea Leopard*. The date is . . ." He scrunched up his face as he racked his brain to try and translate. The Muslim calendar was a lunar one and did not correspond to the Christian calendar. "The date would be in March of this year. I recognize the sigil of His Excellency Lord Zahid bin Mustafa."

Horner's voice and expression were pleasantly neutral when he asked, "Everything is in order?"

Thorton bit his lip and glanced at Tangle. Then he glanced at Achmed. He avoided looking at Horner.

Horner was a sharp observer. "What is it, Lieutenant?"

Thorton swallowed. He had been asked a direct question and could not avoid answering it. He gave Tangle an apologetic look as he explained to Horner, "I don't think Lord Zahid was Minister of Marine in March of this year.'

Horner's bushy eyebrows lifted up to where they would have met his hairline, if his hairline had still been keeping company with his forehead. "Indeed." He looked to Achmed.

Achmed continued smiling warmly. "That is correct. Abdul-Mohammed bin Omar was the Minister of Marine this spring. This is a notarized copy of the letter of marque that was filed at that time. The original is in Zokhara where it must remain for safe-keeping. Zahid Amir is minister now, so he signed the copy."

It was so very plausible. And a lie. Horner received the Arabic paper back and studied it as if he understood it. He asked Thorton, "Do Sallee privateers post bond?"

Thorton was sweating under his collar. "They do, sir."

Tangle unbuttoned the top buttons of his uniform coat and reached into his breast pocket. He pulled out a paper and held it up. "The bond. I paid it. Kasim Rais is my brother-in-law. My wife and other relatives are investors in the ship." He had made certain to study the English he would need for this discussion.

"May I see it?" Horner asked.

"Certainly."

The eunuch moved quietly to bring it to Horner. Once again the English captain reviewed the Arabic with great care. He handed it to Thorton. "Can you read it?"

Thorton studied it. It also was a pre-printed form with the pertinent information written in. "It lists Kasim bin Nakih, and is signed with the name and sigil of the bond-giver, Isam bin Hamet al-Tangueli, the amount, one thousand Sallee sequins, and the date. It is countersigned by Zahid Amir Mustafa."

Horner took the bond paper back, looked at it again, then tapped his finger upon it. "I'm surprised Kasim Rais did not produce his papers when he was arrested."

Achmed smiled again. He had a very natural and believable smile. His expression remained good-humored, as if he were being patient with a slightly dotty friend. "Mister Thorton, when you searched Kasim Rais' cabin, did you search it completely? Or did you stop when you found his strongbox?"

Thorton's face was wooden. "I did not continue the search after finding the strong box."

"Did you search the ship?"

"No, sir. I inspected it for damage and gave orders for repair."

"Given that the *Sea Leopard* was knocked down by the weater and had tossed everything overboard when she ran from the Spaniard, is it not possible that the document was lost, damaged, or destroyed?" Achmed asked.

"I suppose so, sir."

"Did you undertake a concerted effort to locate the missing papers, or to ascertain who had last seen them or had responsibility for them?"

Thorton stiffened still further. "No, sir."

Tangle's brown eyes snapped and he took a step forward, but Achmed raised his hand. "Peace, Isam. We must remember that these officers were themselves in great peril. We must forgive them if they were caught up in other duties and neglected to make a thorough examination of the question. Tell me, Captain Thorton. Did you find any British goods the *Sea Leopard*?"

"Only the Irish girl."

"Was she on a British vessel when she was taken?"

"No, sir. She was on a Spanish smuggler plying between Spain and Ireland."

Achmed smiled warmly at Horner. "That settles my questions. I hope the information is sufficient to secure the release of the *Sea Leopard*."

Horner neatly folded up the bond and marque and handed them over to the eunuch. He bowed to the Sallee envoy. "I must apologize for the inconvenience we have caused you, and I hope it will not lead to any ill feelings. We were only doing our duty to apprehend what we thought was a pirate. I am relieved that you have brought the papers necessary to settle the matter."

Achmed's smile was genuine as he said, "Excellent! I will send Isam Rais aboard immediately."

Tangle smiled faintly, but he remained alert and watchful. He had been bested by Horner once before and he was not willing to be tricked a second time.

Horner unfolded his legs and rose. "I will issue orders to Mister Thorton. We will need to make some arrangements of our own."

Tangle spoke, "You may deliver Kasim and the officers to the *Seven Stars*. They will report to His Excellency. I will go aboard the *Sea Leopard* with my officers and transfer my pennant to it."

"Very good, sir." Horner gave a little bow. "Come along, Mister Thorton."

A very unhappy Thorton followed Horner out of the cabin. "Sir, may I have a word in private with you?"

Horner gave Thorton an enigmatic look. "If you insist. Join me in my boat."

They went over the side into the *Resolute's* boat. Horner took a seat in the sternsheets while Thorton sat on the bench in front of him.

"Isam Rais Tangueli was chained to a Spanish oar aboard the *San Bartolomeo* until April of this year! He couldn't possibly have posted bond for Kasim in March!" Thorton burst out.

"I reviewed the log of the *Ajax* thoroughly when I came aboard. I am well aware of the sequence of events."

"Those documents are frauds!"

"But they are legal frauds. If the Sallee government chooses to backdate them and extend the cloak of legality over Kasim Rais, there is nothing we can do about it. Do you really think the Admiralty will concern itself with the fate of a privateer who hasn't pilfered English goods?"

"I suppose not. But they made me look like a fool!"

Horner patted his knee. "Your friends have gone to great expense to make an honest man of Kasim Rais. Let us hope they are successful."

"Aye aye, sir." Thorton huddled unhappily in his cloak and said nothing more.

CHAPTER 19 : THE LEOPARD'S MASTER

Thorton was glad the *Sea Leopard* would not be forfeit and the men would not be hanged, but he was the object of a certain amount of ill will on the part of Suhail and other members of the crew. Previously he had been resigned to difficulties as long as he remained in British service, but always in the back of his mind was the comforting thought that if it became too onerous, he could desert to the Sallee rovers. Yet Tangle had gone to great effort and expense to protect his odious brother-in-law, and Thorton had come off looking very bad as a result Now that he had offended his friends and patrons among the rovers they would not be so quick to receive him back.

Tangle in his boat with his officers was not far behind as Horner and Thorton in the *Resolute's* boat approached the *Sea Leopard*. The British marines in their redcoats received Thorton as the master of the vessel as he climbed aboard. Abby was there, his hand on the shoulder of one of the ship's boys to help him find his way around.

"Welcome back, Captain."

"Thank you, Lieutenant."

As Tangle and his officers approached the *Sea Leopard*, the British watchman challenged them. "What boat?"

Tangle stood up and called back in his Turkish accented English, "*Sea Leopard*, Commodore Isam Rais Tangueli!"

"Who?" the watchman replied.

Thorton had to speak then. "'Tis true. He's brought the papers. Pipe the commodore aboard."

Six sideboys lined up to receive the commodore. Tangle's booted heels rang on the deck as he came over the side. He stalked between the rows of scarlet-clad marines and their presented arms with a scowl on his face. The corp of Sallee officers followed him up and looked around with eager curiosity.

"I am Isam Rais Tangueli. I am the new master of the *Sea Leopard*. My papers." He presented them to Thorton.

Abby recognized the shadowy figure and knew his voice. "Welcome aboard, Commodore," he replied in surprise.

"All hands on deck," Thorton said.

MacDonald piped the call that brought all the British sailors to line up at attention. Thorton spoke briefly. "The Salletines have brought the necessary papers to verify the identity and nature of the *Sea Leopard* and her crew. They are properly commissioned privateers and will be released. We are now transferring authority to the Sallee captain."

Abby barked, "Attention!" The men straightened up and silenced their murmurs.

Tangle read out his commission that made him master of the vessel. His mellifluous Arabic flowed over all their heads. The Englishmen stared blankly at him. He repeated it in English. He'd had the document prepared in both languages and practiced it so that he could deliver it without error.

The change of officers was made, and the British hauled up their dunnage and got into the boats.

"Peter. Not you. You're going to stay a while."

It was an order, not a request, so Thorton waited nervously. "Aye aye, sir."

"My cabin."

Abby hesitated, too, but Thorton said, "Go on Abby." Reluctantly the blond lieutenant went over the side.

Thorton waited in the great cabin. His things were gone and with them Ra'uf. He missed the man. Above and below he heard the sound of the *Sea Leopard* coming to life. There was the thumping noise of Maynard's peg leg crossing the quarterdeck overhead and the call of Arabic orders. The hold was unlocked and the prisoners brought up into the light of day. They praised Allah when they found themselves in the hands of their co-religionists and freed from fear of the gallows. Men hauled Tangle's dunnage into the cabin and his servant, a slender black eunuch, quietly unpacked the carpets and cushions and desk and other things. Tangle was fond of blue and gold and his things were in much better taste than those that had belonged to Kasim. Thorton had nothing else to do, so he helped the man unpack and arrange things for his master.

After an hour Tangle came into the cabin. He dismissed the servant and stood looking around. He grimaced at the gaudy walls. "I'll have it painted immediately."

Thorton nodded. Tangle stared at him for a while, then took a seat on his sea chest. He pulled up his legs and sat cross-legged like the Turk he was. He unbuttoned his coat to the waist and reached into a breast pocket. "Shakil has sent you a letter."

Thorton's face brightened and he sprang forward eagerly to receive the envelope. He was too intent on the familiar hand-writing to notice the darkness in Tangle's eyes. He broke the seal and opened it up swiftly. Shakil had written in Arabic and translated into Spanish. As he read, Thorton's face fell. When he was done, he looked up with hollow eyes. "Did you know?"

"Yes, I know," Tangle replied. He patted the sea chest beside him. "Sit down before you fall down."

Thorton plunked his butt down on the seat next to Tangle and reread the letter. "He says he cannot trust an Englishman. That my duty will call me to act contrary to the interests of my friends. That he is tired of worrying about me."

Tangle nodded. "He said that to me as well."

Thorton folded up the letter and rubbed the sleeve of his cloak across his eyes. "I tried to save the *Sea Leopard* for you, but everyone was stubborn!"

The great corsair leaned back and propped his elbows on the windowsill. The unbuttoned coat gapped open to show the embroidered front of his white tunic. He stretched out one long leg. "Thank you for the letter. Without it Kasim's fate would have been decided and the *Sea Leopard* lost before we ever knew."

"I tried to persuade Horner to release the others."

Tangle snorted. "He held me with far less excuse. Did you really think you would fare better?"

"You should have let us hang Kasim. That would make things easier for you."

Tangle shook his head. "As much as I would like to be rid of him, he is my wife's brother, and she worries about him. Not to mention, his children live in our house. How could I tell them I let the *ferenghi* hang their father? More to the point, I couldn't let the *Sea Leopard* be condemned. The investors are furious with him. They voted him out and made me captain. I have posted Kasim's bond and I plan to make him forfeit his share of the *Sea Leopard* to pay me back."

"'Tis all right then," Thorton said in relief.

Tangle sat up and glared at him. "No, it is not!" He grabbed Thorton's pigtail and jerked it roughly. "Why, why, why did you tell Captain Horner that Kasim didn't have a letter of marque? He need never have known! You could have sent me your letter and the investors would have taken care of him without hauling the *Sea Leopard* all the way to England to be put on trial for piracy!"

"Ow!" Thorton pulled his hair away from the corsair. "Because he didn't have one," he said stubbornly. "Why should I lie for Kasim? Why should I lie at all?"

"You're going to get yourself killed if you always tell the truth!"

"Honesty is the best policy!"

"Except when it isn't." Tangle waggled a long brown finger at him.

"Shakil is always honest!"

"Shakil has twice the sense you do. He knows how to keep his mouth shut. I confess, I drive him to fits because he must figure out how to accommodate my whims while keeping his conscience pure, but really, a little impurity is good for a man. It keeps him healthy and in the good graces of his friends."

"I don't have many friends."

Tangle smote his thigh. "Have you ever thought why?"

Thorton stared at his knees. "I don't really know why. I try to be good and honest and work hard, but people don't like it. What else am I supposed to do? Be a rogue? Like you?"

Tangle laughed at that. "You're an intelligent man, yet you haven't a lick of sense. You are as blind to people as Abby is to the world."

"I don't like it when people yell at me. Nobody ever yells at Abby because he's blind. If a man is the way he is, shouldn't you leave him alone? You might as well be angry with a donkey because he isn't a horse."

Tangle quieted. "I know it is your nature. I also know that you will never be scheming behind my back or trying to spite me, but you are not a politician. Thank Allah we have Achmed to handle these things. I wanted to slap Horner's sanctimonious face."

"Horner is a good officer."

"Devious, too. I will never forget the way he made me a hostage under the guise of hospitality. Until I got the *Sea Leopard* under my control I thought it was a trick. I was afraid I'd be going to England in the hold along with the rest of the pirates."

Thorton smiled a little at that. "He's the only man who has ever bested you, isn't he?"

Tangle's brow darkened. "You forget the Spaniard that captured me. That makes two. There will not be a third."

"You've never told me about it."

"I never will. I haven't told anyone."

"Why not?"

"Because . . . I am a proud man."

Thorton smiled. "You're as vain as I am stubborn."

Tangle's lips twitched a little as he tried to suppress a smile. "I am the greatest corsair of the age. I don't like being beaten at my own game."

"You're a fine seaman, but you should have seen what I did with the *Sea Leopard*."

That got Tangle's attention. "What?"

Thorton told him about tricking the Spanish off Finisterra.

Tangle laughed at the ruse. "That was admirably devious! I don't think I would have thought of it. But then, I am not accustomed to sailing without guns. A prize crew only, no guns, a hold full of prisoners, and outnumbered by the Spanish! You never cease to amaze me, Peter. You always rise to the occasion."

Thorton smiled warmly back at him. "We're still friends then?"

Tangle smiled and said gruffly, "We are." He ran his hand over Thorton's hair, then leaned forward and gave him a peck on the mouth. The kiss was brief and chaste, then Tangle turned his face to hide his feelings.

Thorton heaved a sigh of relief. He let himself think about Shakil. Unhappiness came bubbling up. He was lonely, more lonely that he had ever been. For the first twenty-nine years of his life he had never had a lover and not known what he was missing. Over the course of single summer, he had briefly had Tangle for his lover, then Shakil. Now he had no one. Being parted from Shakil had been hard, but he had the secret knowledge of another man's love to comfort him in the dark of night. He could remember Shakil teaching him Arabic, the warmth of his body next to him in bed, and the joy of a lover who had a quiet courage, and the fortitude to do what must be done. He could daydream about seeing him again and what they might do together. Such dreams had carried him through many a dull watch and long night. No more. Shakil didn't want him.

But Tangle did. Even though he had jilted the man, Tangle still carried a torch for him. Thorton did not want to be alone anymore. He slipped his hand onto Tangle's thigh and let it rest lightly.

Tangle turned to face him and brown eyes gazed into blue ones. Slowly and deliberately Thorton leaned forward and kissed the man full on the mouth. His eyes closed and his hand tightened on the corsair's thigh. Tangle's arm went around him and pulled him into an embrace.

"I knew it would never work out between you and Shakil!" the corsair said. "I love him like a brother, but you and I are men of action. We need a lover than can match us. That is why we are drawn to each other."

Thorton's heart ached as it beat against his ribs. Shakil's rejection burned him and made his face red with shame. Shakil was unfair. Tangle was easygoing and understood him. "Are you angry with me for jilting you?"

Tangle laughed a little. "You hurt my feelings more than I will ever admit! I do not like losing, Peter."

"You haven't lost. Not yet. Suffered a few setbacks, perhaps . . ."

Tangle knew an opening when he saw it, and he took it without hesitation.

CHAPTER 20 : THE SECRET OF COMMAND

The Sallee rover and the English lieutenant were warm together in the rover's bed. It was a doublewide hanging cot long enough for a man of Tangle's height to stretch out. Hung from chains it swayed with the motions of the ship instead of tipping them out the way a fixed bunk would have.

Thorton whispered, "I don't want to go back."

Tangle raised his head. "You don't have to."

"Alan Abby is the senior surviving officer of the *Adamant*. I expect I will have to testify at his court martial. And the *Resolute* must go to trial, too. Horner and Abby are men I respect and admire. I must help them as much as I can."

"Do you want me to come? I was there. Powell didn't have to die." There was a hardness in his voice.

Thorton wanted him to come to England very much. He also knew that if he did come, he would wind up in the rover's bed again. He ought to be ashamed of that, but he wasn't. He was afraid of being caught, but not enough to refrain from doing it. He cursed himself as fickle and wanton. Maybe Shakil had been right not to trust him. He was in Tangle's bed for no good reason. Thorton did not understand men very well, himself included.

He nodded to his Turkish lover. "Can you?"

Tangle snuggled against him. "I will. I have to attend to Kasim and his officers, and I have to take some prizes, but now that I have the *Sea Leopard* back, I am free to do as I please. Well, not entirely free, but fortunately Zahid Amir is our friend."

Thorton propped on his elbow and noticed something. "What happened to your grey hair?"

Tangle's hair was grown long enough that he could tie it in a short ponytail at the nape of his neck. It was jet black. The older man looked abashed. "Oh, that. I had the barber pluck them out. I don't want to look old."

Thorton tugged the white streak in his beard. "You don't look old, you look distinguished."

Tangle rolled his eyes. "I'm forty-two and starting to look it."

Thorton snorted at that. Tangle was exceptionally lean and fit with broad shoulders, narrow waist, and a robust constitution. He had recovered rapidly from the privations of the galley. He was brown all over, including places where a gentleman ought not be tanned. Thorton was a sallow white under his clothes. He rested a hand on Tangle's hip and stared at the contrast in color. He felt a molly boy next to the rover. The man had a scar the size of a hand that reached from his clavicle to his armpit. His nose had a small hump in it due to being broken, and his entire back was a mass of lines from the bite of a Spanish cat.

"You're not old. You're in your prime." Tangle was in much better shape than most men half his age.

Tangle's eyes grew dark. "Not any more. I'm starting to slip. My joints ache; I know when it will rain. I have trouble sleeping. I cannot abide to see a man flogged anymore. I want nothing more than to be home with my wife and children in front of a roaring fire. I've gotten soft, Peter."

"No one would ever think it to look at you. You are a hale and virile man."

Tangle smiled at that. "I know you never flatter, Peter. Coming from you, it must be the truth." He rumpled Thorton's blond hair.

Thorton smoothed his hair down and smiled shyly. "I miss you. I miss my purple coat. I miss praying in Arabic."

"You miss me?"

"I do. You make me blush, but I miss you all the same."

Tangle laughed. "If those English uniforms don't cure you of modesty, nothing will!"

"What do you mean?"

"They are very revealing."

"No they aren't!" Thorton protested.

Tangle rose. "Let us wash and dress, and I'll show you what I mean."

The two washed in the same basin, then dressed in their respective uniforms. Thorton pulled his coat over his waistcoat and checked to make certain his stocking seams were straight.

"There, that's part of what I mean. Look at how those silk stockings cling to your legs! You have a very fine calf and the silk shows it to perfection."

Thorton gave him a startled look, then turned his leg and looked at it. "I suppose it is a good leg," he admitted.

Tangle smiled appreciatively at the leg, then his eyes roved higher. Thorton blushed to be gazed at so frankly.

"And those breeches. They fit your form and reveal your thighs and groin. The waistcoat is not long enough. I have noticed old Englishmen wear their waistcoats down to their thighs, probably to conceal that they are limp with age."

Thorton's jaw dropped. He was absolutely scandalized by such a remark. His lips moved, but he could only sputter, "That's not why!"

Tangle enjoyed teasing Thorton; the English lieutenant was an easy mark. "I assume, therefore, that young men display their legs because they want them to be looked at. And I do enjoy looking at them. I cannot help thinking randy thoughts, like how easy it would be to do —" he put his hand on Thorton's groin and gripped him "— this!"

Thorton squawked and jumped and pushed the man's hand away. His face was bright red. "You're a scoundrel!"

"Every man must be a rogue when confronted with such a tempting target."

"I don't think so!" Thorton retorted.

"Oh, come now, Peter. How many women are in naval service? You cannot pretend the uniform is for their benefit."

Thorton shook his head violently. "'Tis because an officer must look like a gentleman to effectively lead the lower orders!"

"So you are saying that men are pleased to follow a fine pair of legs. I have no argument with that."

Thorton's face was scarlet. He mumbled, "'Tis the fashion, nothing more. You make it sound scandalous."

"It is scandalous. The Qur'an enjoins us to dress modestly in loose fitting clothes. This is not loose fitting." Again he attempted to tweak Thorton's groin, but Thorton was alert enough to dance away and cover himself with his hands.

Tangle went on. "Look at my uniform. The coat has a full skirt. You can see nothing underneath. Which has been a blessing on more than one occasion — a man cannot control the reactions of his body. But if you had the horn, everyone would know it.

"I don't!"

"You did earlier. I was gratified to see it. I like to know how I'm doing."

"You're horrible!"

Tangle grinned at him. "The white vest comes down just low enough to draw the eye to the groin. The contrast between the blue breeches and white waistcoat forces the eye to observe the location. You're just begging to be ogled."

"No more, I beseech you! You are indecent!"

Tangle sobered. "Now that I think about it, I think it has something to do with British discipline. You demand more of your men than any other navy, and you get it. If a fine pair of legs can get a sailor to pay attention, so be it. An officer must use every tool at his disposal to bend the men to his will."

"That is not why we wear breeches!"

"Do you think Abby and Perry don't know how good they look? They walk like men who expect to be looked at. Are they not well-liked? I don't like Perry, but if I didn't know what I know, I would like him very much. I certainly like his legs."

Thorton started to protest, but then he stopped. Captain Horner was a dowdy man. He was respected, but was he liked? Captain Bishop was not at all attractive in person or in personality. "A captain doesn't need to be liked. Just respected."

"I grant you that if a man must choose one or the other, respect is better than affection. I think you have made that choice, Peter. But wouldn't it be better to be both liked and respected?"

"I suppose it would."

Thorton had a great deal to think about on his way back to the *Ajax*. He was very self-conscious about his body and appearance, and he eyed the sailors aboard the *Leopard's Whelp* worriedly, wondering if they were sneaking peeks at him while they worked the lines and manned the tiller. He thought they might be. He swiftly closed his legs and wrapped his cloak over his knees.

"Cold, rais?" one of the men asked him.

"'Tis chilly," he replied.

"Autumn is here. In the Mediterranean 'tis still warm."

"Indeed."

"Does it snow in England?"

"Yes, it does, although not as much as the Maryland colony where I was born."

What if Tangle was right? The sailor had looked at him because of the way he was dressed and that had led them to chat. Perry had tried to teach him how to make small talk long ago. Usually Thorton cultivated the aloofness of an officer; he thought Horner an ideal captain in that respect. Horner was very able and fair, and Thorton admired him for it, but he did not love him. He loved Tangle, loved him with the admiration and affection of genuine regard. The ideal officer, he thought, would combine Horner's skill and dedication to duty with Tangle's warmth and cleverness. Did he have it in him to accomplish that? He didn't think so . . . but he wanted to try.

CHAPTER 21 : HAPPY BIRTHDAY, CAPTAIN HORNER

Over the next few days the English reconnoitered Eel Buff, took on water and fresh produce, then clawed against contrary winds as they tried to make their way home. Thorton resumed command of the *Ajax* and covertly observed the officers. He saw that Perry and Abby wore frock coats with narrower skirts and smaller cuffs, and that their waistcoats were shamefully immodest. Although their waistcoats came below the waist, they stopped just short of the crotch. When they raised their arms to point out something in the rigging or shoot the sun, it revealed their flies. The sight distracted Thorton the same way a fluttering bit of lace on a woman's bosom might distract a ladies' man. He tried hard to concentrate on his work. Yet now that he had noticed it, he couldn't stop thinking about it. Entirely unequipped with a sense of fashion, he had always known that Abby and Perry were good-looking, but not understood how the cut of their clothes enhanced their physical appearance. Now that he knew, he was jealous. He wanted to cut a fine figure too. He betook himself to his cabin, and with the aid of his shaving mirror, examined himself from top to bottom.

Thorton had had a frock coat made in Port Mahon and he studied it carefully. He discovered that the shoulders were cut a little broader and lightly padded to exaggerate his natural shoulders, and the waist nipped in and the skirts were lightly flared to emphasize the leanness of his legs. It was a good coat, but he was wearing a secondhand white waistcoat that came down to his thighs. He had even pulled his wool stockings over the hems of his breeches and held them in place with garters like an old man. It was convenient and functional, but it was not fashionable. He had bought half a dozen pairs of white silk stockings in a rare bout of personal indulgence when he had his Sallee prize money. He had been saving them for his dress uniform and for battle, but those days were somewhere in the hazy future. Right now he was embarrassed by his appearance. He vowed never to appear in public again dressed in mended woollies. Off they came, to be replaced by silk. On top of that, he wanted a new waistcoat, so he got some old sailcloth and made himself a short one. It would never do on shore, but it was good enough while at sea.

Finally dressed, he surveyed himself in satisfaction. His silk stockings clung to his legs and were tucked under the hems of his breeches while his frock coat still had a crisp newness about it. His new waistcoat was as short as the other young men. He was pleased with the result — he did have a good set of legs. The only thing that could not be mended was the pair of brown shoes he had bought to match the buff and purple uniform of a Sallee rover. Still, he thought himself enough improved to go on deck.

The officers were congregating on the quarterdeck as usual. They all turned to give him their attention and he froze in panic. They must be looking at him, noticing his change of dress, wondering at it, and were about to remark up it. He was starting to turn red when Jackson saluted.

"Signal from the *Resolute*, sir."

Thorton returned the salute and said, "What is it, Jackson?"

"'Thorton to *Resolute*,' sir," Jackson replied.

Saved from one terror only to be thrown into a worse one! He trembled to think of being pinned by Horner's steely gaze, examined from top to bottom, and finally summed up with a condescending, "Hm," delivered from beneath Horner's long nose. There was no help for it. When a superior officer called, he did not expect to be kept waiting while his inferior changed his stockings.

"Acknowledge and call my boat," Thorton replied.

Forsythe greeted him with a worried look as he came aboard the *Resolute*. He spoke in a low and hurried voice. "Thank you for coming, Peter. I didn't know what else to do. Horner's not well." Forsythe was a sturdy and somewhat plodding officer. To take initiative was unusual for him, but he was devoted to Horner.

The intelligence sent a cold dread down Thorton's back. "What's the matter with him?"

If Horner was incapable of command, Thorton, as the acting-captain of the *Ajax*, was going to have to take responsibility to get the battleship, the prize, and the frigate to England. The Bay of Biscay was choppy and a cold breeze was blowing. Autumn might be lovely ashore, but in the Bay of Biscay it could be unfriendly. Thorton's blood ran cold in spite of his cloak and muffler.

"He ordered dinner for two, but just sits there alone, drinking. He hasn't eaten. His food is cold. He won't speak to anyone. We've asked about the sails, but all he said was, 'Do as you see fit.' I put a reef in. Do you think that was the right thing to do?"

"Very sensible," said Thorton. "I had no idea Horner was not giving orders."

Forsythe brightened a little and clung to Thorton's arm. Although he was Thorton's senior, he had no confidence in his ability to command. "What else should I do?"

"Have you called the physician?"

"I did. Horner refused to let him bleed him and said he planned to drink away his malady. The doctor said drinking *was* his malady, but he cursed him, and drove him out."

Thorton was astonished. He had never seen Horner drunk and never heard him curse. He could not imagine what had driven the captain to such an extreme. "I'll call on him."

"Please! I know you'll know what to do."

Thorton knocked on the door to the great cabin. At first there was no answer, so he knocked again. "Go away," came a surly voice that had the same tone and timber as Horner's, but it hardly sounded like him.

"'Tis Thorton, sir!" he called through the door.

"Enter," was grunted from the other side.

Thorton steeled himself, turned the knob and crossed the threshold.

Horner's gangly form was sprawled upon the locker beneath his windows. He had a nearly empty bottle of brandy in one hand and a glass in the other. His head lolled upon its neck like a marble rolling on top of a fence post; at any moment it seemed in imminent danger of toppling off. He was wearing his dress coat with white facings and a very long waistcoat. The boot cuffs on the frock coat were deep and the skirts were full; it had been the height of fashion years ago when it was first made. His woolen stockings were pulled up over his knees and gartered, but one of them had slid down to his ankle. His shoes were lying on the painted canvas rug. The thinning blond hair was pulled back from his forehead, and the forehead itself had a sheen to it. Heavy lidded eyes regarded the younger man.

Thorton advanced into the room and said, "Good afternoon, sir." A glance told him the dining table was set in its best white linen with two places of blue and white china ready to receive the feast. A roasted hen was on a platter accompanied by potatoes, vegetables and fruit.

"I couldn't get a goose, Mister Thorton," Horner said when he saw the direction of his glance. "I had to sacrifice my last chicken."

"What is the occasion, sir?"

"'Tis my birthday, Lieutenant."

Thorton smiled. "Capital news! How old are you, if I may be so bold as to ask, sir?"

"Forty." He looked fifty.

"Felicitations! I wish you many happy years to come!"

Horner drank more of his brandy. "Impossible."

"I do mean it, sir."

Horner snorted. "They all mean it, Thorton. 'Get married again,' they tell me. 'You need a wife,' they say. 'Someone who will take care of you and raise your children.'"

"Have you been widowed long, sir?"

"Five years, Mister Thorton. Five years exactly. My wife committed suicide upon my thirty-fifth birthday." He drank down the last of the brandy in his glass and poured himself another. "The table was all set, just as you see it. That is the fatal tablecloth itself. We were having goose and duchesse potatoes. Those are the very dishes. She was late coming down, so I went up to her and found her fainting in her own blood. She had opened a vein in her arm. The doctor had often bled her for her maladies. She watched and never fainted when he did it. How little did I guess that she was studying to perform the same operation upon herself!"

Thorton had to sit down. He dropped onto the cushioned locker next to the inebriated scarecrow. "I'm sorry, sir." He didn't know what else to say. What else could be said?

"Get a glass. You might as well drink with me and help me eat the goose." Silent tears ran down his face.

Thorton felt the need for a drink, so he got up and got a glass and brought it back. He took the bottle from the captain and poured himself a tall drink. He thought if he had it, Horner wouldn't. Horner didn't need it. He was more than worse for wear, he was completely undone. No wonder Forsythe had called him. Still, he had no more idea than Forsythe what he ought to do with the man. He knocked back some of his brandy and coughed. Then he thought it might be well to put some food into the man. Starving wouldn't help.

"I will be happy to join you for dinner, sir. In fact, I hope that you will join me tomorrow for a rubber of whist aboard the *Ajax*." Horner was very fond of whist.

Horner cocked his head at him and appeared to give the invitation serious thought. "I believe I would enjoy that," he said with alcoholic dignity.

"Well, then. Let's go to table. We'll expect you tomorrow for dinner and cards." Thorton rose.

Horner rose. All the alcohol rushed to his head, and he fell like a stone. He lay unconscious on the floor. Thorton checked to make certain he was breathing, then went to the door and called for the steward and the doctor. Together they trundled him into his cot, removed his stock and shoes, and made sure he was well covered with blankets. The doctor bled the unconscious man a little, then pronounced rest to be the best cure and advised his steward to let him sleep in on the morrow.

"Will he be all right?" Thorton asked anxiously.

Ferncastle chuckled. "The British navy routinely survives drunken captains without mishap. Go to bed and don't worry yourself. Sleep is all he needs. His head will ache tomorrow, but he'll be fine."

Thorton had put a drunken Perry to bed often enough when they shared a room while on leave. He had difficulty imagining the mighty Horner in a similar state, and yet, there he was. He nodded.

Forsythe looked uncertain. "I suppose there is no need change to the quarter-bill. I guess I can do the morning inspection without him."

Thorton patted his shoulder. "You'll be fine."

"Thank you for coming, Peter."

"'Twas no trouble. I'm glad it wasn't serious."

"Yes, thank you."

Thorton went over the side into his gig. It was a relief to know that Horner was merely human, but it made him sad, too.

CHAPTER 22 : MUTINY

The sound of musket fire woke Thorton from a deep sleep. For a moment he lay blinking in his hammock, then the repeated cracks of distant gunshots caused him to leap out of his hammock. He attempted to throw off his nightshirt in the same motion and landed in a heap on the deck under the hammock with his nightshirt over his head. He flung it off, rubbed his smarting nose, and grabbed his clothes. He was into his drawers and buttoning up his breeches when a knock pounded wildly on his door.

"Come!" he shouted.

The marine sentry opened the door and Midshipman Bettancourt burst in. He was a gangly boy of fourteen or fifteen who had served long enough aboard the *Ajax* for his arms and legs to shoot out beyond the length of his sleeves and breeches. He was full of alarm.

"Lieutenant Perry says to tell you there's mutiny on the *Resolute*! They're shooting over there, sir!"

"Go wake the wardroom, everyone of them. Beat to quarters!" He shoved his arms into the sleeves of his shirt as he spoke. The boy ran off without a proper dismissal, but Thorton didn't mind. He was busy jamming his arms into his waistcoat and frock coat without bothering to button them. He seized his sword in one hand and his shoes and stockings in the other and ran out on deck. Before he reached the quarterdeck the drums were rattling out their wild tattoo.

The officers on the quarterdeck saluted him and he raised his shoes and stockings in acknowledgement. "What is happening?"

They all stared to the north where flashes of musket fire could be seen.

"Mutiny, sir. Somebody has control of the quarterdeck, but we don't know if it tis the rebels or the officers," Perry replied.

Thorton puts his things on the roof of the skylight. He balanced on one foot to put on a stocking. "Prepare a boarding party. We must go over their stern before they have the guns in order. Lieutenant Barnes!"

The marine lieutenant was wearing his scarlet coat over his nightshirt as he came on the quarterdeck. "Aye aye, Captain," Barnes responded. Heedless of his bare feet on a cold deck, he ran below and started issuing his own orders.

Posonby came up properly dressed, then Jackson and Abby and all the others. Thorton sat on the ammunition chest and buckled his shoes. "Horner was incapacitated by drink when I left him. I never dreamed this would happen, or I wouldn't have left!"

Abby consoled him. "Nobody knew what they were plotting. They seized their chance while they could."

"But why?" the master's mate asked.

"Same reason Powell put a bullet through his head," Perry replied grimly. "They don't want to face court martial in England. Somebody must be blamed, and somebody will hang for it."

"A battleship!" Thorton exclaimed as he stood up and buttoned his shirt. "Where do they think they can go with an entire British battleship? Do they think they the Spanish will embrace them?"

"If there are any Papists among them, they might," Perry replied.

"Get the boats ready! Douse the lanterns. We must sneak up on them as best we can. Mister Perry, you will command the launch."

"Aye aye, sir," Perry replied cheerfully.

The frigate's lights went out. The scudding clouds alternately covered and uncovered the face of a gibbous moon. Thorton longed for a galley; they could douse the sails, and practically invisible, row up behind the *Resolute* and have a chance of taking her by boarding.

"Make all plain sail. Have both broadsides loaded and ready."

The *Ajax* was undermanned. He would only be able to work one side of the guns at a time. His only hope was that the mutineers were few enough in number they could not properly man the *Resolute's* guns. Otherwise, should it come to a broadside battle, they were doomed. He didn't worry about it. He would do what he must do, or die trying.

Horner was popular with the men and officers of the *Ajax*; they were eager to go to his rescue. They got into the boats swiftly and muffled the oarlocks with their kerchiefs. They rowed stealthily away.

"Lay her along their larboard quarter. Notify Mister Posonby to stand by to run out the starboards guns on my order." The larboard was where the *Resolute* had suffered the most damage during the Battle of Majorca, damage that could only partially be repaired at Gibraltar. Although it meant attacking from the lee, it was her weakest point.

As they drew nearer, they could hear the hoarse shouts of the combatants and the rattle of the implements of war. Musket fire from the quarterdeck aimed into the waist — but who had control of the quarterdeck? The officers and marines? Or mutineers? A sudden cry from the *Resolute* announced that they had been spotted. The stern lanthorn revealed a black flag being run up.

"Run out the guns. Fire upon the quarterdeck as she bears. The mutineers have the conn." Thorton's orders were brisk and his tone matter of fact.

Word was passed. A moment later the gun ports flew open and the guns thrust out their black mouths and spat fire. Tongues of flame six feet long leapt through the dark. At a range of no more than a hundred yards, the shot slammed into the quarterdeck. On the *Resolute*, a cheer went up from the defenders in the waist. They rushed the quarterdeck.

Thorton's heart hammered in his breast he stared at the *Resolute's* lofty side. He waited for a double row of gun ports to fly open and answer shot with double shot. Fortune was on his side; the blank walls of the battleship never opened.

"Back sail. Take position off her larboard quarter."

A new cry rang through the air. "*Ajax!*" the boarders roared as they clambered over the taffrail and stormed the quarterdeck. They had climbed her galleries and sculpture with the aid of grappling hooks and rope.

In a moment it was over. Beset before and behind and with the *Ajax* preparing another broadside, the mutineers threw down their weapons and surrendered. The black flag came down less than a quarter of an hour after it rose. The British ensign rose in its proper place. A mighty cheer erupted from everywhere in the *Ajax* and the *Resolute*. Sailors tossed their hats and waved their weapons.

"Lay alongside. Prepare to grapple."

Thorton climbed up to the *Resolute's* quarterdeck. He found an immensely hungover Captain Horner in command of his own vessel and Perry at his side. Horner gave him a grateful look. Thorton saluted.

"Captain. I am pleased to see you on your feet again!"

"Thank you, Mister Thorton. I am pleased to be on my feet and not murdered in my bed. Your help was timely and greatly appreciated."

"'Twas my duty, sir."

Horner was still wearing yesterday's uniform. He had neither stock nor shoes. His waistcoat was open a few buttons — just the way they had left him in his bed. The tip of his bloody sword rested on the planks at his feet as he rested his hand on the hilt. He spoke with restrained feeling. "Well done, Mister Thorton, Mister Perry, Mister Barnes. Well done. You have the thanks of every loyal man aboard the *Resolute*."

"What happened?" Thorton asked.

"I don't know yet. I woke up when a shot fired outside my door. I grabbed my sword and opened the door to find my sentry murdered and a mob outside. I shut and barred the door against them. I fired through the door when they tried to break it down. When they finally broke it open, I fought them with point and fist. When you fired your broadside they ran from the cabin. I came out and joined the fight for the quarterdeck. They had the advantage and it was a hot fight. Your men scaled the stern and we caught them between two fires. They folded then."

Thorton heaved a sigh of relief and started trembling. He hated himself for it, but now that he saw how near a thing it had been, his knees went weak. "Are you secure, sir? Are your remaining men trustworthy?"

"The marines have secured the ship. I will sort out loyal from disloyal tomorrow. We have the ringleaders. Justice will be delivered at noon. I cannot be impartial in such a matter. I ask you to preside, Captain Thorton."

Thorton stiffened, then nodded. "Aye aye, sir. If you will advise me as to the proper procedure, I will see that it is done."

Horner held out his hand. Thorton clasped it. Horner's blue eyes met his. "I owe you my life, my ship, and my career, young man."

"I'm glad to be of service, sir."

Next Horner shook Perry's hand. "A gallant assault, Lieutenant. Your timing was impeccable."

Perry smiled. His face was grimy from the gunsmoke and his lace was grey. "My pleasure, sir."

Next was Forsythe. "You're wounded!"

"This isn't my blood," Forsythe said about the red stain on the front of his nightshirt.

"Thank God for that." He shook Forsythe's hand firmly.

Horner moved to the next man. "Barnes. My compliments to your men. I'll depend on you to keep order for the rest of the night." Another handshake.

"You may rest secure with me, sir."

"We will make repairs. You may give the loyal men beer after the work is done, Lieutenant Forsythe."

"Very good, sir."

The various officers went their separate ways. The lanterns were lit and the sound of sawing and hammering was soon heard. Horner went below to visit the wounded in the cockpit and to inspect the men in irons suspected of leading the mutiny. Thorton found himself standing alone on the quarterdeck of a British battleship, a position he had never occupied before. The battleship was merely a fourth rate, but she dwarfed the *Ajax*. Her quarterdeck was high above the water. For a moment he dared to dream that some day he would command such a behemoth of the deep.

He had learned one thing during a long and difficult summer — he liked being in command.

CHAPTER 23 : THE CAPTAIN'S JUDGMENT

The great cabin of the *Resolute* was transformed into a solemn chamber. Horner's personal things were moved aside or stowed below. His dining table was set up across the end of the cabin before the windows and covered with a green baize cloth. Acting-Captain Thorton occupied the single chair behind it as sole judge. Horner had recused himself. Thorton was sitting in judgment in his stead. The clerk from the *Ajax* was aboard as clerk of the court and Lieutenant Barnes was in command of security for the event. The *Resolute's* officers were all interested parties and feeling was running high. Although Horner was entitled (and the Admiralty would never have questioned his right) to sit in judgment on his own crew for the crime of mutiny upon the high seas, he felt it best to create as formal and disinterested a set of proceedings as could be managed.

Thorton sat alone. All the testimony had been given. The evidence laid before him was plain. He already knew what his decision would be and what would happen to the condemned men. He had had no trouble in deciding the guilt or innocence of those accused. Still, it was customary to take time to deliberate. Yet the knowledge that he was going to condemn men to death was not what disturbed Thorton.

He sat staring into space and listening to the grey rain drumming against the skylight of the great cabin. The lamps were lit and cast swaying shadows over the interior as the *Resolute* lay hove to, rising and falling on the waves like a bauble on the breast of a giantess. He clasped his hands before him and reflected on the adventures of the last six months that had brought him to this moment.

The British system was the most efficient naval system in the world. It had the most ships, the biggest shipyards, the largest budgets, the most officers and men, and the greatest success. Yet all of this was built upon the backs of pressed men, and Peter Thorton had himself been a pressed man. He had striven hard to excel at the trade into which he had been thrust and risen through the ranks to reach his present status as a very junior lieutenant who was not in the good graces of the Admiralty.

He had converted to Islam out of a sincere conviction that "There is only one God worthy of worship, and Mohammed is His messenger."

He had resigned his commission and accepted a commission with the Sallee rovers. Fortune had briefly granted him pride of place as the captain of a Sallee galiot; he had taken prizes and gained friends in North Africa. How this had all come to pass he did not quite understand, but he knew his personal qualities had impressed the corsairs. The North African corsairs practiced a fierce sort of republicanism where a man advanced by his skills more than his political connections. Noble birth and high rank were advantages, but they did not weigh as heavily as they did in England. A man in Sallee service found them a help to obtain a post, but if he was not equal to it, they availed him naught.

Such men, when placed in British service, provided they did not do something stupid, were nearly guaranteed promotion, wealth, and rank. The merit-based rewards offered by the Admiralty were hungered for by all men but received by few. Look at Horner: thin, grey, haggard, and prematurely old. The only position he had been able to obtain was a substitute captain aboard a frigate during the illness of her actual captain. Luck had put him into even more temporary command of a fourth rate battleship, and bad luck had raised a mutiny under him that was no fault of his own. The mutineers had been very plain in their explanations for their conduct. They feared they would be condemned for surviving the Battle of Majorca when the rest of the British Mediterranean fleet had been destroyed. The least punishment meted out to them would be an end of their livelihoods, disgrace to their names, and poverty. At the worst, the officers would be executed for cowardice and dereliction of duty. The mutineers had planned to flee to France.

Such a situation would not, could not, occur on a Sallee rover. All the men were volunteers, except the galleyslaves, who were still paid a share for their labors. The Sallee Republic did not have the same power over its navy and corsairs; the crimes for which a man could be executed were decidedly fewer in number. Running from a superior enemy was not among them. No Sallee rover would ever have to justify himself to a court martial for saving his ship and the men in her. As aggravated as Thorton was by the uneven quality of the rovers and the maddening unreliability of men who thought they had as much right as their commodore to make tactical decisions, Thorton could not help but think their ways superior. A little more discipline on their part would subdue their many faults while not committing the excesses of the British system. In Lord Zahid, new Minister of the Marine, the Sallee

Republic had a man who would strive for excellence, and the Divan (at least for the time being) was willing to let him try.

At last Thorton made up his mind. He picked up his papers and began to make his notes. Finished, he reconvened the proceedings.

The accused, witnesses, officers of the court, and spectators crowded into the cabin. They were quiet except for shuffling their feet and coughing. All eyes were upon him. The mutineers stared at him with mixed expressions: rage, fear, hope, resignation, sullenness, despair. The officers of the *Resolute* were jittery. Forsythe, acting first lieutenant of the *Resolute*, was white and anxious. Whittacre, the *Resolute's* sole surviving lieutenant, was covered in a grey sweat. His wounds had not killed him, but the infection would. He could not stand and was sitting in a chair. Horner's long countenance was even longer than usual. His usually square shoulders were bowed.

Thorton called the assembly to order. "After a proper and due consideration of the evidence laid before me, the following judgments are made. Step forward when your name is called."

He consulted his list. The first and foremost named was expected. "Francis Mortimer, midshipman."

The man was tall, thin, and black-haired. He was one of the oldest midshipmen in the navy, having never yet passed his lieutenant's examination. A scar marked his forehead and his mouth turned down in a sour sneer.

"I find you guilty under Article Eighteen for leading mutiny against the lawful authority of your captain and sentence you to hang by the neck until dead."

"My lawful captain is dead, and you have no right to sit in his place!"

"Silence!" Thorton banged the gavel.

"I won't be silent! 'Tis a drumhead court. We are nearly home to England — we have the right to be reviewed by the Admiralty."

"Had you committed any crime but mutiny, I would consider it. But mutiny is a summary offense. You will be hanged at the conclusion of the court."

Mortimer's face contorted in rage. "You're nothing but a jumped up pawn, a disgraced renegade, a — " Barnes and his marines grabbed the man and Barnes personally punched him in the mouth to stop his words. Mortimer spat blood and teeth onto the deck and restarted his invective, only to be methodically beaten in the face until he sagged.

Thorton ordered, "Take him out. Clean him up. Keep him quiet."

The marines dragged him out. There was a short pause during their absence, then Barnes returned and the proceedings continued.

"John Jones, master's mate." The man took a step forward. He was a man of medium build, pock-faced, with dark hair lying lank against his neck. He had his arm in a sling and a bandage around his ankle.

"I find you guilty under Article Eighteen of making mutiny against the lawful authority of your captain and sentence you to hang by the neck until dead."

The man had not expected anything else. He gave Thorton a bitter look. "You'll get yours sooner or later," he replied.

Thorton banged the gavel. "Silence! Lieutenant, remove that man."

The convicted mutineer was hustled away.

Thorton gave the crowd a sour look. "The accused are reminded that they have already had the opportunity to speak upon their own behalf and will refrain from making further remarks."

Murmurs responded.

"Abraham Langtry, boatswain." The man stepped forward silently. He was a terrified man of about thirty. Uncombed blond hair formed a long tail down his back. His whiskers were bushy and his chin had not been shaved in two days. His eyes started from his head, and his face was sickly pale beneath his tan.

"I find you guilty under Article Eighteen of making mutiny against your captain and sentence you to hang by the neck until dead."

"No!" he cried. "I have a wife and children!" Tears coursed down his face and he flung himself on his knees before the table. "Mercy, sir! I beg you!"

Thorton's face wrinkled in distaste. He looked around the room for help. A stoic himself, he had no idea what to do with a man who cried. Seeing his uncertain look, Langtry turned to Horner and beseeched him. "Captain, save me! For the love of God!"

"The testimony is incontrovertible," Horner replied. "The safety of the ship is your especial duty, but you connived to deliver her into the hands of the French."

"I repent!"

Thorton banged the gavel down and roared, "Silence! Judgment is rendered. Take him away."

Barnes and his men dragged the man to his feet and out the door.

"Samuel Goldman, able-bodied seaman." Goldman was a simpleton. He understood his work and did it well, but he was easily lead by others, and they were in the habit of taking advantage of him.

He had taken up arms at their instigation, but had laid them down again when called on to do so by Captain Horner.

"I find you guilty under Article Eighteen of making mutiny against your officers, but I accept mitigating factors. I admonish you most strenuously to attend your duty and shut your ears to malefactors. I sentence you to be lashed two hundred times. Offend again and there will be no mercy."

Goldman looked unhappy about his sentence, but he said, "Aye aye, sir," as he had been taught to say whenever addressing an officer.

"Punishment to be carried out immediately. Dismissed!" Thorton banged his gavel.

Everyone but Horner filed out. He remained standing where he was. "Mister Thorton. May I have a word with you in private?"

Thorton motioned away the clerk and guard. He remained seated where he was. "Yes, Captain?"

Horner stepped forward. He gathered himself to say what he felt must be said. "I was drunk and derelict in my duty, sir. You must not withhold the condemnation of the court out of sympathy or any other feeling."

"The Admiralty does not require you to convict yourself, Captain. It requires the testimony of others. All witnesses testified that you were asleep in your bed when the mutiny was fomented, that you resisted to the utmost of your ability, and that you personally lead the party storming the quarterdeck. No one has given any indication that you were intoxicated or in any way impaired in carrying out your duties."

"You yourself had called on me the day before and seen my condition."

"I was not called upon to testify. Even if I had been, I saw you twelve hours before the fighting broke out. You were surely drunk then, but when I came aboard after the fight, you just as surely were not. Your effective exercise of leadership during the crisis demonstrates that you were fit."

Horner held his cocked hat under his arm. His uniform was the ordinary undress uniform; criminal proceedings were not dignified with full dress. "I cannot help feeling culpable. The ship was placed in my charge after the death of her officers and I failed her. I should have rooted out discontent before it grew into conspiracy."

Thorton was silent for a long time. "I was discontent when forced to return to the Service, but you treated me well. I knew I was going to be court-martialed, and I feared I would be hanged, but I did not make mutiny. I submitted myself to the lawful authority of the king and his officers. If you had mistreated me, I would have rebelled, but you were humane and honorable. I cannot believe you treated these men any differently. They leapt to judgment before the court-martial even sat, and so condemned themselves."

Horner drew in a great breath and nodded. "You are right. But still, I cannot rest easy. This should never have happened. I am responsible for these men. I beg you to commute their sentences."

"Captain." Thorton's voice was soft. "I cannot. If you had counseled me to leniency when you instructed me in the operation of justice, I would have. But now that judgment has been rendered, we cannot reverse without looking weak. The men will think they can get up a hue and cry about anything. Vacillate now and we become a ship of quarrels. Discipline depends upon the certainty of justice."

"I carry it on my conscience."

Thorton came out from behind the table. He laid a gentle hand on Horner's shoulder. "You have been keeping too much company with the bottle instead of other men."

Horner flinched. "Since my wife died, it has been my only reliable companion. Only once a year on the anniversary of her death do I indulge to excess. We were nearly home to England and the weather was mild. I did not anticipate trouble."

"You have friends, sir. You should turn to them, not the bottle."

Horner's head drew back and the familiar steel flashed in his eyes. His shoulders squared and his spine stiffened.

"I will take your advice under consideration, Lieutenant." His tone put Thorton in his place. The younger man was only an acting-captain. How dare he advise someone a decade older than himself and far superior in seniority!

Thorton smiled to see him angry. "We still expect to see you for dinner, sir."

Horner had not expected such a response. He hesitated, then said, "On the contrary, it is I who should offer you hospitality. May I offer you a glass of cider?"

"With pleasure, sir."

CHAPTER 24 : THE HEMPEN JIG

Three men condemned to die. Horner and Thorton stood at the rail and watched the scene unfold below. Jones and Langtry would die together, dangling from the yardarms. Their hands were tied behind their backs and the hoods put over their heads. The lines were run from the arm tackles, and the nooses put around their necks. Langtry cried and begged for mercy again, but his tears were ignored. It embarrassed them all to see him blubbering at the end. Mortimer watched the proceedings with hate-filled eyes. He would die last and alone.

At Thorton's command, the drums rattled a long ruffle. At the end of it, a lone gun boomed. The smell of brimstone drifted across the deck as the lazy breeze carried the smoke in a slow stream downwind. The sailors hauled the lines and swung the men up. Their legs kicked convulsively as they dangled in the air and twisted round and round. After five minutes one of the men hung limp, but Langtry still kicked and writhed. One of his shoes came off and dropped into the sea with a small splash.

"The knot's gotten under his chin. He'll never die like that," Horner said.

"Take him down and do it again," Thorton ordered Forsythe.

Forsythe turned pale, but he said, "Aye aye, sir."

"I'll see to it," Horner replied.

The captain swiftly descended the steps. Langtry was lowered, caught with a boathook, and fished in. When the noose was taken from his neck he cried out his thanks for saving him. He could not see with the hood on, but he blessed the sailors, the officers, the captain and everyone. With his own hands Horner turned the noose and set the knot behind his ear. He gave it a snug tug, choking off the sailor's cries. When the man realized what was happening, his horror grew more intense and he writhed and shook his head, getting the rope twisted around again.

Horner snapped, "Hold still, man! The more you fight the more you'll suffer!"

A wail of terror ripped from the hooded throat. One of the red-coated marines punched him in the face. A stunned silence ensued.

"Begging your pardon, sir," the man said to Horner, respectfully touching his forehead.

"Quite all right. Carry on."

The marine set the knot properly behind the left ear and snugged it down firm and tight.

"Haul away," Horner said.

The sailors hauled and the condemned man swung again. He revived and began to kick, but this time the knot was set firmly where it belonged. After a few minutes his kicking ceased.

Mortimer grimly awaited his own turn. He wore his blue frock coat with the white collar of his rank. He had been allowed to change his linen for the court martial, so was neat and clean in his person. His eyes blazed contempt for the man who died so poorly and his own shoulders were square in spite of his hands bound behind his back. As the hood was brought, he gave his horrible glare to each and everyone of them.

"I'll come back and haunt you. You'll see me by night and by storm. You'll hear me whispering in the wind, and you'll feel me in the waves. This is a cursed ship and will be forever more."

Sailors were a superstitious lot; no mortal threat could have moved them more than the supernatural claim. They cringed and drew back in dread. The man who held the noose dropped it. The man who held the hood hesitated.

"If anyone could escape the jaws of hell, it will be him," Whittacre said grimly. "I hate that man." The wounded lieutenant was leaning on a midshipman to witness the proceedings.

"Carry on!" Thorton called.

Apologetically the sailor put the hood over Mortimer's head. "Sorry, sir," he mumbled.

"You'll be the first to see me," Mortimer replied. The man jumped back.

Horner spoke, "He's got them all spooked. Every accident will be attributed to the vengeful ghost of Mortimer. He knows exactly what he's doing, the knave."

Thorton had to do something. He roared, "Avast!"

Everybody looked at him in surprise. He came down from the quarterdeck and walked up to the condemned man, lifted the hood from his face, and pushed his face right into the face of the surprised midshipman.

"If you have something to say, midshipman, you will say it to me, in person."

"I have nothing to say to you," Mortimer replied.

"I thought not," Thorton said contemptuously. He pulled the hood back over the condemned man's face. "Give me the noose."

The man whose job it was to put the rope around Mortimer's neck swiftly handed it to him. Thorton set it around the midshipman's neck with his own two hands.

Addressing the crowd as he worked, Thorton said, "He's a great one for speaking when he thinks no one will stand up to him, but if you face him down, he will yield. He always does. Remember that. Whenever you think his ghost has risen, say to it, 'Hah! You were a windbag when you were alive, and you're nothing but a windbag now!'"

Mortimer would have liked to have said something in reply to that, but Thorton had tightened the noose so snug about his neck that his breath was stopped before he was even hoisted.

"Drum!"

The drum rattled and the gun boomed. The wicked midshipman rose into the air. Thorton checked to make certain all was as well as it could be with a man dangling at the end of a rope, then returned to the quarterdeck. Mortimer was left to dangle while he dealt with the final case.

The simpleton was called forward, stripped to the waist, and bound to the grating. His back bulged as he gripped the wood and bent his head. MacDonald, the boatswain from the *Ajax*, administered the first twelve lashes, then traded off with his mate for another twelve. Back and forth they went with Thorton keeping count. Long before it was over he regretted ordering so many strokes, but having made the decision, he could not back down.

Dr. Ferncastle called a halt after one hundred and eight. He inspected the man's back, then said, "Enough for now."

Thorton nodded. "Very well. Take him to the cockpit. We will complete the flogging when he has recovered." He was glad to have an excuse to stop. The loblolly boys came and helped the man below.

Thorton checked his watch. "Dr. Ferncastle. If you will examine the hanged men, please."

The limp bodies landed on the deck. "Dead," the portly physician reported after checking each one.

"I will read the burial service, Mister Thorton," Horner said.

"As you wish, Captain," Thorton had done as much as he could stand. He did not think he could steel himself to read the Christian service for the dead.

The sailmaker and his mates came and stitched the bodies into their hammocks. The last stitch was taken through the nose to prove that they were dead, and the bottom of the shrouds were weighted with shot. They were laid on boards with the ends propped on the gunwales. The company stood at attention with their heads uncovered. Horner opened up his Book of Common Prayer and began to recite.

"I am the resurrection and the life, he that believeth on Me though he were dead shall live, and every one that liveth and believeth on Me shall not die for ever. O God, by Whose mercy the souls of the faithful are at rest, to the souls of Thy servants who here and in all places repose in Christ, favorably grant the pardon of their sins, that absolved from all offenses they may with Thee rejoice without end.

"We commend into Thy hands of mercy (most merciful Father) the souls of these our brothers departed. And their bodies we commit to the sea, beseeching Thine infinite goodness to give us grace to live in Thy fear and love, and to die in Thy favor: that when the judgment shall come, which Thou has committed to Thy well-loved Son, both these our brothers, and we, may be found acceptable in Thy sight."

The corpses sank into the grey-blue deeps, never to be seen again. Not even Mortimer's ghost rose to torment them; the weather after the hanging was very fair and mild. They had blue sky and dolphins until they reached England.

CHAPTER 25 : IRON MEN

They arrived too late in the day to make the harbor at Spithead. The wind was dying and fog was rising; Horner decided to heave to and enter first thing in the morning. He invited the officers of the *Ajax* and the *Resolute* to sup with him that evening. The masters and their mates had charge of the vessels while the commissioned officers joined their captain for their last night together.

It was a gloomy crew. Horner would have to present his dispatches and logs, and the mutiny was sure to be a mark against him just when he had hoped to post to a battleship at last. Worse, he was likely to be unemployed; he was only a substitute sent out to replace the *Ajax's* own captain, Horace Bishop, while he recuperated from a heart attack. Whittingdon had sufficient power to deny Bishop his place in Gibraltar, but in the weeks Bishop had been home in England he was likely to have rallied support to retrieve his command.

Forsythe, Perry, and Thorton were filled with gloom. None of them would escape Bishop's wrath, but Thorton would be his special target. Likewise, Abby as the senior surviving officer from the drowned *Adamant*, and Whittacre, the senior surviving (but slowly dying) officer from the *Resolute*, would both have to endure court-martial. The former ship had been lost in battle and the latter had run. Both deeds would have to be answered for. Posonby had no such black marks against him; even so, once he set foot ashore, his creditors would be after him. Lieutenant Chagall, who had been loaned to the *Resolute* from the *Pegasus*, was probably the only man happy to see England. The two marine lieutenants, Barnes and Ogilvy, had nothing to fear from the courts-martial, but they felt the gloom of their fellows.

Perry attempted to lighten the mood. "Let's drink a toast to our friends and confusion to our enemies," he said.

"Here, here," they replied, and lifted the wineglasses to their lips. Thorton merely sipped his.

Chagall proposed another toast, "Let's drink to the lovely ladies of England whose arms will soon be around our necks."

Perry and Forsythe were pleased to drink to that, but Abby and Thorton merely raised their glasses. Horner fell into a brown study and raised his cup slowly.

The toasts warmed the company a little, and they began to chat. Thorton narrowed his eyes as Horner talked little and drank much. Being an acting-captain Thorton was seated at the foot of the table or he would have kicked the man in the shins when he raised his glass once too often. Horner did not become drunk in any obvious way, and he did not drink more than Barnes or Chagall, who achieved a state of comfortable lubrication before the evening was over. They finished up with cigars and brandy and a rubber of whist. Thorton, being a good player and sober to boot, emerged victorious.

Thorton rose and said, "I thank you for your hospitality, Captain, but the fog is rising and I must return to the *Ajax*." That was the signal for the rest of them to rise and make their goodnights.

Horner rose also. As Thorton was about to leave, he said, "Mister Thorton, stay a moment, please."

So Thorton waited. Horner waved the rest of them away. "Go on without him. I'll send him over later in my gig."

When they were alone, Horner began slowly. "Tomorrow we arrive in Spithead, and we take our papers to the Admiralty."

Thorton nodded wistfully. "The journey is over at last."

"Not quite over. We may think we know what tomorrow brings, but we can never be certain what will happen tonight."

Thorton glanced at the windows, but he only saw himself and the captain reflected in the glass. He could not see out into the dark and foggy night. "'Tis true, but I doubt the weather will turn foul. 'Tis a quiet night."

Horner stepped up close to him. He was holding his brandy in his hand and took a sip. "What I wanted to say, Peter, is that I have come to value your friendship. Tomorrow I may not have a position, nor do I know where any of us will be sent. I wanted to speak to you while I still could."

Thorton smiled. "Thank you, sir. I think of you as a friend."

"My friends call me 'Evan.'"

"Evan." Thorton savored the name.

"We have not chatted lately."

Thorton shook his head. "No."

"Did Commodore Tangueli bring you news from Sallee?"

"Yes, he brought me a letter." His face fell as he remembered the contents.

"Good news, I hope?"

Thorton shook his head. "No. It was from Shakil. He bade me farewell. He says he cannot love an Englishman."

Horner put an arm around his shoulders and gave him an avuncular squeeze. "I am sorry for you. I know you were fond of him."

Thorton sighed heavily. He put his arm around Horner's waist and replied, "I understand what he means. Tis too difficult to be divided in one's loyalties. I am going to resign tomorrow and go home to Sallee. If they let me."

"Do you think he will receive you back?"

"He might. But I am not certain to renew the suit. I had hoped for more patience from him."

"Ah. He jilted you, and it has wounded your pride."

Thorton flushed. "He broke my heart. I suppose I broke his, but—" He realized he was standing in a position of great intimacy with his superior officer. He took the brandy from Horner's hand and said, "You have had too much to drink, sir!"

"I am not an iron man and neither are you, Peter."

"Brandy will not make you strong, Evan. You must depend upon your friends, not the bottle."

"I am not certain how far I can depend upon my friends. The bottle is a known quantity."

"Your friends will do you good, but the bottle never will." Thorton stepped away to put the glass on the desk.

"That's true, but I confess to having some difficulty with my friends."

"How so?"

"I desire company, but I am not ready for female companionship. Seeing how well you and Shakil conducted yourselves made me consider the company of men. You seemed happy with each other, yet now I find you were not."

Thorton was not sure he understood the man correctly. "Did you ever enjoy the company of men before, sir?"

Horner shook his head. "When I am in the company of women, there is a spark. I think you know what I mean. I never felt such a spark with men. Yet you and Shakil seemed to enjoy a deeper sort of friendship, one elevated above the baser passions. I thought I might enjoy that sort of intimate friendship, but it seems prey to the same vagaries that mar more passionate affairs."

Thorton blushed and ducked his head. "I like to think our sentiments were noble, but I must admit there was a 'spark' as well."

Horner studied him. "You told me that the two of you never violated Article Twenty-Eight."

Thorton blushed a deeper red. It had been true at the time he said it. "Kissing is not mentioned in Article Twenty-Eight. Neither is holding hands nor whispering sweet things."

"I see. So it was more of a courtship than a friendship?"

"It was both. Although my suit was accepted, at least for a while." Thorton's face was burning hot.

Horner studied him thoughtfully. "Is it always that way for you, that friendship mixes with sparking?"

Thorton shook his head. "Some men inspire a spark and some don't. I like some, and some I don't. I like you, for example. I also like Posonby and Forsythe."

"But no spark."

Thorton nodded.

Horner looked nettled. "'Tis not as simple as I thought." He reached for the glass on the desk, looked at Thorton, and let it be.

"Why do you ask?"

Horner gave him a rueful look. "I was thinking about kissing you."

Thorton's jaw dropped. "Me, sir?"

"Would you have minded?"

Thorton was thrown into confusion, but he shook his head.

"I think I shall, just once."

Thorton could scarcely believe his ears, but Horner caught his face in his hands and pressed his lips lightly against his. Thorton shut his eyes and kissed him back. He was thoroughly bewildered but willing to go along. The kiss continued. It went on and on until Thorton was dizzy. When Horner finally broke it, he gave Thorton such a complicated look that the lieutenant went weak in the knees. He backed up until he felt the locker behind his legs and sat.

Horner remained standing with an inscrutable expression on his face. Finally he said, "You're a very good kisser."

"Did I do something wrong?"

Thorton was sure it was his fault He had never expected such behavior from Horner, and yet, it had happened. Somehow it had happened because of Peter Thorton. He reviewed the scene in his mind. He saw now that the whole conversation had been a careful sounding of the depths before Horner presumed to drop his anchor. Now that the anchor had set both men were finding it difficult to get it loose again.

"No, Peter." Horner crossed and sat down next to him. "Forgive me. I was only flirting with you."

"Don't you know what could happen? What if someone suspects? You could ruin my reputation, but you are only flirting with me?"

Horner took his hands. "Forgive me. I was kissing you goodbye. I did not expect to feel a spark."

"I felt it, too," Thorton said unwillingly.

Horner put his arm around him. "I like you very much. If we go our separate ways tomorrow, I will miss you."

"I'll miss you, too."

Horner kissed him again. He pulled the lieutenant against his chest while Thorton wrapped his arm around his neck and held on tight. The kiss blazed long and hot and hard and spread the embers to every part of his body. He was lonely, he wanted someone to keep him company, he liked and respected Horner but was baffled by his advances. Horner groaned and held him tight. He could feel the heat and arousal in the younger man's body.

Horner broke the kiss.

"I am finding it difficult to separate friendship from courtship, or to elevate my feelings to the platonic ideal," the captain remarked with his arms still around Thorton.

"Just remember they'll hang you for sodomy if you don't," Thorton replied bitterly.

Horner blinked. "That does put a damper on our relationship," he agreed. He let go of Thorton and ran a hand through his thinning hair.

"Evan, if you are still flirting with me, please don't. I could hardly bear the fear when I was in love, and that was when I thought I had something worth dying for. But this . . . I don't know what you're doing or why."

"I don't know what I'm doing, either," Horner admitted. "The ideal has crumbled before the real. I have been without companionship so long I am making a botch of it."

Thorton wasn't sure if he dared believe what he thought Horner was saying. "Do you want to make love to me?" he asked nervously.

Horner thought about that for a while. "Yes," he finally said.

Thorton knitted his fingers together and frowned in thought. He was pursued by three men now: Tangle, Abby, and Horner. He liked each of them, yet each of them had their dangers and drawbacks. "I miss Shakil!" he blurted out.

Horner winced. He leaned back against the window sill and crossed one knee over the other. "I have the worst luck," he remarked. There was no bitterness nor self-pity in it. He was simply making an observation.

Horner was the perpetual underdog who could never get ahead in spite of his good qualities; he did indeed have bad luck. It made Thorton want to stick up for him. On the other hand, Tangle was a man who was more handsome and charming, whose randy affection was plain and straight forward without the danger of death — if Thorton ran away to the Sallee Republic. Yet Tangle was also vain and domineering. Abby was lively and handsome but a little too free. He was confident that being the son of an earl would shelter him from the consequences of his deeds. Then there was Shakil, who was sober and modest and hardworking, but who was as stiff-necked as Thorton himself.

Horner was the soul of rectitude, but the righteousness of youth had gone out of him. He was ten years older than Thorton and the rasp of time had filed off his sharp edges. Unnoticed by him, a ladder was slowly working its way down his woolen stocking. He was imperfect in little ways that filled Thorton with the urge to make them right.

"If you want me, you will have to court me. I am not going to accept a sailor's suit when I know he will disappear and forget about me. You will have to convince me that you mean it."

Horner sat up. "I'm not sure I do mean it."

"Then you have to make up your mind!" Thorton replied tartly. He stood up and went to collect his cloak and hat from their pegs.

Horner rose. Amusement glinted in his eye. "The usual way is to pay court until the feelings are certain, not to ascertain the feelings, then pay court!" He picked up the empty brandy glass and tossed it from hand to hand as he watched Thorton clap his hat on his head and sling his cloak around his shoulders.

Thorton paused on the threshold. He watched the glass in Horner's hands, then gave the man a troubled look. "I will not come in second best to the bottle, Evan. If that is my rival, I will have none of you."

Horner stopped the glass between his two hands. "Good night, Mister Thorton."

Thorton did not want to leave things like that, but he did not know how to make them right, either. He crossed to Horner, kissed his cheek lightly, and said, "Go with God, Ebenezer Horner."

His cloak swirled as he turned, then he vanished through the door. Horner held the empty brandy glass in his hands for a long time as he stared at the shut door. Eventually he sighed and put the bottle away. He called his steward to clean up, and said, "Bring me some cider before I go to bed. Those are the new standing orders. No brandy unless I have company."

"Aye aye, sir."

Chapter 26 : The Turk in England

Horner and Thorton reported to the Admiralty office to turn in their logs and dispatches. The loss of the Mediterranean fleet, the mutiny on the *Resolute*, the Turkish defeat at Sebta, the Portuguese actions; the Admiralty wanted to know it all. The questions hammered them until their ears were numb. Other men, other officers, other captains, came and went. The new Mediterranean fleet was fitting out. Nobody offered them positions with it. Leaving the Admiralty office, they stood aside as a detachment of marines tramped along the street with their kits on their backs.

Thorton said, "They didn't ask one thing about the Sallee Republic."

"Eh?" Horner racked his brain. "That's true."

"Isam Rais is right. Britain really doesn't care about her ally."

Horner considered his words as they walked along the street. "I know you have friends there, but the rovers are a small concern."

"If the rovers take Sebta they will have as much control over the Strait of Gibraltar as the Spanish do. Surely that is a concern?"

"But they didn't. And it appears unlikely that they will."

Thorton fumed. "They will take it. Wait until they put Commodore Tangueli in charge."

"He's a very good privateer, but that's not the same as laying siege to a massive fortress."

Thorton stewed some more, but he was forced to admit that he did not know Tangle's capacity for waging large-scale naval warfare. The Sallee rovers were excellent commerce raiders, but that was the lesser half of naval operations. "Do you think you could take Sebta?" he asked curiously.

Horner walked slowly as he stared into space and wrestled with the problem. Thorton was obliged to take his arm to keep him from walking into a group of gentlemen.

Finally Horner said, "With the necessary resources, yes. It means an effective encirclement with no supplies for the Spanish. Starve them out, preferably over winter. It would be long and difficult. The Turks started off correctly, but they were broken and the garrison relieved."

Thorton continued holding Horner's elbow. "I think we can do it. Come with me to the Sallee Republic?"

"Are you enticing me to desert?" Horner asked with a raised eyebrow.

"If you are always going to throw the *Articles of War* in my face, we cannot be friends," Thorton replied crossly.

Horner smiled and patted the hand on his arm. Whatever he might have said was interrupted by a stentorian voice.

"Peter Thorton!"

Thorton knew that voice. Full of dread he turned to look. It was Horace Bishop, rightful captain of the *Ajax*. He was flanked by a pair of burly marines in scarlet coats. One of the two had a red nose and the other had pockmarks on both cheeks. Thorton didn't like the looks of either of them.

"Sir," Thorton said. He slowly raised his hand in a salute. His stomach knotted.

Horner turned to consider the man. He did not know Bishop well, but he knew him. "Captain Bishop. You're looking much better than the last time I saw you. I trust your health has improved?"

Bishop flushed. "I was fine the last time you saw me! Whittingdon had no right to furlough me!"

"Last time I saw you, you had fainted dead on the sand, you cullion-faced coward!" Thorton retorted.

Bishop glared at him. "We have not completed our appointment. I insist upon meeting you upon the field of honor. I have been practicing my aim."

Thorton started forward, but Horner caught his sleeve and held him back. He spoke smoothly, "Captain. The *Ajax* is yours. I implore you to harbor no ill will and to begin anew on a fresh course."

"I will not! That man, that renegade, that bald-faced, lying, son-of-a-bitch has made a laughingstock of me! I demand satisfaction, and I will have it!"

"I don't think he did anything you could not do better," Horner replied in a soothing voice. "Let it go and be friends. He has brought you prize money, after all."

"Worthless! No one in England wants a pair of rat-infested Sallee xebecs!"

Thorton erupted, "They aren't Sallee xebecs, they're Spanish! They don't have any more rats than your own house!"

"You see how he provokes me!" Bishop told his companions. He pulled off his glove and slapped Thorton in the face with it. "You cannot refuse me now or everyone will know you are a coward, you faithless, idol-worshipping dog!"

The glove stung, but Thorton was more exasperated by the man's ignorance. "I am a Muslim, not an idol-worshipper, you damned infidel!" He slapped Bishop across the face with his gloved hand.

"Gentlemen!" Horner cried. "Desist, I beg you! This is not the way to behave in the public street!"

Just then sound of guns boomed across the anchorage. One, two three guns, pause, a fourth gun.

"The Sallee private signal!" Thorton exclaimed.

They all swung around, but the buildings blocked their view. Thorton ran along the street to the dock. Long-legged Horner loped after him.

Bishop found himself blustering alone. "Come back! We haven't set the time and place!"

Reaching the quay, Thorton and Horner watched as three Sallee rovers swept into the harbor. Their great lateen sails were all set and the broad purple pendant of a Sallee commodore hung from the masthead of the first vessel. All her sweeps moved in perfect unison as she rowed in. She wheeled in place to point her bow to the sea and drop her anchors. Her consorts did likewise in a cadence as perfect as the interlocked gears of a clock. The purple ensigns flew from their sterns and the vessels themselves had new paint and bright white sails. They were swiftly brailed up as neatly and efficiently as any British warship.

"Who in the hell is that?" Bishop demanded as he finally caught up to them.

"Commodore Tangueli of the Sallee Republic. The flagship is the *Sea Leopard*. Her consorts are the *Seven Stars* with Achmed Rais Mamoud, Sallee envoy to Britain, and Joshua Rais Foster in the *Arrow*. You remember Captain Tangle and His Excellency Achmed, I'm sure," Thorton replied.

Bishop remembered them very well indeed. Achmed had been his passenger six months ago aboard the *Ajax*. Shortly after that Bishop had fought and lost a duel with Captain Tangle. That event, coupled with getting arrested by the French, had brought on the heart attack that had prevented him from exercising command until he recovered.

"You are pale, Captain," Horner said solicitously. "You must not over exert yourself or you will suffer another heart attack."

"What's he doing here?" Bishop cried.

"He promised he'd come. He's going to testify at the court-martial. He was there, helping us fight a Spanish battleship to rescue the *Resolute*. We succeeded too, even though he only had a galiot and we a frigate," Thorton explained.

Bishop glared at him. "You're a liar and a braggart. No man could beat a battleship with a galiot."

Horner spoke mildly. "I was in command of the *Ajax* at the time. We harassed the Spaniard until the *Resolute* made her escape. You are welcome to attend the court-martial. I'm sure you will want to know everything that happened to your ship in your absence."

"I will attend. Mark me, I will!"

"Then you must delay your request for satisfaction because the Admiralty has a prior claim upon Mister Thorton. That supersedes any private demands. Now, if you will pardon us."

Horner and Thorton walked along the dock to the end and waited. After the obligatory visit from the harbor officials, Tangle and Achmed came ashore. They were accompanied by an honor guard of Sallee marines in short brown jackets and purple pantaloons. They grinned to see Thorton. Tangle was as tall as ever in his snowy turban and purple coat. He grabbed Thorton by the shoulders and kissed him enthusiastically on both cheeks.

"Peter Rais! You are well?"

"Very well." He would have said more, but Tangle was in an expansive mood; he even grabbed Horner's hand and shook it.

"And you?" the corsair asked the older Englishman.

"As well as can be expected," Horner replied. He was a like a cat that has been petted against his will, but his innate dignity saved him.

Achmed in his green coat said, "Peace be upon you and yours. I see your prizes at anchor. Have they been auctioned yet?"

"Not yet, but soon," Thorton replied.

"Excellent. I will bid on them."

Tangle spoke to Thorton in low Arabic so Horner would not understand. "I am glad to see you again. You're not in trouble with the English, are you? Have they accepted your resignation?"

"I have not tendered it yet. I am waiting for official business to conclude."

Meanwhile, Achmed smiled and spoke tranquilly to Horner in English. "I trust you had a safe journey home?"

"I'm afraid not," Horner replied. "There was a mutiny. Some of the warrant officers were discontent."

That got Tangle's attention. "What happened?"

"Lieutenant Thorton sent a boarding party over the *Resolute's* stern and we suppressed them. We hanged three," Horner replied.

"And?" Tangle demanded.

"That's all," Thorton said.

"I forgot I was talking to the two most taciturn men in England. Out with it! I want the whole story."

Thorton and Horner looked at each other. By mutual unspoken agreement they declined to tell the whole thing. Thorton distracted Tangle with a new topic. "You'll never guess who wants to see you."

"Who?"

"Bishop!"

"Bishop?" Tangle had to ransack his brain to remember the man. "Oh, Bishop! Am I going to be sorry I didn't shoot him when I had the chance?"

"That's strange," Thorton said when they reached the street. "He was here a moment ago. I wonder where he went."

"He'll turn up again, count on it," Horner said. "In the meantime, you must be thirsty. May I buy you a cider?"

"Cider would be delicious," Tangle replied.

CHAPTER 27 : THE WIDOW'S PORTION

Thirteen captains sat behind a long green baize table. They wore their dress uniforms with white facings. A crowd of officers in formal dress filled the benches. Only admirals warranted dress uniforms during a court martial, but the loss of the Mediterranean fleet was grave enough to warrant it. Walters was dead and Wolfe was in a Spanish prison, but the proceedings were going to impact heavily on their reputations. Absent though they were, the admirals were going to be on trial.

More men in civilian dress, a few women, and the Sallee officers in their turbans filled the room to capacity. Sunlight streamed through the tall glass windows and bathed the room in light and heat so it almost seemed a church. The polished wooden floor and maple wainscot gleamed and the brass fittings of the furniture and windows shone like amber. For three days they had listened to the testimony of the surviving officers, civilians, ordinary seamen, and even the Salletines.

"The court calls Mistress Anne FitzGerald."

A whisper went around the room. A pair of marines pulled open the carved wooden doors and called her name.

She hesitated on the doorstep. She was clad from head to foot in dark grey with a white fichu around her neck and shoulders. The mistress of a dead admiral could not wear mourning for him, so she had added pink and white striped bows to the outfit at the neck and on her hat. The hat was a wee black thing perched upon a blonde wig. Blond ringlets were arranged around her swan neck. Her face was powdered white, but her eyes were red. An artificial mole was located high on her left cheek and almost appeared to be a tear. She had applied no rouge or lipstick. She trembled as she looked around the room. The soft susurration of her weedy silks was the only sound as she made her way to stand in the dock. Her hands clenched the rail before her as she faced the thirteen men who were sitting in judgment upon her lover, supporter, and destroyer.

She took her oath with both hands clinging to the Bible. The opening questions were the usual, name and residence, where was she at the time in question.

"Port Mahon, in Minorca," she replied. "I was keeping house for Admiral Walters."

Walters was a married man, and his widow and one of his sons were in the audience. The court did not ask her to explain her position in any further detail. "Did he discuss naval matters with you?"

"When they pertained to myself, he did. Usually he confined himself to general remarks such as he might make to any person."

"Did he make remarks to you during the preparation for the departure from Minorca?"

"He did not. He was bed-ridden and I was given to understand Admiral Wolfe was in command."

"Did you see Admiral Walters in his bed?"

"I did, sir."

"What was his condition?"

"He was very poor. The ball had lodged in his lung and he was ill. Sometimes he was faint, sometimes he raved, and sometimes he prayed."

"Did he know you?"

"He did, sir."

"Was his speech sensible?"

"No, sir. He raved and spoke wild things. He was not in his right mind."

"What sort of things did he say?"

She was silent and her face was drawn. "He reproached me, sir." Tears began to streak down her face. "He accused me of making an intrigue with the Turk which I never did. Captain Tangle saved my life when the freight wagon wrecked my carriage. All I ever did was thank him for saving my life, but Johnny was jealous."

Mistress Walters hissed. She had dyed her fashionable dress to the blackest hue and wore a wrap of sable furs. Her bonnet was burdened with black bows and her brunette hair curled around her neck. Her son was a solid gentleman in a captain's coat and restrained white wig. He put a hand on his mother's arm. He wore a black band of mourning upon his left arm.

"To the best of your knowledge, who gave the orders to evacuate Port Mahon?"

"Admiral Wolfe. He came to me himself and told me for my own safety I must go aboard the *Essex*. We had to hurry and couldn't pack up the house because the French were coming." The *Essex* was one of only three vessels to limp home. Her captain was among the dead.

The testimony from the naval officers had already established all the particulars of the day; the arrival of the French, the departure of the *Ajax* ahead of the other vessels, the departure of the fleet, and so forth. No one was alive in that court who could tell them anything about the decisions made at the highest level; the responsible parties were either dead or in a Spanish prison.

"Did Admiral Wolfe tell you why?"

"He said we couldn't hold Mahon with the forces we had, and he hoped the French would do a better job of it."

"He voluntarily handed over Mahon to the French?"

She was uncertain on the point. "A French boat came with a messenger. I don't know what they said."

They could not elicit any more useful information about Mahon from her. They moved on. "Tell us about the Battle of Majorca."

She took her handkerchief from her reticule and dabbed at her face with it. "It was dreadful. I was sent down to the cockpit with my daughter. We were put in the gunner's cabin. It was very dark and smelled foul. We had to stay there for hours. We heard the guns firing, and the screaming of the wounded. A great many men were brought into the cockpit and we could hear them shrieking. I put my hands over my daughter's ears and sang hymns as loudly as I could to try and block the sound from her. We cried and cried!"

The cockpit was forward of the gunroom. Both were below the waterline, which made them safer than any other place on board the vessel. The thin partitions between the cabin and the cockpit would not have muffled the sound of a man screaming as his leg was cut off. The court already had the casualty reports; they did not need a woman's hysterical version.

"Yes, yes," the president of the court said as she cried. "There now, don't cry. We have no further questions. We are sorry to distress you. You may step down."

She gave them a little curtsy and stepped away from the dock.

Mistress Walters hissed, "Hussy!"

Two points of color appeared high on Mistress FitzGerald's cheeks. She didn't look at the widow as she made her way down the aisle.

"'Tis an insult that she dares wear mourning for him," the widow said loudly enough for the people around her to hear.

"Mother," her captain-son said softly.

"I'm only saying what we're all thinking," she replied.

Anne FitzGerald had to pass her, but she couldn't bring herself to do it. She stopped just in front of the woman and said, "What I'm thinking, I won't say," she cried in a passion. "We all know what a cold and carping woman you are and that's why he preferred the Mediterranean over England!"

Mrs. Walters leaped to her feet and cried, "How dare you! You horrid slut!" She slapped Mrs. FitzGerald in the face. Her black glove came away covered in white face powder and left a smeared streak of makeup on her rival's face.

Anne FitzGerald shrieked, "You villainous virago!" She pulled Mrs. Walters' hair.

"Ow!" the widow cried.

Captain Walters tried to interpose himself between the two women, but his mother got around him and pulled Mrs. FitzGerald's hair. The blond wig came away in her hand and she held the blonde curls the way a savage of the New World might hold his enemy's scalp.

Anne FitzGerald grabbed it back. "That's mine, you thief!"

Mrs. Walters would not relinquish her grasp and the wig shredded. Golden strands of hair floated to the floor. The room erupted in pandemonium. The president of the court banged his gavel and shouted for order but nobody paid any attention to him. The supporters of the admiral's wife (and they were many) shouted, "Fie on you, whore!" and "You're the reason Walters is dead!"

Mrs. Walters was very capable of fighting her own battle. She shouted, "Harlot! Murderess!"

Anne FitzGerald had her own partisans. Although they were fewer in number, they were more active, chiefly because they were led by Commodore Tangueli. He leaped to his feet and pushed his way among the blue-coated officers and red-coated marines who were spilling into the aisles.

"I killed your husband," he told the widow coolly. "If you think I was wrong, say it to my face. Don't take it out on a defenseless woman."

Mrs. Walters was only five foot two, but the giant Turk looming over her did not intimidate her in the least. She tried to slap him, but his hand flew up and blocked her blow.

"Adulterer!" she shouted at him.

"I have never laid with any woman but my wife, and I will not take insult from you or any *ferenghi!*"

Captain Walters cried, "Unhand my mother!"

Where Tangle went, Thorton followed. "'Tis true. He never did. I know him."

"Liar! Barbarian!" Mrs. Walters shrieked at the big Turk. She hit him with her reticule.

The gavel banged and banged again. "Order in the court! Sit down! Everyone! Sergeant, arrest anyone standing up!"

Perry grabbed Thorton's arm and hauled him back into the benches as marines waded into the mob.

A redcoat used his musket butt on Tangle, but the Turk punched him in the nose. Red-blooded Englishmen would not sit still for a turban-wearing foreigner to assault a marine and swarmed into the aisle. The Sallee marines who had accompanied Tangle rose up and starting fighting the redcoats. Thorton would not desert a friend. He leaped into the fray. Abby was not completely blind; he could tell a red coat from a purple one. He shoved a red-coated marine right in the middle of his cross-belts and sent him stumbling against a British officer. Surprised to be attacked by one who was supposed to be on his side, the officer cursed and threw the man back. The president banged his gavel again and again, but it was too late. The melee was general.

Later — much later — blue coats, red coats, purple coats, and brown coats were all thrown into the gaol together.

CHAPTER 28 : JUDGMENT

Thorton spent the night in prison and didn't like it one bit. That Tangle and Abby and others he knew were in there with him didn't make it any better. Several naval officers and marines had spent the night in the cell along with them and a stony cease-fire had endured until they were all bailed out. Achmed bailed out Tangle, Perry bailed out Abby, and Horner bailed out Thorton.

Thorton and Horner went to the inn where they were staying. The younger man hastily shaved, washed, donned a clean shirt and fresh stock, combed his hair, then hurried without breaking his fast to the Admiralty building. Perry and Abby had arrived before them and saved them seats. They squeezed into the pew with their friends. Abby was pale and a little faint. Thorton patted his shoulder and whispered, "It will be all right, I'm sure."

Court was called to order. The formalities were observed, then the president of the court read out the judgment, "This court-martial finds the following items: 1) that Vice Admiral Jonathan Walters was incapacitated by the wound suffered when dueling Commodore Isam Rais Tangueli at Minorca and that therefore command was vested in Rear Admiral Nathaniel Wolfe. 2) That Admiral Wolfe generously returned Port Mahon to our allies the French who had lost it to the Spanish earlier in the summer. 3) That the Mediterranean fleet was perfidiously ambushed by the Spanish fleet off Majorca. 4) That due to the superior force of the Spaniards, and the debilitated state of our fleet, victory belonged to Spain through no error on the part of the commanding officers. This does not absolve the individual captains of responsibility for their actions during the course of the battle. They will be dealt with one by one. This court has adequate information laid before it to address only the matter of the *Essex*, *Adamant* and *Resolute*. Summon Lieutenant Whittacre."

A small table was placed in the middle of the floor and covered with a green cloth. The sergeant-at-arms laid Whittacre's sword on the table with the hilt pointing towards the door; he had been found innocent. The audience sighed with pleasure.

The marine guard opened the door and called, "The court summons Lieutenant Gerard Whittacre!"

The ashen-faced lieutenant entered. He was supported bodily by a friend on either side. When he saw the sword, hilt-first, he gave a glad cry and collapsed. He never regained consciousness.

The court addressed the unconscious man. "This court finds you not guilty of any wrongdoing. You were obedient to your duty and your captain. The decision to flee was made by Captain Oberon, and on him alone, may God have mercy on his soul, does the responsibility lie."

Whittacre's friends carried him out. A week later they would serve as his pallbearers and lay him in the ground with a good name and clean reputation.

"The court summons Lieutenant Alan Abbersomewhitham." The president of the court could not wrap his tongue around Abby's Welsh name and butchered it badly.

Thorton whispered to Abby, "They're laying your sword with the hilt towards you!"

Abby straightened up and edged into the aisle. Thorton guided him to the table, then left him and returned to his seat. The blind lieutenant still wore gauze around his eyes as he listened to the judgment.

"The court finds the captain and crew of the *Adamant* not guilty on any charges, and commends them for their gallantry in doing the utmost that could be done against the Spanish fleet, to the loss of their lives and ship. The court mourns the loss of Captain Alexander James and the officers who perished in the line of duty. It further commends Lieutenant Alan Abblewithymath for his dedication to duty, not only aboard the *Adamant*, but for assuming the place of a fallen officer on the *Resolute* and continuing to do his duty, which ultimately resulted in serious injury and the loss of his sight. The court grants promotion to the rank of master and commander and permanent furlough on half-pay."

Abby listened to all this with his head held high. When he heard his promotion, he trembled, and when he heard he was pensioned off, he sagged. "Let me have a position, I beg you, sirs! Do not force me to retire!"

The president spoke kindly, "We admire your dedication to duty, Commander, but there is no place for a blind officer in the Service. You may rest comfortably upon your laurels secure in the knowledge that you have served your country to the utmost. We are grateful for your sacrifice."

The half-pay of a commander was better than the half-pay of a lieutenant, but with two hundred pounds a year in allowance from his natural father, the Earl of Falmouth, the money was of no importance to Abby. He stepped forward and groped until he found the hilt of his sword. "Thank you, sirs." He turned around and wandered away from the table. Thorton hastily came up the aisle to guide him.

Next the *Essex* was absolved; she had fought until broken, then limped to Sardinia and home.

The court rustled. Men who had held their hats on their knees started to stretch their legs in anticipation of leaving, but the court was not done. "The court calls Isam Rais Tangueli, Commodore of the Sallee Navy.

Tangle gave a startled look to each side, but nobody but the officers of the court knew why he was being called. He stepped up with a wary expression.

"Although at great disadvantage and under no obligation to do so, you gallantly hazarded yourself and your vessel to assist in the rescue the *Resolute*. The court extends its thanks and commends your valor."

Tangle pressed his hand to his forehead and bowed deeply to the court. He spoke something in Arabic. The court could not understand it, but the flowery tone made them think he was returning the compliment. The Turk finished by speaking English, "Thank you, gentlemen."

After he returned to his seat, the court called Captain Horner. The dour officer stepped to the dock.

"The court wishes to commend the officers and men of the *Ajax* for their gallantry in rescuing the *Resolute*. They faced great odds with courage and resourcefulness. They are an example to us all."

Applause broke out. Some of the officers stood up and called, "Here, here!" The Sallee rovers they had given grudging respect, but their adulation was granted without reserve for the men of the *Ajax*. They had risked their lives to come to the aid of their fellows in spite of the danger of pitching a frigate against a battleship. The feisty little frigate was the hero they craved to redeem the ugly debacle in the Mediterranean.

The crowd showered the officers of the *Ajax* with attention as they spilled out of the courtroom. Abby was thumped on the back and congratulated on his promotion.

"Damn me! We're popular!" Perry said in happy surprise.

Horner accepted the accolades with laconic modesty as he was mobbed by blue coats.

Thorton, being a mere lieutenant, blended in with the crowd better than a captain like Horner, so he was able to slip away. He would have gotten clean away had he not been stopped in his tracks by the auction notice tacked up on the bulletin board in front of the Admiralty office. The *Santa Casilda* and *San Idelfonso* headed up the list, but at the bottom was, "*Ajax*, frigate. French-built As is. Cracked keel."

Tears streamed down his face. After all that they had been through, the *Ajax* was going on the block. She had been a good and faithful mistress to him, rising to every occasion and surviving every vicissitude. To see her stripped and sold like a slave on the block was painful to behold. He was still standing there when Horner caught up to him. The captain wondered to see his silent tears, then read the poster. He put his arm around younger man's shoulders. Neither of them spoke for a long time.

Thorton sniffled, pulled out his blue-checked handkerchief, and wiped his nose with it.

"Ships are casualties of war as much as men," Horner said.

Thorton nodded. "'Tisn't fair that we get commended, but she is to be sold. She won't fetch a good price, not with a cracked keel."

Horner tugged his shoulder. "Let's go back to the Scarlet Hen. We'll have a drink."

Thorton allowed himself to be pulled. "I guess I'll write a letter to Shakil and tell him how it has all turned out. Then I'll write my letter of resignation. I was thinking about buying a new uniform with my prize money, but not any more."

"It could be a very long time before the Admiralty answers your letter, and they might refuse. I would buy the uniform if I were you."

"I want my purple coat back."

"I'll buy you a ticket to the theater. They're playing *The Beggar's Opera*. 'Tis a rascally comedy, but perhaps it will cheer you up."

"I've never been to the theater," Thorton said.

"Never?"

Thorton shook his head, "No, not ever. But I did play the role of Polonious when we read *Hamlet* aloud in school."

"I am very fond of *Hamlet*. My wife and I named our son 'Horatio.'"

"Poor fellow. Does he suffer very much?"

Horner chuckled. "No more than 'Ebenezer' did when he was at school." He hooked his arm companionably into Thorton's. "Let's find a tailor and buy those tickets. Then we can help Abby baptize his promotion in proper style. We ought to look well for him if not ourselves."

CHAPTER 29 : AFFAIR OF HONOR

Thorton and his seconds met Bishop and his seconds at the Tennis Court early on Saturday morning. The grass was tipped with frost. It was cold and Thorton had donned flannel drawers beneath blue wool breeches. He had a long-sleeved wool waistcoat under his uniform coat. His plain black cloak was over it all, a blue-plaid muffler was around his neck, and his cocked hat was on his head. He had a pistol borrowed from Abby that would serve his purpose very well.

Perry and Forsythe were his seconds. Horner, Jackson, Tangle, and Aruj were witnesses. Bishop had a pair of seconds with him, along with the two thuggish marines who were pleased to make some extra money by accompanying him and intimidating anyone that the surly captain chose to bluster at. Bishop was well-dressed in a dark blue wool cloak and cocked hat with gold braid around the brim. His cockade was crisp and new. He and his seconds looked very respectable and substantial while the shabby officers and their Moorish companions looked like rogues and ruffians.

Fortunately Bishop didn't recognize Aruj as his former Midshipman Archibald Maynard; the boy lieutenant was wearing a beige and brown striped burnoose with the hood up over his turban. The burnoose was so long that only a few inches of his peg leg showed beneath the garment's hem. Aruj hated Bishop and loved Thorton with the black and white certainty of youth. The danger of arrest could not keep him away. A body of Sallee marines, sniffling in the cold, was there for his protection.

The seconds met to confer regarding the details of the duel. Bishop threw his cloak over his shoulder to reveal the fine frock coat laden with gold braid and the epaulette on his shoulder. He was one of a handful of naval officers who had adopted French fashions in their uniforms. Apparently he thought he cut a fine figure. He strutted halfway across the tennis court to confront Thorton.

"I fully intend to blow a hole in you that no surgeon can ever close, even if I have to press the gun to your breast to do it," he boasted.

The seconds all turned to look at him. Tangle translated for the benefit of the Sallee marines. Horner's mouth turned down at the corners. Thorton made no response.

Seeing himself the object of disgusted gazes, Bishop did not retreat. "I have been practicing my aim, and I am sure I can plug you where it will do you the most harm. If you do not answer me, it is because you are afraid."

Thorton untied the strings of his cloak and handed it to Horner. "If that's the way you are going to conduct yourself then we ought to wrestle in the mud like pigs."

"You are no gentleman! You came up from the gundeck."

"I rose on merit. You apparently rose on hot air." Thorton pulled the pistol out of his coat pocket and began to examine it. The flint and steel were new and clean and the barrel was a shiny blue-black. Silver tracery decorated the barrel and the grip was mother of pearl.

Bishop's seconds hurried over to him. "I entreat you, sir. Say no more. The duel will settle all scores."

Bishop allowed himself to be led back to the other side of the tennis court. The red-haired man stayed with him while the dark fellow finished speaking to Perry and Forsythe. They returned to their respective sides.

Bishop and Thorton removed their coats and hats. Horner received the younger man's clothes and stood like a valet with Thorton's cloak over his arm. "God be with you, Peter Thorton." He leaned forward to give Thorton a brief kiss of Christian friendship upon his cheek.

Thorton gave Horner a lopsided smile. "Thank you, sir."

He handed the pistol over to Perry and Abby to inspect and load, then stepped away and swung his arms and twisted his body to warm himself up. He had selected the waistcoat especially with the duel in mind; it moved freely while keeping him warm against the cold. It was a handsome mustard-colored waistcoat — not regulation, but he had felt free to take liberties with the regulations when he was at risk of dying. The Admiralty could reprimand him when he was dead. Once he was limbered up he squared his shoulders and accepted the pistol back. He checked the load and priming. Satisfied, he held it at his side.

Bishop had a very fine, long, white, silk waistcoat on over his linen shirt and dark blue breeches. He had his own pistol. It was plain and serviceable. His wig was neat and short with his own hair tucked into a black hair bag at the nape of his neck in the French fashion.

The two foes met in the middle of the tennis court and turned their backs to each other. The seconds ranged along side them to inspect the position, then stepped back to the sidelines. With no net, the tennis court was a flat and fine ground with woods on one side, a clubhouse on the other, and bowling greens and target range on the remaining sides. It was lightly frosted and the grass crunched under foot, but as the sun rose and broke over the tree tops the frost began to melt. Rays of sun touched Thorton's blond hair and made it shine like gold. No breeze stirred and the birds and squirrels were still.

The young lieutenant stood as still as a statue with his pistol in his hand.

Forsythe called out, "Gentlemen! One last time, we beg you, abjure this quarrel and make your peace!"

Bishop snorted, "I will not!"

"Three times you have come to the fatal ground. You won't leave it alive this time. Your luck has run out," Thorton replied.

The red-haired man called out, "Gentlemen! Ten paces please!"

They stepped off the distance. Bishop was a shorter man and he deliberately took short steps to reduce the distance in order to improve the chance of hitting his target. Thorton had long legs; he stepped off the distance with stately strides.

"Turn!" Forsythe called.

The two combatants turned to face each other with their pistols at their sides. Forsythe pressed a gloved hand against his face where a bit of perspiration gathered in his hairline in spite of the cold. Then he pulled out his white handkerchief and held it before him. "May God forgive you both."

He let the handkerchief fall.

Thorton had seen duels fought before. When Bishop had faced Tangle, Tangle had held his fire. Bishop had missed. Tangle had compelled his apology, then discharged his ball harmlessly into the ground. The second time Tangle had stood against Admiral Walters he had turned his body to present a narrower target to the other man who was reputed to be a decent shot. He had taken a ball in his arm anyhow but delivered a mortal wound to his opponent.

Thorton did not have the cool bravado of the Turk nor the hasty excitement of the belligerent Bishop. Although Bishop raised his pistol and squeezed off a shot as fast as he could, Thorton raised his pistol with both hands and took deliberate aim. He squeezed the trigger a second after Bishop.

Red bloomed directly over Bishop's heart. He staggered back and fell down. The pistol dropped from his hand and lay on the cold grass beside him. His seconds rushed forward.

"He's dead!" they called.

Perry and Forsythe ran to Thorton. "Peter, are you hit?"

Thorton stood as still and white as a statue and made no reply.

Perry and Forsythe looked him over front and back, then Perry gave a cry. "Here!" He hooked his black-gloved finger into the tear in Thorton's sleeve. "Right through the sleeve! He isn't hurt, thank God!"

Thorton sucked in a deep breath and looked at Perry. Then he looked at Forsythe. "I killed him?"

"You did! A perfect shot," Perry assured him.

"Instantly," Forsythe agreed morosely.

The cloaked figures of Bishop's seconds stooped over the corpse. The marines came forward with the dead man's cloak. They used it for a stretcher and carried him off the field of honor.

"God forgive me," Thorton replied. "I have killed a man. I am no longer angry and I repent what I have done."

"What? Don't castigate yourself. 'Tis Bishop's foolishness that brought him to this end," Perry urged him.

Tangle and Horner and all the others swarmed onto the tennis court. Horner quietly helped Thorton into his coat and hat, then hung his cloak around his shoulders. Thorton huddled in his cloak.

"Well done, Peter," Tangle said.

"We're finally rid of Bishop," Aruj exulted.

None of them understood his mood except Horner. The older man put his arm around his shoulders. "Let's go back to the inn," he said gently.

Thorton took a deep breath and said softly, "Thank you, sir."

CHAPTER 30 : THE PERILS OF MISS ALLEN

Bishop was right — the xebecs had little market in England. They sold remarkably cheaply. They were bought by Tangle and Achmed, who, having come prepared to buy back the *Sea Leopard*, bought two Spanish xebecs for less than they had feared they would have to pay for one. They were jubilant at the prospect of selling them south and making an immediate and handsome profit. Fortunately, the Spanish battleship was worth more than all the small prizes combined. Unfortunately, the Admiralty did not care to buy it. Three-fourths of its ships were laid up in ordinary since the conclusion of peace with France the previous year. A French agent bought it cheaply.

The gloom of the British officers was in inverse proportion to the happiness of the Sallee rovers. The less the rovers paid for the prizes, the less the officers received as prize money. Worse, the money was diluted by being shared among all the ships in sight at the time of the action. A lieutenant's share amounted to little more than sixty pounds. Still, it was enough to re-equip themselves, although it was nowhere near close to putting a dent in Posonby's debt.

Horner and Thorton had reason to be annoyed still further with Bishop; although he had not been present for the battle, he was the duly commissioned captain of the *Ajax*. He had demanded — and received — his share. For a while it appeared that the Admiralty would cheat Thorton of his captain's share even though he had commanded the *Ajax* to gain the victory. He produced his warrant making him acting-captain of the frigate and the Admiralty secretary was forced to yield.

Thorton and Horner, and blast him, Bishop, too, (or more precisely, his estate) were awarded over five hundred pounds each. The sum went a long way towards reconciling them to their loss of employment and a winter to be spent on the beach on half-pay. For the time being they had prize money to spend, Abby's promotion to celebrate, and no duties whatsoever to fulfill. They decided to make merry.

Thorton came into the room he shared with Abby to find boxes and tissue paper everywhere. The barmaid was in there with another woman in a state of dishabille. The barmaid was hauling as hard as she could on the laces to tighten the corset on the other woman.

Thorton coughed. "Pardon me, ladies, but I think you are in the wrong room."

The berry brown maid grinned at him. "No mistake, sir. I'm 'elping Miss Allen with 'er stays."

The strange woman held onto the bedpost. "Tighter! I must have a nineteen inch waist and I don't care if I suffocate for it!"

Thorton knew that voice. "Alan?"

Brandy hauled the laces hard again. She even put her knee into the small of Abby's back. The commander gasped and couldn't answer. He was wearing a shift that stopped short of his knees with the corset over it. White silk stockings encased his legs and went up over his knees and were held in place by rose garters. His blond hair was done in ringlets artfully arranged across his brow and around his neck. He grinned from ear to ear while Brandy tied off his laces.

Thorton gaped at him. "What on earth are you doing?"

"Getting ready for the theater." He turned his back to Thorton. "Haul my laces. You're a man, make me feel it! I'm sure you can pull them tighter than Miss Brandy."

Thorton had never even seen a corset before. Not when it was being worn, anyhow. He had, on one or two occasions, when he was too young to understand why men were supposed to stay out of the yard on laundry day, accidentally stumbled upon his mother's unmentionables when they were hanging on the line. Gingerly he stepped forward, untied the laces, and gave a little tug.

"Not like that, you're loosening them! Haul them tight! Brace those yards hard round!"

So Thorton hauled the laces tighter and tighter until Abby said, "oof" in a happy voice. Then he stood aside as Brandy put a a froth of white petticoats and violet dress over Abby's head. The dress was trimmed in black lace. Abby and Brandy pulled at the front until he had a modest semblance of cleavage, due mostly to his waist being cinched in so tight that his form was forced to assume the shape of an hourglass. A white fichu went around his shoulders. A black velvet ribbon and cameo was tied around his throat and covered his small adam's apple. Next came the bonnet. Thorton was forced to admit that from the rear it was a very credible imitation. Meanwhile Brandy powdered his face white, painted his eyes and lips and cheeks into a perfect imitation of womanhood, and even gave him an artificial beauty mark near the corner of his right eye. She gave him the glass.

"Behold Miss Abigail Allen!" the barmaid exclaimed.

Abby preened before the mirror. The white powder had paled his tan face and the rouge heightened his cheekbones. Lipstick had turned his mouth into a perfect bow.

"Why are you doing this?" Thorton asked in bewilderment.

Abby pouted prettily and stomped his foot. "That's not what you say when introduced to a lady." He held out a lace-gloved hand. "You bow over my hand and say, 'I am delighted to meet you, Miss Allen.' Do it. Practice. We shall make a gentleman of you even if you did come up from the weather deck."

Thorton took the proffered hand gingerly. "I am delighted to meet you, Miss Allen," he replied. He bowed awkwardly.

"No, no. Put one leg back and bend the knees a little. Keep your back straight and incline from the hips. Try it again."

So Thorton tried again. And again. And again. He practiced until Abby was satisfied. 'Miss Allen' curtsied very prettily in return. Then Brandy hung a black lace fan on a string around his wrist, and finally, the black wool shawl was wrapped around his shoulders. When all was done he was the very model of a fashionable young lady.

"Go see if Tangle is in the public room. He's my escort," Abby directed him. "Not a word to anyone! I want to see if I can fool them."

Brandy grinned at him. "You'll fool them all. I swear it. You are perfection, Miss Allen."

Thorton went and peeked down the stairs. He saw Tangle's purple coat and came back to the room. "Isam Rais is ready. But Horner's down there, too." He had a knot in his stomach.

Abby bit his lip. "I'd rather not meet Horner just yet. Go down, get him to leave. He's waiting for you."

So Thorton descended the stairs and wondered what on earth he was getting himself into. He smiled bravely enough at Horner, who smiled up at him as he descended the stairs. The captain had overcome his usual frugality and splurged on a new uniform and silk stockings. The undress frock coat with its leaner, modern style suited his thin frame.

Horner offered him an arm. "Ready?"

"Aye aye, sir."

Thorton accepted the arm and they went out as if they were bosom friends. They went straight to the theater and into their box. Thorton began to relax; Abby might get away with it after all. He wondered how Tangle had taken it when Abby came tripping down the stairs in his violet dress. Well, that wasn't his problem. He tried to pay attention as Horner chatted about the theater. Finally the curtain went up.

The play was a proper scandal. Miss Polly Peachum was the daughter of a receiver of stolen goods and had had married a highwayman without her parents' consent. Her parents connived to have the highwayman arrested in the hopes that he would be hanged and leave their daughter a rich widow, but the scoundrel denied her in favor of her rival. A cavalcade of pregnant whores, each claiming to be the highwayman's wife, came to plead for him, causing him to choose the gallows over matrimony. In the most flagrant case of *deus ex machina* known to European theater, the highwayman was saved and lived happily ever after with his only legal wife, Polly.

Thorton had thought his own amorous peccadillos to be the very depths of scandal, but *The Beggar's Opera* showed him that he was an amateur where concupiscence was concerned. He understood why his opponents censured him so strongly; they suspected him of far worse than he had ever imagined.

After it was all over, Thorton remarked, "Now I know why they say the theater is a corrupter of public morals."

"'Tis not an edifying piece, but it does serve to amuse," Horner agreed.

They collected their hats and cloaks and stepped out onto the mezzanine. They spotted the turban of the Sallee commodore towering over the lesser forms of Englishmen. A black bonnet was with him.

Horner noticed immediately. "There's Commodore Tangueli. Fie on him! He asserted himself so forcefully in the courtroom I believed him, but there he is with a pretty miss on his arm!"

Thorton, who knew the full facts on both sides of both cases, opened his mouth, thought better, and shut it. "I am sure 'tis only social," he said weakly.

"Let's go meet her," Horner said and started over.

Thorton squawked and hurried after him. "I think we ought to leave them alone. 'Tis no affair of ours," but Horner was not a man to change course at the behest of a mere lieutenant.

Tangle saw them coming and gave Abby a warning. The cross-dressed commander turned to face Tangle and kept his back to the officers as they approached. Horner had a view of blonde curls, shapely waist, and the back of Abby's bonnet. It was a fine figure and he did not mind looking at it.

"Good evening, Commodore," Horner said pleasantly. "I hope you and your companion have enjoyed the play."

"Peace be upon you, Ebenezer Rais. We are enjoying our evening very much. And you?"

"I'm well, thank you. May I beg an introduction to your lovely companion?"

Abby could not ignore such a polite and reasonable request. He turned part way round, but the bonnet's brim was as effective as a set of blinders. It prevented Horner from getting a good look at his face.

"Miss Abigail Allen, may I present Captain Ebenezer Horner, formerly of His Majesty's frigate *Ajax*?" Tangle said. "Captain Horner, Miss Allen."

"Delighted," Abby said in a voice so low Horner could barely hear it. 'Miss Allen' extended a lace-gloved hand.

Horner took it and bowed elegantly over it. In his new uniform he cut a handsome figure. *"Enchanté.* I am delighted to make your acquaintance, Miss Allen. Commodore Tangueli is lucky to have such a charming companion for the evening."

Tangle smiled warmly. "Fortune favors the bold."

Abby turned away from Horner. He tugged the white streak in the corsair's beard playfully and murmured something that made Tangle grin, but Horner could not hear it.

Horner was scrupulous about matters of etiquette. "May I beg leave to present Mister Peter Thorton, formerly third lieutenant of the *Ajax*?"

Miss Allen extended her hand to Thorton and murmured something unintelligible.

Thorton bowed over the gloved had as he had been drilled. "I'm delighted to meet you, Miss Allen." He wanted to drag Horner away before the charade was up. "Shall we get something to drink?" he proposed desperately. He tugged Horner's elbow.

"Would you care for a drink, Miss Allen? They have champagne," Horner asked.

"Champagne would be lovely," Miss Allen replied in a soft voice.

They left the Turk and the cross-dressing commander to go over to the bar. Thorton said, "Let's go back to the inn. I don't feel like drinking. Leave the Turk to his amours."

"She must be an actress or other low sort. I would hate to think the Turk had succeeded with one of Britain's better daughters," Horner replied.

Thorton did not like to hear Abby discussed in such terms. "I am told Miss Allen is the daughter of an earl!"

Horner gave him a look of surprise. "Really?" He glanced back at the bonneted figured. "In that case, we must rescue her from folly."

Alas, but Folly had stolen a march on them. Tangle thought drinks a good idea and had left Abby alone while he went to fetch them. Lieutenant Barnes was taking advantage of his absence to ingratiate himself with Miss Allen. Abby opened the black lace fan with a supple flick of his wrist and hid behind it. The two blue eyes looking over the edge of the lace only served to entice the marine further.

Horner slowed his step and put a hand on Thorton's shoulder. "Hold a moment. The Army has come to the rescue. We'll see if he can drive the Turk from his position."

"We don't want a quarrel," Thorton said anxiously.

"Barnes can hold his own. He is an officer of the marines. Besides, he has friends." Horner nodded to the knot of red-coated officers who were watching Barnes' sortie.

Tangle noticed the direction of Horner and Thorton's gaze, and turned his head to look back at Abby in worry. When he saw the marine attempting to enfilade the commander's position, he abandoned the idea of refreshments. He charged straight for the violet dress. Abby took Tangle's arm and smiled up at him. The black fan went flick-flick-flick and Barnes was obliged to retreat. He regrouped with his red-coated friends.

"The Turk has entrenched his position and thrown up a breastwork I see," said Horner. He reached the serving table and received two glasses of champagne.

Thorton took nothing for himself. He was positive now was not the time to dull his wits with alcohol. Horner returned to 'Miss Allen' with Thorton trailing him anxiously.

Abby was fanning himself violently with the black lace fan. His face was flushed and his eyelids were drooping. It hardly seemed the face of a man at all; it was the face of a woman about to faint.

"Drink this, it will revive you," Horner said. He offered the glass.

"Thank you." Abby put out his hand and groped to find the glass.

Horner stood stock still. He had not recognized the face, but he recognized the blind groping. Abby took the glass and lifted it, but it slipped from his hand. Tangle and Horner both tried to grab it but missed. The glass shattered on the tile floor. Abby crumpled and Thorton leaped to catch him.

Abby was shorter and slimmer than the average man, but he was bigger than the average woman; Thorton couldn't hold him. They went to the floor together. Thorton held the swooning commander in his arms and Abby's head fell back. His Adam's apple was not prominent, but with his head hanging back like that it was obvious above the black velvet band. Tangle swiftly picked up his head and tucked it against Thorton's shoulder, but it was too late. Horner saw it.

The shattering glass and fainting woman attracted attention. Barnes and his friends immediately came to offer their assistance.

Tangle whispered to Thorton in Arabic, "We've got to get him out of here!"

Horner stood up and spread his arms to block the gawkers. "Stand back, let her have some air."

"What happened?" Barnes asked anxiously.

"She is overcome by the heat. Lieutenant, would you be so kind as to engage a coach for us? We will take Miss Allen home."

"Of course!" Barnes immediately darted away.

"Here are smelling salts!" a dowager lady exclaimed and shoved them under Abby's nose. "Let me help, poor dear."

Abby woke with a jolt. He blinked and sat up. He did not know the people gathered around him; he saw shadowy shapes and heard strange voices. "Peter?" he whispered in a panic.

"I'm here, Miss Allen," Thorton replied.

Horner intercepted the dowager, "Thank you, dear lady. I think we have everything in hand. We will get her home. Can you stand, Miss Allen?"

Tangle and Thorton took Abby by the elbows and hauled him to his feet. The commander grabbed Thorton's arm and clung to him. Tangle gave Thorton a glare, but Thorton was oblivious.

"Miss Allen is my escort. I will attend her." The corsair offered his purple clad arm.

Abby kept hanging onto Thorton. Either he did not see the proffered elbow, or he did not feel steady enough to release one support to seize another.

Barnes returned. "I have a carriage for you."

Abby whispered in Thorton's ear, "Get me out of here!"

Horner took charge. "Lieutenant Barnes, Commodore Tangueli, if you will clear a path, please."

Barnes and Tangle gave each other the kind of look that said they would just as soon see the other pitch headfirst off the mezzanine, but they smiled politely and started shooing people out of the way. Horner came to Abby's other side and helped Thorton steady him down the steps. Reaching the coolness of the outdoors Abby revived a little and let Tangle hand him up into the coach. The Sallee rover and the naval officers climbed into the coach with him. Unseen, Barnes hopped on the boot with the footman. A shilling bought the footman's silence. They rode together all the way to the Scarlet Hen. Barnes was sorely puzzled when the carriage stopped at the inn but slunk away into the darkness before he was detected.

CHAPTER 31 : ON THE BEACH

Tangle scooped Abby up into his arms and carried him up the steps to the room the crossdressing commander shared with Thorton. Thorton followed but paused as his own door shut in his face. He was standing undecided in the hallway when Horner came up at a sedate pace. The captain stopped beside the blond lieutenant.

"Did you know what he was up to?" Horner inquired.

Thorton blushed and stammered, "I tightened his stays."

Horner pinched the bridge of his nose. He held it for a long moment. "So you supported and encouraged him in this folly? What were you thinking?"

"Me? He was already into the corset and curls when I found him!"

"You should have stopped him."

"How? He's a grown man. Besides, he's my friend."

Horner stared at Thorton. Several things chased through his mind, not the least of which was that Thorton hadn't an iota of sense where other people were concerned. "I am going to have a few words with Commander Abby."

He rapped authoritatively on the door. Without waiting for an answer, he opened the door and pushed into the room. Thorton swiftly followed him — and ran into his back as he stopped short.

Abby was sitting in Tangle's lap. He was dressed in his shift but had shed the corset. He had white silk stockings up over his knees fastened with garters. He wore dainty high-heeled black ladyslippers. His hair was still in curls and his arms were around Tangle's neck. His head snapped around at the unexpected entrance. Tangle groaned like a man much put upon.

Horner said in a severe voice, "You have some explaining to do, Commander."

Abby glared at the captain. "No, I don't. The matter is between Isam and me and none of your business."

Horner snorted. "Frankly, Commodore, for a man who only a few days ago vowed your faithfulness to your wife, the situation hardly becomes you."

Tangle replied smoothly, "I said I had never lain with any woman but my wife, and I told the truth. Alan is not a woman."

"You haven't laid with me at all!" Abby cried. To Horner he said, "If you must know, I was trying to seduce him. You're interrupting me."

"The skirts were for me?" Tangle asked in surprise. "But I like a man in uniform."

"What? I did this for nothing?" Abby smacked the rover's nose with the fan.

"Ow!" Tangle complained and rubbed his nose.

Horner stared at the two, then turned around and walked out. He nearly ran into Thorton, but the younger man jumped out of the way. Thorton threw an anxious glance at the quarreling couple, then ran after Horner.

Horner entered his own room with Thorton close on his heels. The captain hung up his cloak and hat. He knelt on the hearth and struck a spark into the kindling. It caught and the fire began to warm the room. He took a taper and lit the lamps. Then he pulled a chair away from the table and sat down. He let out a rueful laugh.

"I appear to have stumbled onto something I would rather know nothing about."

Thorton drew up a chair next to him. "Alan set his cap for Isam a long time ago."

"You've known all along that Alan was an epicene?"

Thorton floundered. "What's an 'epicene'?"

"'Epicene' is the grammatical term for something possessed of both genders. Lately we have come to apply it to gentlemen of a similar nature."

"We do?" Thorton asked in surprise. "You mean, he's not the only one?"

"You didn't know?"

Thorton shook his head.

"The tipstaves arrest mollies from time to time and put them in the pillory. They are a source of amusement and outrage to the public. I own I have never seen one as pretty as Abby in the pillory, though. The ones I saw were such graceless whores I wonder they ever fooled anyone."

Thorton gave Horner a wounded look. "Don't talk about Alan that way! He's not a whore. Besides, I doubt his father, the earl, would ever let him go to the pillory."

Horner gave him a twisted smile. "That may be true. But the rest of us aren't fortunate enough to have earls for fathers. We must guard our reputations."

"I don't care. I always get in trouble no matter how hard I try to be good, so it doesn't matter. I would rather have friends."

Horner gave him a level look. "Your friends will come to an unhappy end sooner or later."

"What of it? You're unhappy already. I don't want to wind up like you."

Horner stiffened. "I don't like your tone, Mister Thorton."

"Are you happy? Do you have friends? What are your prospects in the Service? You've been furloughed. Where is the reward for your virtue? But it doesn't matter. No man is perfect and neither are you. Can't you forgive us for being human? I know Abby and Tangle will stand by me, so I stand by them."

The silence grew. The fire talked to itself in a series of pops and hisses. Horner stared at Thorton for a while, then his eyes turned inward. When he spoke his voice was so quiet he seemed to be speaking to himself.

"I have striven to be the best officer I can. I like to think I have accomplished something and that my name means something. But my last two commands were temporary warrants with no hope of another any time soon. Seniority will make an admiral of me if I manage to live long enough, but at this rate, I'll be sixty before I retire as an admiral without distinction of color."

Thorton said nothing.

"I'd like to have the better pay of a battleship commander, but I like the freedom of a frigate and the chance for prizes. I'm not old enough to want the comfort of a large cabin more than I want the liberty of independent action."

Thorton smiled. "I like galiots and corvettes and frigates and especially xebecs. I like action. I saw how much paperwork you and Forsythe had to do for the *Resolute*. I'd rather ply my guns than my pen."

Horner chuckled. "To hell with them all. I'll take my chances in the heat of action." He leaned over and kissed Thorton full on the mouth.

Thorton sat still in complete shock, then his eyes closed and he kissed him back. His heart beat faster. Horner was not a man to do things by half-measures. Thorton felt his certainty and it fanned his ardor. The kiss grew longer and hotter.

Horner broke the kiss at last. "Will you spend the night, Peter? I think your own bed is going to be busy, so you may as well share mine."

Thorton swallowed hard. He glanced involuntarily at the four poster bed with its canopy and muslin curtains. He looked at Horner again, then nodded.

Horner's knee was pressing against his. His hand came to rest on the lieutenant's thigh. "We might not sleep."

Thorton blushed. He cleared his throat self-consciously. "I wouldn't mind . . . but the *Articles* . . ."

Horner brushed a hand over the younger man's hair. "We are on furlough, and you've tendered your resignation. I don't think the *Articles of War* apply anymore."

Thorton brightened. "That's true. I'll stay, then." His heart hammered in his chest as he said it.

Horner had been married eight years before being widowed. He knew what he was doing as he undressed Thorton and took him to bed. All the same, he was surprised when Thorton did something for him that his wife, a good and decent woman, had never done. Much later they both slept very soundly.

CHAPTER 32 : THE AMPHITRITE

Thorton and Horner slept late. When they woke, they disported themselves again. Precisely at the most inconvenient moment a knock sounded on the door. Horner groaned and Thorton buried his face in the pillow. The rap sounded again, sharper and longer.

"Do you suppose they heard?" Thorton asked softly.

Horner kissed his shoulder. "We have been quiet enough, and even if they have, 'tis none of their affair."

Tangle's voice called through the door. "Captain Horner? Are you at home?"

Thorton muttered something. Horner sighed and eased off. "I'll get rid of him."

Just as Horner was slipping naked from the bed and reaching for his dressing gown, Tangle rapped again, opened the door, and stuck his head in. "Captain Horner?"

Wrapping his dignity around himself along with his dressing gown, Horner said, "You have disturbed my rest."

Tangle's brown eyes flashed with amusement as he realized what he had interrupted. "Sorry, Captain, but the Admiralty sent a note to Peter. I'm looking for him."

"I believe I can find him," Horner replied gravely. "Leave the note with me and I'll see that he gets it."

"Did Peter get another room? He didn't have to. I didn't spend the night with Abby."

"You didn't?"

Tangle shook his head. "I made it clear to Alan that I prefer Peter. He didn't take it well. He's been pouting ever since."

"How very awkward," Horner replied.

Thorton buried his face in the pillows to muffle any noise that might involuntarily escape him. He wished Tangle would leave.

"What room is Peter in? I'll go knock him up."

"That's not necessary. I'll let him know."

"I want to talk to him."

Thorton couldn't stand it any longer. He sat up in bed and hurled the pillow at the Turk. "Just go!" he shouted.

Tangle turned in surprise and caught the pillow in the face. It fell, and he gaped to see Thorton naked in Horner's bed. He turned back to Horner. "You sly dog! I had no idea!"

"You still have no idea," Horner replied composedly. "The note?" He held out his hand. Tangle surrendered it. Horner carried it to Thorton.

Thorton broke the seal and read. "I'm summoned to the Admiralty at nine of the clock this morning to meet Admiral Sir Charles Leggott. What time is it?"

Tangle fished out his watch. "Eight thirty. You're going to be late."

Horner rang the bell. "We've got to get you cleaned up."

Thirty-five minutes later Thorton was admitted to an office in the Admiralty building. He waited with his cocked hat under his arm. The man at the desk pulled his bifocals down his nose and looked over them at the younger man. "Lieutenant Peter Thorton. You're late."

"I'm sorry, sir. I was at the theater last night and rose late."

"No excuse. I wasn't even in town last night, but I'm still here on time."

"Aye, sir." Thorton stood stiffly and stared at the wall over the man's head.

The stranger was a man of middle age, good-looking in a well-polished way, with a short white wig featuring two rolls on either side of his face. He wore an admiral's uniform made out of fine dark blue wool and heavy gold braid. It gleamed with the luster of real gold, the stuff was practically solid bullion. He, too, had adopted the French fashion of epaulettes. His eyes were brown and he had heavy cheeks and the start of a paunch, but he gave an impression of solidity, dignity, and wealth.

"Do you know who I am?"

"Not specifically, sir," Thorton said apologetically.

"Charles Leggott. I'm the new Vice Admiral of the Mediterranean fleet." He held up a folded paper. "I want to know what this is."

Thorton blinked. He was impressed and worried to meet Admiral Walters' replacement, but he didn't know what the paper was. "I don't know, sir."

"Your letter of resignation, that's what!" the man cried in exasperation. He threw it down on the desk like a poisonous thing.

Thorton cringed. Then he squared his shoulders and continued staring at the wall. He had thought his resignation would be processed by a faceless bureaucrat in London. He had not expected to have to answer for it personally.

"I have read every dispatch, every newspaper account, interviewed every witness, and listened to every rumor and every bit of gossip. I think I have a very good idea of the events that unfolded this summer."

"Aye aye, sir," Thorton said since it seemed he was supposed to say something. He trembled in his shoes and kept staring at the wall over the man's shoulder.

"The *Ajax* was the only victorious vessel in the Mediterranean theater, and you were acting-captain when she whipped a pair of Spanish xebecs. You are not resigning."

He ripped up the paper and let the pieces fall on his desk like confetti. Thorton watched the falling shreds in despair.

"I want the *Ajax* back at sea. I believe that success should be rewarded, not sold on the auction block. Unfortunately, that idiot Montague has no sense at all. All he cares about is money. I'm informed one of your Sallee rogues bought her. Since you are on friendly terms with them, you are going to act as my agent to buy her back. We'll reimburse him whatever he paid, plus any reasonable expenses he may have incurred in outfitting her."

He handed a paper to Thorton. "This is your commission authorizing you to make the purchase. He only paid five hundred pounds for her. You're authorized to go to a thousand. Don't tell him that. Haggle with him. But buy her back today."

Thorton took the paper and looked at it. "Who's going to be her captain?"

"Not Bishop. I owe you thanks for shooting him. The man was a nincompoop. By the way, the matter of the courtroom brawl is being dropped. Don't make me regret it."

Thorton was feeling dizzy from the whirlwind approach of Sir Charles. "Aye aye, sir."

"Dismissed."

Thorton saluted and fled.

The Sallee fleet in Spithead was sizable. Four xebecs, a frigate, and a galiot were lying at anchor together. Thorton hired a wherry and went out. He saw that the *San Idelfonso* was being used as a sheer hulk to fit a new foremast in the *Ajax*; they were re-rigging her as a xebec. It would be easier to keep the squadron together if they were all lateen-rigged. He was intercepted by a guard boat rowing around the flagship.

He recognized the curly-haired young man. "Kaashifa!"

The midshipman in his purple jacket recognized him too. "Peter Rais! Are you coming back to us?"

Thorton shook his head. "I tried, but they refused my resignation. I'm here on business. Who bought the *Ajax*?"

"Oh, that was Kasim Rais. He sold his share of the *Sea Leopard* to get the money to buy it."

"Not Kasim! I need to see Isam Rais."

Tangle was busy, but not so busy that he didn't have time for Thorton. He laughed to see him again. "Ahoy, there. And congratulations on your conquest!"

Thorton blushed bright red and muttered, "'Tis not a thing for congratulations!"

"Still, I'm glad to see you having some sport. You need it. You will be a pleasanter man for it. And I'm glad Horner was favorably disposed towards you all along. I wish I had known. I wouldn't have worried so much when he arrested you."

"No! He is not like you and me. 'Twas an unusual circumstance, nothing more. But stop! I need your help. I am here at the order of Admiral Leggott." He told him of his mission.

Tangle accompanied the English lieutenant over to the *Ajax*. Kasim Rais folded his arms over his chest and looked down his nose at Thorton even though the Englishman was taller. He was dressed in a large turban, brocade coat of many colors, and mustard-colored pantaloons. His curly beard was neatly combed and completely black.

Thorton spoke Arabic and gave a little bow. "Peace be upon you, Kasim Rais. I've come on official business from Admiral Sir Charles Leggott. He's the new admiral of the Mediterranean fleet."

Kasim was pleased to be approached by an admiral's messenger. It suited his sense of self-importance. "I can grant the Admiral a few minutes."

Thorton switched to Spanish because his Arabic wasn't good enough. Tangle translated for him. "The Admiral would like to buy back the *Ajax*. I am authorized to reimburse you for the cost."

Kasim glared at him. "No!"

"I understand you may have spent some money outfitting her, so we can reimburse you that as well."

"Absolutely not! I am captain of the *Ajax* now! I bought her fair and square and I'm not giving her up, you dog!"

"I'm not a dog. I'm a Muslim the same as you."

Kasim glared at him and acted like he would spit, but he glanced at Tangle out of the corner of his eye and refrained. "We have nothing in common, you damn catamite."

Tangle glared at Kasim and did not translate, but Thorton had encountered sexual insults before and knew what he said. The two Salletines started to argue in Arabic.

"Rais! Let me offer you a small profit for the price," Thorton interjected.

"How much?" Kasim asked.

"Five hundred and fifty pounds for the *Ajax*, as is."

Kasim spit over the side. "I can't buy a ship in Zokhara for so little. I'll sell for ten thousand pounds. Not a shilling less."

"You're a preposterous man. Six hundred."

Kasim's eyes glinted. "You really want it, eh? Very well. Raise your price."

Thorton shook his head. "Tell me how much you want."

"I already told you. Ten thousand pounds."

"Then you're ten thousand pounds foolish. I'll give you one thousand pounds for her."

Kasim scoffed. "She's worth ten times that and you know it."

"No, she's not. The Service could buy a brand new frigate at that price. She has a cracked keel. She sold cheap for a reason, rais."

"You can kiss my ass and your admiral, too. Meet my price or there's no sale."

No amount of arguing would move Kasim. The English lieutenant had to go back to Leggott in defeat.

Sir Charles looked up from his desk. "Well?"

Thorton licked dry lips. "I regret to inform you that Kasim Rais is demanding a price of ten thousand pounds sterling. He would not entertain my offer."

"Ridiculous! What does his commander say?"

"He has no commander, sir. He is a privateer. Commodore Tangueli assisted me, but he can't force a privateer to do anything."

"Damn privateers. They're a plague on every nation. Very well. Are you satisfied Commodore Tangueli tried his utmost?"

"I am, sir. Kasim Rais is a difficult man."

"Very well. I didn't think we'd get her back at a price we'd be willing to pay." The admiral picked a stack of forms and starting filling in the blanks.

Thorton was relieved that the admiral did not appear to be angry with him for his failure, but wasn't sure if he was dismissed or not. He remained standing silently. He was reminded of the time he had once been sent to the masthead as a midshipman and been forgotten about until after dark.

Leggott rang the bell and his secretary came in. "Copy these."

The secretary said, "Aye aye, sir."

The secretary settled on the other side of the desk and both of them plied their quills. Thorton remained as he was. Finally the papers were done. The secretary tied them with red tape and put them in a leather pouch.

"Deliver these to Captain Horner," Leggott ordered.

"Aye aye, sir."

The secretary said, "Sign here."

Thorton signed the receipt for the dispatches. He was intensely curious to know what was in them, but he was glad that Horner was getting some kind of post. There were a lot of packets in there; probably some of the other officers were getting assignments as well. He put the precious bundle into his coat pocket.

Arriving at the Scarlet Hen, his stomach rumbled at the smell of ham steaks and beer. It was dinner time. He had missed his breakfast running around all morning. Noon was gnawing at his insides. Fortunately, dinner time also meant that Horner and the other officers were easy to find. They were gathered around a long table in the front room.

"Peter!" Perry hailed him. "You're just in time. Holla, what's that you've got?"

"Orders, I think," he replied. He presented the pouch to Horner. "These are for you, sir."

Horner rose and took the bag. "Thank you, Lieutenant." He went upstairs to his room.

Thorton took Horner's chair and helped himself to the man's plate; he was hungry. After a few minutes the chambermaid came down and whispered to Thorton. He went upstairs to Horner's room.

"Sir." He saluted.

"Your orders, Thorton." Horner handed him the packet.

Thorton pounced on it and tore it open. "Lieutenant on the frigate *Amphitrite*!"

"Yes." Horner had the packets laid out neatly in order of rank. "Tell the gentlemen they may come up at their convenience to receive their orders. Please sign here."

Thorton signed for his orders. "And you, sir?"

Horner's face was perfectly bland. "Why don't we call the officers so I only have to explain myself once?"

"Aye aye, sir."

In a state of high excitement he hurried out. He was only halfway down the steps to the common room when he waved violently and called, "Orders! All of you, come up!"

The former officers of the *Ajax* bolted from the table and ran upstairs.

"Gentlemen! No stampede, please!" Horner rebuked them as they piled into his room.

They calmed themselves and stood to attention.

"Mister Forsythe. Sign here." Forsythe signed and received his packet with trembling hands.

"What did you get, Albert?" Perry asked.

Forsythe was too nervous. He hadn't opened his yet. "I don't know."

"Mister Perry." Perry leaped across the room and signed for his papers.

"Mister Blakesley." The sailing master stepped forward more calmly than the younger men.

"Doctor Ferncastle." The physician stepped forward eagerly.

"Reverend Pennybrigg." The parson had not expected to get a position; chaplains were not considered indispensable to the Service.

"Mister Jackson," Horner said with clipped efficiency.

The midshipman signed and received his own packet.

The rest of the orders were passed out and a general noise of breaking seals and rustling paper rattled through the room. Only Abby did not receive a set. He stood quietly by the fire with his back to them. Still, he could not resist looking over his shoulder at them.

"What have you got?" the officers asked each other.

"*Amphitrite*. You?"

"*Amphitrite* here!"

"Me, too!"

"What about you, Chagall?"

"Ordered back to the *Pegasus* on the *Amphitrite*."

"Same here," said Posonby.

They all turned to face Horner. "What about you, sir?" Perry asked respectfully.

Horner's dour expression never faltered.

They held their breaths in fear of bad news. "Don't keep us in suspense, sir," Forsythe begged.

Finally Horner grinned from ear to ear. "Captain of the *Amphitrite*."

They cheered.

CHAPTER 33 : THE QUEEN OF THE SEA

The officers made haste to quit their rented rooms and move to the *Amphitrite*. Except Chagall. Being a passenger he had no obligation to work. He preferred to disport himself in the city until the vessel would be leaving. Posonby was likewise a passenger, but Horner told him very sternly he was going aboard where his creditors couldn't have him arrested. (And he couldn't spend any more money.) Captain Horner and his officers piled into a rented boat while two more boats followed in their wake with their sea chests and furniture. Abby came with them. They were such a company of friends that they did not think to exclude him.

The *Amphitrite* rode at anchor with the rest of the Mediterranean fleet. They were all fitting out. So far they had their yards crossed and their lines reeved. Work continued with hammering and sawing, the bawling of petty officers giving orders, and lots of paint being applied. Her rig, square sails on the main and fore masts and a lateen on the shebeck yard crossing the mizzen, made her easy to pick out from the other ships.

She was long and sleek and low to the water. Not as low as a xebec, but as they came across her head they saw that she was fine and slim with an exceptionally graceful curve to her body. Her figurehead featured a half-naked goddess with pink shells to cover her breasts, long green hair trailing down, and a rose-colored garment draped around her nether parts. She had a pair of crab claws extending from her brow like horns in lieu of a crown.

"Look at those curves!" Perry whistled.

"I don't think she's any beamier than the *Ajax*," Thorton said.

Forsythe said, "But she's longer. Look, twenty-eight guns on the gundeck, and another eight on the castles. Thirty-six all told."

"Twelve-pounders, I think," Jackson observed.

"Thank God for that," Perry replied. "I would feel puny with a set of nines."

Horner surveyed his new command. He noted her hull was solid with few signs of repair, her paint fresh, and her ornaments classically Greek. "Row around her," he commanded.

Passing abaft her stern they saw she had a small gallery off the captain's cabin, an unusual feature in a frigate. The railing was a series of Greek keys. The transom's decoration featured a nearly life-sized Amphitrite on the larboard and her husband, the sea-god Poseidon, on the starboard. Seahorses, scallops, seaweed and ribbons decorated the arch. The wardroom below had five high square windows and each was topped with a hemispheric scallop shell. The transom and counter formed a perfect oval. The ornament, smaller and less ostentatious, continued under the wardroom windows. The rudder was topped with a carved seahorse. All the decorative ornaments had the possibility of clashing, but they didn't. They melded together in a lush and sensuous portrait fit for the Queen of the Sea. Whoever had designed her loved ships and knew the sea; he had designed her with his whole heart.

"She's beautiful," sighed Forsythe.

"I don't mind losing the *Ajax* so much now," Perry said.

The boat rowed around to her starboard side. The watch hailed them. "Ahoy the boat! Who goes there?"

"*Amphitrite!*" the lieutenants called back in triumph.

Horner rose from his seat in the sternsheets and let them look at him. On deck the standing officers and seamen would be scrambling to welcome the new captain aboard and wondering what kind of man he was. The boatswain's pipe shrilled and hands came running to line up.

Horner climbed the accommodation ladder and came in through the entry port. It was nice to have an entry port, although it would be a weak point during foul weather or combat. He was able to step onto the deck with the dignity befitting his rank instead of slithering over the gunwale like a deserter. He strolled between the sailors who formed the honor guard; she did not yet have her contingent of marines on board. At the end he was met by the master and his mates. They saluted. He raised his hat in return.

"Captain Ebenezer Horner. My commission." He pulled it from his breast pocket.

"Martin Bracegirdle, master. Welcome aboard, sir." Bracegirdle was a short round little man with short dark hair and mustache. His face was ruddy and genial. He wore a dark blue frock coat with a falling collar. He looked like a shopkeeper.

The junior officers clambered up the battens and manropes into the vessel behind the captain. Introductions were made all around, then Horner said, "Assemble the hands."

The pipes trilled and all hands lined up. It was only half the crew she needed and the deck was a mess with lines and pieces of wood. The carpenter had been at work building new trucks for the forecastle guns. Horner unfolded his commission and read it aloud in firm voice. He was now their lord and master, and only the King, through his representatives in the Admiralty, could overrule him. Not even God could contradict a captain on his quarterdeck. He folded up the commission.

Horner felt it was incumbent to make a speech. "I regard myself as a firm but fair taskmaster. Do your duty as you have been taught, and you will have nothing to fear. If you don't know your duty, ask. I don't expect a man to do what he doesn't know. But once you have learned it, I expect you to do it cheerfully and well.

"We will not winter at Spithead. We go out in advance of the new Mediterranean fleet and will be placed at the disposal of Commodore Whittingdon in Gibraltar. God willing, we will arrive before the autumn storms begin. The sooner we get to sea the sooner you will be enjoying the warm and sunny waters of the Mediterranean. Keep that in mind as you work."

They all brightened. Activity in the mild Mediterranean was infinitely preferable to an English winter spent at anchor.

Bracegirdle called, "Three cheers for Captain Horner! Hip, hip, huzzah!"

"Huzzah!" they shouted back. A few of the more enthusiastic fellows threw their caps in the air.

"Very good. Dismiss the hands. Gentlemen, stow your dunnage. All commissioned officers and senior warrant officers to meet in my cabin in half an hour."

"Aye aye, sir."

They went their separate ways. The stewards were left to stow the sea chests and other things. The officers prowled over the vessel examining everything and asking questions. Bracegirdle answered their questions with great pride.

"She's a hundred and thirty-five feet between perpendiculars, her greatest beam is thirty-six feet, and she drafts sixteen feet."

"That's almost ten feet longer than the *Ajax*, but hardly any wider or deeper!" Perry exclaimed.

"She used to be a privateer. We captured her from the Dutch," Bracegirdle explained.

"How fast?" Thorton wanted to know.

Bracegirdle smiled complacently. "Thirteen knots. She can really fly."

"Is she crank?" Abby asked.

The master shook his head. "She's a sweet sailer. She likes a light to moderate breeze over her quarter. She rolls in heavy weather, though. You don't want to keep too much sail aloft when the weather is lively."

They extracted all the essential details from the master, then trooped below to examine their berths. They had a handsome staircase leading below with just enough headroom in the wardroom for Thorton to stand up between the beams. Their cabins were a trifle larger than the *Ajax* and the deal bulwarks were hinged to swing up out of the way when clearing for action. A pair of twelve pounders shared the second cabin on each side. The first lieutenant's and the master's cabins had windows and roundhouses, but the master's cabin was cut a little short to provide a walkway so that the rest of the officers could reach the privy on that side.

A small amount of ornament continued on the inside: scallop shells were carved at the head of the pilasters around the windows, and seahorses were carved into medallions set in the middle of the louvered doors to their berths. The walls were painted pale green and the woodwork was white. The mizzenmast was located just forward of the bulkhead that separated the wardroom from the gundeck. That permitted a large table with a green and white checked cloth to occupy the center of the space without interruption. Doors with arched tops lead to the gundeck, passing on either side of the the companionway. Green wool curtains tied back with gold tassels screened the doorways. It was almost as gracious as a drawing room. Almost, but not quite. Sun dogs reflected from the water and danced across the deckhead.

"This is a mess that is going to have to spend some money to live up to the surroundings!" Perry announced. "How much shall we subscribe?"

They all had prize money. "Thirty pounds," suggested Forsythe. It was a moderate sum for a mess; some messes subscribed fifty.

Thorton was busy opening lockers. "What about dishes? Tablecloths? Teapots? We're going to have to equip her from scratch."

That made their faces droop. "Ten pounds for equipment, and thirty for food?" Perry suggested.

"That will eat up most of your prize money," Thorton said.

"Five pounds for equipment and twenty for victuals?" Forsythe suggested.

"Bracegirdle must have had something," Perry said.

"I think we ought to equip her new and not take castoffs. I'll buy the dishes and tablecloths," Thorton announced. With his captain's share of prize money he had almost as much as the rest of them put together.

Perry whistled. "The pinchpenny speaks!"

Thorton glared at him.

Jackson pulled out his watch. "We need to meet Horner. We don't want to be late."

Horner's had a handsome stateroom with a bulkhead to separate his sleeping chamber from the dayroom. A dark green curtain screened doorway between them. The walls were painted pale green and the woodwork white. The woodwork was carved more elaborately than the wardroom. It was a very handsome cabin with just enough headroom for a tall man to stand upright as long as he minded the beams. He had no table or chairs, but he had a secretary desk. He had no cushions for the locker tops, either. It was a very Spartan cabin.

"Tell me how you find our new command," he addressed them.

Forsythe gave a report of the particulars they had learned from the master. Horner listened, then passed out assignments. Forsythe was first lieutenant, Perry second, and Thorton third. They were content with the arrangements. Forsythe would oversee getting the ship ready, Perry would go ashore to requisition all that they were supposed to have from food to powder to hands, and Thorton would go ashore to make purchases for the officers and to equip the wardroom stores.

"Which reminds me. I've got a warrant for MacDonald, and I'll want notices drawn up calling the *Ajax's* crew to serve. They'll get the volunteer's bonus if they agree to join up. Thorton, take care of having the posters printed."

"Aye aye, sir."

"Any questions?"

Abby spoke up. "May I take passage to Gibraltar with you, sir?"

"The wardroom is going to be crowded with Chagall and Posonby. I leave it to you, gentlemen. Do we have room for Mister Abby?"

"He can berth with me, sir," Thorton volunteered.

"I'll take Posonby," Forsythe offered.

"I guess that means I get Chagall," Perry said.

"Very well. I agree. Any further questions? No? Dismissed."

As they rose and filed out, Horner said, "Mister Thorton, bide a moment."

Thorton waited until the other officers left. "Sir?" he asked.

"I need some furniture. Pick out a good table with several leaves and chairs for me. I'd like a pair of linen tablecloths for it, one fancy, one not. I'd also like an easy chair. You can spend up to seventy-five pounds to equip me. I'll write you a letter to act as my agent."

"Aye aye, sir."

A silence fell. Horner ruminated for a while, then said. "We are going to sea, Mister Thorton. We are not on the beach anymore."

"That's true, sir."

"I'm afraid Article Twenty-Eight comes between us."

Thorton licked suddenly dry lips. He nodded. "I understand, sir."

"I did not mean to trifle with you. I honestly thought it would be months before we received a post."

"I know, sir."

"That will be all."

"Aye aye, sir." Thorton saluted and made his exit.

Chapter 34 : Collision in the Solent

The *Amphitrite* raised anchor on a dreary morning in October. She ran slowly down the Solent with just the fore course; the main course was fouled. That was Perry's division. He swore and ran to fix it. It wasn't a pleasant task, not with snow mixed with sleet falling from a leaden sky. Slush accumulated an inch deep on deck and a stiff breeze was blowing out of the north. The officers were wrapped in tarpaulin coats and wearing sea boots, but the slush soaked their feet. The ordinary sailors were even worse off. They had to climb the slippery ratlines and inch their way along the cold, slushy yards. The main sail was finally cleared.

"Put the idlers to work sweeping the deck," Horner said.

"Aye aye, sir. Idlers to the brooms! Clear the slush off the deck!" Forsythe called.

Reluctantly men came out of their hiding places and into the raw wind.

"Stand by to set the fore topsail," Horner said in a conversational voice. He stood at the quarterdeck rail with his gloved hands in a muff. He had his collar up and a dark red muffler around his throat.

Now it was Thorton's turn. "Stand by to set fore topsail!" he bellowed.

The first man up found himself clinging to the yard as the footrope sagged beneath his weight. He was short enough and the footrope slack enough that he could barely get his arms over the yard to hang on. He certainly couldn't work like that.

Thorton roared, "Those horses want mousing! Why the hell do I even have a crew? I should have done it myself, ye sons of bitches!" He stormed up the shrouds to supervise the setting of the sails himself.

Above him men moved out along the yard to take their positions. Each man's weight on the footrope caused it to flex and sag in a new spot. The footrope was supposed to be stationery, but it kept jumping and changing position as each new man added his weight to it. They fumbled for footing, then one of them lost his grip on the slippery yard. With a yell he plummeted to the deck.

Thorton made a grab, but his fingers only brushed the man's jacket. The man crashed to the deck and a wave of slush splattered the sailors standing nearby. There was a moment of horrified silence.

The figure groaned and writhed.

"He's no dead!" a black sailor called.

Thorton held tight to the slippery shrouds. He squeezed his eyes shut and took a deep breath. He had a duty to do and so did the men aloft. The men on deck would take care of the fallen man. He continued climbing to the yardarm.

"Mind yourselves, men. And mind the man next to you. We're lucky Davy's not dead. Let's not repeat the accident."

Some of the men pulled at the gaskets to loosen the sails, but some didn't. "'Tis madness to be up in this weather!" a small bald man complained. "We'll all be killed!"

Thorton snorted. "'Tis nothing. 'Tis disagreeable, nothing more. Here, I'll help."

The sailors gave him startled looks when he edged out onto the footrope, but they moved over to give him room. He balanced carefully on the horse and untied the gasket in front of him. The men followed his example and the sail came loose and hung in its gear.

One of them said in a low voice, "Looks like he knows something about how to set a sail."

Thorton was making a gasket coil to hang neatly in front of the sail. "I should. I was captain of the foretop before I was called to the quarterdeck. Remember that. Do your work well and you could earn promotion. Horner's a fair man. You have a better chance with him than most captains."

They stared at him in amazement. They were a snaggle-toothed, pock-faced lot. Not one of them could read or write. "You were before the mast, sir?"

"I was a pressed man like the rest of you." He moved back to the shrouds. "Now come along. We'll mouse the horse when the weather clears."

They made their way down. Below them other hands were hauling the lines to trim the topsail. Reaching the deck Thorton inquired after Davy, but he had been taken to the cockpit.

"Broke his back, poor sod," a man told him.

Thorton wanted to visit him, but he couldn't as long as he was on duty.

The *Amphitrite* skimmed along. The Solent became increasingly choppy as they ran toward the Channel. The wind kicked up and she heeled. Men puked in the scuppers; vomit mixed with slush. Thorton yearned for Mediterranean heat and a seasoned crew. Many men from the *Ajax* had chosen to volunteer with them, but they compromised only half the crew.

He climbed back to the quarterdeck and saluted. "Topsails set, sir."

"Very good," Horner replied. He said nothing about the accident.

"We'll mouse the lines when the weather clears, sir."

"See that you do, Mister Thorton."

"Aye aye, sir."

It was not a rebuke, but it felt like one. With a million things to do in readying the ship, mousing the lines had escaped notice. Thorton felt bad about it, even though it had been the boatswain's job.

They suffered through a miserable set of maneuvers. They wore ship and tacked, let out and took in sail, and raised and lowered the topsails for hours. Everyone was thoroughly drenched and frozen by the exercise.

Horner said, "Enough. Change the helmsman. Let's go home."

Forsythe leaned over the rail and shouted, "Relief to the helm!"

The *Amphitrite* was rather old-fashioned; her helm was located in the coach, right before the mizzenmast and just aft the companionway. The coach provided the helm with a certain amount of shelter, but required her to be conned from above since the helmsman couldn't see anything. Not that it mattered in this weather; visibility was down to a quarter of a mile. The new helmsman came and took his place while the other one left it to go below gratefully.

They made their way close-hauled back up the Solent. They did not expect to meet anyone in weather like that, but they did.

"Sail fine on the larboard bow!" the lookout sang out. "Two cables!"

Horner pulled out his glass and studied the murk. All the officers did the same. The stranger was lateen-rigged. Shadowy in the distance behind her was another set of triangular sails.

Perry said, "Your rovers picked a hell of a day to weigh anchor."

Thorton shrugged. "The wind's over their starboard quarter. 'Tis the perfect point of sail for them. At this rate they could make Brest by suppertime tomorrow."

The two vessels were on course to pass abreast of each other, but Horner didn't trust the weather or his green crew. He decided to give the other vessel wider berth.

"Helm starboard two points."

"Helm starboard two points!" Forsythe called.

The new helmsman put the wheel over the wrong way.

The head of the *Amphitrite* swung into the wind. Everyone who was paying attention realized what was wrong and shouted a cacophony of criticism and orders. "Helm hard over!" "Wrong way!" "What the hell are you doing?"

The helmsman shouted back, "Ye said 'larboard!' and larboard it is!" He cranked the wheel as far as he could.

Horner shouted, "Belay that! Helm, fall off!" but the luffing of the sails drowned him out.

The *Amphitrite* hung for a moment and Thorton prayed for her to miss stays and stall, but she didn't. She tacked through and came onto her new course directly into the path of the xebec. The sails were taken aback and slatted violently. The foresail split.

The main topmast shuddered, wood cracked, and it toppled. It hung from its lines and dangled like a spear waiting to pierce through the deck right to the bottom. Perry was hard on Thorton heels, shouting, "Trice up the maintop!"

The xebec was close enough they could make out her sodden purple pennant: the *Sea Leopard*. She had been sailing complacently along, knowing she had the right of way and assuming that the *Amphitrite* would be competently handled. Now she clawed to windward in desperation. She was a shallower vessel than the *Amphitrite*; she made more leeway. The wind and tide continued to push her towards the British vessel.

Understanding his error at last, the helmsman corrected. He cranked the wheel hard over the other way.

"Belay that!" shouted Horner.

More cries rose up.

Forsythe bellowed, "Silence on deck! The cat for the next man who speaks out of turn!"

Having come around onto her new tack her only hope would have been to keep bending her course and hoping that she could turn tightly enough to evade the *Sea Leopard*, but when she tried to tack back, she luffed up and stalled. She did not have enough way on her after her previous turn. She was now sitting directly in the *Sea Leopard*'s path.

Horner tore halfway down the ladder to where he could see the helm and shout directly at him, "Port the helm! Brace those yards sharp!"

"I'm sorry, sir! I thought you said 'larboard!' afore," the helmsman cried.

The bow watch shouted, "Collision!"

"Prepare to fend off! Boathooks out!" Thorton shouted back. He scrambled up to the foredeck.

Half a dozen men got the long pikes out and prepared to brace against the impact. On the *Sea Leopard* the tinny clatter of the triangle sounded with extreme urgency. Her men had the boathooks out, but to no avail. The *Sea Leopard*'s bowsprit ran under the *Amphitrite*'s and tore out the watersail. The *Amphitrite*'s well steeved bowsprit rode up over the *Sea Leopard*'s prow and they fouled each other's headsails. That is to say, they fouled the *Amphitrite*'s jibs and the *Sea Leopard*'s foresail. The boathooks braced, but the two vessels weighed hundreds of tons each; mere muscle power was not enough to stop them. The bows clashed together with a wooden thunder that knocked Thorton off his feet. He sprawled on his back on the slushy deck, scrambled and slid in the icy mess, and got to his feet again.

Horner and Tangle climbed onto their respective foredecks to survey the mess. Tangle shook his fist and swore at them in Turkish. Remembering his English, he shouted, "What in the hell are you doing?"

"My apologies, Commodore. We made a mistake. May I respectfully suggest you set a stern anchor?"

The two vessels were locked together and slowly drifting towards the Isle of Wight. Tangle looked around at the mess and barked orders in Arabic. He said in English, "We're going to row out of it. If that doesn't work I'll drop a stern anchor."

The sweeps came out. The forward ones pushed against the *Amphitrite* while the others splashed into the sea. The Turkish drum beat the cadence and the men put their backs into it and rowed. Slowly the *Sea Leopard* backed up. Meanwhile the second Sallee xebec hove to and the orderly line of Sallee ships held their positions while their commander worked to disentangle himself. Had it been a line of green British ships putting to sea, a secondary collision would have been likely. Horner had taken his crew out on a training exercise for good reason.

The *Sea Leopard*'s fore antenna snagged in the forward shrouds of the *Amphitrite*.

"Avast rowing!" Horner bellowed.

Tangle was watching; he saw it. He shouted orders in Arabic and the rowers held water. Thorton and his crew jumped forward, slid in the slush, and started pushing and pulling at the shrouds and antenna. Their boots skidded on the wet deck and Thorton fell onto his hands and knees. He swore like a sailor.

"Ease the shrouds a little, Mister Thorton, and mind your language," Horner directed.

Normally the shrouds were kept snug but not tight; Horner did not like harpstrung standing rigging. Thorton and his men took a few turns on the turnbuckles to gently ease the shrouds. Yet the wind was coming over that side, so however much they loosened them, the wind blew the mast further and it tilted more to leeward. The windward shrouds never did ease up. The lee shrouds went slack and hung in curves while the mast slanted.

"I'll set an anchor," Tangle said.

That done, the vessels twisted slowly until they were streaming downwind from the anchor. The swinging caused the *Amphitrite*'s bow to turn more towards the wind and the fore stay took tension. That eased the shrouds and they were able to work the *Sea Leopard*'s antenna back through the shrouds and free it. The *Amphitrite* slowly dragged her bowsprit along the prow of the *Sea Leopard* with a loud and unpleasant scraping of wood, then drifted free. A ragged cheer went up on each side.

Tangle shook his fist at them, "You ruined my paint!"

Thorton went out on the *Amphitrite's* bowsprit and inspected.

Horner called to him, "What's the damage?"

Thorton hung on tightly to the head rails as he leaned out to look under the bowsprit. The last thing he wanted was to go overboard. "The spritsail is shredded and foul. The starboard clew is torn out and the sheet's in the water. The prow of the *Sea Leopard* went right through it."

"Retrieve the sheet. We'll jury-rig. Tighten the shrouds first."

"Aye aye, sir."

The *Sea Leopard* had problems of her own. Her forestay had parted and some of her headrails were broken. The headrails were not inconsequential; they provided footing for men working the foresail. A xebec carried a considerable amount of canvas well forward of her foredeck. Her foresail was torn down low where the antenna had fouled. Tangle surveyed the damage in disgust.

"Douse the sails. Out oars. We're going back to Spithead." This was all said in Arabic, but Thorton understood him. He translated for Horner. A minute later and Arabic signals were flying from the *Sea Leopard* to the rest of the Sallee fleet. They all put out their oars, turned around neatly in place, and rowed back to port.

Thorton envied them. He had to jury-rig then beat back up the Solent. The *Amphitrite* had four sweeps for maneuvering in harbor and that was it. They did not get back to their anchorage until three hours after the corsairs. Once back, they had to mend the damage. That required embarrassing explanations to the Admiralty and reparations to Tangle. Thankfully, Tangle did not press charges, although he did express himself in voluble Turkish to Horner who comprehended his meaning well enough even though he didn't speak a word of Turkish. With the bad weather turning worse it was days before either vessel was ready to sail again.

CHAPTER 35 : THE BLOODY ENSIGN

The *Amphitrite* battled contrary winds and foul weather for twelve days. She beat her way down the Channel and across the Bay of Biscay with snow, sleet, and rain sweeping over her in turn. When the sun appeared it was a white and watery orb. Mornings they often woke to find the deck and rigging completely iced up. Gradually as they struggled southward the days warmed so that the ice would melt by noon and they could climb the soggy rigging. Tempers were short and the landsmen were sick all the time. Accidents were common. Many men wound up with their ankles wrapped or their wrists braced from falling on the ice. The cold took its toll and they hid below decks and had to be chased out and started to work with the tawse or rope end.

The *Amphitrite* groaned in the choppy seas and leaked prodigiously. They were constantly at the pumps. Men who had once been proud of her good looks began to curse her for being as wet as a French whore. In such conditions she showed none of her good traits; she wallowed in the troughs of waves, showed no speed, and rolled more than British seamen thought proper. They swayed in their hammocks when they slept and their tables swayed when they ate. They often had cold meals because the weather was too rough to light the cook fires. The crew was sullen and the officers snappish. Only Horner remained indifferent to the weather.

Finally, on the twelfth day, the weather broke. The sky was as blue as Chinese porcelain without a trace of cloud. A vigorous sun beamed down and the rigging and sails began to steam as water evaporated in the warmer air. Men stood with their faces turned up to soak up the welcome sun, then dragged their wet things on deck to air them out and dry them off. It was chilly in the shade and damp, but slowly, very slowly, the sun dried them and they began to feel almost comfortable.

"Deck! Smoke on the southern horizon!" the lookout hailed them.

The officers were all gathered on the leeward side of the quarterdeck to let Horner have his walk on the windward side. Horner stopped his pacing and came to the leeward side with his glass in hand. Those who had spyglasses pulled them out. They could see a low white cloud on the horizon rising into the sky like a small thunderhead. They listened, but heard nothing.

"A fire at Eel Buff?" Perry suggested.

Horner replied, "I doubt we have been fortunate enough to find Eel Buff when we haven't been able to shoot the sun in three days. 'Tis either a burning ship or the coast of Spain." Spain would mean a navigational error of a hundred miles. Hardly unusual, especially given the weather, but Horner prided himself on doing better.

"I'll go to the masthead, if you please," Thorton volunteered.

"Please do."

Thorton swarmed up the damp ratlines, crawled around the futtock shrouds like a proper seaman, and joined the lookout in the top. From that height he could see more than the deck, but the smoke was rising from beyond the horizon. At that distance it meant something larger than a single ship was burning. A fleet on fire? He slid down the backstay and came to report.

"Helm two points to leeward, please," Horner ordered.

The *Amphitrite* came around on her new heading and began to gain speed. The wind was over her starboard quarter and she grew a creamy white mustache as her bow wave built up.

"I'll have all plain sails," Horner said conversationally. "Keep a sharp lookout."

The commands were made and echoed along the length of the ship. All the canvas shook out and dropped drenching loads of cold water on the men below. She gained speed and flew over the billowy sea with the grace of the goddess she was named for. Everyone's mood improved.

"Deck! I can see three columns of smoke now!" the lookout cried.

"Mister Thorton, would you be so kind."

"Aye aye, sir," Thorton replied, running for the shrouds before the order was even completed.

This time they had come close enough that he could make out the pyramids of white sails that were warships. He counted seven. Adding three columns of smoke meant at least ten vessels had joined in battle. He was too far away to make out the ensigns. "Deck! Seven vessels under sail, plus three burning! Five are pursuing two on a course southwest, all sails set!"

"Colors?"

"Not yet, sir!"

Horner called, "Come down, Mister Thorton." When the blond lieutenant arrived on the deck, Horner suggested, "We should have just enough time for a rubber of whist after our dinner, gentlemen."

Half of them groaned. To play whist with Horner was an acute trial to men who could not remember what cards had been played or to deduce what cards their partner must be holding by the way he played. Horner was a superb whist player.

"Couldn't we dance, please, sir?" Perry asked. "'Twill warm the blood."

Horner considered, then grunted his agreement. "Very well. But you'll dine with me, won't you gentlemen?"

They were all jittery over their meal of cold meat and raw potatoes. With the foul weather they'd had no practice with the guns. Should they have to fight they'd be in a bad way. They kept listening and yearning to go up and take a peek. Horner alone was unflappable. He dined and made small talk as if it were any other dinner. Thorton tried to imitate his phlegmatic demeanor. After thirty minutes they washed the food down with beer, then Horner said, "Mister Perry, you may call the fiddler to the weather deck."

Perry was up and out of his chair like a shot. Horner wiped his fingers carefully on the linen napkin. "Mister Perry is an avid dancer. Let us join him on deck. Commander Abby, may I have the pleasure of your company for a dance?"

"Certainly, sir," Abby replied and rose. He took Horner's elbow and let the man lead him out on deck. They filed out with him.

Horner asked for a stately minuet and the fiddler and fife obliged him. The dancers rose gracefully on their toes, then eased down again. Horner and Abby approached, presented their left arms, then Horner turned Abby through a slow and graceful three-quarter turn. Had Abby been wearing a dress it would have allowed him to display the elegant sweep of his skirts, but as it was, he could merely show a good leg. The midshipmen were pressed into service as ladies to partner with the commissioned officers, of which there was a superfluity, thanks to having so many passengers on board. Thorton found himself partnered with Midshipman Niall Jones. A mere thirteen years old the boy knew nothing of minuets and had to fumble his way along by watching the other dancers. Thorton made hands signs and hissed at him to help direct him, but it was not the pleasant experience it could have been. Perry, who was an excellent dancer, was partnered with midshipman Lemuel Jackson, who proved a passable dancer for the minuet, except that he kept forgetting he was supposed to be a lady and kept trying to lead.

They were in the middle of the reversed S figure when the masthead lookout shouted, "Deck! Spanish colors!"

The dance immediately halted. Thorton and the others ran to the quarterdeck and hauled out their glasses. The fiddler and fifer waited.

"Musicians stand down," Horner ordered. The man never lost track of anything.

The red and gold of the Spanish ensign could be made out on the squadron of five vessels that chased two more. The fleeing vessels were hull down and well south.

Horner snapped his spyglass shut. "Whoever flees the Spanish must be a friend of ours."

"What can we do?" Forsythe asked. "We are one frigate against a fleet of five."

Thorton called up, "Masthead! What colors on the burning ships?"

"None. They're struck."

Thorton surveyed the ships with his glass. The sails and rigging of two were already burnt; their masts were poles wreathed in smoke and supported no yards or pennants. The nearest vessel was burning in the bow, with a lateen yard crossing her mizzen. The antennas of the foremast and main were shattered on her deck and trailing over the side.

"She could be a French galley . . . Their privateers are likely cruising this area with Eel Buff as a base," Perry ventured.

"There is something familiar . . ." Thorton began. "By God! 'Tis the *Ajax*!"

Half a dozen officers clapped glass to eye and stared at the vessel nearest them. She was still three miles distant. She had raked masts for a lateen rig now, but the shape of her bow and the line of her quarterdeck was unmistakable.

"My God. You're right," Horner said.

"What shall we do?" Perry asked.

"Hoist the Spanish colors. We shall go in under a ruse and render what aid we can."

The Spanish ensign was pulled out of the box and raised up. It made them all uneasy, but they understood their danger. The false flag was the only cloak that could protect them from the more numerous Spanish.

Horner gave another order in a pleasant tone. "Studding sails, please. We may be able to save a few rovers if we make haste."

They closed warily with the burning *Ajax*. Those aboard had not given up; a gun pushed its nose through the gun port and barked at them.

"Haul down the Spanish colors. They have served their purpose. Hoist the British ensign. Keep a sharp eye out for the Spanish. If one of them falls behind or turns our way, I want to know instantly."

The red and gold of Spain came down to be replaced by the white ensign of England. They came near the frigate's stern; they wanted to be as far away as possible from the fire. Kasim Rais shouted over the quarterdeck rail at them in Arabic. He pointed and gesticulated.

"Send help," Thorton translated. "He wants help fighting the fire."

"Very well. You may send the launch with thirty men. It will return with any wounded. Mister Thorton, since you speak the language, you will lead."

"Aye aye, sir."

He called out his petty officers and men, and took midshipmen Bettancourt and Jackson with him, along with every bucket the *Amphitrite* had. They boarded the derelict *Ajax* and formed bucket brigades, one under the command of each midshipman, to add their powers to fighting the flames that consumed the forecastle. The Sallee sailors were already pumping and throwing water on the flames, but they could not quench the fire.

Thorton went to the quarterdeck. He stopped dead in his tracks when he saw the inert figure sprawled on the planks. He knelt swiftly. "My God! Isam!"

He touched the man's brow, but there was no response. He put his head down to listen and feel for breath; nothing. He put his head against the commodore's chest; he heard nothing. He looked up and tears started in his eyes. "What happened?"

"Gun exploded," Kasim Rais replied. "The Spanish have taken Eel Buff. They've got a squadron stationed there now. They came after us."

A bloody gash ran across Tangle's dark hair and down the side of his face. His turban and part of his scalp was torn and strewn on the deck. A great puddle of blood surrounded his head. The brown eyes were closed, and the face was composed as Thorton had never seen it, not even in sleep. The high brow was smoothed of all lines and the nose with the small hump where it had been broken years before was a long line to the slightly parted lips. Coagulated blood soaked the hair and beard along the right side of his face. The broad chest neither rose nor fell. The strong arms lay slack in their purple clothes while the gold lace on his chest gleamed brightly in the sunlight. Pieces of the shattered gun and carriage lay on the quarterdeck. The flagstaff was broken and the purple flag with the white crescent moon and star was torn in several places and smudged with black marks as it draped over the taffrail.

Thorton wept as he folded the mahogany dark hands on the corsair's breast. He used the cuff of his coat sleeve to wipe his face. "We must give him a proper burial."

Kasim's face was grimy with gunpowder and smoke. His multicolored coat was stained with blood and ash. He looked away for a long time, then said, "My sister loved him. We'll bury him in the bilge and take him home, if we can save the ship."

The *Ajax* was settling by the stern. She creaked ominously and the men fighting the fire between her decks and on her weather deck retreated as the fire advanced.

"We will take off your wounded, sir. Isam Rais with them. If you can save the ship, we will return them to you."

"Do it," Kasim replied curtly. Then he walked forward to stand at the rail and watch the fire fighting efforts. The massive length of the main antenna was sprawled over the side and the forward end was burning. "Send the antennas overboard!"

The sailors looked up, broke off their fire fighting efforts, and gathered to hoist up the mighty spar and heave it into the sea. The burning end splashed and hissed as it hit the water. With the antennas gone, they had more room to work, but the fire crackled and heat curtains danced above the deck.

Thorton gathered up the torn and bloody ensign and lifted the fallen corsair onto the purple silk. He wrapped the body, then called for some of his own sailors to help him. They knotted the silk ends of the great flag, then carried the corpse down the ladder and into the launch. Wounded men were put into the boat along with their dead commander.

The forward hatch collapsed with a great shower of sparks and a cry sounded from the men below decks. Panicking men ran aft and came up the rear companionway to escape the inferno below. Confused cries in Arabic and other languages spread the panic on deck. Kasim watched as the English kept plying their buckets. Their boy officers exhorted them to do their duty and throw more water on.

"Abandon ship," Kasim Rais ordered. He descended the ladder from the quarterdeck.

The triangle began to beat a tune Thorton had never head before, but he knew what it meant. He shouted, "*Amphitrite*! Fall back! Tritons, abandon ship!"

Bettancourt and Jackson gave up their work, collected their men and buckets, and came back to the launch. They climbed in with the wounded and the launch stroked back to the *Amphitrite*. The *Ajax* launched her own boats and the crew piled into them, but there was more crew than there were seats in the boats, even with thirty wounded taken off by the English. Horner was watching; he sent the gig and cutter to the aid of the *Ajax*.

The launch arrived at the *Amphitrite*. A boatswain's chair was waiting for the wounded, but they lashed the body of the dead corsair into it first and Tangle was hauled up. Thorton scrambled up the battens and onto the weather deck. He knelt beside the purple clad corpse and wept bitter tears.

Abby knelt on the other side and asked, "Who is it?"

"Tangle," Thorton replied. He peeled back the purple silk to show corsair's bloody face.

Abby bowed his head and began to pray. "Our Father, Who art in Heaven, Hallowed by Thy name, Thy kingdom come, Thy will be done, on Earth as it is in Heaven . . ."

The wounded rovers turned out to contain a number of Englishmen who had been hired to help take the purchases to Africa. They were a mixed lot of black, white, and brown who spoke half a dozen languages. They were all taken to the cockpit.

Horner came down. "Mister Bettancourt, Mister Jackson, take the launch back to the *Ajax*. Rescue as many as you can."

"Aye aye, sir." The middies went back over the side.

Horner stood gazing at the fallen corsair, then removed his hat. He held it over his heart and said, "A giant has fallen and an age has come to an end. The world will not see his like again."

"I'll stitch the shroud myself, sir," Thorton said.

"Of course." Horner returned his hat to his head. "Pass the word for Weatherby and his kit."

The sailmaker came up, but Thorton didn't let him or his mates help. He borrowed the man's tools to sew the corsair into the purple shroud himself.

CHAPTER 36 : THE PURPLE SHROUD

Thorton started at the foot and neatly whipped the edge of the purple Sallee flag to itself. He bound it snug around Tangle's lower legs, boots and all. He kept sewing up past the knees and muscular thighs. A pang struck him as he remembered how virile and vigorous the man had been. He bitterly repented of his own uncertainty and stubbornness that had not let him fully enjoy what had been offered when he had had the chance. Now it was too late.

"His wife is pregnant. Seven children and a widow!" Thorton finally sympathized with the wife who had been his rival for the corsair's love.

The *Amphitrite*'s officers gathered round to watch.

"Say what you will, but he was a man," Abby said.

The officers nodded agreement.

"He was a rogue of the better sort," Perry grudgingly admitted.

Thorton bit off another piece of thread and stitched the purple across the man's groin, up to his waist, and across his lean belly. Another thread continued up over the hands resting on the chest and then to the collarbone. He shuddered as his fingers felt the stiffness of the beard beneath the silk. Although the rest of the body was slack, the beard still bristled. It gave him a cold frisson down his spine. He opened the silk to reveal the majestic visage. Tears ran down his face and dripped onto the silk. He sniffled and rubbed his nose with his sleeve.

He fumbled with the needle, dropped it, picked it up and dropped it again.

Abby knelt beside him and gave his arm a squeeze. "I'm sorry, Peter. I know he was dear to you."

Thorton nodded. "I learned so much from him. He was a damn fine mariner and a leader of men. Nothing was impossible for him."

The launch bumped along side, then more wounded were swayed up in the boatswain's chair. Kasim Rais came aboard. He paused when he saw the British gathered around the purple figure with their hats off. Some of his officers hurried over and let out a keening wail. Slowly Kasim joined the group. He pulled out a big white silk handkerchief and rubbed his face. It came away black and his face was none the cleaner.

"What happened?" Horner asked him in Spanish.

"The Spanish have taken Eel Buff," Kasim replied in bad Spanish. "They chased us, caught three, boarded two. We were on fire, so they left us while they chased the others. They caught them and set them on fire."

"The *Sea Leopard*?" Thorton asked, forcing himself to thread the needle again.

"Running with the *Seven Stars*. Isam Rais was on board the *Ajax* to meet with me. He couldn't get back to his own ship when the Spanish attacked."

Thorton took a deep breath to steady his hand, then closed the purple silk over the rover's face. Steeling himself to complete what he had begun, he braced the needle. It was the English custom to put a stitch through a dead man's nose to prove that he was really dead. With grim determination, he plunged the needle through the tip of the commodore's nose.

A muffled moan came from within the silks and Tangle's head twitched.

"He's alive!" Thorton shrieked. He swiftly withdrew the needle and tore open the purple silk to reveal the corsair's frowning face. He was still unconscious, but the piercing of his nose had made him groan. Many hands tore at the silks and knives came out to shred the purple shroud and free the wounded man. Even Kasim Rais knelt and helped claw the purple silk away from the fallen rover.

Somebody poured a bucket of water over the rover's head. His eyes blinked open and he stared upward with unseeing eyes.

"Isam! Isam!" Kasim shook his shoulder.

"Isam! Rais! Habibi!" Thorton called and squeezed his hand.

A cheer went up from a dozen throats and more hands shook the wounded man.

"Gentlemen! Easy, if you please! If you must do something, carry him to my cabin," Horner admonished them. "Dr. Ferncastle!"

Eight men picked up the edges of the purple silk and carried the semi-conscious rover into the great cabin. He was put into Horner's hanging cot. Ferncastle arrived in his green coat and chased out everyone but Horner, Thorton, and Kasim. He examined the head wound, inspected the corsair's eyes, and felt his pulse.

"He needs to be bled a little and his scalp stitched. It looks a bloody mess, but he is merely stunned from the explosion and has a good chance of recovery."

The mariners retreated and left Ferncastle and his mate to tend the unconscious corsair.

Eventually Thorton and Kasim were allowed back in. They both stood watch over the sleeping man, but Tangle did not recover consciousness that night. Horner had a hammock slung for himself in the day room and hammocks slung for Thorton and Kasim along side the convalescent corsair. By mutual agreement, Thorton and Kasim took turns sitting up with the man. Any moan or movement brought them to their feet to attend him. In this manner they cared for him, and even managed to get him to drink a little water. He was never sensible, although at times he seemed aware of their presence.

At dawn, Horner came into the sleeping chamber to get a clean shirt and drawers. He put a gentle hand on Thorton's shoulder. "Mister Thorton. There is nothing more to do. Do not exhaust yourself. He is in God's hands. Or Allah's, according to his belief."

Thorton rose tiredly. He was stiff and sore from not sleeping, but he nodded. He shuffled into the day cabin.

"You're not yourself. Here's a shirt. Let me help you get dressed."

Thorton let Horner help him out of his old shirt and into the borrowed one, to wash his face and shave, and to share his breakfast. It felt good to be helpless and let someone else coddle him. Once he had eaten some oatmeal and had a little beer, he revived.

"Thank you, Captain."

Horner smiled. "I am pleased to help, Mister Thorton."

"Do you think he will recover?"

"Dr. Ferncastle is optimistic. He says it looks worse than it is."

Thorton took some comfort from that. "I thought I would lose my mind when I saw him dead on deck like that. His head was lying in a pool of his own blood."

Horner's gaze turned inward and he nodded. "I mourned when my wife died, even if our marriage was unhappy." He reached for the brandy. They each had a shot, then he put the bottle away.

Abby came and knocked on the door. He was admitted and allowed to sit with Tangle. Kasim was tired and cranky; he ate breakfast, washed, then crawled into his hammock and slept. He'd lost a ship and regained a brother-in-law. It did not seem a fair trade to him.

Thorton went out on deck. The *Ajax* had burned to the waterline and was drifting as a dismasted and blackened hulk. The *San Idelfonso* and the *Santa Casilda* were sunk. The Spanish had boarded them and done a thorough job of their destruction. Debris floated on the water. There was no sign of the Spaniards, nor of the *Sea Leopard* and *Seven Stars*.

Horner surveyed the scene. "We must reconnoiter Eel Buff and make a full report. Make sail, course northwest by west. We should raise Eel Buff about noon, if Kasim Rais' calculation of our position is correct. Get the hands a hot meal before then. Let them have apples as a treat, it will help their mood. Feed the guests the same."

"Aye aye, sir," Blakesley and Forsythe replied.

Horner continued giving orders. "Mister Forsythe. Many of the rovers are hired British hands. Sort them out. If there are any able to work, ask them to volunteer. Add them to the quarter-bill; we may need them if things get hot around Eel Buff."

The *Amphitrite* was jam-packed with men; in addition to taking the men off the *Ajax*, they had spent the night picking up survivors from the other vessels and searching the area. Although the *Ajax* had suffered heavy casualties when bombarded by a Spanish battleship, the majority of her crew was still alive and about half of them were able to work. Most of the ratings were Englishmen. Parliament had not authorized much expansion for the navy to fight Spain and the merchantmen were winding down their seasons to wait out the winter, therefore a good many unemployed sailors had been willing to let somebody pay them to go to the Mediterranean where they could spend a warm winter chasing pretty women.

A marine guard came up, "Begging your pardon, sir, but one o' them blackamoors is babbling Spanish. I don't know what 'e wants, but 'e said Mister Thorton's name."

"I'll go see." Thorton descended the windward ladder and found Lieutenant Suhail at the bottom. The blackamoor leaned on the rail to ease his left leg. His face was carefully neutral as he waited for Thorton.

"*Salaam, Suhail,*" Thorton greeted him in Arabic. "How are you?"

Suhail had a medium complexion, short cropped nappy hair, and no turban. He had tied a white cloth over his head. He wore a short azure jacket above tan pantaloons. The left leg was stained brown from the blood he'd spilled. The torn fabric hung down and exposed a portion of his muscular brown thigh with a white bandage.

"I'll recover. Took a ball in the thigh. The officers want to know if we can come up to the quarterdeck. We're badly crowded."

"Let me ask Horner Rais."

Permission was granted, so Lieutenant Suhail struggled up the steps. The word was passed, and several other Moorish officers, some no more than boys, straggled onto the quarterdeck. Thorton made introductions. The pale-faced Englishmen greeted their swarthy guests politely, but their startled looks showed they were not accustomed to men of color serving as commissioned officers. French turned out to be the common language as most of the British officers and several of the Salletines spoke it. Horner inquired after their welfare and called for chairs. The ship's carpenter swiftly threw together some hammock chairs and they were brought up. The wounded men eased into them with grateful sighs. One of their servants was allowed to attend them; he was a French boy about thirteen years of age.

Perry's lip curled and he whispered to Thorton, "It isn't right to see white boys waiting on black men."

Thorton glared at him. "I'm a quarterblood myself, but you shared a room with me!"

"You aren't black, Peter. You're only part Indian, and the Indian is superior to the African in capacity."

"This Indian has held command over you, so mind your manners!"

Perry glared back. "You're third lieutenant to my second, and I'll pay you to remember it!"

Thorton's head jerked back. He snapped a salute and said, "Aye aye, sir!" He stalked over to stand next to Suhail.

CHAPTER 37 : THE CHASE

"A sail! Fine on the port bow!"

Every man on deck tensed. Thorton, who had just started down the ladder to the weather deck, paused and looked over the side. He could not see anything in the hazy distance.

Horner looked over the quarterdeck rail and asked, "If you would be so kind, Mister Thorton."

"Aye aye, sir." Thorton swung up into the main shrouds. Joining the lookout in the top, he pulled his glass and scanned the horizon. He watched it a while. The strange vessel was white dot on a course perpendicular to the *Amphitrite*, running southeast as they ran northeast.

"Course southeast!" he called down. He continued watching.

"Chase her," Horner said. "All sails, please."

The *Amphitrite*'s cloud of canvas broke open over head. She threw up a froth of spume from her bow wave and every man felt the rush in his veins as she tore along. The wind whipped their hair and filled their coats with cold.

"Toss the log."

"Ten and a quarter, sir!" Jones squeaked as his voice broke.

At such a rate they were sure to overtake their prize, but she had a goodly head start. There was nothing to do but wait.

Perry was officer of the watch and remained on deck with Horner. He pulled out his spyglass, but he couldn't see anything. Horner began to walk the quarterdeck at a stately pace. Fifteen paces aft, turn, fifteen paces forward, turn again. Back and forth he went at a slow stroll.

After a quarter of an hour, Thorton called down, "Lateen sail, sir!"

"Spanish galley?" Perry asked.

Horner paused to consider. "Possibly." He removed his own spyglass from his pocket and examined the horizon.

As Thorton watched, the strange vessel suddenly turned onto a new course: southwest. To pursue her they would have to tack back and forth across the eye of the wind.

"She's seen us! She's running to windward!"

He swiftly wrapped his arms and legs around the backstay and slid down to the deck. He dropped lightly to the wood and ran up to Horner. "'Tis the *Arrow*, I think."

"Are you sure?"

"No, but I know how to find out. With your permission, sir, I'll fire the Sallee private signal."

"Carry on."

Thorton ran down the companionway to the orlop deck, stuck his head in the gunroom, and said, "Carson! I need four guns ready to fire a signal, instantly."

The gunroom officers — gunner, boatswain, purser, carpenter, sailmaker, midshipmen — rose from their seats. "Are we clearing for action?"

"No. I think 'tis a Sallee rover. We need to signal them."

Thorton went up again and hurried to the foredeck. He met Midshipman Sinclair there. The lad was about eighteen or nineteen. His light brown pony tail hung down his back and he had a mustard stain on the front of his coat from hastily trying to shove the rest of his food into his mouth as he came on deck.

"I need four guns, quick to make the Sallee private signal."

Sinclair said, "Aye aye, sir," and ran down the forward companionway, bawling for his subdivision. Down below his men left their hanging tables, dodged among their shipmates, and ran up to answer the call. They pulled the six pounders back and pulled the tampions from the muzzles. Barefoot boys ran up with the cartridges.

Finally, five minutes after the order was given, the first gun spoke. A few seconds later, the second boomed out. A few more seconds, and the third gun belched smoke and fire. Thorton counted off a pause of ten seconds, then gave a curt nod. "Fire!" The last gun boomed.

Thorton ran to the foremast top and studied the distant vessel. She continued on her course. He knew all on board must be anxiously peering through their glasses at the strange ship. What did they make of her? Was it the *Arrow*? Was she a prize in Spanish hands? Or did she fear a ruse by the Spanish? Or was it entirely a stranger?

Thorton hurried to the quarterdeck to report.

"I'm sure it is the *Arrow*, sir."

Horner said, "Break out the studding sails. Course southwest as close by the wind as you can lay her."

"Aye aye, sir," Perry replied.

The sailors swarmed aloft to set the studding sails. As the additional sails caught the wind the *Amphitrite*'s speed increased.

"Heave the log," Horner said. He stood at the binnacle with his hands clasped behind his back. He was as calm as if he were standing in a public park surveying flowers, but the smile on his face betrayed the love he felt for a good fast ship as she flew through the water. The *Amphitrite* leaped over the seas. Her slim form shot ahead and she ran as lightly as the goddess for which she was named.

"Twelve knots, sir!" Midshipman Jones reported.

"What speed can the *Arrow* make?"

"Ten at best, sir," Thorton replied.

Horner did the math in his head. If they were on the same course, they would overtake her in an hour. But she could run a point closer on the wind than they could. At the end of the hour, they would be abreast but more than two miles distant. Still, they could get upwind of her and bear down on her. Once they had the weather gauge, she would be theirs. She knew that. She would deny them the weather gauge by running northwest. That would take her towards Eel Buff.

"Very good. Gentlemen, I suggest you take your dinner. Let the men eat before we clear for action. This will be a long chase."

"Thank you, sir."

They retired below and ate quickly while they could, washing it down with red wine. Thus fortified, they donned their better uniforms so as to cut a more imposing figure to their own men, and if necessary, the enemy. Properly attired in silk stockings with their pistols primed and ready in their coat pockets, they came back on deck.

The fugitive vessel saw them closing and made her tack to the northwest. The sails thundered in the luff, but the *Amphitrite*'s head swung around onto the new course and she continued her pursuit. Again the galiot's advantage of sailing a point closer to the wind meant their courses slowly diverged. Yet the *Amphitrite* had such an advantage of sail that the galiot's escape was by no means certain. Once they headreached her they would have the weather gauge.

The chase went on. By noon they sighted Eel Buff to the north as a low grey-green mass on the horizon. The galiot shied away and ran southwest again. Now they had a new worry. They must be visible to the watch tower on top of Eel Buff.

"Hoist the Spanish colors," Horner said.

The red and gold of Spain flew over their deck once again. That a Spanish frigate should pursue a lateen-rigged stranger was perfectly appropriate. No vessel came out of Eel Buff. Slowly they gained on the galiot. The *Arrow* ran northwest once more.

The officers waited tensely. Horner remained serene. He had not gone below, but he had accepted bread and cheese and eaten them neatly while standing on the quarterdeck. He studied the wind and sky, glanced back at Eel Buff, then gave his order, "Course due north."

The *Amphitrite* flew like a giant bird. Spume flew from her bow and the wind blew over her starboard quarter. Their hair ribbons blew out sideways. Eel Buff loomed larger. The galiot tacked again, cutting away from the island. She was not Spanish then, or she would be seeking refuge under the guns of Eel Buff. The *Amphitrite* swept after the smaller vessel like a hawk stooping on a dove.

"Cast the log."

"Cast the log, aye," said Chambers. He had replaced Jones at the changing of the watch. Half a minute later and he said, "Half less thirteen."

The officers all looked at each other and grinned. She was the fastest vessel they had ever served aboard. "I'll thank you to tighten the lee sheets just a bit, Mister Perry."

That was done, and the *Amphitrite* gained a trifle in speed. Within the hour Eel Buff had fallen behind the horizon. "Lower the Spanish flag," Horner directed. They were glad to remove the enemy ensign.

The *Arrow* was just ahead of them, a half mile distant, no more. She flew no ensign, but they could see purple coats on her quarterdeck through their glasses.

"Hoist the white ensign," Horner directed.

The white flag went up and streamed behind them. The British jack was in the canton.

"Fire a challenge."

The signal gun puffed out a cloud of smoke and thunder of noise. The vessel did not slow nor make any token of submission.

"Pass her on the starboard," Horner directed.

Once they had pulled abreast, the officers of the *Arrow* — for it was truly her — could see their flag and make out their uniforms. Thorton took off his hat and waved so that they could see his blond hair. Aboard the *Arrow* the purple ensign rose and the white crescent and star could be seen streaming in the breeze. The *Arrow* spilled her wind then, and the *Amphitrite* spilled hers. They eased together until there was half a cable between them. Thorton waved and the purple-clad officers waved back at them.

"May I go over, sir?"

"Invite them to join us," Horner replied.

"Begging your pardon, sir, but two of the lieutenants are Englishmen. They won't come over."

"Very well, Mister Thorton. You may go over." He gave Thorton a long penetrating stare. "You will return, won't you?"

Thorton had become so accustomed to British authority that desertion had not entered his mind. Now that Horner had said it, he gazed with longing at his former command. His tongue ran around his lips as he remembered the people aboard her: Lieutenants Aruj, Foster, and Nazim, the midshipmen and crewmen, the men he had rescued from a Spanish galley, his own capacious cabin, and the right to love as he pleased. He gazed at her with yearning.

"Belay that, Mister Thorton. Mister Suhail!" Horner said crisply.

Thorton gave him a bewildered look while the African officer limped forward. "Sir?" He had learned a few words of English.

"Lieutenant Suhail, please make arrangements for the *Arrow* to take off as many of the Moors and Turks as possible. We'll keep the Englishmen ourselves." He spoke French so that the black officer would understand him. "Mister Chambers. Make a signal, 'Send boat.'"

It was the light-skinned Lieutenant Nazim that came aboard. An African man with keen features, hazel eyes, and a slender build, he clambered up the accommodation ladder with ease. The other rovers descended to the weather deck to meet him and jabber in their own language. They informed one another of their various adventures and clapped each other on the back. The officers of the *Arrow* had been in dread. Not expecting to meet any British ship, they were certain that the *Amphitrite* was a Spanish coastguard. When she had hoisted the Spanish colors near Eel Buff, they had been certain of it.

A sudden hush fell over the crowd as a lean dark figure emerged from the coach. Putting his hands out to push off the passageway walls for support, Tangle shuffled onto the weather deck. His head was bound with a white bandage and the right side of his beard had been shaved to let the surgeon stitch up the gash along his jaw, but he was awake. In a display that none who saw it would soon forget, Nazim got down on all fours and bade the corsair to sit on him. Tangle did. With the lieutenant for a seat, Tangle listened to the reports of the various officers in Arabic.

CHAPTER 38 : ASSAULT ON EEL BUFF

The sun was going down in the west and the moon had not yet risen. The *Amphitrite* approached Eel Buff with the Spanish colors flying from her flagstaff. Two cables behind her came the *Arrow* with the Spanish ensign mounted above the Sallee ensign, an apparent captive of a Spanish frigate. The lieutenants had turned their cuffs down so that the white lining did not show. The midshipmen had turned their collars up to hide the white inside. At that distance they hoped the sentry on top of mountain would not be able to tell their uniforms were not cuffed and trimmed in red in the Spanish style. Being blond and speaking excellent Spanish, Thorton was posing as a Spanish lieutenant and prizemaster for the *Arrow*. Lieutenants Foster and Aruj were on deck and visible while Nazim and the other officers of color stayed hidden.

They curved around the west side of the island at a distance of two miles. Both vessels were cleared for action and every man was tense at his post. Marines and Moors stayed below decks or crouched below the gunwales to stay hidden. As they rounded the northwest point, they came in view of the fortress that sat on a ridge overlooking the harbor and guarded its entrance. The hill was only about a hundred and fifty feet above the water and had gently sloping sides. Behind it the ridge rose higher to join the mountain that made up the principle bulk of the island. The fortress was mud brick and housed a garrison of two hundred men and twenty twenty-four pounders. Approaching to within a mile of the fort, they made the Spanish recognition signal. In a prodigious (and very useful feat of memory) Thorton had memorized a captured Spanish signal book the summer before. They held their breaths and hoped the signals had not been changed.

The answer was given, the signal flags barely visible in the gloaming. Iridescent white foam bubbled on the wave caps and the breeze was fitful and failing. The *Amphitrite* gave her salute, followed by the *Arrow*. The fortress replied. The *Amphitrite* stood off and the *Arrow* passed her and entered the harbor mouth. The entrance to the harbor was notoriously shallow; it surprised no one that the *Amphitrite* dropped her anchors outside. It was not even strange that she rigged springs on them, either. When there was no telling what might come out of the night, she must be able to maneuver even if at anchor. The *Arrow*, being a type of galley, had the shallow draft and rowers necessary to enable her to enter the harbor.

The Spanish harbormaster and the health inspector came out in a gig together and boarded the *Arrow* without suspicion. Thorton met them as they came over the gunwale and greeted them in perfect Spanish as they set foot on his deck. "Welcome aboard the Sallee rover *Arrow*. I am Lieutenant Peter Thorton of the British navy. You are my prisoner."

The marines leveled their muskets and the Spaniards dropped their jaws. "I protest!" the harbormaster exclaimed. He was a slender pale man with fine light brown hair and blue eyes. He wore a long black coat and matching breeches with a dove grey waistcoat above grey silk stockings.

"Duly noted. Take them below." The marines escorted them below decks. More marines pointed their guns at the men in the gig and ordered them aboard. Slowly they climbed up the battens and into the vessel. All the Spaniards were confined below.

Thorton turned climbed back to the poop deck and gave his orders. "Run her on the beach. Marines stand by to disembark."

The galiot rowed onto the beach without opposition or any sign of interest from the shore. Lights were lit in various establishments and the taverns were doing a lively business. That boded well; it meant soldiers were on leave to roister in the town rather than keep watch. The more of them drunk in the taverns, the better for the attackers.

"Launch the rocket."

Aruj gleefully lit the fuse. It sparked and glowed in the dusk, then shot into the night sky with a shriek and burst red over head. Immediately the first gun from the *Amphitrite* roared. Three seconds later and the second gun spoke. In the fortress the alarm was immediately sounded and everyone ran to their posts and looked out at the *Amphitrite* bombarding them. Another gun spoke.

In those few seconds, while the Spanish were looking out to sea instead of into the harbor, the Sallee soldiers rushed over the side and onto the beach. Making the beachhead was the most vulnerable time; the minutes of confusion that reigned in the Spanish headquarters were enough for them to run for shelter amid the buildings with Kasim Rais leading them.

The fortress' guns were all pointed out to sea or into the harbor entrance. It would take a few minutes before they could turn some of the guns around to batter the *Arrow*.

Tangle spoke in Arabic, "I have the deck, rais. Take your force ashore."

Thorton flourished his fingers in the Muslim way. "You have the deck, sir." He went to the weather deck, and shouting in English, cried, "Tritons, follow me!" The Englishmen followed him over the sides. They splashed through shallow water onto the beach.

A few Spanish soldiers ran out of the taverns and took shots at them, then retreated back inside. Kasim's force was already rooting them out. Thorton had been afraid of that. Kasim reacted to what was in front of him; he did not keep the long range goal in sight. That was why he was given the task of securing the beachhead while Thorton led an English party through the streets and up the hill to the fortress. A portion of the Muslim force moved with him, setting up sentries, taking to the rooftops, and guarding the cordon along which he would have to retreat. Somewhere in the darkness he heard the crash of doors broken open and a woman screaming. He gritted his teeth and kept going. What Kasim's men did was on his head. Tangle had ordered no looting; the Sallee commodore would deal with him later.

Suddenly he heard the thunderous roar of the *Arrow's* twin thirty-two pounders. Instinctively he startled and looked for cover, then sheepishly recovered himself. He hoped the men were not laughing at him, but they had jumped, too. The fortress had her guns limbered up and answered the *Amphitrite*; the thunder of artillery echoed from the hills. Lurid red flashes lit up the evening.

Thorton's column came out from between the houses and onto the dirt track leading up to the fortress. Dusty trees lined the road. A hundred yards of woods lead to a barren pasture that surrounded the fortress. They kept under the eaves of the trees, but the Spanish launched rockets and in the red glare, caught sight of movement in the trees. Muskets barked and balls tore through the leaves overhead.

Thorton took shelter behind a tree at the edge and surveyed the ground they had to cross. The *Arrow's* guns spoke again; Tangle had her off the beach and she was shelling the fortress in support of the attacking English. A shot slammed into the pasture and tore up a divot as it went bounding through the tall grass. Ironically, the Spanish rockets helped the Sallee gunners find their marks. A second ball buried itself in the dun colored wall to the right of the gate with no discernible damage.

Thorton passed the word and they hunkered down to wait. He kept his ears peeled as he listened to the *Amphitrite*'s guns pounding at the fortress and the fortress answering in kind. More balls plunked into the pasture closer to the fortress, then dropped inside the fort. He wished he had some way to communicate with the *Arrow* to direct her fire more carefully, but all he could do was wait and trust Aruj's gunnery. He had trained the boy himself, and he had been promoted to lieutenant of a Sallee rover at the age of fifteen because of his skill in gunnery.

A thirty-two pound ball smashed squarely into the gate and the men who saw it gave a cheer. Thorton whirled on them. "Silence! I'll have the names of every man who so much as farts without permission!" They quieted.

Thorton detailed two marines. "You two, come with me. The rest of you, stand silent. Chambers, see that they obey. I'm going to see if I can see the ships."

Silent nods and a whispered, "Aye aye, sir," responded.

Thorton and his escorts began moving furtively through the autumn trees. "Silently!" he hissed as the marines stepped on leaves and sticks and shoved their way through brush.

Remembering his boyhood jaunts gunning for ducks and other sports in Maryland, Thorton moved as stealthily as a red Indian through the undergrowth. Once he had worn moccasins and put his feet down toes first to test the ground and not set his foot until he was sure of silent and secure footing. He did the same now. It took him over a quarter of an hour to work his way through the woods to see the sea.

The *Amphitrite* was still at anchor. She swung on her springs to bring one broadside and then the other to bear. Her range of movement was small and the Spanish had found her range, but half their shots were falling harmlessly into the sea. She had lost her mizzen topmast, but he was too far away to make out much more than that. He watched the Spanish gunnery a bit longer. The gunners in the fortress were slower and not as accurate, but their balls were bigger. When they hit, they hit hard. He turned to take a look at the *Arrow*. She had a few oars out and was rowing back and forth to confound the aim of the gunners in the fortress. The fortress had managed to work a pair of guns around to bear on the harbor, but they had not found their range as yet. More balls rained on the fortress from both ships.

Thorton worked his way back to his men. The wall of the fortress was twenty feet high on this side, and the gate was damaged but not broken. He must time his rush to the point where the ships had done the maximum possible damage to weaken his target, but had not yet been fatally wounded by the fortress. The advantage was to the land force; although the ships had more guns, the fortress had heavier guns and stronger defenses.

Musket fire on the beach rattled in a sudden volley. The two guns pointing into the harbor boomed out. Things were getting hot down there. He turned to his men and hissed, "Now!"

They leaped from their places and rushed across the pasture. Teams of two carried makeshift ladders. They rushed past him as he turned to beckon to them. He joined the silent rush to the wall. The ladders went up and men scrambled up them.

He drew his sword and pistol and shouted, "For God and King!"

"For God and King!" they roared back. The British swarmed up the ladders. The defenders fired down on them.

Balls whined around Thorton as he ran along the base of the wall. "Up, up! Go, go!" he shouted at them. Men swarmed up. Other men fell back dead or wounded. "Press on!" he shouted. "Force the wall!"

His men threw themselves at the ladders. The Muslims troops that accompanied them reloaded their muskets as fast as possible to fire at the defenders. The best marksmen had been given to him to make this assault. A man fell at Thorton's feet to writhe and gush blood from his throat. He felt a ball snatch at his sleeve, but no pain. A ladder toppled down, overturned by the Spanish defenders. A body fell to the ground with a heavy thud and lay groaning. On the wall above his head British tars battled Spanish soldiers. The rattle of swords and the bark of muskets punctuated the fight. Thorton found himself at the foot of a ladder and ran up it, sword in hand. Before he was halfway up Spanish defenders seized the top and cast the ladder away from the wall. He crashed onto his back and the ladder landed on him. The wind was knocked out of him and he lay stunned for a moment.

"Sir! Lieutenant! Mister Thorton!" somebody shouted at him. Then, "Fall back! *Amphitrite*, fall back!"

Chambers thought he was dead and was taking command. Thorton threw the ladder off himself, groped for his sword, and heaved himself to his feet. The Moors laid down a covering fire as the marines ran.

Thorton swore and swore again, then called, "Retreat! Tritons, to the woods and regroup!"

CHAPTER 39 : SECOND ASSAULT ON EEL BUFF

The Spaniards on the wall shook their muskets and jeered at them. They thumbed their noses and made other rude gestures as they mocked the British hiding in the woods. Thorton rubbed his face on his sleeve and gazed bitterly at the fortress. He had a hundred and twenty men, plus casualties left moaning on the field. His ladders were all overturned and abandoned in the tall grasses. The naval bombardment continued and Spanish jeers turned to screams as a cannonball struck the wall and killed a man instantly. Others were wounded. The *Amphitrite* and *Arrow* continued their assaults. They were counting on Thorton to take the fortress.

"Damn it all!" he swore in despair. He rubbed his back where it hurt due to the ladder fall.

The sound of motion caused him to turn his head ready to yell at the men, but what he saw was Kasim Rais coming up the road at the head of a force of eighty men. He trotted up to Thorton. He was breathing heavily and perspiring from the jog up the road, but he was still in one piece. His lip curled as he surveyed the scene.

"Why haven't you taken the fortress, you worthless sodomite?" he snarled in bad Spanish.

"We were repulsed!" Thorton snapped back in perfect Castilian Spanish. Kasim always grated on his nerves. Irritation stiffened his spine.

Kasim spat on the ground. "Bah. Damn *ferenghi.*" He turned to his men and shouted in Arabic, "Let's show the infidels how real men fight! *Allahu Akbar!*"

"*Allahu Akbar!*" went up the ululating cry from eighty Muslim throats.

Kasim shouted, "Follow me!" He turned and ran out from between the trees. His troops surged after him.

Thorton watched in dismay as they passed him. He turned to his own men. "Damn you lazy wench diddlers! Are you going to stand there and let them shame us like that! Forward!" he roared.

Chambers cried, "*Amphitrite!*" and a hundred throats shouted back, "*Amphitrite!*" They jumped up and ran after Thorton and Chambers.

The Muslim turbans could be seen gleaming white in the gloaming as the forces spread out and ran through the tall grass. They found ladders and dead men, and threw the former against the walls while leaping over the latter. At the top the Spanish pointed their muskets and fired down into them. Artillery shells continued raining into the fort.

Thorton drew his pistol, took aim at a dark-faced Spaniard leaning out to tip the ladder away from the wall, and fired. A dark smear of blood blossomed in the man's face and he fell back and disappeared. British marines knelt on one knee as they fired their muskets and picked off Spanish defenders who had to expose themselves to attack the ladders. Ghazi warriors fought their way onto the parapet and Kasim Rais' voice could be heard bellowing, *"Allahu Akbar!"*

"Damn him," Thorton said. "If he can do it, I can do it."

Sword in hand, he swarmed up a ladder. This time he made it to the top. He came over the lip of the parapet to find hand to hand fighting raging. Another artillery shell fell into the fortress and the floor beneath his feet shuddered as the supporting wall gave way. He leaped and crashed into a Spanish soldier and they wrestled. Mud bricks disintegrated and that section of the interior wall gave way. Thorton and his foe tumbled down amid the dust and debris. Thorton kept rolling and leaped to his feet. Covered in dust, he stabbed the Spaniard as he was rising.

Spanish defenders turned to look at him. He had lost his cocked hat, it was dark, and he was filthy. In his perfect Spanish he gestured with his sword, "What are you doing? The fortress is lost! Retreat!"

That threw the defenders into confusion. Some of the men ran into the barracks and others ran for the gate. "Open it! Run for your lives!" he urged them.

They lifted the bar and one of the heavy wooden doors swung open. More artillery shells landed on the walls and in the courtyard. Stone chips flew and stung his face, legs, and hands. With the door open, he gestured and called to the other Spaniards, "Save yourselves!"

A Spanish officer in his blue and red coat pointed his pistol at Thorton and shouted, "Die, coward!" and fired.

Thorton dodged away. The ball whined and buried itself in the mud bricks beside him.

"Stand your ground!" the Spanish officer roared.

Thorton didn't wait. He ran to the center of the courtyard and hacked at the flagpole with his sword. The flag halyard parted and the Spanish flag fluttered down. Balls whined around him. He ran for the breached wall and dove over the rubble to the shelter of the darkness within. A spatter of pistol balls smacked into the rubble around around him.

The Spanish guns continued roaring. Overhead he heard Kasim Rais shouting and the patter of footsteps as the invaders ran along the parapet. More balls smacked into the wall around them. Somebody shrieked and fell. He grimaced as his back gave a twinge and he stumbled. Still holding his sword, he peeked out.

British tars were forcing their way in through the open gate. The Spanish defenders were gathering on the seaward side of the fortress and shooting back. He listened, but no more shells were falling on the fortress even though the Spanish were still working at least ten guns. The falling of the flag had signaled the *Amphitrite* and the *Arrow* to stop their bombardment, friendly forces were inside the fort.

Thorton took a great breath and shouted, "Surrender!" in Spanish.

"Death first!" the Spanish officer roared back at him. The gun carriages creaked as they turned the guns around to point into the interior of the fortress.

Kasim's party reached another gun and overwhelmed the crew. They turned the gun halfway around so that it pointed along the parapet. Spanish gunners abandoned their posts and fled or leaped down from the walls. Kasim touched the linstock to the fuse and a moment later the gun roared and belched a tongue of flame eight feet long. The twenty-four pound ball screamed the length of the parapet and burst through the wall at the far end.

The defenders were in disarray and the attackers had the upper hand. The Spanish officer surrendered.

By dawn arrangements had been made. Tangle came up to take command of the fortress with fresh Muslim fighters. The Spanish prisoners were locked into the holds of the *Amphitrite* and the *Arrow*. They divvied up the prisoners, half to each, and thus each would have some head money for their efforts. The town was happy to welcome the liberators. They had been in dread of the Spanish auto-da-fé and welcomed the Muslim promise of tolerance.

Thorton entered the *commandante's* office. Tangle was sitting at the cherry wood desk writing his dispatches with a fine quill pen made from the pinion feather of a swan. He looked up and smiled tiredly. Lines of pain deepened the crow's feet around his eyes. His head was still wrapped in a bandage and the wound to his jaw was red and angry.

"Congratulations on a successful action, Lieutenant."

"Thank you, but Kasim Rais deserves the credit. He lead the second assault. Without him we would not have taken the fortress."

Tangle's smile grew strained. "My wife will be pleased to hear about her brother's valor." He dipped his quill into the inkwell and scratched some more words on his paper.

Thorton stepped up to the desk. "Are you all right?"

Tangle put the quill into the inkwell. He looked at Thorton with a haggard expression. "I do what I have to do."

"Until you collapse. Have you had any sleep?"

"No." Tangle's head hung heavily. He picked up a clean piece of paper, drew it to him, then picked up the quill and began to draw. Watching him, Thorton saw a face take shape on the paper. Long curls of hair framed a profile that was classically Greek in its good looks.

"I miss my wife." He slumped over the desk in a faint.

Thorton came around and shook his shoulders, then dragged him upright. Tangle's eyes flickered open and rolled in his head. Thorton put a shoulder under his arm and dragged him to his feet.

"To bed," he said firmly. "You're wounded and need your rest."

He staggered to the door, looked around, found a hallway with rooms and a cot in one. He laid the corsair down on it.

"Dispatches," Tangle protested. "Not done."

"I'll take dictation," Thorton replied.

"Your Arabic is terrible."

"I know my alphabet and all the words are spelled exactly like they sound. I don't have to understand it to write." He fetched the papers, quill, and ink. He settled on his knees and used a wooden footlocker for a desk.

Tangle lay on the cot with his arm over his eyes. He spoke slowly and carefully. The quill scratched on paper. He waited for Thorton to write, spelled out words when needed, and explained the meaning. He was sending dispatches to the *Sea Leopard* and to Zokhara. Those were substantially the same, except the *Sea Leopard* was directed to return to Eel Buff. The last letter was the hardest. Tangle was writing to his wife.

> *Beloved,*
> *I don't know what rumor will reach you before this letter does, but please know that I am alive and well on Eel Buff. We have suffered some vicissitudes which are damaging to our fortunes, but we have captured Eel Buff from the Spanish and expect to make up our losses through possession of the island.*

I doubt we can hold it for long, but since I plan to ransom it to whomever will pay first, we don't need to hold it for long. French, Spanish, Portuguese, English, I don't care who buys it.

You will be pleased to know that your brother Kasim conducted himself gallantly in the assault on the Spanish fortress. He was first to surmount the walls.

When this business is concluded I will come home for the winter and I promise you that I will not leave until after our child is born and you are recovered from your travail. I am looking forward to spending the winter with you and the children and I am loathe to even think of leaving. Give my love to the children and my affection to Shakil.

Thorton discovered he was at peace even as he penned his former lover's letter to his wife. Once upon a time he had been jealous of Jamila, but she had always treated him well. Tangle loved her dearly even if he did flirt with men. The man was loyal in his affections and that meant his friendship for Thorton was just as true and long-lasting as his love for his wife.

Tangle watched him through bleary eyes. "Do you want to send a message?"

"Tell Shakil that I hope he is happy and well," Thorton replied.

Peter Rais sends his good wishes to Shakil and hopes that he is happy and well.
I remain forever
Your loving husband
Isam

When Thorton was done, Tangle said, "Read it back."

Haltingly Thorton made out the phonetic pronunciation of the words on the paper. He could understand only part of what he had written. Tangle signed it with his formal sigil. That done, Thorton copied it, sealed the letters, called for messengers, and sent them away.

Tangle laid down again.

"I'm weary," the younger man whispered. "Can I lay down with you for a few minutes?" Thorton had not slept all night, either.

"Of course."

Thorton crawled onto the cot next to him and the corsair's arm wrapped around him. They both fell asleep instantly.

CHAPTER 40 : PARLEY

A cannon spoke in the distance. A few second later and another gun spoke. After a short pause a third gun spoke. Thorton and Tangle woke from their sleep and scrambled up. Tangle swayed and groaned with his hand to his head.

Thorton leaped to his feet and blinked in the bright light of day. "What time is it? What is happening?'

"Give me a hand up," Tangle said. Thorton hauled him to his feet, then ran out of the room and down the hall. He reached the front door, looked back, and saw the corsair leaning on the doorframe of his sleeping room. He came back, pulled Tangle's arm over his shoulder and helped him out.

"'Tis the Sallee warning signal. It came from the sea." Tangle groaned.

All around them men were running for the walls. The men on duty peered out to sea, but the could not see anything but the *Amphitrite*. Tangle and Thorton climbed up the steps and looked out.

A young man in a turban and short purple jacket ran up to Tangle, pressed his hand to his brow and said, "Mirror signal, rais. Four sail, due east, five miles. Spanish flag." The bulk of the mountain concealed the eastern sea from their view.

Tangle and Thorton swore in their respective languages. "They were sleeping up there," Tangle said bitterly. They were all tired from the night action, lookouts included.

Thorton looked over the wall to see the *Amphitrite* hauling her anchors. He racked his brain. If he ran for the town and grabbed a boat, he might be able to reach her before she ran from or fought the Spaniards. That was where he belonged. He didn't move. It was no fault of his that he had been caught on land. Didn't he have a duty to the British that were helping to hold Eel Buff? He couldn't get them all off. If the Spaniards caught them in open boats it would be a slaughter. The wind was out of the northeast; the Spanish must be making at least five knots. They would come up in about an hour.

He straightened and Tangle felt the resolution in his spine. Thorton asked, "Are you going to hold the fortress or do you want to be taken off?"

Tangle straightened as well. "We're holding."

He shouted in Arabic and a pale-faced Sallee midshipman in a short purple jacket ran up. He received the orders in Arabic, then took off at a run to carry them down to the *Arrow*. The orders were simple enough, "Clear the harbor. Fight or flee as you think best. We are holding the fort."

The first Spanish vessel cleared the end of the island as they watched. She was sweeping around to the west with the wind over her starboard quarter. Her three masts were set with topsails and her two decks were high above the water.

"Battleship," Thorton groaned.

Tangle pulled his spyglass out of his pocket. *"Nuestra Señora del Mer.* The flagship of the Spanish fleet that took Isle Boeuf. She's a two-decker with seventy-four guns."

Thorton shuddered. Her single broadside carried as many guns as the entire armament of the *Amphitrite*. Most of them were of heavier caliber, too. Following her like chicks after a hen were three frigates.

"Ha. They've suffered! 'Twas seven vessels before. Now there's only four. I wonder what happened to them?" Thorton said.

"I wonder what happened to the *Sea Leopard* and the *Seven Stars*," Tangle replied.

The *Arrow* rowed out of the harbor mouth, saw what was out there and closing, and took to her heels to run behind the western corner of the island. The *Amphitrite* was running too. All sails out she beat the *Arrow* to the corner, but she wore around and presented her broadside with all guns run out to cover the retreat of the smaller and slower galiot.

Tangle said, "We're going to the mirror station."

They hiked slowly around the parapet to the small tower. Tangle gritted his teeth and climbed laboriously up the wooden ladder to the flat roof. Thorton came up after him. They could see more from that vantage, but the shoulder of the island did not let them see further than the northwest corner. They had a good view of the tower on top of the mountain, though.

Tangle barked Arabic at the signalmen, "Make a signal, 'It is the enemy who is without issue.'"

It was a tedious process to spell out the message with the proper number of mirror flashes, but fortunately Arabic could omit the vowels and still be understood.

Aboard the *Amphitrite* a line of signals ran up. "English signal, sir," Thorton said.

Tangle leaned on the wall and watched. "What's he saying? I can't concentrate."

"'God is on our side,'" Thorton translated into Arabic.

Tangle grunted. "I'd like to think so, but I've been wrong before."

"Spanish signals, *kapitan*," the signalman said respectfully.

Thorton studied the flags raised. "Spanish flagship, 'Truce declared between England and Spain.'"

"No!" Tangle cried. "Those perfidious English! How could they do it?"

Thorton continued translating. "'*Amphitrite* to Spanish flag, 'Do not understand.'"

After a pause, the Spanish answer went up, "Go in peace."

Horner replied, "English forces in Eel Buff."

To which the Spanish responded, "Send boat."

Tangle said, "I'm not letting them meet. I need your men to help hold Eel Buff. Messenger! All batteries! Open fire on the Spanish."

The messenger flew down the ladder. Tangle and Thorton climbed down a little slower. They met Kasim Rais and other officers coming up to meet them.

"Concentrate all fire on the flagship. The frigates are of little consideration unless they try to land."

"Sir! I must protest!" Thorton replied.

"Your protest is noted. Carry out your orders."

The Muslim officers called orders in Arabic and men began to move purposefully. The magazine opened up and powder and shot began to flow onto the walls.

"Isam, I must obey my captain."

Tangle fixed him with a firm gaze. "You're a Muslim. Will you let your brothers in religion perish at the hands of the Spanish and make no move to help them?"

Thorton stopped as if struck. "I'll stand with you, Isam, but the British need to go back to their ship."

"You forget. We hired them. They aren't your men, they're mine."

"Some of them belong to the *Amphitrite*."

"I don't have time to sort them out. You came ashore with us and you're staying with us."

The first gun roared from the fort. The shot dropped short of the *Mer*. A second gun spoke and whistled through her rigging. A white flag went up her flag halyard. Tangle swore in Turkish. He did not say anything else for a minute, and two more guns roared out from the fort. The Spanish fired a rocket, but their guns did not answer the fort's assauLieutenant

"She wants a parley!" Thorton exclaimed. "You cannot fire on a white flag."

"Cease fire," Tangle ordered. The message was shouted from gun to gun. The fortress fell silent.

The Spanish fleet held its position as it made another signal. "Send boat," Thorton translated.

"What in the hell do they expect?" Tangle grumbled. "We're not surrendering. But I suppose it is chivalrous of them to offer terms." He sighed. "Kasim!"

Kasim Rais appeared. He was wearing the same coat as yesterday and dirt smudged the brilliant colors. His turban was dirty, too, but he himself was hale and full of energy.

"The Spaniards want a parley. Stall them as much as possible. Ask for ransom. Thirty thousand sequins is a fair price. Insist we need it for our honor and to make up our losses. See if you can find out what happened to the *Sea Leopard* and the *Seven Stars*. If there's any chance they might come up, I'm holding the fort."

Kasim snorted. "That's the battleship that mauled us two days ago."

"I know. But she has lost some of her consorts. She has also used up part of her powder and shot. The frigates may not be significant. If we can form a wolf pack, we can take the battleship by storm."

"Only if the xebecs come up," Kasim replied pointedly.

"It is your job to find out what you can about them. We need to know."

Kasim chewed the inside of his cheek and his curly black beard bristled. He eyed the Spanish fleet. "I'd just as soon run the bastard through."

"I share your feelings. But not yet."

"May I go to the parley?" Thorton asked.

"No," Tangle replied shortly. "Messenger! Make a signal, 'Envoy coming.'" A boy ran to the signal tower.

Thorton had to watch as a fishing lugger carried Kasim and his bodyguards out to the Spanish fleet. The *Amphitrite*'s gig carried Horner to the meeting. He stared through his spyglass as the fleshy Kasim climbed up the battens, and a few minutes later the gangly

Horner went up. Horner was a man who was all knees and elbows, but he climbed like a spider.

"What I wouldn't give for a good storm blowing out of the Bay of Biscay," Tangle mourned.

Thorton fanned himself. "'Tis warm today. If it gets any warmer, we might have storms tonight."

"I doubt it. My joints don't hurt. We're in for several days of fair weather," Tangle replied.

They waited. It took over half an hour for the boats to make their way to the *Mer*, then discussions on board lasted at least an hour. It was approaching noon, so the Spanish captain invited them to dinner. The Muslims in the fort went to prayers, then dinner. Tangle and Thorton prayed, ate, and napped. They woke when a messenger came to tell them the boats were returning. Eventually Kasim reached the fort.

"Well?" Tangle demanded. He was slouched down in the chair behind the *commandante's* desk with a vinegar plaster against his aching head. His eyes had dark circles under them and his face was drawn tight with pain. Kasim, Thorton, and the other officers stood in a semi-circle before him.

"Spain and Britain have declared a truce while they discuss Portuguese independence," Kasim announced. He planted his feet wide and put his hands on his hips and glared at Tangle as if it were his fault.

Mixed emotions played across Tangle's face. "'Tis well for Portugal, but ill for us. What else? What about the French?"

"Negotiations with the French are not progressing."

"What about the *Sea Leopard* and *Seven Stars*?" Thorton asked.

"They ran for the Portuguese frontier and met up with a Portuguese fleet under Admiral Henrique, Duke of Coimbra. The Portuguese mauled the Spanish; they didn't have news of the truce. An advice boat came out of Coruña as the Spanish were heading north and told them. The Spanish squadron is ordered to hold Eel Buff against the French, who are expected to launch a counterattack."

"What did they say to ransom?" Suhail demanded.

"They refused. They pointed out their superior force and said they saw no reason to pay for what they could take."

"What terms do they offer us?" Tangle asked.

"The English can leave and take the wounded with them. They will even let us abandon the fort and go out in the *Arrow* with twenty-four hours grace. After that, we're fair game."

Tangle shifted the brown paper and vinegar on his head. His eyes were tense with pain. He stared into space and tried to think. "What deadline do they give us?"

"Sundown. They commence the assault tonight."

"We're tired enough already. They can shell us through the night, exhaust us, batter this fort to smithereens, and land at first dawn. That's what I would do."

"We can't hold it," Lieutenant Suhail said. "We should accept their terms. They're very good terms. We'll get away with our skins."

"We've lost three ships! We deserve compensation for that!" Kasim objected.

"Loot the town," somebody said.

"Ha, the Spanish looted it already. There's nothing left!" Kasim replied.

The discussion became general. Tangle closed his eyes and let the compress lay on his head as the noise flowed over and around him.

Thorton watched him. "Isam," he said softly.

Tangle opened his eyes.

"Accept their terms. You have a pregnant wife at home. The season is drawing to a close. Go home. Rest. Recover. Enjoy your family." Thorton spoke very softly.

"This cruise has nearly ruined me. I don't mind the loss of money so much as the loss of prestige. My reputation is broken if I do not salvage something from it."

"Then raid on the way home."

They spoke soft Spanish. The other officers stopped talking and craned their ears to hear what they were saying.

Tangle's expression hardened. "We hold Eel Buff. Ransom, or a river of Spanish blood."

"*Kapitan Pasha!*" Suhail protested.

Nazim said, "I stand and fall with Isam Rais. No Muslim will ever run from a Spanish dog, no matter how loud he barks."

"You may take the crew of the *Amphitrite* off, Mister Thorton. But the men I hired stay with me."

Thorton saluted. "Aye aye, sir." He wanted to say more, but he knew the corsair had made up his mind. He turned swiftly and left the room.

CHAPTER 41 : THE SPANISH HOSTAGE

Horner handed Thorton a brandy. Thorton took it and knocked it back neat in one gulp. The two stood in silence in the coolness of the *Amphitrite's* great cabin. Sunlight streamed through the stern lights and dust motes danced. Two stern windows had their glasses swung up and hooked to the deckhead. The faint sea breeze played over the room with a refreshing coolness. Neat as ever, Horner had no papers or other loose items on his desk or anywhere. He put the plug back in the bottle of brandy and returned it to his cabinet.

"He's stubborn to the point of foolhardiness," Thorton said bitterly.

Horner's mouth quirked slightly. "I would do the same. Eel Buff is strategically significant."

Thorton gave him a surprised look. "You would?"

"I did in the Sea of Alborán, if you recall. He had me badly outnumbered."

"You tricked him and took him hostage, though."

Horner nodded.

"I doubt he can take the Spanish commander hostage. The man would be a fool to leave his ship."

"We might be able to help him."

"How?" Thorton said.

"Stall the Spanish."

About about half an hour before sunset the *Amphitrite* signaled for parley. Her request was accepted and Thorton put off in the gig. They rowed leisurely across the sea to the *Mer*. Thorton was in no hurry, but eventually he arrived at the Spanish battleship. He was admitted to the great cabin.

The Spanish commodore's accommodations were luxurious. The rich were very rich in Spain, and he was one of them. Captain Morales was a small pale-haired man with a thin mustache, goatee and watery blue eyes. He almost disappeared in his blue uniform with red lapels, but his cravat was made of excellent lace that spilled over the front of his red waistcoat. The cabin was warm to the point of stuffiness thanks to a portable iron stove. Woven tapestries of hunting scenes decorated the walls and oil paintings in heavy gilt frames depicted stern faced men and women in the dress of a previous century. The only sign the vessel had been in combat was wood boarding up one of the stern windows.

Captain Morales had been at supper. A pair of serving boys, one black and one brown, were clearing away the remains of his dinner. He had had his officers as guests to judge by the number of white china plates. The lace tablecloth was long and elaborate. The chandelier that hung over it was made of hundreds of crystals that scattered dogs of light throughout the cabin.

"Lieutenant Peter Thorton, of His Britannic Majesty's frigate *Amphitrite* at your service, sir," Thorton said in Spanish. He swept his hat to the side and bowed elegantly with one foot behind the other as Abby had drilled him. He could not help but feel a rustic compared to this lord of the sea.

The captain had a glass of wine dangling in his hand. "What may I do for you, Lieutenant?" the man asked him. His eyes roved over Thorton from head to foot and took in every inch of him.

Thorton felt self-conscious under his gaze and hoped the seams of his stockings were straight. Then he castigated himself for letting the smaller man intimidate him. He drew himself up to his full height and was glad there was enough room that the top of his head merely brushed the deckhead. He tucked his hat into the crook of his left elbow.

"I understand you have orders regarding Eel Buff. However, His Britannic Majesty has preferences regarding Eel Buff as well, and therefore we beg leave to communicate with our king before you commence any action."

Morales eyebrows shot up. "An extraordinary request. Why should I allow it?"

"Britain prefers that Eel Buff not return to the hands of the French or Spanish for obvious reasons. We regard it preferable for a small power, like the Sallee Republic, to hold it, as we believe they are least likely to be able to do damage to our commerce."

"England and Spain have a truce, Lieutenant. England need not fear for her commerce on our account. May I offer you wine?"

"Please," Thorton replied. "It seems to us an arrangement might be made that is suitable for both sides."

"I hardly see how, but I will entertain your proposition."

Morales' servant brought Thorton a crystal cup emblazoned with a coat of arms featuring chevrons and lion's head. "Your arms, sir?" Thorton asked.

Dark was falling outside the windows. The battleship was silent aside from the usual creak of wood and the watchman crying the hour. There was no rumble of great guns nor the scrambling noise of a vessel clearing for action.

"They are. We are an ancient and noble house going back to the Crusades. My ancestor was knighted for resisting the Moorish advance on Tabanos."

"*Salud,*" Thorton said. He raised the glass and sipped the wine.

"*Salud,*" the commodore replied and drank again. "Please, have a seat." He settled into one of the royal blue velvet easy chairs. Thorton hesitated, then settled into the other. "You speak excellent Spanish. Were you educated in Spain?"

Thorton shook his head. "No, I was pressed into Spanish service. I was aboard the *Marigold.*"

"Ah. I remember that vaguely. She was running contraband in the West Indies, as I recall."

"Supplying Jamaica," Thorton replied. "Legitimate supplies."

The captain waved his wine. "An old argument." He sipped and watched Thorton over the rim of his cup. "There was a Lieutenant Peter Thorton on the *Ajax* this summer."

"That was me." He racked his brain to recall the lesson that Perry had given him so many months ago about making small talk. "You burned the *Ajax* two days ago. I was sorry to see it."

"Tell me how the *Ajax* came to be in the hands of Sallee rovers."

Thorton shrugged. "Her keel was cracked, so she was sold at auction. Kasim Rais bought her. He survived, by the way. So did Commodore Tangueli. He was visiting Kasim aboard the *Ajax.*"

Morales grimaced. "If I had known the notorious corsair was aboard, I would have pummeled her until she sank. I thought he was aboard the *Sea Leopard.*"

"The fortunes of war, eh?"

"Yes, indeed. The fortunes of war are very strange. After my bad luck of the last few days, who would have thought the Turk's catamite would be delivered to me?'

Thorton's eyes flashed and he jumped from his seat. "I am no such thing!"

"But you are my prisoner, so sit down. We shall discuss your predicament like civilized men."

Thorton wrenched open the door to the stern gallery. Crystal shattered behind him as he threw down his glass and dove over the rail into the cold sea.

"Guards!" Morales shouted.

Thorton went down and down into the chilling sea, turned and looked up at the dark bulk of the ship above him with the light from her stern lanthorn turning the sea to gold.

Morales stood in his gallery shouting, "He dove in there! Shoot him! Kill the sodomite!"

Thorton swam along the side of the *Mer* and clawed his way to the surface. His head broke water. He saw the gig thirty feet ahead of him and hissed, "Morris!"

The cockswain turned around and looked at him in surprise.

Thorton held a finger to his lips. "Cast off," he said softly. He swam quickly for the boat, but above them some of the Spanish crew were looking over the side in search of him.

"*Allá!*" someone shouted and pointed. The Spanish marines loaded their muskets and the boat began to row frantically away from the side. The British marines in the boat were already locked and loaded; they raised their muskets.

"One by one! Make them keep their heads down!" Thorton called.

Spanish marine leaned over the side and took aim. Thorton dove under water. A ball splashed into the water near him. He swam under water as long as he could until forced up to breathe. The marines in the gig were shooting back. At that short range casualties were inevitable. Thorton crawled over the stern and was helped in by many hands.

"Row!" he croaked, short of breath.

The Muslim battery on Eel Buff opened fire. Spanish marines whirled around as the first shot ranged near their bow, then a second overshot them. It sent up a fountain of water ten yards from the gig.

"Row! Damn you for a pack of lazy whoresons! Move!" Thorton shouted at them. The British sailors put their backs into it and the gig shot forward.

A shot crashed onto the deck of the *Mer* and a man screamed high and shrill. The Muslim gunners had the range and more shots peppered the battleship. Spanish drums beat and whistles shrilled. All hands ran to their quarters. Thorton was grimly pleased at the thought of Morales' finery being upset in the commotion. He watched the lighted battleship falling behind as the British rowed as hard as they could to get out of musket range.

"Damage report!" he barked.

"'Ere's Morton, shot in the arm, sir."

"Let me have a look."

"I think it went clean through, sir," said the wounded man.

Thorton pulled his checked handkerchief out of his pocket and tied it around the man's forearm. "That's a good thing, my lad. Better than hitting a bone."

"Aye, sir. Stings a bit, it do."

The Spanish turned their attention to fighting the Muslims and let the English boat go. By the time they reached the *Amphitrite* Thorton was breathing normally and was able to climb up the side with a certain amount of dignity in spite of being soaking wet. He delivered his report while dripping on the quarterdeck, then Horner sent him below to get changed.

Abby met him at the companionway. "What happened out there? You're wet!"

So Thorton told him all about it as they descended to the wardroom. His damp clothes clung to him and Abby helped him to peel them off in the privacy of their little berth. It was odd to shed his clothes so casually while gunnery thundered across the sea and reverberated from the hills. He sat on his sea chest and let Abby kneel before him to unbuckle the sodden shoes. "I've lost my good hat," he mourned.

Abby laughed. "You can afford another one, Mister Prize Money!"

Thorton laughed at that, too. "I suppose I can. I might even buy you a bonnet," he teased.

"I'd like that," Abby smiled up at him.

Thorton's heart did a slow lurch. He was unattached, male, and had had a narrow escape. The infernal racket of battle made him restless and keen for action, but he could only wait. The English were neutral parties. Slowly he leaned forward and kissed Abby's mouth.

Abby closed his eyes and kissed him back. His arm went around Thorton's neck. Thorton was wet and half undressed. He pulled the warm firm body of the other man against him. "I'm cold," he whispered.

"I'll warm you up," Abby promised. He proceeded to do exactly that.

Later they snuggled together in Thorton's hammock. It was very pleasant to have someone to cuddle with in the evening cool. The guns continued to bark at irregular intervals. Abby dozed. He was a sailor, he could sleep anywhere at any time. Thorton twined his soft blond hair in his fingers.

"Alan," he said.

"Mm?"

"This is very comfortable."

"Mm, yes it is."

"I'm not in love with you."

Abby yawned. "I know. It doesn't matter."

"Are you sure?"

"I've slept with worse men for less reason."

Thorton gave him a strange look. "Why?"

Abby laughed. "I get the horn as bad as any man."

"I'm growing fond of venery myself. I never thought I would."

Abby laughed again. "Most men find it comes naturally and at an early age."

"Feh. I am not most men," Thorton said crossly. "Let's go up and watch the battle."

CHAPTER 42 : THE END

Horner was studying the hills of Eel Buff through the night glass. It was an awkward view since the night glass turned things upside down, but it showed them more clearly than a standard glass. He lowered it with a thoughtful look. As Thorton and Abby came on deck they saluted. Horner returned their salutes abstractedly.

"Your Turk is a clever fellow," he remarked.

"How so?" Thorton asked.

"He's hauled his guns up the mountain. They're in the trees and probably dug in. The Spanish can't elevate their guns high enough. They've been trying, but they're taking fire without doing the Salletines any damage."

"The clever bastard!" Thorton swore in admiration. "I thought he was going to die for nothing, but he might not die after all! The Spanish are going to have a hell of a time attacking on a foot."

"Surely you can compliment a man without swearing, Mister Thorton. I have not pressed you before, but a gentleman should be able to express himself without resorting to profane language."

Thorton blinked. Not a talkative man to begin with, depriving him of profanity eliminated half his capacity for speech. "Aye aye, sir." A suggestion from a superior officer was as good as an order.

"I think cider and a rubber of whist on the quarterdeck is in order. It will provide a pleasant way to wile away the evening as we watch the battle."

Perry and Chambers groaned.

Horner fixed them with a stern looked. "I have humored you enough with dancing. It is time for whist."

Thorton said, "As you wish, sir."

A pair of sawhorses and some planks were brought up to form a table. A green and white checked tablecloth was laid over it. Chairs were brought from the captain's cabin to seat four men. Chagall was keen to take a hand and asked Posonby to partner him. Horner drafted Perry as his partner much to Perry's dismay. Thorton found himself out for once. Horner sent for his humidor and passed around excellent Cuban cigars. They smoked and played in the golden light of the stern lanthorn.

The wind died and the night was cool and mild. A crescent moon rose in the east and gave a ghostly luminance to the scene. The *Nuestra Señora del Mer* had her boats tow her out of range of the Muslim artillery. The guns fell silent, but the clouds of gunsmoke hung in the still air. They could smell it even at a distance.

Thorton leaned against the port rail and watched in silence. Abby came and slipped an arm around his waist in a brotherly gesture. Thorton smiled at him.

Horner said, "Since the gunnery has stopped, let's have the fiddler up."

The fiddler had been blind with cataracts in both eyes, but now, thanks to Lord Zahid, he could see again. He was one of many men that had chosen to follow Horner into his new command. He bowed deeply. "What song, gentlemen?"

"Something slow and sweet," said the captain.

The man put his fiddle into the crook of his arm and began to draw out a stately strathspey. The gentlemen sat smoking their cigars and listening. Posonby left his cards face down on the table while Horner sorted his quietly. The captain puffed on his cigar, then held it in his left hand as he looked up to watch the fiddler. The yellow lamplight was kind to him; it glowed upon his blond head and sculpted his face into strong areas of light and shadow.

Thorton looked up at the diamond stars and felt the slowly cooling evening on his cheek. "I could never be a landsman," he remarked. "They don't have nights like this."

Murmurs of assent answered him.

The fiddler continued playing and a mist began to rise from the sea. Tendrils hovered like ghosts above the glassy waters. The Spanish fleet lay becalmed with their own lanthorns glowing at a distance of two and a half miles. No lights appeared on the hills of Eel Buff. Thorton murmured a soft prayer in Arabic for his Muslim friends. Abby yawned and leaned against him. Thorton was tired, too; he'd had very little sleep the night before. He shook his head to clear the cobwebs.

"Deck!" cried the lookout. "A sail! North northeast!"

Forsythe was officer on watch. He stepped forward to the rail and called out, "What course?"

"South!"

The ship couldn't be seen from the deck. Horner considered his cards, then sighed. He laid the cards down. "I regret not being able to play out this hand. I would have made a small slam."

The others gaped at him.

"How do you figure, sir?" Posonby asked. He did not have Horner's ability to calculate the hands.

Horner rose from the chair. "I'm afraid we must clear for action, gentlemen."

Forsythe bellowed, "All hands, clear for action!"

The fiddler continued playing a haunting Scottish melody while the officers got up and the servants came to fetch the furniture. The officers went below to change their wool socks for silk stockings, to put on dress coats and good hats, don their swords, and prime their pistols. Thorton checked that his seams were straight. Victory or defeat, they were officers and gentlemen, and they looked it.

Abby helped him dress and said, "You cut a very fine figure, Peter. You have grown in stature since I first met you."

"Do you think so?"

"Yes, you are developing a certain verve. This uniform is cut much better than your old one and the lace is excellent quality." He stood on tiptoe to kiss him on the mouth. "You cut a dashing figure these days."

"I didn't always," Thorton said ruefully.

"I'll teach you to carry yourself like a gentleman. You have an innate dignity that serves you well. Don't let anyone fluster you and remember that if you appear cool, people will believe that you are cool."

"Like Horner and Tangle."

"Exactly."

Abby picked up Thorton's hanger and wrapped his arms around his waist. The sword belt settled above his hips and Abby buckled it. Then Abby took out his own best hat, the one with a bit of ostrich feather around the brim and a line of gold lace and put it on his head. The naval cockade was full and crisp. Thorton gave him another kiss, then went out and climbed the companionway to the deck.

Slowly the fleet crawled into view. They were coming out of the north-northeast at a walking pace. Each ship — and they were ships, he could see that much at least — had all canvas set. The breeze was so light they barely moved, and yet, one by one their sails came up over the horizon, followed slowly by their hulls until they could be seen in their entirety. When a ship was fully manifest in spite of the soft blurring of the faint haze, another sail appeared over the horizon to follow it in the soft white gleam of moonlight.

The breeze carried the sound of drums from the Spanish to the patch of sea where the *Arrow* and the *Amphitrite* hung on the corner of Eel Buff.

"Beat to quarters," Horner said. "Fiddler stand down." The *Amphitrite's* drums sounded and the fiddler ceased his playing and went below.

"Wear ship."

The sails shook out and the *Amphitrite* began to fall off and turn before the wind.

A single spitfire leaped from the forecastle of the flagship of the strange fleet. The *Mer* replied in kind. Thorton pulled out his spyglass and studied the upside-down scene. He lowered his glass and stared at the night, then raised it again. He looked at Horner. Horner said nothing, just watched. The glow along two levels of the stranger's decks showed that her gun ports were open; the light was the glow of lanterns in the interior to light the crews at their guns. They were too far away to see the guns themselves, but the opening of the gun ports could only mean that loaded guns were run out and ready for action.

On the quarterdeck of the *Amphitrite* the officers were tense with suspense. Below them the men finished stowing all that needed to be stowed and went to quarters. Aboard the *Arrow* similar preliminaries were made.

Due to the weakness of the wind, it took the strange fleet hours to draw near. The Spanish made up their minds long before they arrived and fled. They set every stitch of canvas and ran southeast for the coast of Spain. They were expecting a French counterattack at Eel Buff and clearly did not think themselves strong enough to resist it.

Eventually the twelve strange warships loomed close enough for them to identify the white ensigns carried on their flagstaffs. A cheer went up. The Mediterranean Fleet had come out.

The following day they dined aboard the *Windsor*. Admiral Sir Charles Leggott kept a handsome table covered in snowy white linen heavily adorned with lace. It could seat twenty with all the leaves in. His chairs were covered in black needlepoint with a pattern of pink English roses, and his china continued the rose pattern. Commodore Tangueli had the seat of honor and various captains, officers, and senior ward officers sat around the table. Thorton was glad that Abby had coached him in better manners. Fortunately, it was easy enough to chat; they wanted to know all about the assault on Eel Buff.

Much later, a drunk but happy Tangle was poured into a boatswain's chair to be lowered into his own boat. Thorton helped to make certain he was secure, then asked, "Why so happy, rais?"

"The *ferenghi* admiral agrees that Sallee ought to keep Eel Buff. They don't want France or Spain to have it, and they might buy it from us, if we can keep the Spanish off it. The *Arrow* will carry dispatches south. You'll have dispatches to take back to England, poor sod. 'Tis cold there. I'm going home where it is warm and the beds are soft."

"Who is holding Eel Buff?"

"Kasim Rais. He wants to be a hero. I'm letting him. I want to see my wife and sleep in my own bed."

"Godspeed, Commodore."

"Allah defend you, Lieutenant."

"And you, sir." He leaned forward and softly kissed Tangle on each cheek in the French fashion.

Tangle kissed him back. "I'll miss you, Peter." Then he went over the side.

The *Dart* shot away with a strong pulls of the oars.

Two British frigates peeled off from the larger fleet to support Eel Buff. Although Spain and England were technically at peace, a show of strength would do much to protect Eel Buff from the Spanish. Or French.

Horner stepped out of the coach. He watched Thorton watching the corsair depart. The sound of lusty Turkish singing came through the night, slowly trailing away as the small boat disappeared in the night.

"'Tis a lively tune," Horner remarked.

Thorton smiled. "He can stay in tune even when drunk. He has a good voice."

Horner put a hand on his shoulder. "We might see him again."

"We might."

"Come. Let's go back to the *Amphitrite*."

"Aye aye, sir."

Back in his own berth, Thorton made love very passionately to Abby. He felt as if he had lost something. No matter how he tried to assuage the feeling, amorous exertion did not satisfy. At last he lay still and stared into the dark while Abby slept. He gave the man one last kiss, then crawled out of the hammock, got dressed, and went on deck.

He found Horner smoking one of his Cuban cigars at the taffrail. "Good evening, sir. Can't you sleep?"

"No. What about you?"

"I can't sleep either. There must be another adventure waiting for us somewhere out there."

Horner smiled crookedly. "I'm sure there is."

"I want to find it."

"We will."

The two smiled at each other, then at the night.

THE END